Mr. Gallion's School

BOOKS BY JESSE STUART

Man with a Bull-Tongue Plow
Head o' W-Hollow
Beyond Dark Hills
Trees of Heaven
Men of the Mountains
Taps for Private Tussie
Mongrel Mettle
Album of Destiny
Foretaste of Glory
Tales from the Plum Grove Hills
The Thread That Runs So True
Hie to the Hunters
Clearing in the Sky
Kentucky Is My Land
The Good Spirit of Laurel Ridge
The Year of My Rebirth
Plowshare in Heaven
God's Oddling
Hold April
A Jesse Stuart Reader
Save Every Lamb
Daughter of the Legend
My Land Has a Voice
Mr. Gallion's School

FOR BOYS AND GIRLS

Penny's Worth of Character
The Beatinest Boy
The Red Mule
The Rightful Owner
Andy Finds a Way

Mr. Gallion's School

by Jesse Stuart

McGraw-Hill Book Company
New York   Toronto   London   Sydney

*Dedicated to ten thousand
high school youth who taught me
more than I taught them*

Education is a race between civilization and catastrophe.

H. G. WELLS

Contents

Mr. Gallion's School

Chapter One

The School Bell Rings Again

Puffs of warm July wind came through the car to fan George Gallion's face and his woolly arm that rested on the open window. The car was new and powerful—it had 300 horses under the hood. Grace drove up to the summit of the overpass that spanned the railroad tracks. Directly beneath them, the Ohio River stretched like a white ribbon in the broad green valley.

"How wonderful it is that we're both alive and together, and we don't have to worry about anything any more—except," Grace said, "your health."

"Worry is the worst of all diseases," George said. "It can kill you. I'm not worrying about my health, and don't you worry about it."

They drove on in silence, down the overpass now, onto a straightaway which led into Main Street and the center of Greenwood. It was the first time in two years—since his illness—that George had been here.

Made of dull-gray pavement and colorless brick buildings, Greenwood is one of the oldest towns of Kentucky. Even in this fast-changing mid-twentieth century, most of its 1100 inhabitants are the direct descendants of its first settlers a hundred years ago. Here the mountaineers and the river people still meet, marry, fight, love, die. It was here, too, that so much of George's life had been spent. He remembered the days when Greyhound boats carried passengers on the river and the Negro stevedores sang as they loaded freight. He used to watch huge horses pull loaded draywagons up the steep bank with sparks flying from their steel-shod hooves. He glanced to his left at his

wife's old home, standing coolly back from the street, surrounded by elms. He remembered he had walked to school
years ago, beside her.

"Here's home, Grace," he said.

"Not any more. The Valley is far dearer to me now."

Down Main Street in the shade of giant elms, the non-
descript houses on either side blocked the Ohio River breezes.
Elm leaves hung motionless in wilted clusters from the interlocking elm branches above Main Street. Large elm roots were
exposed at the bases of the trees, coiled like huge reptiles en-
joying the penciled spots of sunlight that found holes in the
canopies of wilted leaves. On the windows and doors that faced
the courthouse square were the familiar names of merchants
and professional men they knew. Seats donated by the town's
local politicians were filled with men who sat, whittled, and
talked.

"This old town does look good," George said, smiling. "It's
good to see the old names and the familiar houses."

Grace drove around the square up the other side and parked
in front of Tad Meadowbrook's barbershop.

Grace got out and hurried around to the other side to open
the door for George, but he was already easing himself out
slowly. George had both feet on the street and he straightened
up slowly while she put a coin in the parking meter. Grace was
an attractive woman, tall and slender, with large hazel eyes, a
wide thin mouth, and a strong chin. She was in her mid-forties
and her once-brown hair brushed back from her face was
streaked with gray.

"George, Tad's barbershop is full," she said. "You want to
wait or come back later?"

"No, I'll get my hair cut now."

"Yes, I know, you want to hear the gossip."

His blue summer suit was wrinkled and his shoes needed a
shine. He was six feet tall with broad shoulders, a short neck, a
large head and long deep-set gray eyes.

"You bet I want to hear the gossip. I want to hear some man-
talk."

"I'll go in with you."

"Sure you haven't some shopping you'd like to do?"

"Not today," she replied, smiling. "I want to learn why you like barbershop talk!"

As they walked across the sidewalk together she put her hand in his. "It's the best place in the world to hear what's going on," he said. "Tad has more news in an hour than the *Greenwood Times* prints in a week. I'd rather hear Old Tad talk than read the newspapers, anyway. He never slants the news. He's the most authentic reporter in the Tri-State."

"Here's the step," she said. "Go easy! Remember what Dr. Vinn told you."

The barbershop was the bottom half of the square two-story building. There was a big sign on the door in block black letters with red trimming: TAD'S BARBERSHOP. TODDLE IN AND TALK WITH TAD. HE'S THE BEST BARBER YOU EVER HAD.

Tad left the chair where he was cutting the hair of a man George didn't know, came over and opened the door.

"Come in, Professor and Mrs. Professor," he greeted them warmly with a big grin. He held a long cigar between his gold front teeth. "I've been thinking about when I'd get to cut your hair again. It's been a long time since you've been here. How're you feeling, Professor Gallion?"

"Could whip my weight in wildcats," George Gallion said with a wan smile.

"I don't know about now but I remember when you could," said the young man at the other chair. "You sure poured it on me once. Remember?"

"Ken, I didn't recognize you," George said. "You've grown up and lost a lot of hair. You've lost yours and we've held ours, haven't we, Tad? But our hair has changed its color a little."

"Yes, mine used to be black as a stove pot," Tad said, smiling. "Women used to wish for my wavy black hair! Now look. White!"

The stranger in Tad's chair looked at his watch.

"You want a haircut, Professor?" Tad asked. "If you do you'll have to wait awhile!"

"George, maybe we'd better come back later," Grace said.

She looked around at the row of men. The chairs were filled and several were standing. She was the only woman in the shop. On every patch of wall were hung pictures of pin-up girls, many of them dating back to the 1940s. In the corner of the shop were rifles and shotguns Tad traded or sold when he wasn't busy. Near them was his five-string banjo which he would play sitting in his barber's chair when he needed customers. Sometimes people danced in the streets to the dance tunes he played.

"No, I'll wait," George said.

"Then I'll get you some chairs," Ken said.

"Professor, I didn't introduce you to the fellows around here," Tad said as Ken came from the back of the shop with two wooden stools.

"I've always said, Professor, if I could have been with you longer I'd never have been in this shop with Dad cutting hair," Ken said.

"What's wrong with barbering? It's a good profession."

"I want you all to meet my friends, Professor and Mrs. George Gallion." Tad addressed the room at large. "He used to be principal of Kensington High School, and I started cutting his hair then. When he was there we never had all this trouble like we're having down there now. Right, Professor?"

"What's wrong at the school?" George Gallion asked.

"What isn't wrong with it, Professor, would be a better question." Ken said. "The trucks that take soft drinks and milk won't even go there any more! The boys down there rob the trucks! They walk out of the school and just take what they want when a truck comes in."

"You're kidding me."

"No, Ken ain't kiddin' you," Tad said as his scissors now moved swiftly over his customer's head. "He's right, Professor. I still live over in Kensington. That school is the talk of the town. We was just discussing it 'fore you came in. The kids down there tell the teachers what to do. Right in the middle of a class some tough kid'll git up and say to the teacher, 'Now, we've had class in this room for thirty minutes and the next thirty minutes we'll go outside under the shade of them locust trees and finish the class.' And, Professor, they just git. Poor teacher can't do a thing about it!"

"Where is the principal?" George asked. He began biting his lower lip.

"Now, don't you get all worked up over it, George," Grace said. "You're not principal of that school now. It doesn't concern you."

"It does concern me. It concerns everybody."

"Well, there's nothing you can do about it now," she said. "So why worry about it? Leave it to younger principals and teachers."

"They can't find teachers who'll go there and stand the abuse for the low salaries they get," put in one of Tad's customers who was standing near the window.

Seems like I ought to know you, George Gallion thought. He looked at this big square-shouldered man in a business suit. I know I've seen you someplace before.

"Do they have the same people living down there they used to have?" George Gallion asked. "Have all the people I used to know there twenty years ago moved out and strangers moved in? What's the cause of all this trouble?"

"I'd say seventy percent of them are the people you know," Ken said, as his customer stepped down from the chair. "I'd say the youngsters raising all the hell down there are the sons and daughters of the boys and girls you taught there twenty years ago."

"Then I must have done a rotten job," George Gallion said.

"No, Professor, it's not that," Ken said. "They let 'em do as they please. They don't have any discipline. Nobody seems to be interested or to care what goes on. Teachers don't tell them what to do. They tell the teachers!"

"But what about the principal?" George Gallion asked.

"Well, he won't be there this year," Tad said. Tad's customer got down and another stepped into the chair. "They don't have a principal. Can't get one. Well, I heard some young inexperienced fellows wanted to tackle it."

Then a smile came over George Gallion's face. He glanced up across the barbershop at his wife. Her face was strained.

"I could handle that school with one hand tied behind me," he said. "If they're the sons and daughters of the students I had, they're not outlaws. They've got good stuff in 'em."

"George, you couldn't be thinking about taking over that school," his wife interrupted. "You must think of your own health. Remember your last two years!"

"No, I'm not thinking about going back," he told her. "Only about what I would do if I were there. I can't forget what Ken said about no one seeming to care what goes on. I'm thinking about the fine kids I taught there. I haven't forgotten many faces. This shouldn't happen to those people. When I went there it was as rough as you said it is now. I had teachers who were as interested as I was. We changed that school until it was one of the best. Now, from what you say it's gone back to the jungle again."

"Professor," Ken said, waving his buzzing clippers, "I've told them down there they need you back. You remember when I kept running away from school and you told me if I did it again, you'd use the board of education on me? I wanted you to expel me. You told me you'd make that decision. Well, I tried you again, and honest, when you got through with me I looked to see if flames were shooting from the seat of my pants. Boy, I hated you for a while, and then the hate died. After you left, what happened? I walked out when I wanted to. I got kicked out. Then, Dad would see that I went back. But I got expelled for a double amount next time. Then I got so far behind I drifted out of school. Later I learned about discipline in the Army. It was some shock too!"

"I agree with you, Ken, we must have discipline," said the big man who was standing near the window. "I think that's the main trouble down at Kensington. Our young people down there are growing up like uncultivated corn. Put corn in the same field and cultivate one half and let the other half go and see the results. Kensington High School right now is the part of the field that was planted and not cultivated."

"The Professor could handle the situation even if he has been sick," Ken said. He raced his electric clippers up the other temple. "Yes, he can handle the place with a hand tied behind him!"

"Who are the young fellows wanting to be principal?" George Gallion asked.

"One is Harvey Winthrow," Ken said.

"I remember Harvey," George Gallion said. "He could never make up his mind. A man's got to work fast on a lot of small decisions in a big school. He's not the man. I taught him and I know. He'd make a good classroom teacher."

"Little Tommie Fillis wants it, and he qualifies," Tad said. "He got a big master's degree in college. He's a well-eddicated dood."

"I remember him too." George Gallion smiled. "When he ran away from school, I went to his home and he was hiding in the clothespress. I pulled him out and took him back to school. He never ran away again. But he won't make a principal of Kensington High School. He's too young and not a good enough student to work with veteran teachers."

"George, why are you so interested in who takes it?" his wife asked.

"Because I like school problems." He avoided her eyes.

"George, you don't think anybody can handle Kensington High School but you! Times have changed and the world is not like it used to be. You're thinking back twenty years ago! You were a young man in good health when you took that school over."

"Yes, and you know why I took it over, Grace. They had trouble. They had a scandal that got into all the newspapers. The chips were down when I went there. A high school principal has got to like a problem or he should stay out of administrative work. If he's a principal, he's going to have more problems, even with a little school, than the executive who heads a big business. His problems are with human lives. A principal is the hub of the wheel and his teachers are the spokes. He'd better be strong. He'd better make decisions. No, I'm not the only one who can handle Kensington High School! I do know the people there and . . ."

"You *used* to know them," she interrupted him.

"Even if I wanted to be principal of Kensington High School, I couldn't get it," he said. "I disciplined John Bennington, who's now Greenwood County Superintendent, when he was a teacher on my faculty. I used to treat him pretty rough about his not getting his reports in on time." George stopped a moment and then continued thoughtfully. "Now, I can tell you one of my students who could discipline the school. Banks Broadhurst can handle it. On the football field he fought for inches when he couldn't gain feet. He was a good student and he could make decisions and stand by them."

"They've tried to get him, Mr. Gallion," said the big man against the wall, "but too late. He'd signed a contract with some large school in Ohio to coach there next year. He asked for a release, but they wouldn't release him."

"I can understand that," George Gallion said.

"Ever discipline Broadhurst, Professor?" Ken asked.

He chuckled as he made the scissors sing over his customer's head.

"No, Ken," he said. "But I took him to college and gave him five dollars. That's all the money he ever got, and four years later he had a degree. He didn't have any help and he was from a broken home."

"How can you remember so many?" Ken said.

"Because I've always been interested in my boys," he replied "I sometimes wish I could forget some of them, but I can't."

"Professor, I can cut your hair now," Tad said as his customer got down from the chair. Tad smiled and brushed the loose hair from his white coat. "It's been a long time since I cut the Professor's hair. Who's been cutting it for you, Professor?"

George Gallion pretended not to hear the question. When he started to climb up in Tad's barber chair, Grace got up to help him.

"No, I can make it all right." He climbed up awkwardly. "It's good to be in your chair again, Tad," he said, grinning. "Good to hear all this news about Kensington High School too, even if it is bad news."

"Well, we're telling you the truth," Ken said. "The high school situation is all they talk about in Kensington. This is July and they don't have a principal. They don't have teachers. There's talk that the school won't open in September. If it does and if one of the young fellows I mentioned gets to be principal, you'll see classes all over the hillside and down on the banks of the Tiber River."

Tad clipped George's long graying hair. It fell in wisps onto his lap and down around the chair.

"How old are you now, Professor?" Tad asked, "if ye don't mind my asking?"

"Not at all," he replied. "I'm forty-nine. But I still can handle Kensington High School!"

"You don't have to go back to schoolwork, and you shouldn't," Grace said. "You're just able to get around, so why *t*hink about it?"

"I can't keep from thinking I'm needed," he told her. "I'm thinking perhaps too much money and soft living has caused all that trouble down there."

"Yes, half the lads at Kensington High School have cars now," Ken said. "They drive away when they want to and burn the rubber on the highways. Big problem there last year was parking space."

"Only the coach and one of our teachers had cars when I was there before," George told them.

"I told you the world had changed," Grace said. "Your ideas are too old, George."

"Character and discipline are never old. We've had these for five thousand years!"

"If I had known you were going to get all worked up in here over a problem . . ."

"You would have cut my hair at home," he interrupted.

George's mind flashed back to the times she had cut his hair when he was propped up in bed. He remembered too, the first time she cut it his hair was nearly down to his shoulders. This was after the long weeks under the oxygen tent and flat on his back, not allowed to move.

"By this time, Mrs. Gallion, you should have learned to be a good barber," Tad said.

"She's next to you, Tad." George laughed. "She did a good job."

"I want him to guard his health, Mr. Meadowbrook," she said.

"Can't blame you for that."

Now Tad had finished with him. George got down from the chair slowly.

"A Tad Meadowbrook haircut," he said, looking into the mirror at himself. "This is like old times again. You used to give me courting haircuts that wooed my wife, Tad," he said, trying to joke the serious look off Grace's face. "That's how I got Grace. You gave me traveling haircuts, farming and teaching haircuts! You make people look better, Tad! You are a successful man in this world. You've done something!"

"Oh, thank you, Professor," he said, laughing. "Now, I want you to come back again soon. Come back and bring Mrs. Professor."

All the customers had gone from the shop except the big man who leaned against the window. He still stood there smiling. When he smiled, his lips parted like an unzipped billfold so everyone could count his missing front teeth.

"Mr. Gallion, I'd like to speak to you alone a minute before you leave," he said.

"All right, let's step outside," George told him.

While they moved outside, Grace went back to the car.

"I don't want your wife to hear what I am going to say," he said softly to George.

"I don't keep any secrets from Grace. You can speak in front of her."

"I'd better not. I know how she feels," he said, "and I can't blame her. I don't want to hurt you but I used to know you in Kensington. I sold insurance there in those days. Two of my brothers-in-law went to school to you. Remember the twins, Ned and Ted Traylor?"

"I thought I knew you," George said. "You're Orman Caudill!"

"I'm chairman of the Greenwood County board of education now," he explained, "and we're really up against something at Kensington High School. Honest, I don't know who we are going to get to handle the school. And if you are able, I'll go to the superintendent's office right now. You said John wouldn't accept you because you'd disciplined him when he taught for you. Last week he said he wished for a man like you to take the school over. We can't pay you what you might ask us. I know you've made big money, but if you are interested and have the health, would you consider taking the school over? I can sympathize with you. I've had a heart attack too and if I don't get somebody who can handle that school, I'm going to have another one."

"I've got a doctor and a wife who'll have to pass on me," George said, smiling. "Each has a vote, and I'll have one."

"Your wife will be against your going."

"My doctor will have the deciding vote," George said. "Maybe I did say too much in there. Maybe I bragged too soon about handling it with a hand tied behind me."

"Would you even consider going back?" he asked George.

"Yes, if my doctor will okay me."

"When can I have the word from your doctor?" Orman said.

"I'll phone him," George said. "I'll let you know this afternoon."

"I'm going to hurry down to the office and tell John," Orman said enthusiastically. "The board meets Monday night and we have to hire somebody. We're desperate."

"He wants you to take the principalship of Kensington High School," Grace said when George went to the car.

"Right."

"Are you going to do it, George?"

"If I can pass the physical," he told her. "I am needed and I'll go back."

"Two years ago, you know what happened. Only by a miracle of good doctors and people's prayers are you a living man. I'm your wife and I stood by your bedside. I remember you in the oxygen tent, forty-six days on your back. One year in bed. Then, this past year you've spent convalescing. I remember your first step, because the nurse and I helped you take it. You screamed and said pins and needles were sticking your feet. And now you're interested in this school, George—I know you! We made a mistake coming here. I should have cut your hair again. George, you can't go back."

"You're my wife, Grace, not my doctor."

"I'm against it from the start," she said. "This will finish you."

"Let's get to a phone," he said.

"We don't need the money, George; we have security. You won't live to enjoy it."

"I've heard security in this country until I'm sick of it," he replied sharply. "That's all I hear these days. Economic security, social security, psychological security! Enough to last us to the end of our days. I've never known of anybody starving to death, but I've known people to rust out because they were afraid to live."

"What salary did he offer you?"

"None. I never asked him. I'm needed."

"You're egotistical."

"Maybe I am. Let's drive over to the telephone exchange where I can put in a phone call."

Tears welled up in her eyes as she drove down the street.

There was silence between them now. When George got out, she got out too while he called Dr. Charles Vinn of Toniron, Ohio.

"George, is the building all on one floor?" Dr. Vinn asked him.

"No, there are two stories."

There was a long silence on the line. "I think it would be all right if you don't climb stairs. It's obviously something you want to do very much. But remember you had a double infarct. I'm sixty-eight now and have had only three patients survive this. You have as much scar tissue on your heart as a man can have. Think you can handle a high school?"

"I believe I can," George said. "If I see I can't do it, I'll resign. But it's a challenge, Doc, and I'm needed."

"You have my okay and you won't have to take a physical there. I'll send my okay to your local doctor."

"Thank you, Dr. Vinn." He hung up the receiver. "Two in my favor," George said smiling. "I'm in, if the superintendent and school board will hire me."

"You're in," Grace said sadly. "I've been married to you seventeen years and I thought I knew you. All I have to say is, this country is hard up for high school principals when a man of your physical condition has to return." She was almost crying. "You are my husband and I love you. I hate to see something happen to you."

"You're so right when you said this country is hard up for principals. For schoolteachers, too," he said, taking her by the hand. They walked out of the exchange onto the street. "It's damned hard up. You won't find any shortage of men in the professions where the big money is."

She waited for him to get into the car. "They're smart. You're not. You're a do-gooder and you're going into something blindly. Everything is against you. What can you gain? You're going back to where you started twenty years ago."

"Maybe so," he said. "I'm trying to do something for the kids. I'm not trying to promote myself."

"Your doctor won't even permit you to drive a car, yet he allows you to accept principalship of a problem school! It doesn't make sense."

"I don't believe in that old theory a school has to get bad before it can get better," George said as Grace drove down Main Street. "I think the moral bottom can drop out and it can stay that way." But she didn't answer, so he sat in silence as she drove.

Grace slammed on the brakes and the car jerked to a stop under a large elm by a parking meter. They were in front of the Greenwood County school superintendent's office, a now shabby building which was once the home of a prosperous undertaker. This headquarters of educational enlightenment for thousands of young Americans was the most dilapidated of all the public buildings in Greenwood County.

"Well, we're here, he said. "Are you going in with me?"

"You bet I am. I might have something to tell the superintendent and that snaggled-toothed board member that hung around up there in the barbershop."

When he stepped on the rickety porch and opened the door, she was beside him.

Chapter Two

The Hub and the Wheel

Lined against the wall in the small office was a row of chairs filled with waiting people.

Just like it used to be when I was superintendent of this county, George Gallion thought. Every person here has a problem or he wants something. The superintendent is the wagon's tongue. He pulls the wheels with the hubs and spokes.

John Bennington and Orman Caudill were talking when George and Grace entered.

"Mr. and Mrs. Gallion," John said as soon as they entered. "It's great to see you here! Let's go over to my cubbyhole where we can talk."

This small, graying man in a plain business suit, with trousers worn slick at the seat and coatsleeves worn threadbare at the elbows, led them into a small inner room which had perhaps once been the pantry in this old house. There was a small table in the center with six chairs around it.

"Have seats," John Bennington said, looking up with owlish eyes from behind his thick-lensed glasses. "This is where I meet with members of my Greenwood County school board. Here's where our decisions are made."

Grace Gallion looked around at the bare, chipping walls, the bare light bulbs hanging in their sockets.

"Mr. Gallion, I just can't believe you might go back to Kensington High School," John said. "It sounds too good to be true!"

"I had no such intentions when I came to Greenwood to get

a haircut," he said. "But Kensington High School is now barbershop talk, John. When a school gets to be barbershop talk something is radically wrong. Very few people will praise a good school, but everybody will push one deeper when it's stuck in the mud."

"How right you are," Orman said. "People have worn paths over my grass from all directions to report what goes on in Kensington High School. A lot of the reports I hear can't be true."

"Mr. Gallion, when will you know whether you can take the school or not?" John asked.

"John, I am happy to report I already have two votes out of three. I know I'm not as physically strong as I once was, but I believe Kensington High School will be an easy task."

"You must have had a good report from your doctor," Orman said, grinning.

"George hasn't told you all," Grace said. "Dr. Vinn told him not to climb the steps to the second floor. He told him if he felt the least bit tired to resign immediately. My husband wants to take it, regardless of the consequences."

"Well, of course we want him to. He's the right man—the only man—for the position. But we don't want him to wreck his health. We know what he's been through. We have licked many problems, but Kensington High School is such a headache that I hoped—"

"How about teachers?" George asked.

"They're scarce, Mr. Gallion," John Bennington said. "We're scraping the bottom of the barrel. Several of our teachers are still so limited in training it's hard to get them even provisional certificates from our state department of education."

"I won't have any trouble getting qualified teachers for Kensington High School, will I?"

"You might have a little trouble, Mr. Gallion," John Bennington said thoughtfully. "It's not the same as it used to be when I taught for you. There were ten teachers then for every job. And, of course, a teacher without a college degree wasn't even considered for a high school position in this state twenty years ago."

"And now?" George asked.

"The situation is tragic for all our youth, Mr. Gallion," John Bennington continued. "We've got a lot of big problems ahead of us in this country when this generation grows up. Our youth are not disciplined and educated now the way we used to do it. In some of the one-room rural schools last year, we sent as many as five different teachers to one school. We had to send uneducated, unqualified teachers out—young people mostly—and the pupils ran them off. I'm telling you the facts behind closed doors. No wonder my hair has turned almost white in two years. And I have ulcers too."

"You mean you don't have elementary teachers either?" Grace Gallion asked.

"That's true, Mrs. Gallion," he answered softly. "When we can get a college-trained teacher, we almost shout. We struggle hard to go back and get the experienced old-line teachers. That's why we want your husband."

Orman Caudill laid the application form on the table. George Gallion pulled his glasses from his inside coat pocket and put them on. "I never used to have to wear these bifocals before I had that heart attack," he said. He fumbled in his inside coat pocket for his fountain pen. "It's been a long time. This brings back memories. I'm sure I'm equal to this task. I believe there're a lot of exaggerations about the educational situation now." Then he stopped writing and looked up. "Do five board members have to pass on me?" he asked.

"Don't worry about that," Orman Caudill said. "You've taught four of them. I'm the only one you didn't teach."

"You know, Mrs. Gallion, this might interest you," John Bennington said while George filled in his application. "Back when your husband was county school superintendent, he rode horseback to my little one-room rural school and he made a talk. He said, 'The time will come someday when this county will have consolidated schools. Some young man is going to be superintendent and put this over.' I said to myself right then, 'I am going to be that superintendent to give Greenwood County its consolidated schools.' So I ran three times before I was elected superintendent of Greenwood County schools. This is my third year in office and I am happy to say that this year we have completed the last consolidated school. Not one child will go to a one-room school. This year we have eleven consolidated elementary schools. Your husband's former pupils voted five to one to raise their taxes for this school program. Now do you wonder why we want him to help us? What we wonder about is paying him what he is worth."

"Pay me what you pay the principal of East Greenwood County High School or even less if you want to," George said. "Don't tell me what you're going to pay me. Let's see if I can go back where I left off twenty years ago and do the job."

"I didn't know the situation was so bad," Grace Gallion said.

"I told you, dear, it was rough. When the papers are filled with the faults of the schools and people who have never been teachers start telling school people how to run the schools, then it is time for all of us older teachers to go back."

"Do you have a degree, Mrs. Gallion?" John Bennington asked.

"Yes, I have a degree in elementary education and I taught second grade for eleven years," she said. "But I haven't taught for seventeen years. I'm not up on any of the new teaching methods."

"A college degree in elementary education and eleven years of experience, Mr. Bennington!" Orman Caudill almost shouted with enthusiasm. "It's a prayer answered! We can't get a second-grade teacher for Kensington Elementary—that's the school just across the highway from Kensington High School. Won't you come back too, Mrs. Gallion?"

Grace stared at him.

"You mean that you want me too?"

"Want you?" John Bennington said. "Want you? Do we want you? Get her an application, Orman! You're an answer to a prayer!"

"You're needed too, Grace," George said. "You're one of the best elementary teachers who ever walked into a classroom. We can drive together, morning and afternoon, five days a week."

Grace looked skeptically at George.

"George, if you are determined to go back and there's a vacancy in my field, what else can I do?"

"It's not the school administrators' fault we can't pay teachers enough in Appalachia, one of the poorest parts of America," John Bennington said. "This is the people's fault. About half of the people don't care whether we have good schools or not. While about half of the other half want something for nothing. It takes money to have good schools."

"I used to think," George said, "we could build our country into a modern civilization that would rival the old Greek civilization. We have athletic competitions and we honor our athletes just as much as they did. But our love of learning and our desire to create fall sadly behind the ancient Greeks'."

Orman Caudill placed an application on the table in front of Grace.

"I'm so behind the new methods," she sighed. "I'm not young any more and I've never dreamed of going back to teaching again."

"Mrs. Gallion, I'd like to say something here," John Bennington added, tapping the table with his fountain pen. "We really need your type of teacher. The older teachers are better qualified than the younger ones we have to take. The young ones haven't had any teaching experience. Many have had only one year in college."

"Well, since my husband is determined to go back, I'll go with him," she said. "But I admit I don't want to do it."

"Monday night the Greenwood County school board will

pass on your applications," John Bennington said. "You will have to have written statements from your doctors regarding your health."

"I'll have them Monday morning," George told him.

"Then you'll be our new principal of Kensington High School," he said proudly. "And you'll have our number one headache!" He paused. "I don't know the things you plan to emphasize, Mr. Gallion. I doubt you'll have time to emphasize anything new. If you can find a faculty and a way to keep the kids in the classrooms we will be pleased."

"I won't have the trouble you think," George said firmly. "We'll move forward."

"That's the only way you can move," John Bennington assured him. "Kensington High School has gone as far backward as a school can go. The situation there is one of moral disintegration. We even thought of delaying its opening in September. We actually thought we might have to close that school and not open it at all."

"Now I'm getting downright eager," George said.

"Mr. Gallion, you know Orman Caudill is running for re-election in the Kensington District," Bennington said. "Unless Kensington High School is improved we have conceded his defeat. Your going there might save one of my best board members. You take over Kensington without any strings attached. You run it. Make it a school again if you can."

It was already late afternoon. Grace went into a rear office to collect her materials. The two men continued to talk.

"How many will be enrolled in Kensington High School, John?" George asked.

"Approximately five hundred. Of course, we are never sure of these figures, Mr. Gallion," he added cautiously. "It's hard to pinpoint the number, due to new people moving in down there. Two industrial plants and a dam in the Ohio River are bringing in new families."

"But Kensington High School's capacity is three hundred. If we have five hundred down there this year, I don't know where we'll put them."

"Space is a problem down there, Mr. Gallion, but we've added some since you used to be there. Now we have the Ag building. Beyond the Ag building is the shop. We have a nice two-room block building outside where another class can be taught. And then," he continued, choosing his words carefully, "we planned to move three or four pre-fabs from the atomic plant and put them directly behind the school for classrooms. So I'd say space won't be exactly your problem. You'll have additional space in these outbuildings."

"Hauling flimsy pre-fabs a hundred miles for schoolrooms? What about the roofs after they reach here?"

"We get them cheap from the government," John said. "I don't know about the roofs. This is the best we can do."

"We'll lose time changing classes," George sighed, "when pupils have to go that far between classes. It will be rough out there in winter weather too. Now about my teachers," he continued. "I haven't talked to you about them. I suppose a few didn't return from last year?"

"Yes, Mr. Gallion, that is quite true. Several are not coming back and perhaps it's just as well! I'll show you the number we have signed up."

George followed the superintendent into the main office.

"With approximately five hundred pupils down there, I'll have to have at least twenty teachers. I'd like to have one teacher per twenty-five pupils. I'd rather have one teacher per twenty pupils."

"How do you figure it that way, Mr. Gallion?" John asked.

"By past experience."

"Here's the list, Mr. Gallion," John said, giving him a single sheet of paper.

"You mean this is all, John?" he raised his voice as he scanned the sheet. "You mean. . . ?"

"Yes, Mr. Gallion," he interrupted. "This is the list."

"Only six of twenty-three coming back." George looked at the short list, unbelieving.

"I've just found how much I knew," Grace said, as they walked to the car. "Mr. Dunnaway, the head, admits he's not an elementary school man. After I talked with him, he started asking me questions. So I guess I am needed," she sighed. "With all the transition from the one-room to the consolidated schools this year, I can see a horrible mess! You've got us into it, too, George!"

George was silent as she drove up Main Street.

"I wonder what my associates will be like. I'm one of the few who will have a college degree in elementary education in my school. We'll have nearly three hundred pupils," she continued. "I'm in for trouble, George."

"Did you get any new materials?" he asked her.

"Not anything more than what I learned years ago," she replied. "The material I got here isn't as good as the old material I used to have. How did you get along?"

"Terrible," he sighed. "You know what? I'll have to admit already you had a point in your argument about my going back. Did you know that Kensington High will have approximately five hundred pupils this year and I have only six teachers? Of the six teachers, one is eighty-four years old. Another has high school grades I'd be ashamed to show you. He went four years to college, played football, but doesn't have a degree! I'll have to hire fourteen new teachers. But I'll find them!"

"Where?" She looked quickly at him. "Didn't I read somewhere in the paper that all the Kentucky schools are desperate for teachers? Principals and superintendents are scraping the bottom of the barrel for teachers. Now where will you get them? Kentucky is low on salaries."

"Where teachers can't be found, I can find them." He spoke with confidence. "Good teachers I used to know couldn't get jobs. There weren't any. I had to turn them away! I wish they were here now. I agree with you and John Bennington and everyone else who says the world has changed. Teachers are such scarce commodities, and the demand is so great they own the market."

"But where are you going to find fourteen teachers, George? You speak with such confidence! Tell me where you'll find them."

"First, I'll try to fill each position with a college graduate," he said. "I've always staffed my high schools with college graduates."

"What if you can't get them now?" she asked. "Then what?"

"I'll fall back to my second line of defense," he said.

"What's that?"

"I'll take teachers who haven't degrees."

"What if you don't get them?"

"I have a third line of defense."

"What in the world is a third line of defense?"

"That one is my secret," he replied. "I'm going to do the job. I have the will and I'll find the way. I'm determined to pull Kensington High School back up where it belongs."

They were almost home now. They turned onto a small dirt road, on both sides of which the long green acres of their farm stretched.

"Who's going to take care of all this?" she said. "We'll both be away from home so much!"

"Land can take care of itself more efficiently than youth. And," he added, avoiding her glance, "you and I will be human conservationists instead."

It was early the next morning that a car came up the hill beyond the house. The wheels spun and threw dirt in two earth-colored arcs. The car door opened and a tall young fellow with short red hair standing up like stickers on a chestnut burr got out and came toward George, smiling. His brown eyes sparkled like earth-colored agates in the sun. He was dressed in brown sport slacks and a short-sleeved brown sport shirt which was open at the collar.

"You're Mr. Gallion, aren't you?"

"Yes, I am."

"I'm Don Webber," he said. "I'm coach at Kensington High School. It's out everywhere in Kensington that you're going to be our principal this year. We get the news before it reaches the papers."

"I'm glad to see you!"

"I've come to see how you feel about athletics," he said. "I want you to be frank with me. I've never had any cooperation before."

"You'll get my cooperation," George said. "I think sports are wonderful for young men. I'm all for it!"

"For winning teams?"

"Yes, if you can produce them," George replied. "If you can't produce them, I won't hold it against you. But I like good teams."

"You know Kensington High School won three basketball games and four baseball games the year before I took over?" he said. "Lost every football game. Our teams were called sick chickens and hard-luck teams! Since I've been coach it's not been that way."

"Wonderful," George complimented him.

"I don't enjoy being a loser," he said.

"Your talk suits me," George told him. "You've whipped your problem, but I understand I have a big one before me."

"You sure have."

"You help me, I'll help you," George told him.

Don Webber grabbed George's hand. "You're talking my language now."

"What do you coach?" George asked.

"All three major sports," he replied.

"Teach any subjects?"

"Five. And I kept a study hall too."

"Good teacher?"

He looked at George and laughed.

"Do you read much" George asked.

"Best-read teacher on Kensington High faculty. Check last year's library cards, and you'll see."

"Have you got your athletes reading?"

"I'll say I have. Best-read pupils in school." He looked George in the eye. "I've heard about you. I just wanted to look you over. I never want another year like last year. I wanted to look you in the eye to see whether I'd work for you or not."

"How do I look? How about my eyes?"

"You look all right. You've got a good eye. I judge character by the eye."

"Do you believe in discipline?"

"A coach has to believe in discipline. What do you think?"

"You'd better believe in discipline," George warned him. "We've got a task ahead, if my information is right."

"Suits me." He grinned. "I believe we'll get along."

"Now what, George?" Grace said. "What are you going to haul in that truck?"

"Nothing, darling," he replied.

"You're driving?" she questioned him.

"Sure I'm driving," he said. "If I topple over I won't hurt anyone but myself. So I've decided to take a little trip and do my own driving."

"Let me take you in the car."

"Not this time. I'm the only one who can do this."

"What is it? Why is it so important?"

"I'm going to Kensington to hunt teachers."

"I'll take you."

"I'm going alone."

"George, I'd like to go with you."

"Not this time, darling," he told her. "I want to go alone.

Some people I want to see. I want to know something of the situation in Kensington High School. I can find out better if I'm alone."

He drove away in his old farm pickup down the lane to the Valley Road. He looked in the mirror and he could still see her standing at the end of the drive watching the truck.

This is life again, he thought. I'm beginning to live. I've never felt better than now. Rusting out will kill a man. If there are any teachers at the bottom of the barrel I'll find them.

George pulled the truck to the curb in front of Kensington Elementary.

"Thunderation and tarnation," the old man said as he walked over to the pickup. "Old Gordie kin hardly believe his own eyes! Is that you, Mr. Gallion?"

A broom was across his shoulder, a big pipe was in his mouth, and his slouched black hat was pulled low over his big ears.

"Yes, Gordie, that's my name."

"On my honor, I'm glad to see yuh," he said. He dropped his broom and stepped up to shake George's hand. "Oh, I reckon I know what happened. I know why you're here."

"When did you find out?"

"Saturday," he replied.

"I didn't know myself then. How did you find out so soon?"

"Ah, Mr. Gallion, you know me." His old inky eyes sparkled. "A little bird tells me. You ought to remember how I could get secrets when you couldn't."

"You could find out more than any man I've known," George said. "What goes on down here? What's the news?"

"Ah, Mr. Gallion," he sighed. "It's not like the old days, when I was custodian over there for you. The situation here is the worst I ever seen. Mr. Gallion, it's the worst place for talk I ever seen. You can't believe nobody. What's the matter with people any more?"

"You tell me," George said. "I'd like to know!"

"Kensington High School is worse off than hell." He

wheezed hoarsely on his pipe. "The bottom's done gone out of the place."

"Are you working here?"

"Now it ain't that I was fired from over there. You know I'm seventy-five and all. The place gave me the creeps. I tell you, Mr. Gallion, I couldn't stand them tales. I told John Bennington since he didn't have nobody for Kensington Elementary I'd come on over here."

"Who's disturbing the peace over in Kensington High?"

"If you don't know now, you'll find out." He spat and knocked the ashes from his pipe. "It's that Riddle! See that block building over there?" He pointed. "He'll decide who'll teach in that building. Now wait and see! Why, Mr. Gallion," he whispered, "that Riddle has a snake's forked tongue and each fork will tell a different lie at the same time. He's been in Kensington High too long, Mr. Gallion!"

"A forked tongue, huh?" George laughed. "I don't know Mr. Riddle."

"Watch him, Mr. Gallion. He's pizen. One fork of his tongue will salve you while the other will broadcast that you are a sonofabitch! Pardon my language, Mr. Gallion; I'm just warning you. But don't you mention my name!"

"I won't," George promised. "I'll keep my eyes open, too."

"You'd better not shut them once," Old Gordie shouted. "If you do you're a goner! He's pizen, I tell you! He told I kept a dirty schoolhouse and I oughta been retired ten years ago."

"Did he tell that on you?"

"He shore did, Mr. Gallion. I'm about as good a man now as I ever was. He told I had a pension with my job and slept most of my time in the furnace room!"

"Anybody else talking over there?"

"Hardly anybody left over there to talk," he said. "The place got so bad about everybody left. Jest a few old scrubs and creeps still hangin' on."

"Where did they go?"

"Better jobs over in Ohio."

"Can you tell me where I can find teachers? Do you know a real good one who's not been hired yet?"

"No, I can't, Mr. Gallion," he said, filling his pipe again. "Well, there's Dolores Binford lives up the road. Finished college and taught at the high school last year. But I hear she's gone over to Ohio, too."

"Has she been hired yet?"

"I don't rightly know, Mr. Gallion."

"Where does she live?"

"Seventh house up left side of the road."

"What ever became of Alice Nottingham?"

"She's gone, Mr. Gallion," he replied. "She went across the river two years ago. One of the best teachers at the school, too."

"I agree with you, Gordie," George said. "I used to work with her. Where does she live?"

"In Kensington, same old place."

"I'd like to have her this year."

"You won't get her, Mr. Gallion," he said. "Old Gordie knows what he's talkin' about. She gets big money over in Ohio. They like her an awful lot over there. So my little bird told me."

"They're all about gone," George sighed. "What about Irene Dumfries? What happened to her?"

"Quit teachin', Mr. Gallion."

"It's a shame she's quit," George said. "She was a wonderful English teacher. I'd like to have her, too."

"You'll need all the good teachers you can get and then some, Mr. Gallion. See that patch of woods over there in Kale Manning's cow pasture? That's where they'll hide on you. First day of school them woods will be filled with boys."

"You think so, Gordie?"

"Oh, yes, Mr. Gallion. If you don't have enough good teachers. Last year it was a plumb sight. Ruined Kale's white board fences climbing over 'em with their muddy shoes and all!"

"We can stop that this year. And you can help me."

"I'll do all I can," he said. "See, that's the only way they can leave the hill without your seeing 'em. They go through the pasture and over to that little store up the road there. They all got money to spend. Seems as like money burns their pockets."

"Could I ask the merchant not to serve them? Would he cooperate?"

"Well, you know how that is, Mr. Gallion." He shook his head. "That won't work so good. Merchants like to sell."

"I'll keep a check on every pupil in school," George said. "I'll know where they are every minute." He got up to go.

"Drop in any time you're down this way," Gordie said. "But don't come too much after school starts, come to think of it. People'll get the wrong ideas if they see us together too often."

"I'll watch that, Gordie," he said. "I won't put you on the spot."

He got into his truck, turned left onto the Lane Road, and came in behind the Kensington High School building. The two-story brick structure looked like an ancient fortress upon a low hill. George drove slowly, looking over this schoolground that once held so many of his dreams. During his two years' illness he had often thought of the school. He saw now the new, ugly buildings that had been erected behind the main school building since he had taught there.

He pulled up beside the main building and got out of the car. He stood in front of the gym in astonishment. Almost all the window panes had been knocked out or broken. Birds were flying in and out of the building.

You've had some bad treatment, old girl, he thought. He remembered this schoolhouse when it was beautiful. He tried to open the pair of rear gym doors, but they were stuck. He went to the front door, which faced the Ohio River; it was locked. He looked up at the windows on the front side. There were a dozen broken panes. He looked for a minute from the front steps through the window into his old office. It's in shambles, he thought. What has gone on here? Old Tad and Ken weren't lying.

He walked around in front of the building, looking down over the green acres of Kensington High School playground. The grass had not been cut and the grasshoppers flew up here and there in July heat so intense it glimmered. He walked to the door on the east side. This door was locked, too, and he tried to shake it open. *I'd like to go in there, he thought. This school holds dreams for me. I remember their faces. I remember the years.* Memories of the youth he had taught here and the teachers who had worked with him welled up within him like heated water about to boil. All that had once been so full of life and so beautiful had come to this broken-windowed emptiness. He went back to his truck and drove over the hill.

He parked in the drive of the seventh house on the left above Kensington High School, got out and rang the doorbell. A young woman came to the door.

"Are you Miss Dolores Binford?"

"Yes, I am."

"I'm George Gallion. I'm looking for teachers for this year."

"Well, Mr. Gallion," she said, "I've just signed a contract to teach in Ohio next year."

"Too bad," George said. "I hear you are a good teacher and I'm going to need you. But if you've already signed a contract . . ."

"I have," she interrupted him. "I wouldn't want to go back there anyway."

"What do you teach, Miss Binford?"

"French and Latin," she replied.

"Oh, languages," he said with enthusiasm. "A Latin teacher! I want to emphasize languages."

"Mr. Gallion, I like your enthusiasm," she said. "But how can you get pupils to take Latin?"

"How can I get them?" He was astounded by her question.

"They should *want* to take Latin! I won't have any trouble."

"I can see you don't know the pupils in Kensington High School," she told him. "I do."

"I used to be principal there eighteen years ago and we certainly had Latin," he told her. "We didn't have any trouble then."

"That was a long time ago, Mr. Gallion. Now they tell us what they want to take. They don't want Latin. They say Latin is too hard. They want easy courses."

"How many did you have in Latin last year?"

"Mr. Gallion, are you trying to be funny?" she asked him. "Don't you know?"

"Know what?"

"Latin just isn't taught in Kensington High School any more," she said. "There's no one to take it!"

"I'll put Latin back," George told her. "I know its value more and more as the years pass. And, Miss Binford," he added positively, "I'll find a teacher and I'll get pupils and we'll have the languages."

"Well, well, if it isn't you, George Gallion! Come in."

"How are you, Alice?"

"Fine, George," she replied. "And you?"

"Worried," he answered her as he went inside. "Worried! Worried!"

"If all reports are true, I know why you're worried."

"They're true all right," he said. "I'll be principal of Kensington High School this year."

"It's a rough school now."

He remembered Alice Nottingham well. He remembered when there were problems in the school. He had seen her stand and look so steady and straight at a pupil until he thought her green eyes would drill holes where she was concentrating her gaze. She was plump, redheaded, and rugged as a storm-ridden oak in winter on a high hill.

"Every report I have had agrees with yours," he said. "So it will be a challenge."

"Why did you go back?" she asked.

"Alice, I'm needed."

"You certainly are," she said.

"Alice, you can shoot straight with me. You were never afraid of a school problem. Why did you leave Kensington?"

"For three reasons," she answered him. "I don't want to teach in a school where I wouldn't send my own son. I like organization, discipline and a good curriculum. Then, if you noticed when you came in, I live in the same area but in a different house."

"Yes, this is the nicest one I've seen in Kensington," George said.

"John and I are paying for it," she explained. "Maybe I'm a little selfish, but I think teachers are entitled to at least a few of the better things of life. A teacher is more respected in the classroom and in the town if he lives in a decent house. So I went to Ohio where I make $1600 more a year than I made in Kensington. Can you blame me?"

"Of course not. But you know why I'm here. I want you back."

"But I've signed a contract. Even if I wanted to go back it would be hard to get a release now. They don't have time at Northwest High to get a replacement for me."

"They have as much time to replace you as I have to get a dozen teachers," he told her. "I'm in a desperate situation."

"You're putting me on the spot."

"Of course I am," he admitted. "You know why? You know the pupils and you know the parents. Here I'll need all sorts of information before the year is over, and you can supply that information."

"What about Mr. Riddle? He's been up there a dozen years or more now."

"This is his adopted county; he's not one of the people here. Your people go back to the pioneers. We need you on the faculty."

"You flatter me."

"No, I'm not flattering you, but I will flatter you any way I can to bring you back from Ohio. If your principal knew how badly I needed you, he'd release you. I'd like to encourage him to give you the toe like we teachers used to get around here!"

Alice Nottingham laughed.

" 'The toe,' " she repeated. "That used to be a familiar expression, but I've not heard it in a long time."

"Can't you come, Alice?" he pleaded. "Really, I need you."

"No, George, I can't, she said softly. "I'm paying for my house. I'm paying tuition for Bill and . . ."

"Bring Bill back to Kensington High with you," George interrupted her. "He belongs in Kensington."

"No, he doesn't, George. You say I'm a good teacher. Well, let me say what I think. When a school cannot give a pupil what he needs, the best thing to do is take that pupil out. When a school fails all the pupils, then either change the principal and faculty and strengthen the curriculum or close the school."

George Gallion stood silently taking it all in.

"I don't believe in being sentimental," she added. "The secondary school is important—most important in moulding a youth's life. My son was running wild. No discipline. He couldn't get what he wanted."

"Can he get everything he wants at Northwest High School?" George asked.

"He's not in Northwest High School. That's another thing. Problems arise in a school where teachers are forced to teach their own children. I have Bill enrolled at St. Mary's in Dartmouth."

George was silent.

"You're a public school man, George," she explained. "St. Mary's is a church school. It's Catholic. We're Protestants. I've been a public school teacher since I've been eighteen. I am the same age as you are. Yes, I know what you're thinking."

"No, you don't either," George said. "It would take pages to write what has flashed through my mind in a minute. St. Mary's is good. But give me four years and the teachers and see what happens! They won't be running away from my school. The young and eager will be wanting to come!"

Now she was silent.

"You know, Alice, what we used to have in Kensington High School?"

"That time is so far away and so long ago, George." She sighed. "Eighteen years in a changing world when we've been through two wars . . . you won't be going back, George, to the world we knew in Kensington High."

"Alice, do you see any possible way of working with me?"

"George, if I had signed a contract to work for you, what would you think if I walked out just a month before school began? You wouldn't like it, would you?"

"No, I wouldn't," he admitted slowly. "But Alice, this is war for me. I'm fighting for something."

"You don't have to do it, George," she interrupted him. "You could stay home and take it easy."

"My wife has told me that so many times I'm about to believe it." George raised his voice. "You're wrong and she's wrong. I can't stay home and take it easy. If I had you and a few others we could pull the school through the worst this year."

George rose. Alice stared at the carpet, then she looked up slowly until her green eyes met his.

"I can't do it, George."

"I'm sorry, Alice," he said. "If you ever change your mind, let me know the minute you do. And if you can think of an available teacher, let me know."

"I'll do that," she told him. "I'll steer anyone I can your way for Kensington High School!"

"Everything but yourself," George said, forcing a little smile. "And it's you I want most. Well, good-by!"

"Good-by, George."

She followed him to the door.

"Fred Laurie won't be back at South Dartmouth High," she said. "I don't think he's got a place yet. You might get him."

"Not the Fred Laurie I used to teach in Kensington High? He's not a teacher, is he?"

"Yes, he's the same one. One can never tell what a boy will do. He's the last one in that school I ever thought would be a teacher, and I'm told he's excellent."

"Why's he leaving South Dartmouth?"

"Same old story," she said. "Pay! He has a wife and child to support."

"I don't think he'll teach for me," George said. "You know why."

"It's been so long he won't hold it against you," she said. "Since he's become a teacher he'll understand more about teachers' problems now."

"Yes, maybe," George said. "I'll go see him anyway. Thanks."

"Mr. Gallion, you mean you really want me to teach for you?"

"Why do you think I've come to see you?" George said.

Fred Laurie was a huge man, six feet five inches tall with a florid complexion, brown thinning hair and a tight firm mouth. He towered over his former teacher.

"You wonder why I am a teacher," he said. "I know you can't believe I am. You know what made me a teacher?"

"No, I've not the least idea."

"Your fist."

"Do you mean that?"

"You almost beat the hell out of me."

"Well, you'd whipped every big fellow in school and grownups on the streets! You were a terrible bully. And you almost whipped me."

"Not any more, Mr. Gallion," he said, smiling. "I'm a teacher, and a good one, I hope. You know, I've taught school for years and I've never had a boy come to me as rough as I used to be. Boys can't pull any tricks on me. I know all their tricks, and then some!"

"You must be good in discipline."

"I certainly am."

"I'd like you to come teach for me."

"The world has changed. I never thought this would happen. I've said to myself a thousand times since you lowered the boom on me, 'I'd like to thank Mr. Gallion for what he's done for me.' But you went away and I did too. Sounds silly, doesn't it? I've told people about this and they've laughed at me."

"Will you consider teaching for me?"

"I'd consider it an honor and a privilege."

"I'm really delighted. I didn't think you'd want to work for me," George said quietly. "Now I must be going. I'm trying to find teachers. I've got another stop to make. Didn't you have Mrs. Dumfries in English?"

"Sure did," he smiled. "I thought she was a tough one then, but I know what a good English teacher she was."

"I hear she's not teaching, and I want her to return to Kensington High this year."

"You're out rounding up a few of the old ones, huh?"

"Yes, and the young ones," George replied. "You're teacher number nine and I have to find eleven more. If you hear of any prospects let me know."

"Sure will, Mr. Gallion."

The afternoon was almost gone. George drove the little truck up the Tiber Valley Road, turned left on a lane where tall corn grew on one side and on the other a herd of whiteface cattle ate lush grass. Here was a prosperous farm with large barns and a neat white farmhouse. He parked in front and walked up on the porch and rang the doorbell.

"Mr. Gallion, I am surprised to see you here," Irene Dumfries said, smiling.

"Mrs. Dumfries, I've come for something."

"I've heard you'll be principal of Kensington High School this year."

"That's true. And I'd like you to come there with me."

"You flatter me. I gave you lots of trouble by failing so many."

"I've heard it was unpopular to fail a pupil in the present set-up," George said.

"You've heard right, Mr. Gallion. The curriculum has been watered down until education is tasteless. Now, in its weakened form which any pupil with half a brain ought to master with ease, if a teacher fails a few pupils she's criticized. I went back and substituted last year. I soon got fed up with the situation."

"So you're not interested in going back?"

"No, I'm not. I'm wondering why you are."

"I'm needed."

"No doubt of that! Just how much can one man change the present situation?"

"Plenty!"

They faced each other in the living room.

"Won't you sit down, Mr. Gallion?"

"No, it's too close to your suppertime. I know you're getting supper. I smell food cooking."

"Maybe you can't conceive of my being a farmer's wife," she said with a smile.

"It is difficult. I think of you being more at home in the classroom than any place."

"I used to love to teach. Not any more. You'll get a letdown, Mr. Gallion, when you go back. You're in for some surprises."

"We taught their fathers and mothers."

"I know we did, and that was something very difficult for me to understand," she explained. "Is it that long ago since we were in Kensington High School working together? We made out the curriculum. We told the pupils what to take. Now they tell us what they want to do."

"Only a weak-kneed principal will submit to that kind of monkey business!"

"I'm afraid there are a lot of weak-kneed principals nowadays. Another thing I never thought I'd ever run up against. Parents who know their children do not deserve to pass will make demands on the principal that he put pressure on the teachers to give their children passing grades."

"Mrs. Dumfries, after hearing you talk I'm more anxious than ever to be back in Kensington High School," George said. "Can't you go back with me?"

"I can't get interested again after last year's experience," she said. "Besides, I can't afford it. My little salary would just lift us into a higher tax bracket."

"This is true with us, too," George told her. "My wife is going to Kensington Elementary. Our combined salaries put us in a higher bracket too."

"Is your wife going back too?"

"She sure is!"

"I think that is very commendable of both of you," she said. "But with our daughter away, I'm needed here at the farm. I'm sorry, Mr. Gallion, I won't be available this year."

"I need eleven teachers," he said. "If you change your mind please let me know immediately."

"Eleven teachers," she repeated as if she were shocked. "You can't find eleven teachers now, can you? As scarce as teachers are, will you be able to open Kensington High School in September?"

"Yes, we'll open Kensington in September."

"I'm sorry I can't help you," she said. "I wish I could. You're up against something. Really you are."

"Yes, I have a problem. It's been good to see you. I hope you can see your way clear to teach again."

"Good-by," she said.

I might have to fall back to my second line of defense, he thought. I will make many more contacts before I do. But I am beginning to see that possibility.

"Where are you going on a Sunday morning in that truck?"

"Not to church," he said. "I'm going to find a teacher."

"Where this time?"

"South Dartmouth," he replied. "I want to see her before she goes to church."

"I wouldn't hunt teachers on Sunday."

"But I will."

"Every day I read where schools are not going to open because of teachers. Let the public do something."

"My school will open," he told her. "The public is a sleeping monster. You have to twist his tail and then sometimes he won't wake. He likes to sleep."

"Your work in one little school can't solve the problem."

"You'll be surprised what my work in one little school can do."

He started the motor, and was off down the lane with a trail of soup-bean-colored dust swirling after.

The Blevins' old stone house was one of the largest in this quiet, pleasant town. George rang the doorbell. A well-dressed man about his own age came to the door.

"I'm George Gallion. You're Bertice Blevins, aren't you?"

"Yes, I am," he said. "Won't you come in?"

"I've come to see Mrs. Blevins."

"I've been planning to go see you," he said. "I work for the Home Milk Company. I've heard you're principal up at Kensington High this year, and I'd like to have your milk business if you can keep the boys away from the trucks."

"We'll do our best to protect the trucks that bring us supplies. The superintendent and board of education do the purchasing of school supplies."

"Now I wonder if your wife has accepted a teaching position," George asked. "Is she here?"

"Yes, she's out in the garden," he said. "She's not reemployed yet. She's considering a change. Let's walk around where she is."

"Mr. Gallion, we met several years ago," Edna Blevins said. "Maybe you don't remember. We met when you were principal of Kensington High School and I was a beginning teacher there. My sister Claris used to teach for you at Greenwood."

"Well, after the years we meet again," George said. "If you

are not re-employed, I'm most anxious to have you in Kensington High this year."

"I've never taught anywhere but in South Dartmouth High," she told him.

"You must be a pillar in the school," George said.

"I don't know whether I'm a pillar or a whipping post," she said.

"I hear you are considering a position in Ohio," George said.

"Right," she said.

"You have a fine home here. Looks like you folks are getting along all right."

"We have no children," Bertice Blevins said. "We both work, and work hard."

"Have you done all this work around here?"

"Yes, we have," he replied proudly.

"Now, if you consider staying on in South Dartmouth High School, I'll not try to persuade you to teach for me," George told her. "I know you're needed there."

"I've been there so long I'm taken for granted," she said with a sigh. "I'm considering a change. And I'm offered $2000 more salary across the river. I can cross the bridge morning and afternoon, and stay home and teach."

"Confound that bridge," George said. "That bridge is hurting me."

They all laughed.

"We can't match your salary," George said. "But you do have to pay toll crossing the bridge night and morning. Figure up and see what you can teach in Kensington High School for. We won't take you for granted. If we had more money we'd meet what they've offered. Yes," George added, "if I had more money to offer teachers I'd match anything Ohio offers for you. But I've got an idea. In addition to raising your salary all we can, I'll see Superintendent Bennington and see if we can give you our milk business, Mr. Blevins."

"That would be fine," he said, pleased.

"I'll go right now," George told them. "I'll be back as soon as I can and report to you."

Then George drove back up the Ohio River Road to Kensington where he turned off onto the Tiber Road. He drove to John Bennington's house.

"Yes, we'll let him have the milk business for Kensington High School," John Bennington said. "We can't go above $3300 in salary. Now, Mr. Gallion, bargain with him at first on delivering milk to Kensington High School. To supply milk for five hundred pupils is a good bargaining point. But to get her, we have four more elementary schools with a total enrollment of over a thousand pupils. But hold back on these elementary schools. We might need the milk trade on these to bargain for another teacher! I'm glad you thought of that deal," John continued; "she's one of the best teachers in the state."

"You folks go on to church and I'll go back to South Dartmouth in a hurry."

George got into his truck and was off again down the Tiber Road. When he got back to South Dartmouth, Edna and Bertice Blevins had just returned from church.

"I've just seen Mr. Bennington. He said you were a good man and worked for a good company and he was sure it could be arranged for you to get the Kensington High School milk trade if Mrs. Blevins could teach for us."

"How many pupils in Kensington High School this year?" he asked George.

"At least five hundred," George replied. "Maybe more."

"It will add a lot to my route," he said with enthusiasm. "Give us time to think it over."

"And give me time to think," she said. "So many of my former pupils make daily visits here begging me to return. My pupils depend on me and I love them."

"When can you let me know?" George asked.

"By Wednesday," she said.

"Don't you cross that bridge," George said jokingly. "I'll be here Wednesday."

George was going back to his truck when another thought came to him. He turned and called back to her.

"Mrs. Blevins, what is Claris' married name, and her street address?" George asked. "I remember her quite well. I might get her too."

"I don't think there will be any use to try," she told George. "Her husband is a doctor and they have two small children."

"Confound the income tax brackets," George said. "And confound the bridge! Would she return to her teaching just out of the goodness of her heart?"

"Go see her," she said. "She's Mrs. Emmett Torrence, and she lives at 527 Chestnut Street."

"It will be worth a try," he said. "She's a good Latin teacher. There's no Latin in Kensington High School but I'm going to add it to the curriculum."

I won't have any trouble getting Claris, he thought as he drove over the Dartmouth Bridge. Among all these well-dressed people driving nice cars, there must be teachers to fill our classrooms. He drove across Dartmouth toward Chestnut Street.

"Sorry, but no more teaching for me," Claris said to him. "I have two small children and they need me. Besides," she added, "all I'd make would go to the government for taxes." George couldn't persuade her to return. She gave George the name of three "prospects" who were retired teachers and lived in Dartmouth.

He left hurriedly and drove to the address of the first one.

"After fifty years teaching on a salary so small I wasn't able to save anything, I am now on a small pension that will hardly pay my rent and buy me food. Don't you think, young man, I've contributed enough?" the elderly woman asked George.

She closed the door in his face. The second prospect, who had been retired two years, met him at the door with a cane in her hand. She was crippled with arthritis. He wondered if Claris had played a trick on him. He didn't follow up the third prospect. The hour was late. Lights had come on over the city and he had a long drive home.

Monday morning George drove to Greenwood where he stopped at the superintendent's office.

"Mr. Gallion, we have an application here for band director," John said.

"Where is he from?"

"Indiana."

"He can't be very much," George groaned. "If he is acceptable they'd hang on to him there."

"Yes, he is, Mr. Gallion." John Bennington was very positive this time. "My son-in-law, who was a music major, says this man is excellent."

"What's his name?"

"Shan Hannigan." He gave George the application.

"Here's the catch," George said. "He's not a college graduate."

"Mr. Gallion, he's an Army regimental band conductor," John said with emphasis. "He's plenty good."

"Why didn't he stay in the Army? He's not old enough to be retired."

"A physical disability, Mr. Gallion," he explained. "He's had the same thing you've had."

"Oh, well, then," George said quietly. "Maybe he's a do-gooder too!"

"Well, not as much as you might think, Mr. Gallion. We'll have to make concessions to meet his salary demands."

"How much?" George asked.

"Four thousand," he replied. "Band directors come high on Kentucky's education market. There's a lot of bidding for them."

"What about your son-in-law who's a music major?" George asked.

"He's getting $5000 in Indiana."

"I hate to fall back to the second line of defense." George spoke stoutly. "Damned if I don't. I hate to be a second-rater. I have pride in my school, my pupils and my teachers. We're in a hell of a situation!"

"Will you accept Shan Hannigan?" he asked. "Other schools are bidding on him. We have to work fast."

"I'll have to accept him," George replied. "John, this situation is serious. Can I use your phone to call the State University and colleges to see if they have teachers?"

"Yes, you can use my phone," he said. "But Mr. Gallion, there will not be any use to call. I've already done it."

"But I know many of the college presidents personally. I've spoken in their assembly programs. I've spent nights in their homes. Personal contact might pull a dozen white rabbits from the hat."

But each call brought the same reply: there was no one.

"What in the hell has happened to one hundred ninety million Americans?" George shouted irritably. "Don't we give a damn about our youth? Can't somebody work for something that doesn't have the almighty dollar sign!"

On Wednesday George drove through Greenwood and stopped at John Bennington's office again.

"John, have you had any report from South Darmouth?"

"Yes, just a few minutes ago," John replied, pursing his lips. "The news isn't good. Mrs. Blevins is staying at South Dartmouth High School. The school board met there last night and gave her extra work so they could increase her salary legally above the state's salary schedule."

George was silent.

"First I offered Bert Blevins the milk trade at Kensington High School," John continued, moistening his lips with his tongue. "When he said he wasn't interested, I offered him four additional elementary schools. Even with supplying milk for seventeen hundred pupils, I couldn't bargain with him for his wife's teaching services. They must have given her a good raise to hold her. Mr. Blevins said the pupils and their parents were beating a path to her door begging her to stay."

"Maybe they'll wake up and learn to appreciate a good teacher," George said. "I'm glad she's staying there. She's needed in that school. But what are we to do?"

That afternoon when George walked inside the Math Room he greeted his teachers, seven men and two women.

There was old Garrett Newell, eighty-four years old now, whom George had known when he was a student in Greenwood High School. He was at that time superintendent of the Rosten City schools and George thought then he was an old man. There was Coach Don Webber, and Fred Laurie. They and Marcella Waters were the only ones he knew well.

"Marcella, I'm glad you're here," he said. He walked up the aisle and shook her hand. "John was a little reluctant to let you teach for me this year," he said.

"I'm glad you encouraged him to let me come. I like to teach. And right now," she added, "teachers are so badly needed."

"And you must be Delbert Bennington," he said to the young man sitting near her.

"Yes, sir, I am," replied the man as he rose from his chair. He was in his early twenties and looked more like a student than a teacher. He was small with a shock of coarse black hair, a narrow mouth, and large expressive blue eyes.

"I've never taught in high school, Mr. Gallion," he said warmly, shaking his principal's hand. "Dad came after me and told me this was a must. So I'm here."

"You had a good job, too, but now you will have a more exciting one."

"If I can't do this work, my company will take me back. I have this understanding with my boss."

"I hated to put the pressure on your dad to get you, Delbert. I hate for you to cut your salary in half, and you with a wife and child, but others have used pressure to get things of less value than good teachers. Now we have nine instead of seven teachers." George walked forward to face his little faculty. "If any of you can think of an idle teacher any place, let me know. Maybe we can manage with nine more. We have hardly a month left before school starts."

"Do you suppose we'll be able to get enough teachers?" Gus Riddle asked.

"Mr. Riddle, if you hear a rumor Kensington High School won't open in September be sure to spike it! This school will open. I have the third line of defense up my sleeve."

"Mr. Gallion, I'd like to know what that is," Fred Laurie said.

"All of you may soon know what it is," George said as he sat down on a knife-scarred chair arm. "We might have to resort to a last-ditch stand."

His nine teachers were as quiet as trees on a sultry summer day when no wind stirs. There were questions on their faces. Garrett Newall's deep-lined face was grim and serious. His gnarled hoe-calloused hands rested on the arm of his chair.

"Most of you are veterans on the firing line," George said, interrupting their silence. "I want to talk to you about teaching. Each of you will have a full teaching load in addition to other responsibilities."

"Mr. Gallion, I take instructions from the State Department of Agriculture on what I'm allowed to do," Gus warned.

"In addition to their orders, you might have to take some extra assignments from me."

"I do a lot of work here," he said.

"I don't question that," George explained. "Since there is so much to do, each might be asked to add more work."

Gus looked at George and his blue eyes looked doubtfully toward the cobwebbed ceiling. Don Webber looked at George and smiled.

"Mr. Riddle, teaching is a many-sided vocation," George continued. "Good teaching goes beyond the expected. Just for an example, all of you, no matter what you teach, should be English teachers at all times. I like the word *dimensional*,"

George explained. "A good teacher must be an inspiration. He must approach his pupils in many different ways to inspire them. If he can excite and inspire them half of the battle is won. He won't have many discipline problems."

"I agree with you on that," Garrett Newall said. His heavy words eased from his wrinkled mouth over the worn stubs of discolored teeth.

"Don't let the word *dimensional* throw you," George continued. "I like to use this word to cover what I mean. A teacher should have many sides. And until education becomes a passion it is only routine."

"You don't mean to give the pupils a lot of fluff instead of factual knowledge?" Charles Newton asked. He had been at Kensington for several years.

"Not at all, Mr. Newton," he replied. "If a boy pushes a woman teacher aside and goes through the door first when he leaves the classroom, what would you do?"

"I'd call him aside and explain to him his manners were atrocious."

"That's good teaching too," George said in a complimentary tone. "From what reports I have had on Kensington High School, we have moral disintegration. This should not be or have been."

"We have worse than that," Gus said, shaking his head. "We'll do well to put a few facts into their heads."

"Give them the regular prescribed courses," George interrupted, "and for greater dimensions give them plenty of other things—manners, honesty, and encouragement. Inspire each one if you can to reach up and out for better living and the best things in life."

"That's just so much sweet talk," Gus said. "It sounds all right to speak before teachers or to put on paper, but to put that into practice is something else."

"If some of that had been put into practice, Kensington High School wouldn't be in its present condition," Fred Laurie said.

"I agree to that statement too," old Garrett Newall said. "I've been right here all the time. I've seen the foundation props go from under Kensington High School."

"What will you do when pupils won't mind you?" Gus asked. "Expel them."

"No, no, no," George replied emphatically. "Never expel! That's what they want. Take them into your confidence and try to discipline them with words."

Gus laughed.

"Mr. Gallion, you didn't discipline me that way. You used to be as rough as a crosscut saw," Fred Laurie said.

"How many times did I talk to you first?"

"About a half dozen times," he replied.

"Then I had to use other measures," George said.

"We'll never use harsh discipline until the higher one fails," George said. "I won't suspend pupils, because they need to be in school. We'll handle discipline right here! When a pupil becomes unruly you send that pupil to my office. I'll handle him with your help."

"This school will be better off with from three to seven percent of the hoods and bums kicked out and never allowed to return," Gus said. "If I were principal, I'd kick 'em out!"

"I would too," Charles Newton agreed with Gus.

"Where would they go?" George asked. "What would they do? They'd loaf in Kensington and get into something. They'd soon be a menace to society."

"But we'd save this school," Gus retorted.

"What about saving everybody?" George asked.

"Not those who will never amount to much, Mr. Gallion," Charles Newton said. "After they get through school, what will they be? This isn't a reformatory, but a high school."

"From what I've been told it isn't my kind of a high school," George said. "It's not even a good reformatory. But if we make good citizens out of them, we've achieved. We've done something great. This goes back to dimensional teaching. You might arouse an interest in each pupil of this group until he can find himself. When he finds himself he will be different."

"I agree with that," Fred Laurie said. "That is just what happened to me. That's why I am a teacher."

"You don't agree with Mr. Gallion, do you, Mr. Laurie?" Charles Newton said. His cheeks were flushed. "You don't agree that we can possibly reform the hoods?"

"I certainly do," he replied. "I was once a hood."

"I agree with Mr. Gallion," Garrett Newell said. "Good discipline can change youth. In my day we had hoods too, only we'd never heard them called that. I know what he's talking about."

"Don't you believe in the same kind of discipline for all pupils?" Charles Newton asked.

"I do not," George replied. "It won't work. People are different. What will work wonders on some won't touch others."

"That shows partiality," Charles Newton argued. "All of them should be disciplined alike."

"Now if I know a pupil who would rather be spanked than expelled I might expel him," George said. "When one won't listen to reason in our higher frame of discipline and we must resort to the lower frame, he will not have any choice in the kind he is about to receive."

A hush fell over the room.

"Can you, as teachers, stand discipline?" George asked, breaking the silence. "Would you leave me if I were to discipline you? Would you leave me, as much as I need you?"

Old Garrett Newall's crinkled lips spread into a smile.

"I might have to discipline you," George said. "You might have to discipline each other. You might have to discipline me. I won't be offended. We have to work together and with our pupils to rise higher and higher. Our theories in education can be no higher than the teacher who puts them into practice."

"You're not poorer teachers either because you don't get higher salaries," George continued. "You should be paid more, but a better salary is not a guarantee of better teaching. Many of you are here not for better salaries, but because of your love of teaching. I think you will be dimensional teachers. Remember," he continued, "you never enter the classroom alone. There is always somebody following you."

"And who is he?" Gus Riddle asked skeptically.

"The man or woman you really are," George said.

George waited in his truck across the street, and when John Bennington arrived at nine to begin his day he overtook him at the door.

"Have you found another teacher?" George asked.

"No, I've not," he replied. "Have you?"

"No, all my last contacts have been disappointments. Now I'm willing to accept teachers with some experience and without degrees. Time is eating away at us!"

"Come into my office and let's discuss this situation."

"I hope you can re-establish decency and order down there." John Bennington spoke quietly. "And say nothing about what we are saying behind these walls. If you do, it might cost me votes."

"It won't cost me any votes," George said emphatically. "But for your sake I won't publicize the situation. John, you're younger than I am. I'll tell you how to buy good will."

"Tell me," he said eagerly.

"Do a two-fisted job, that's how. Lift this educational system to a higher standard even if it puts you out on a limb. Don't be petty and don't be afraid. Hell's fire, John, people hate a coward!"

"I remember when you sat where I sit now." John Bennington spoke with soft guarded words. "People were after you with guns. I go easier with people and give them more of what they want and hold on to my salary, which is the best I've ever had in my life."

"And you won't last, either," George told him. "You can't

fool the people. They like a fighter who stands for something. Look at rubber-stamp congressmen in this state! They're out. Don't be a rubber-stamp county school superintendent."

"You would have been killed if you had stayed on here," he told George. "I don't want to die. No job is worth dying for."

"I never think about that. I've barely missed death several times but I'm still here. You just can't be a rubber stamp, John! We can't go back. We have to start all over for more reforms."

"You asked me if I had any news this morning," John said. "Yes, I have news of a different sort, I don't know whether it's good or bad news. The figures have been revised on the number you will have in Kensington High School. You'll have approximately one hundred more than we have anticipated."

"Six hundred pupils for a schoolhouse that was built for a capacity of three hundred," George said. "Two hundred fifty pupils are as many as we ought to have in that building. That means more teachers, too."

"I could hardly sleep over this weekend for thinking about what to do with six hundred in that school building. Have you any suggestions?"

"Since there's no basement to put them in, cut a hole through the roof and have classes up there," George said.

"We couldn't do that. What about rainy weather up there? And what about their jumping off and maybe committing suicide over grades?"

"I was just trying to be funny," George said.

"Pre-fabs from the atomic plant are the only answer."

"Get them in a hurry."

"What about teachers? Teachers! Teachers!"

"Yes, teachers," George sighed sadly. "Would you look over all your elementary schools, check qualifications of your teachers and see how many have had high school teaching experience?"

"Mr. Gallion, we have very few college graduates in the elementary schools."

"I've given up my first objective," George sighed. "I have to fall back to the second one. I hate to retreat to the third."

"What is the third objective, Mr. Gallion? You have me puzzled."

"Student teachers in high school, John," he replied. "Kensington High School will open if we do this. And we should all hang our heads in shame. Our country, a giant among other countries, goes out with an honest heart and an open mind to save her neighbor, when she's losing herself at home."

"What will I do for replacements in the elementary schools?"

"Pull them up from the ranks," George told him. "Education begins at the bottom. I need the better-trained teachers in the high school where pupils are more advanced."

George Gallion had deep sympathy for this small man who had once taught for him. He was up against problems that George had not had to face twenty-four years ago when he had occupied this same position. Now, John Bennington was apprehensive of getting three board members in his favor elected in the autumn election. His fears of what lay ahead, in the uneasy transition to consolidated schools, had aggravated his ulcers. He leaned heavily on George Gallion's decisions and advice.

He was a small man, who was struggling with a burden too much for him to handle. He was running for office again to save a school program he had worked hard to get, and he was afraid to speak his thoughts. But George Gallion wasn't running for anything, and he dared to speak out, regardless of the consequences.

"Now, will you check your elementary school faculties and see how many teachers you can find?"

"Yes, sometime today; I'll let you know tomorrow."

The cardinals woke George at the crack of dawn when they left their nests for the feed boxes. The pewees gave their familiar calls as they strained the fresh morning air for the camp-

winged moths to feed their famished young. Grace fussed because George let the birds wake him so early, but she always got up then too.

Each day he received letters from people who wanted to come and teach for him. A newspaper interview he had given to the *Dartmouth Times,* pleading for teachers, had been reprinted in the papers from coast to coast. After reading the replies he didn't find one applicant who he felt was qualified to meet the teaching standards and discipline problems which he was sure he would have in his school.

Six of these applicants were college graduates; three had master's degrees, and one had a doctor's degree. All had graduated from first-rate American colleges, including Harvard and Oberlin. Not one had spent the best of his productive years in secondary schools. Only one was under seventy-five years of age. These people had the pioneer teaching spirit, but age was against them, especially in Kensington High School where the problem of discipline would test the weakest spoke in the wheel.

At eight o'clock he paid another visit to John Bennington. John greeted him with a smile.

"Mr. Gallion, I believe we have three teachers for Kensington. Not college graduates. All women. Come into my private office."

John closed the door behind them. They sat down at the table and John Bennington laid down before him a descriptive sheet about each teacher.

"Ann Rockland. Three years of teaching in a one-room school, where she had taught all from the first through the eighth grades, two years of college, good disciplinarian, physically strong and a teacher of integrity."

"Since we can't do better we'll have to take her," George muttered. "If something should turn up, John, and I get a qualified, experienced teacher to replace her before school begins, will you take her back to the elementary schools?"

"Yes, gladly," John replied, crushed. "If you can replace all three I'll gladly take them back."

"Not enough college work here, John," George muttered, shaking his head. "Maybe I can use her with the beginners."

"There just aren't any teachers, Mr. Gallion."

"How much experience has Elizabeth Haskins had?"

"Five years. I've used her since she graduated from high school. She's one of our better one-room rural teachers. She can handle the rough situations. She's a fiery, tall redhead. She'll fool you, Mr. Gallion!"

"I hope she gives a good account of herself. I'm dubious."

"Now the last one, Mr. Gallion," he said softly. "I wasn't too sure about her. We have to take a chance here."

"Leota Barton. Three years of college, married, two children, thirty-eight years old, has fifteen years of elementary teaching experience," George read. "She's the best qualified of the three."

"That's not it, Mr. Gallion. She's moved here last year from another county. Her husband just got through serving a sentence. She's a fine woman, I believe," he continued, "but sensitive of what it will do to her and her two children if this is known."

"Where is her husband now?"

"He got a job away from here."

"Her predicament might hurt her teaching," George said. "But how can we do any better?"

"These three teachers have handled rough situations," he explained. "They've taught and handled some rough eighth-graders."

"You've got some elementary principals I'd like to have."

"But I can't spare them, Mr. Gallion. What would I do for leaders? What kind of students would we be sending to the high schools? You will take Leota Barton?"

"Only because I have to," George sighed. "We've had to fall back to the second line, John."

"I'll send them down to Kensington High School for the meeting tomorrow. Shan Hannigan, the bandman, came in early this morning and I told him and he'll be there."

"Thirteen teachers and six hundred pupils in a schoolroom built for three hundred. Everything is against us, but we'll have to find a way!"

George Gallion went early for the Wednesday afternoon meeting. When he drove up the Hill, there was a car there with Indiana licenses. A wiry, dark-haired man introduced himself as Shan Hannigan.

"Mr. Gallion, I am a band instructor and this is all I can do in a schoolroom," he said. "In this field I'm sure of myself."

"I almost didn't take you," George told him. "I accepted you because I couldn't do any better."

"I understand you couldn't. I'm not a college graduate. I'm only a sophomore in college. A sophomore at fifty, but I'll have my degree before I'm too old to retire from schoolwork, or leave this world."

"If you had been a college graduate we couldn't have got you. You would have stayed in Indiana. Right?"

"I was offered a position there, but I wanted to get away from home. I was offered a better salary than I am getting here."

"Maybe this question is personal, but do you teach for a living?"

"I don't mind your question," Shan Hannigan replied, pushing a lock of hair back from over his eyes. "I'm retired from the Army on a seventy-five percent disability. My wife and I don't have any children. My mother-in-law stays with us. I'm a carpenter and I make cabinets and such, no big jobs, of course."

"Well, that's something," George said, warming to this new teacher.

"I've been looking around here for a place to have my band

room. I'd like something on the outside of the main building."

"Have you found anything outside? What about one of the pre-fabs?"

"Sound would blast those thin walls out," he replied quickly. "The nearest to anything I can use is that block building. I hear they practiced band on a few old instruments in the gymnasium last year."

"Can you build a band at this school? Can you produce the first year? Now let me tell you"—George spoke so fast he wouldn't let Shan Hannigan interrupt—"if you can, you'll be the first one in the history of this school to have what I think is a first-class band. If I thought you could, you could have that block building, one all the classroom teachers want."

"Let me tell you something," he said. "I like a challenge. If you've not had a good band here, I can do what the others have failed to do. I can build one the first year. I can build one that will stir a pupil or teacher until he'll want to rise and start marching! I can produce a marching band."

"Then you're my man," George told him. "Let your music speak. A good band can bring us together when we disagree on everything else."

"I see you're going to be a cooperative man. The real reason I didn't take that position in Indiana was, I didn't like the way the principal talked. I'd have gone back to carpentry before I'd have worked with him. I can't spend the rest of my days in retirement."

"I'm like that, too," George said. "How can men as young as we are be retired for little physical disabilities? I doubt we'll have a teacher in this school who really has to teach for money."

"I've already found that out," he told George. "I understand you just about have to take culls like myself."

George smiled. "But I'm going to give a cull like you the best building here on the Hill, because I've got faith in you."

"One thing more," Hannigan added. "I've checked over all

the instruments we have here, and we don't have half as many as we need. The ones we have are in such poor condition I can't get a clear tone on one."

"See John Bennington, the superintendent, and ask him how much he can get the county school board to allow you for new instruments and for having the old ones repaired," George told him. "You'll find places over in Dartmouth where they repair band instruments."

"I'll repair the instruments myself," he said. "I can do that as well as anybody."

"Wonderful!" George was pleased. "Don't tell the superintendent or anybody on the school board yet. Make out two expense items and present them. Then, you repair the instruments and take all the money they allow you for this and put it into new instruments."

"I've got a better idea," Hannigan said quickly. "I'll have so many out for band after we get started, I'll take the money appropriated for repairing old instruments and buy old ones in need of repair. I can get these for one-fourth the cost of new ones. I'll repair these myself until they'll play as good as new."

"It's a great idea," George said, slapping Shan Hannigan on the shoulder. He looked up at George and grinned like a possum. "You and I are going to get along."

As they stood on the steps, the three new teachers arrived together. Ann Rockwell was a plump, pretty woman in her middle twenties. She wore her hair in a knot low on her neck, and her eyes were as blue as deep water.

Elizabeth Haskins was tall and extremely thin, with hair the color of flames. Her eyes were as green as those of a cat. Her cheekbones were angular and prominent and her hands and fingers were long and thin. She had an intense and nervous look that made George slightly apprehensive.

Leota Barton was in her late thirties but looked much older. Her black hair was beginning to gray in little wisps and her large brown eyes looked as sad as a scolded cocker spaniel's. Her dress was drab and ill-fitting. She looked like a woman who had had much trouble and little happiness.

"I'm sure of my teaching in the elementary grades," Ann Rockwell said. "I'm not sure how well I'll do in high school."

"Be positive from the minute you step into a classroom," George told her. "Mrs. Rockwell, if you could teach all the grades in a one-room school and discipline the pupils and handle the problems you had there, Kensington High School ought to be easy for you," George said. "Besides, you won't have to teach on a much higher level than last year. You won't have the discipline problems you had last year. You can send them to my office now."

"I hope I don't have as many problems as I had last year," Leota Barton sighed.

"I had them too," Elizabeth Haskins said. "I found most of my problems were caused by the parents. They need to be educated and disciplined more than their children."

George looked at her. Her nervousness seemed to vanish. When she spoke now she seemed intense, but self-assured. I think I can use you, George thought. I'm going to put you, a woman teacher, in that pre-fab building on the far end of the schoolyard back next to the woods where there will be trouble. I believe you will handle the situation better than a man.

"Everybody should be getting here any minute," George said, looking at his watch.

In the wake of swirling dust in this dry August weather, cars were moving slowly toward the building on the Hill. Gus Riddle got out of his car waving a newspaper in his hand.

"Have you tried to use the phone today, Mr. Gallion?" Gus asked breathlessly.

"No, I haven't."

"You won't use it," he said, "Take a look at this!"

He gave George a copy of the *Dartmouth Times.*

"Phone strike, huh?" Gus was positive. "Dartmouth is a big labor town and my Kensington neighbors work for the Home

Telephone Company. Ah, we like a good strike around here."

"I like a telephone too. What will we do without one?"

"Looks like everything is against you, Mr. Gallion," he said. "You know Kensington High School has been called the hard-luck school. Looks like you might be a hard-luck principal!"

"Maybe so, but you shouldn't be telling all the difficulties we have to face before these new teachers." He grinned. "Let me introduce them to you."

"It's really an event to get four at once," Gus said. "The profession must be getting popular again."

"Since everybody is getting here we'd better go inside, where you will have seats," George said, and unlocked the door.

They went into the math room. The three new women teachers sat together. Gus sat against the wall and close to the door next to Shan Hannigan. They were meeting for the first time, and eyed one another closely.

"Mr. Riddle, I'm glad I got up here early," Shan Hannigan said. "I've got a big problem solved."

"What one is that, Mr. Hannigan?"

"I've got a band room outside."

"Which one?" Gus asked. "One of those pre-fabs?"

"No pre-fab for me. I got the block building."

"But that's two classrooms." Gus reddened. "We've always used the gym for band practice."

"Not this year," George interrupted.

"This place is crowded, Mr. Gallion," Gus warned, his lips trembling. "You know that! If you don't, you'll find out very soon."

"Yes, it's more crowded than you think," George told Gus. "We have a new estimate on the number of pupils. We'll have six hundred or more."

"Two rooms for the band!" he muttered angrily. "And six hundred pupils. A phone strike. Not enough teachers. A plague worse than struck Egypt has hit Kensington High School!"

"Maybe miracles will save us," George said.

"We don't have a Moses-hero to lead us out of the wilderness," Gus snapped. He turned and glared coldly at Shan Hannigan.

George looked at his watch.

"Now that you are all here we'll start the meeting," George said. "We've got a surprise for you—four new teachers!"

"Four new teachers and one hundred more pupils," Gus sighed. "We're running and yet we're standing still."

"Where will we put the extra hundred?" Mary Wallingford asked. She had been at Kensington for ten years.

"We have the promise of more pre-fabs being moved over from the atomic plant," George explained. "Two have already been moved in."

"I don't believe in miracles," Gus said. "Only a miracle can save us from going to pieces here. That block building would make two classrooms."

"I made that decision," George said firmly.

"Regarding that point I have no more to say, then," said Gus, and turned his face away.

"I believe it is better to have my music practice separated from the main building," Shan Hannigan said quietly. "After all, I didn't make the decision of taking so much space. But I won't have too much space. I'll be crowded. I'll have so many wanting to join the band there won't be standing room."

"We have some bigger problems than the block building," George said. "This phone strike will hurt us. Maybe they'll get it settled."

"I don't believe it will be settled soon," Fred Laurie said. "My wife works for that company. The union has a lot of grievances."

"I wonder if the union would let us make emergency calls," George said. "We will have calls that are a matter of life and death with six hundred pupils in such crowded conditions."

"No, you won't be able to use the phone," Fred Laurie said. "The cable has been cut in eight places."

The day following the teachers' meeting, George Gallion

began another frantic search for teachers. His gray pickup truck sailed over the highways in southern Ohio, into West Virginia and into the hill and mountain counties of his native Kentucky. From August 10 to the first of September, Sundays included, sunshine or rain, he didn't miss a day following a tip for a teacher or contacting school officials in towns, cities, and counties. Most of the teachers he saw were not qualified or were getting a far higher salary in Ohio and West Virginia than his own state would pay.

Many of the teachers he saw knew him by reputation. They had read his articles in educational magazines in the past years and their pupils had read his stories in their textbooks, yet these things were not of any help when his state's teachers' pay rate was next to the lowest in the United States. He had never expected to use his own personal reputation as an educator and writer to help him obtain teachers when he had accepted the position as principal of Kensington High School. Now he changed his mind. He decided to do anything he legitimately could to get teachers for his school.

As the days passed swiftly and Kensington High School's opening date was fast approaching, at least twice a week George met with John Bennington, who was also conducting his own search for teachers. Each time he went into the office he heard the same report. "Nothing favorable, Mr. Gallion." George knew he faced the greatest teaching problem in a career which had begun when he was seventeen years old. He had managed a problem one-room school alone then but could he now, at forty-nine, manage another problem school, the largest school in his county? Would he have to fall back to his third line of defense? He knew his school would open. It *had* to open.

Gossip had circulated that he had gone broke and had to return to teaching. He had learned this when Tad Meadow-brook refused to take pay when he returned for his second haircut. Tad, who kept abreast of all the gossip, explained to him that he had heard that poor business deals and doctor bills had wiped the Gallions out and that he had been forced to drive a pickup truck, which people had come to recognize all over the county. Now that the wind and the sun had tanned his face, George didn't look as if he had ever had an illness.

"Well," Tad explained to him, "folks figure a man who's got plenty to live on won't go over to Kensington High School unless he's broke or losing his mind. And your wife is goin' to teach, too, so they figure you didn't lose your mind, but your money. See? Why else would you do such a crazy thing? That's what they're sayin'."

Early Saturday morning, Grace and George Gallion left the Valley in their gleaming new sand-colored car. Grace had refused to let George take them in the pickup truck to their last teachers' meeting before school began on Monday.

"Well, they won't believe we're broke now," George chuckled.

Grace turned from the Valley onto State 1. She said nothing.

"You look nice this morning," George complimented her. "That dark suit and that pretty little hat are very becoming. I never saw you prettier!"

"You've got what you want, George," she said, breaking her silence. "You've got me back teaching school. Really, I can't see the point. No wonder people think we're broke! That's not funny to me, about Tad's wanting to give you a free haircut. You might think it's funny, but I don't. No wonder people are talking."

After a minute of silence, George ventured, "Try teaching, Grace, and if you don't like it, resign. I know I'm the cause of your going back."

"George, you've been feeling well. Since you've known you would be principal of Kensington High, you've just about run the wheels off that old truck, going day and night, trying to find teachers. Let someone else do it. Your life and health are more important."

"Baby, you look so sweet and nice and I'm so in love with you, I don't want to quarrel on this wonderful day," he said gently. "I want you to love me as much as I love you, as long as we live. You know I feel wonderful to be alive. I can't wait to meet this challenge ahead of us. All these kids need us. Honest, never in my life have I ever been needed so much before! Never anywhere, any place in the eleven years you taught, were you needed then as much as now. I've been out and I've seen the crumbling of our educational system. I know people are beginning to attack its weaknesses, but they can't kill its strength. I just have to get back to it. I can't stand to see it fall apart."

"We're just two little people, George."

"You've told me that before," he said. "We can't live snugly in our shells with a little security. In an ignorant world, no one is secure. When all the people in the world are enlightened and given the right and freedom to think . . ."

"There'll be no more trouble in the world," she interrupted him. "I've heard that many times before too. You're always trying to change the world. When I married you I didn't know you'd never stop, never relax. Look at the things you've written that have come to nothing. Look at the experiments you've tried. George, you get on one of these wild tangents and you don't realize you have a home, a wife and daughter. You don't know we exist! Now you can't tell me they couldn't find someone to take Kensington High School over. You jumped at the chance to get it! We're needed? Needed, my foot! After all we've been through since we've been married, we're entitled to some peace. George, you're even better to your livestock than you are to me and yourself! You've retired your horses, fed and cared for them and never had a bridle on them in five years. Now, am I right?" Her hazel eyes were full of fire.

"You're right about the horses," he admitted. "But I don't want to retire," he said, raising his voice. "I'm not going to retire! I'm not a horse. And neither are you. I'm a human being. And human beings can think, reason, and act, and they're good for something if they keep their senses and are willing to think and act until the day they die. I'm no damned corpse yet!"

There was no one outside the Kensington High School, where there were several parked cars. George looked at his watch. He was ten minutes late. The teachers were inside waiting for him. He got out and watched Grace turn the car and start down to Kensington Elementary School before he went up the steps.

When George walked into the room his teachers were trying to work out a temporary schedule. They hardly noticed George when he entered.

"Mr. Newall, you have six straight classes in math," George said. "You don't have any rest period."

"I asked for that, Mr. Gallion. I can't see how there will be a rest period for any teacher on this faculty."

"Next Monday we cross the Rubicon," Gus Riddle said, grinning and looking up. "We're now getting ready to cross into a hostile school year. Everything is against us." He shook his head negatively as he looked at George. "I can't say that I look forward to this year."

"I'm not allowed by state law to teach a class," George said. "But there's no state law to tell me I can't be a good substitute."

"You won't have time to teach a class," Gus Riddle snapped. "Not if this year is like last year. You'll have too many problems."

"You still want me to take a class in Latin, Mr. Gallion?"

"Definitely yes, Mr. Newton."

"But if I don't get enough students for the class?"

"You'll have a class, Mr. Newton; Latin has to be included in our curriculum."

"As badly as we need the other subjects taught? Latin over bookkeeping?"

"Yes, Mr. Riddle! Latin must be taught."

Gus Riddle shook his head.

"I'd like to have German, French, and Spanish taught too," George added.

"Ah, Mr. Gallion," Gus sighed, "we can't add more."

"Mr. Riddle, you have small classes in agriculture," Don Webber said. "You're restricted by government and state controls on what you can and cannot do. I'd like to have a schedule as easy as yours for once. Look up there, Mr. Riddle, at my schedule. I've got five classes in history and a study hall. There won't be enough hours in the day for my work. I'm head coach of football, basketball, and baseball. Three major sports. And if I don't win, off I go!

"You're right on all but the last count," George interrupted him. "I won't pressure you to win. I know what a load you have. You've got all you can do. I'll give all the help I can. Fred Laurie, you used to be a good football player. What about helping Webber?"

"Look at my teaching schedule," he said. "I don't have a free period."

"We will be working after school hours, Mr. Laurie," Don Webber said. "All the country boys who have to ride the buses will be gone. But the Kensington boys, and several from the county whose father or mother or brother will come after them, will stay late for practice. We start practice at three in the afternoon, and sometimes it's dark before we leave the field."

"Well, I never coached," Fred Laurie said.

"Be my assistant and learn. I can certainly use you."

"I don't mind trying," he said. "But it looks like I am going to have a full day."

"What about a librarian?" Gus Riddle asked.

"We just don't have one," George said.

"Well, all of the teachers won't be able to teach six classes," Gus said. "Somebody has to keep study hall."

"The biggest study hall we have is the library," Miss Wallingford said. "So the teacher in charge of the big study hall will also have to serve as librarian."

"Yes, until we can find a librarian," George added.

"And if we never find one?" Fred Laurie questioned.

"Then we just won't have one," Mary Wallingford said. "I'll have to train students to work in the library."

"What about books?" Gus said. "I have a better library at home than we have here. They used their knives last year, Mr. Gallion, to cut pages from the books. They threw them in the wastepaper baskets and they were carried down to the furnace and thrown in. That old cuss Gordie we had for a custodian last year nearly got burned up diving after a book he'd dumped into the furnace."

"Don't tell me they did that too," George said.

"I'd like to see you stop it without a good two-fisted full-time librarian," Gus said. "Actually, a male librarian is needed."

"Well, if we don't have enough books, you know we can't stand to have any burned," George said. "So, each teacher who has charge of study hall in the library is librarian for that period. Each of you who has study hall in the library meet with Miss Wallingford. She will select students who will assist untrained librarians who will have to be librarians, disciplinarians, answer student questions, and above all keep an eye out for the book-burners."

There were smiles from the teachers. Gus Riddle shook his head again.

"Mr. Gallion, that's awfully makeshift," Gus said. "I don't think it will work; the state program won't let us get by."

"We'll ask the state department to send us a librarian if they don't okay our plan," George answered him quickly.

"Yes, have them send us some teachers too," Fred Laurie said.

"We have to make our own program if we open this school," George said. "And next Monday morning this school will open."

"We're back on the second line of defense, aren't we, Mr. Gallion?" Gus said with a wink. "I told you we would be."

"We're farther back than that, Mr. Riddle," he replied. "We've got to fall back to the third line."

"Among the numbers of the rooms up there I see Pre-fab No. 1, Pre-fab No. 2 and Pre-fab No. 3. I've been out and looked at those pens. The roofs leak. They have no heat, no water out there! But they can come to the schoolhouse for water and rest rooms. September and a part of October will be warm. And when it rains they can use umbrellas."

The teachers glanced silently at Gus Riddle and then at George Gallion.

"You know, Mr. Gallion, that block building out there has two fine classrooms," Gus continued. "It has heat, light, and water is close and there's a nice partition running through it. It's a mortal shame to make a band room out of that fine building which we need so badly for classrooms."

Shan Hannigan jumped to his feet. He was trembling and his face was pale. "Mr. Riddle, you keep talking about that block building. I would like to know what you have against a good high school band? Or is it something personal you have against me?"

"I don't have anything personal against you, Mr. Hannigan," Gus said. "But I don't think we should give the band priority over classrooms when they are at a premium here."

"The ear is most important in music. I have told you before that we couldn't practice in one of these small pre-fab buildings. Take a horn out there and blow it—the sound will burn your eardrums!"

"Why not practice in the gym? They used to do that here."

"I'm against that," Don Webber interrupted quickly. "How could we ever practice basketball down there? We'll be down there as soon as football season is over. In fact we have to use it now."

"Yes, and the pupils have to eat there at noon," Marcella Waters said. "You know that little cafeteria room won't hold thirty pupils."

"Blame me for the decision about the block building," George said. "I made that decision. That is where the band will practice. I want each of you to shine before pupils of this school and before the public. And I shall work, too, to strengthen all the departments, to add languages, higher math, and sciences. This year we're bringing back chemistry. Next year we'll get physics. This year we're having second-year algebra and Latin and other languages if I can find teachers."

"Sweet talk, Mr. Gallion," Gus sighed. "You haven't been in school work recently. When I hear such sweet talk it does something to me. Don't you know, pressure will be put on you until you have to graduate students who don't make sixteen units of required and elective subjects?"

"It won't be put on me. Each graduate will have sixteen units, which is what the state requires, and he will have to have a C average before he will be permitted to graduate."

"Honest, these teachers' meetings are like old-time revivals," Garrett Newall said. "I like them. We're getting stirred up, and we need to be stirred."

"Since we don't have enough teachers we have to fall back to the third line," George said. "I know you don't like to retreat, but we are forced by circumstances to fall back to the third."

The teachers were silent.

"Those among you who were here last year, help me find student teachers who are smart enough to discipline and to teach freshmen, and, maybe, sophomore classes. You've been wanting to know my third line of defense. This is it. Don't tell me the names of the ones you'd recommend now. Give some thinking to this over the weekend."

"But they will have to go to school too, Mr. Gallion," Elizabeth Haskins said.

"There will be seniors taking four subjects who will have two study halls," George Gallion said. "We can find enough good students from these study hall periods to teach these classes. It will give them teacher training, valuable experience, and perhaps make better students of them. This kind of responsibility will give them a new purpose in life, perhaps even make teachers out of them."

"That's an idea," Fred Laurie said. "It's a good idea!"

"What do you think about it, Mr. Riddle?"

"I'm against it," he said.

"Do you have any other plan?"

"No, I do not, but it's going to make it tough, Mr. Gallion," he said. "Won't these younger students rebel when they're taught by classmates? And what about discipline? Can they discipline? Can they discipline their own classmates in the classroom?"

"This school must open," George said. "I have known it would from the start."

"But what kind of school will we have?" Gus asked. "It's like the blind leading the blind."

George stared hard at Riddle, then turned away. "I've got another important matter to bring up here. Have you given any thought about phone service to this school? Is there any chance of that strike being settled before Tuesday?"

"Mr. Gallion, there is no end in sight," Gus Riddle said. "It's hard to tell when we'll have phone service in Kensington again. Haven't you been reading the *Dartmouth Times?*"

"No, I haven't. I've hardly had time to read a newspaper."

"You ought to. Each afternoon I read where more cables have been cut on the other side of the river. Public telephone booths have been destroyed and telephone poles sawed off even with the ground. It's terrible, Mr. Gallion! We miss the phone service in Kensington. And what'll we do up here without phone service?"

"I believe I have found the substitute for telephone service." George had waited to bring his idea up at the close of the meeting. "I've given the situation some thought, even if I haven't read the newspapers."

"Substitute for phone service? I'd like to know what that would be."

"Those hot-rodders we have, Mr. Riddle," George said. "Invite every last one to bring his car. Welcome all of them! Now we can *use* the cars those youngsters have—to carry messages."

This announcement hit like a bombshell at first. Then, suddenly there was an outbreak of laughter.

"I can't get over this one," Gus Riddle said. "What if an irresponsible hot-rodder breaks his neck? Will the school be responsible? Who'll pay for the gas?"

"They'll pay for their own gas," George said. "They'll be glad to do this, so they can bring their cars."

"You've got it all figured out, Mr. Gallion?"

"Sure have, Mr. Riddle; we can't afford not to stay one jump ahead. We've got to be a dozen jumps ahead of the students."

"It will be more trouble."

"No, Mr. Riddle, this will be turning one of our worst problems of last year into an advantage," Garrett Newall said.

"We've done a lot today," George said. "We can't do much more until we get the student body here so we can put our ideas into practice. Our schedule will have to have many changes too. We're having to work by trial-and-error method. When we cross the Rubicon Monday, let's hope for the best."

Chapter Three

Crossing the Rubicon

Monday morning, the first day of school, George and Grace were up before daylight, and ready to leave at seven. It was a 26-mile drive to Kensington, and on the way they had to drop their daughter Janet at Greenwood High, where she was a freshman.

There was only one person on the Hill when George arrived. He came smiling toward George in the corridor.

"I'm Herb Hampton, the new janitor," he said in a soft voice. "You don't know me, but I know you. My wife went to school to you. Irma Spears."

"Oh, yes, I remember Irma," George said. "She was a nice girl, brown hair, smart, friendly, a good sense of humor."

"That's her!" Herb Hampton was tall, extremely thin, and slightly stooped. He looked frail. He had come to work in well-shined shoes, white shirt, and neatly pressed though much-worn trousers.

"There are a few questions I want to ask you," George said. "Will you tip me off when you see things going on around here that aren't exactly right?"

"Sure will."

"Now be careful when you do," George said. "Don't ever let the pupils be afraid of you. Get their confidence. But when you see something that is an emergency, such as a fire in the building, get word to me or my secretary in a hurry."

"I'll stop any fire-setting myself," he replied quickly.

"Do you smoke?"

"No sir; never have."

"Good; then you'll have a good nose for smoke. Tip me off on smoking. Keep me informed. I am a principal who has to see and know everything. I have to know what goes on. These first days will be trying. They'll be a mess. Now don't get discouraged. Hang on. It will take time to pull out and level off. Stay with us. You're in for a tough assignment. And there's something more," George added. "I know every foot of floor space except the block building, shops and the new pre-fabs out there. I know you can't do all this work alone and that you will be up against it. But you'll get some help—student help. I'll see that you get the best."

"That's wonderful, but how will you do it, Mr. Gallion?" he asked.

"I've always made work an honor instead of a punishment," George explained. "I never punish a student or pupil by giving him a labor assignment. My workers will have to have good character and be on the honor roll before I'll give one permission to use a broom. When work is an honor a student likes to do it, and others envy him. This makes others pull up their grades so they might have the privilege of using a broom, mattock, shovel, spade, or hoe."

When George went into his office, Sadie Markham, his secretary, was already there. She was a graduate of the high school, and had been its secretary for three years. A round, bustling young woman, she had the reputation of being a first-rate and efficient secretary and of being somewhat hard to handle.

"I'm glad you're here, Sadie. I have so many things for you to do today."

He took a notebook from his pocket.

"This morning Miss Wallingford will give me a list of a dozen girls to work in this office," he said. "There will be two office girls for each period. Be sure that one for each period can do errands. This is your own personnel, for your help. You will need them."

"Now we must hurry along before teachers and pupils start arriving." George talked rapidly as he read his notes. "Glance often at the boiler-room window down at the elementary school today. Watch for Old Gordie to wave a book across the window. Count the number of times and report it to me. Get me that message as soon as you can. Don't let anybody hear you. Don't breathe this even to a teacher. Be sure you watch that window and talk only to me.

"Now, one of the girls who is going to help you will cover this building each period during the day after our first classes are made up and check to see if anyone is absent," George went on. "First thing in the morning, both office girls will check the home rooms to get absentees from home-room teachers. Then we can check the absentees in class against the home-room absentees to see who is skipping class. I understand there was quite a bit of this last year."

"More than a bit," she admitted with a wry little smile. "That was the beginning of the trouble here. Skipping school couldn't be stopped."

"We won't have that this year."

She smiled faintly.

"There will be another list of student teachers, Mrs. Markham," he continued. "I'll want you to go to each of the teachers who were here last year and ask for names. I'll want this list this morning just as soon as you can get it."

"You know, Mr. Gallion, I'll have to keep a financial record of all the food that comes in to the cafeteria and all the money we take in," she said. "This is going to be quite a load."

"But everybody will be loaded," he told her. "Select two girls, or three or four girls who need free lunches, to help you in the cafeteria. They must be honest and fast figurers. You're going to have to detail much of your work to pupils."

"I've got so much to do now, Mr. Gallion, I don't know whether I can do it or not."

"You'll be able to do it all right," he told her. "And be prepared to take a class over when and if we don't have a teacher

or a student teacher. We've got to use you for just about everything. If you can't do it at first, you can learn."

Gus Riddle was smiling when he walked into the office.

"Well, the battle begins," he said.

"Step over here and look, coming up the lane road," George
said.

"Troublemakers," Riddle said. "That's the hot-rodder caravan. Look at the old cars! Every model and make from the T-
model to the Cadillac! Somebody ought to be out there to see
they park right."

"Have Delbert Bennington do that," he said, looking at his
notes. "He doesn't have a home room. Have him take the
names of the drivers too, and the makes of the cars. Tell him to
have someone at the shop to make a board and put a nail on it
for each key. Have each owner's name printed by his nail. Tell
Delbert to ask for driver's licenses and report to me anyone
without a license."

"I don't know whether I can do all of that or not, Mr. Gallion."

"Detail part of it; this has to be done. The buses haven't
begun to come yet. Students will be pouring into this building
like flood waters in a few minutes. We have to work fast."

"Well, is there anything else, Mr. Gallion?" he asked. His
voice had a sharp edge.

"Yes, yes, yes, there will be other things," George said
quickly.

"When can I get all of this done?"

"We've got all day for it; if we can't get it done today, we've
got tomorrow. When you build a house you've got to have a
good foundation. This house has to go up in a hurry, but if we
don't lay a good foundation our house might fall. If you have
any time left, help home-room teachers with the registration."

"A man can do only so much," he grumbled, as much to
George as to himself.

George did not answer. He looked at his watch. It was ten

minutes of eight. "Let's go outside and see what's going on," he suggested.

More teachers came up the hill. There were hot-rodders too, and down at the intersection of the lane and the U.S. highway, an orange-colored bus with black trimmings slowed and flashed its signal lights. The windows were down and heads and hands were sticking out. The pupils were hollering and waving, and the noise was deafening as they poured out of the buses. How full of vigor and young life, George thought.

"Listen to that, won't you?" Gus said. "Yelling like young hellions!"

"Sounds good to me," George said. "They're not deadheads. That noise is sweet music to my ears again."

"You'll find out about sweet music," Gus said. "After you hear it awhile you'll get damned sick and call it noise like the rest of us!"

"They're getting together, Mr. Riddle," George said. "Many have not seen each other since last year. Watch them! They're glad to see each other."

Another bus flashed its signal lights and turned in. Pupils with their heads and hands out were yelling and waving to the pupils ahead. Another bus followed and another and another, until a long caravan, loaded to capacity with youth, rolled over the lane road, around the loop and up to unload at the west corridor entrance. The two stood in silence on the steps while pupils poured from the buses like chickens flying from a crowded coop.

The students had all been assigned to their rooms when Gus Riddle again entered George's office.

"Just wanted to tell you, Mr. Gallion, I detected some gambling among the freshmen and sophomores. What will it be with juniors and seniors?"

"You mean cards and money?"

"Mr. Gallion, they wouldn't be gambling for fun. They were matching coins."

"What did you do about it?"

"I walked over to them and they stopped."

George made a note in his notebook. "You think that will be a big problem here?" he asked Gus.

"Yes, it definitely will be one of the worst," he said. "And the reason I came out here in the corridor, I saw smoke boiling up from the boy's rest room like a cloud. You'd better make another note, Mr. Gallion," he said, grinning ironically.

He looked at George as if to say: "And you will never stop it, old man."

"I won't have to take a note on that one," George told him. "I'll remember."

"What about lunch? Will you ring a bell?"

"No, I'll send an office girl to the home room which has finished first," George said. "That way we won't crowd the serving lines too much."

Gus laughed loudly. "Crowd the cafeteria," he repeated, laughing again. "You've never seen a lunch period here. You want them to eat in the gym, don't you?"

"No, since they'll be so crowded and hot down there why not let them go outside?" George said.

"It will be like last year, Mr. Gallion," he said. "They'll be all over our sixty acres and hell besides! They'll be smoking, chewing, gambling, and necking! Won't be just the students, either." He spoke seriously, shaking his head. "You will run a risk. The hoodlums will be dropping up here at noontime. Loafers and hoodlums who never went to school but like to drop in at noon and see the girls."

"Let's try it today," George said. "I want to observe the behavior of this student body."

"You're the boss. Just as you say, but I wouldn't do it that way."

Gus started to walk away. When he reached the steps that went down from the corridor into the gym, he stopped suddenly and turned around.

"Mr. Gallion, I forgot to ask you what you wanted me to do now."

"Go upstairs and help with the seniors," George told him.

"They must be having trouble up there getting their schedules made out so they can graduate."

"Haven't you been up there yet?"

"Not yet, Mr. Riddle," he said. He decided not to mention to Gus his doctor's orders about climbing steps. "You're going to have to help me, Mr. Riddle. Where I don't have time to go, I must send you. You know this school and pupils better than anyone. You have seniority on all of us here."

"I have that all right," he said, smiling. And he turned and started down the steps.

Back in his office, George had begun looking over his mail when Coach Webber rushed in.

"Mr. Gallion, we have the juniors all registered," he said. "We have their schedules arranged."

"Good going," George complimented him. "Mrs. Markham, when lunch is ready, let the juniors go first."

"The junior class is one of the best I've ever seen in this high school," Coach Webber said. "We help them and they help the teachers."

George took the book lists. "Here," he said, giving the book lists to Mrs. Markham. "You take these lists. We'll send a messenger to Greenwood to the superintendent this afternoon. We'll order books just as fast as the lists are made out."

"But who'll take the message, Mr. Gallion?" Mrs. Markham asked.

"A hot-rodder messenger," he replied. "Get one who is registered. Put the time down when he leaves. Put it down when he returns. Which reminds me, Coach," George added. "Don't we have Enic Zimmerman's son in this school?"

"We sure do," he said. "He's on my football team."

"Let me see his permanent record card, Mrs. Markham."

"Ah, Mr. Gallion, I'm sorry you've asked for that," Coach Webber said. "I need Don Zimmerman."

"I think we need him in more ways than one," George said.

"He's not a good student," Coach Webber said. "But honest,

he's a ball carrier. He's a blocker. He's everything in football . . ."

"But I understand there's some question about his being able to graduate this year," George said.

"Here, Mr. Gallion," Sadie Markham gave him a permanent record card with many red marks. "It doesn't look too good."

"I'll say it doesn't," he said. He looked at Don's grades for the first and second years. Then he turned the card over. "His junior year is a little better, but Don Zimmerman is going to need help. Coach, if you know Enic, ask him to come up. I want to see him."

"Yes, Mr. Gallion," Sadie Markham said. "You know, his name's been in the paper every day since this telephone strike started. He's one of the top leaders there."

"I used to know Enic mighty well," George said. "We were young men together around here. Strange now to think that he and I would need each other. Coach you tell him to see me as soon as he can."

As Don Webber left, he passed Delbert Bennington waiting in the hall. His long black hair stood on end like the needles of a scared porcupine. "I hear you wanted to see me, Mr. Gallion."

"Do you have a list of pupils who drove cars here this morning?" George asked. "Did you check their driver's licenses?"

"Forty-one students' cars out there, Mr. Gallion," he said. "Five didn't have driver's licenses. I've got the lists right here."

"How are you getting along with the seniors?"

"All right now," he said. "They act like babies. I can't believe they're seniors and told them so. Every boy in that class needs discipline. He needs military service. Tried to get funny with me when I walked in, but they know better now. I might be smaller, but I can lick any boy in that class!"

"When will you be through up there?"

"Just about through," he said. "Fellows like Don Zimmerman are giving us the trouble. Some don't have enough credits, even if you allow them to take five, to graduate this year. They want their grades changed, blame the teachers that failed them and just about everything else. There are a few decent ones," Delbert went on, with a shrug. "But I've never seen so many in one class who want something for nothing."

It was noon when George found himself alone in his office for the first time. He looked from his window at the blue sky, taking deep breaths of fresh air at the open window. The moment was precious and short. There was no time for anything but the immediate, the concrete, the problematic. He walked out into the corridor.

From where he stood, he could watch the students pouring in and out of the cafeteria, carrying trays of food. The noise of the pupils was like low thunder in the corridor as they laughed, talked, and pushed each other in line. Many went outside while a few walked back to their home rooms. A few went down into the airless, hot gymnasium. Many boys walked outside without entering the cafeteria.

"Mr. Gallion, you know why those fellows are going out?" Gus Riddle whispered. "They have to smoke before they eat. Can't stand it any longer. Wait just a little while and then step outside. You'll see why I suggested it was best for them to stay inside."

"I'll get a lineup on them in just a minute," George said. "You go ahead and get your lunch so you can help me. I'll need you. I'll walk around the building and catch them."

"One more thing, Mr. Gallion," Gus said. "You know I've told you about those hoodlums who hang around the school at noontime. They'll be out on the grounds today. You'll see them in a few minutes."

George walked out onto the school steps, and saw something he had never seen before. He didn't have to go behind the building to find them, nor to the 60-acre wooded area behind the school where a few used to try to hide out and smoke when

he was a younger principal here. They stood near the door—
was it forty, fifty, sixty boys?; there were too many to count—
all of them smoking cigarettes, pipes, and cigars.

"All right, fellows. George's voice was firm and loud. "I
didn't think I would have to tell you that there wouldn't be any
smoking on this schoolgrounds. There is a state law regarding
the use of tobacco on any school premises."

Not one of them spoke up. A few threw their cigarettes down
and crushed them out with their shoes. Many kept on smoking.

"Did you hear what I said? No smoking!"

There was a sullen silence.

"Don't throw anything down on the schoolgrounds. Bring
everything up here and put it in this trashcan. Knock your
pipes out, stick them in your pockets, take them home this afternoon and leave them. You won't be needing them here. All
right, now!"

"By God, I'll let you know I have my rights," one of the
boys said. His beltless pants hung low on his hips, and his long
hair was oiled down flat on his head.

"You," George said, laying his hand down hard on his shoulder, "I want you in the office!"

"Oh you do, do you? Just try and make me."

"You're going," he said, shoving him forward. George was
either stronger than he had thought or this fellow was very
weak. "You go in there and wait for me."

The youth walked sullenly along, muttering something under
his breath. On the steps he stopped and looked back. The others walked slowly over and dropped their cigarettes and cigars
and knocked their pipes out into the trashcan.

"Fellows, I appreciate your cooperation," George told them.
"There'll be no penalty for this, but after tomorrow morning
there will be. I'm afraid we didn't understand each other."

"Mr. Gallion, we smoked here last year," one said.

"But not this year," George told him.

"What about the teachers?" another asked.

"We won't break discipline by doing anything we don't allow you to do."

The young fellow laughed. "You mean that?"

"Go tell Mr. Hampton, the janitor, I want to see him," George told one of the boys.

George looked over the schoolgrounds. Here and there, scattered over the sixty acres, he saw groups of four and five youths squatting on the ground, clustered together in a circle. He watched two motorcycles turn in at the lane road, followed by two old-model wheezing, sputtering cars. When the motorcycles pulled up at the corridor steps, George saw one young man with a ring in one ear, a sport shirt open to his waist, and a broad belt, studded with ornaments around the middle, that supported tight-fitting pants. Behind him perched a girl, in a low-neck blouse and tight pants.

"You go to school here?" George asked the driver.

"Nope, just visiting," he said. "I used to go here."

"Finish?"

"One year," he replied.

"What do you do now?"

"What's it to you?"

"Plenty," George said. "I'm principal here. We don't want or need your type of visitor. Get the hell off."

"That's a welcome for you, ain't it?" he said to the girl behind him. He started the motor. "You can take this school and ram it," he said, as the wheel spun and gravel flew.

The motorcycle behind him started, too, and they followed each other down the Hill.

"You want me, Mr. Gallion?" It was Herb Hampton.

"Look out over these grounds," he said. "Look at the far corners, at the smoke ascending as if from Indian hogans in early mornings on the desert. Go back there then, Mr. Hampton, and guard the rest room."

"Well, what do you think now, Mr. Gallion?" Gus Riddle blinked his eyes in the sun and grinned. George hadn't heard him arrive.

"It's just as you said," George sighed disgustedly. "I broke it up here. But look out there."

"Well, what do you want us to do?" Gus asked.

"I want you to check two strange cars that came on the grounds," he told him. "They're out back someplace. I know they turned in here, but they haven't come around the circle road. Mr. Bennington, I want you to walk from one group of boys to the other and break up that gambling! Break up the smoking!"

Gus sighed. "It's the same old thing. I'd like to find the cause and cure for this gambling."

"Just as soon as they're through with their lunch, we'll call 'em back to their home rooms," George said. "We'll cut their time short."

"You'd better not, Mr. Gallion," Gus warned. "You might have a strike on your hands. You know how they strike around here. They'll openly defy us. You've been away from all this too long. Young people are not like they used to be."

On his way back to the office, George passed Don Webber in the hall.

"Coach, come into the office with me," he said.

When they went inside, the youth he had sent in was waiting.

"I thought you were never coming," he said to George. "I don't like to spend my noon hour waiting in this dump. I like a break with the fellows."

George was grimly silent. He locked the door, switched on the lights, and pulled the shades down to the sills. He went without speaking into the supply room in his office, a place he was told was the safest place in the school building to keep locked. He came out with three paddles.

"No, no," the young fellow said, rising up from George's swivel chair. "Cut it out. I won't take that!"

"Fellow, did you ever hear of the board of education?" George said.

"Say, this isn't funny, mister!"

"I'm Mr. Gallion to you."

"You're not anything to me."

"You get over that table. Lay down with your ass up! We'll see what I am and who I am to you!"

"What's this all about?"

"You ought to know," George said. "You know what you said out there on the schoolground. Profanity is a part of your language. Now get up there and the sooner the easier and better it will be for both of us."

"I won't do it," he said.

"You want this board or do you want my fist? You're a man, but you act like a baby."

"I'm gonna quit this damn school."

"You won't be leaving until we've settled this affair."

The youth got his breath fast and hard. He hissed at George like a snake.

"Get across that table," George shouted, laying his hand on his shoulder. "Lay over there."

He shoved him across the table. Then he came down with the board.

"You hit me!" he screamed.

"Lay back down there," George said. "Another lick for lying."

This time the boy did not even flinch. George took the boy by the hand and helped him up from the table.

"First spanking you ever had in school?" George spoke softly. "How did you miss a good spanking before now?" George asked him. "You're arriving late. Before I was your age I'd had at least a hundred."

The youth smiled.

"It's like this," George told him. "You know the language you used you could not use at your home, even on the street, and you used it on these schoolgrounds. Swearing is a substitute to show you are somebody. Actually, it shows a weakness. The man who doesn't swear has something else to offer to show he is a man. You ever go out for sports?"

"Why don't you try out for football?" Don Webber said. "You're tougher than you think. What about it?"

"You've got guts," George told him. "But I don't like your haircut, though, that goo on your hair, and your pants hanging down that low. Aren't you afraid you'll lose them?"

The youth smiled wanly.

"I want you to stay in this school," George told him. "We understand each other now. I am sure this will never happen again. No one knows this but us. See, no one could look in. And we don't talk. We want to understand each other. What's your name?"

"Orrin Burton, but they call me the champ."

"Let's see you really be one," George said, and patted him on the shoulder.

He unlocked the door while Don Webber raised the shade and switched off the lights.

In the crowded corridor George nearly collided with Mrs. Markham scurrying from the cafeteria with a tray of food.

"I've not had time to eat until now," she said. She stopped in front of George and Coach Webber and held her tray close so it wouldn't be knocked out of her hands. "Mary Davidson counted the registration this morning and we have six hundred twenty-five pupils."

"That's a record here," Don sighed. "Where are we going to put them?"

"Cut a stairway up from the library and put them on the roof," George said.

"That would be nice and breezy up there in this hot weather, but they might get rambunctious and shove each other off," Don said.

"Only thirteen teachers and six hundred twenty-five pupils," George said. "We're twelve teachers short of an average faculty and sixteen teachers short of a competent one."

Mrs. Markham took her tray into the office.

"Coach, something else I've thought to ask you," George

said. "Do you have a couple of strong-armed football players, boys we can trust to fight their classmates if they must?"

"I've got plenty who will fight," he replied. "What's up?"

"Supply trucks come in this afternoon with tomorrow's cafeteria supplies. Our students will be going from classroom to classroom. The truck drivers will have to leave their trucks to carry in supplies. I suggest we don't take any chances! What do you think?"

"You're right. We won't get supplies if they raid the trucks like they did last year. We've probably got boys somewhere in this school now planning to raid the trucks. I've got the right fellows. One is a tackle and one is a fullback. They're both good kids."

"All right, just as soon as the first afternoon period starts, you station those boys right here in the corridor door and give them instructions," George said. "Tell them to report to each truck driver and tell them what they are standing there for and the drivers will know we mean business and won't hesitate to bring us supplies."

George walked out on the steps again and stood at a point from which he could watch the main corridor if he looked in one direction; in the other direction he could see the athletic field and beyond down to the Tiber River. Herb Hampton was policing the boys' rest room. Gus Riddle and Delbert Bennington were somewhere in the large area to the rear where the block building, shops, and the pre-fabs were. Garrett Newall and Charles Newton were in the upper corridor. Miss Wallingford had locked her room and had gone to the library. Marcella Waters was on duty on the east end of the first corridor keeping watch over the girls' rest room.

Last year girls had assembled here, had marked the walls and had played havoc with everything they could, even packing the commodes with toilet paper until a plumber had to be called. If the commodes were stopped, they complained they had no toilet facilities, so that buses had to be called to take them home. In ways like this, the students had disrupted and demoralized the school.

He walked around to the front where Don Webber had the pupils under control. The streams of smoke out on the open yard had ceased. Pupils had gone to the foliage on the Tiber River bank and George wondered what else was going on back there. He didn't have a teacher he could spare to send to investigate. He walked around the building again, this time faster than before, and the Hill looked like a picnic ground filled with happy young picnickers. He saw papers blowing over the ground. He made another note. These are our children, he thought. We are responsible for every last one, good, bad, or indifferent. *This is the greatest raw material in America to shape and mold. This is America's future. The weeds must blossom as well as the flowers. If the teachers can stand the pressure, we'll do the job.*

When Coach Webber blew his football whistle, some of the students came running. Others walked reluctantly toward the building. They poured into each end of the corridor and through the front door until the corridor was jam-packed. Many who had played ball were hot, perspiring, and breathing fast. A long line formed at the water fountain on the first-floor corridor. Many whose home rooms were on the second floor rushed to get to the one fountain spigot up there. There were only four fountains in the school for six hundred twenty-five pupils. After the pupils had cleared the first corridor, Gus Riddle walked in with a dozen boys in front of him.

"These tried to hide out, Mr. Gallion," he said.

"I didn't hear the whistle," one said.

"That's the old excuse," Gus scolded. "What were you doing behind the Agriculture building? Thought you'd hide until we got inside and then you'd go over the fence! Now get in your home rooms in a hurry," he shouted. "Never let this happen again!"

"We'll have a checkup, Mr. Riddle," George said. "We'll know when one is absent."

"Ah, some of them won't care what you've got, Mr. Gallion," Gus spoke irritably. He mopped his September sourwood–red face with an enormous handkerchief. "They won't take advantage of the opportunities they have. I've told you before and I say it again, we ought to get rid of some of this dead wood. They're not here for any good. They're deadheads, no ambition—just here to give us trouble!"

"Mr. Riddle, we'll have a teachers' meeting just as soon as school is out today," George said. An argument would be pointless now. "Bring up problems that you see here at the meeting."

As soon as George was back in his office, he asked Mrs. Markham to get the absentee lists. "This list will be checked with the home-room lists made out this morning. Mr. Riddle, maybe, didn't find all out behind the shop. Maybe they escaped through the Tiber River bank foliage at noon. This noon hour is a problem."

"Noon hour here, Mr. Gallion, has always been a problem," she said.

"Make this note, too," he told her. "Have Mr. Hampton set chairs on the gym floor."

"Chapel program, Mr. Gallion?"

"Right. We need to get together with the student body as soon as possible. Some things I want to tell them."

"Have someone check the teaching schedule," George added, "and when a class doesn't have a teacher, put a student teacher there and tell him or her to take over tomorrow at this period. And you'd better call your student teachers in here. Get them now. Don't ring the bell until you have them here. When you get them to the office, ring the bell. I'll be here in the corridor if you need me."

The bell rang and pupils poured from the home rooms into the corridor. Overhead, George heard low thunderous sounds of scurrying feet.

"Remember this is your first-period class," George shouted above the din of mixed laughter and voices. "All of those who do not have a teacher, wait until one is sent." He repeated the announcement over and over.

Pupils went out at each end of the corridor toward the band building, Agriculture building, the shop, and the three prefabs.

George hurried back to his office where a dozen student teachers were waiting.

"Mrs. Markham, check the schedule," George told her. "See if there is a class without a teacher."

"Two classes, Mr. Gallion, one in algebra and one in English."

"How many of you have first period free in the morning?" George asked the student teachers standing in the office.

Four hands went up.

"How many are good in algebra?"

One hand went up.

"Go take the algebra class," George said to a husky young fellow. "Looks like you ought to be out for football; what's your name?"

"Frank Fairman," he replied. "I'm out for football. I'm a fullback."

"Here, take this record book," George told him. "You're a teacher now. I'll help you if you need me. Meet with the teachers in the math room after school."

"I'm Janet Pennington, and I'll take the English class, Mr. Gallion," a tall blond, blue-eyed girl volunteered.

"Fine, Janet. Here is your record book," he said. "You're a teacher now and meet with us at three-thirty, in the math room."

"Here is a freshman arithmetic class in the second period," George said. "Here is another class in algebra and another one in freshman English."

"Send anyone to the office who won't behave," George told them. "We'll help you all we can."

"I'll take the algebra class," said a young boy. "I'm Lester Bowdin, a senior."

Lester Bowdin was about five feet eight, a 185-pound senior with yellow corn-silk hair which he combed straight back. His blue eyes were bright and alive.

"You don't play football, do you, Lester?"

"Yes, sir, I'm center on the team."

"What kind of grades do you have?"

"I hope to be valedictorian of my class," he replied.

George looked at him. "How many children in your family?"

"Eleven," he said, grinning. "Mr. Gallion, I want to learn something about teaching."

"You'll soon be on the firing line, young fellow," George said with a wink. "All right. Now all of you go and meet your classes. You'll know what to do."

He watched the young student teachers go from his office to meet the emergency in the classrooms. This was the third line of defense, the last place to retreat. He observed the shifts of classes for the rest of the day. Then he walked wearily to the end of the corridor where a stream of pupils passed him, a swift-flowing river of humanity, on their way to the long lines of buses.

But the day was not yet over. The teachers assembled in the math room as soon as the long caravan of orange-colored buses rolled over the Hill.

The twelve student teachers were grouped together on one side and the regular faculty members were scattered over the room. Gus Riddle had his chair well up front. Shan Hannigan had moved as far away from Gus as he could get.

"We crossed the Rubicon, Mr. Riddle," George said. "What do you think about the invasion on the other side?"

"She's rough, man, she's rough," he said. "But not any more than I have expected all along. You know I've told you. That noon hour and sixty acres is a tough assignment."

"We've got to do something about that," George said. "I've made some notes. Can't we cut the noon period to thirty minutes?"

"What? Do you want a revolt?"

"The pupils can leave a half hour earlier," Fred Laurie suggested.

"You'll see," Gus retaliated.

George twisted nervously in his chair.

"It's the hoodlums that come on the ground at noon," Gus said. "You know we had to chase a dozen away."

"Make it sixteen," George said. "I put two motorcycles off."

"Then you saw the crowd of boys hiding out that I brought in at noon," Gus said, shaking his head sadly. "I found a dozen more behind the shop."

"I say, Mr. Gallion, we expel those for good who play hooky," Delbert Bennington said. "I wonder if anybody else agrees with me."

Several hands went up.

"I disagree with all of you about kicking them out," George said. "You know how I feel about this. If there were phones in their homes I'd call their parents. They know we don't have phones and they take advantage."

"We had phones last year and it didn't matter if we called their parents," Charles Newton said. "I quite agree with Mr. Riddle. About ten percent of them ought to be out. We'd have a better school."

"When you kicked them out last year where did they go?" George asked.

"They loafed in Kensington, Mr. Gallion," Marcella Waters said. "They played pool. They played the pinball machines. They drove up and down the road in old cars and on motorcycles."

"Then you want to kick them out?" George asked. "Isn't the environment of this school better for them? Why are we here? Why are we teachers? Keep one thing in mind. All of these pupils are our future. It is up to us to mold and shape them. Teachers, I tell you," George spoke softly, "we can't make finished products out of all, but you'll be surprised how our good training, if we can give it, will influence their lives. In secondary schools we have more influence than the elementary schools and colleges in shaping youth. This is the time that counts most for them. I'm not for kicking them out as long as I believe they have a chance." There was silence. "Besides," George added, "we'd be playing into the hands of the pupils. They want to be suspended. They want us to kick them out of school so they can lay the blame for their failures on us. Let's put the responsibilities for their futures on them."

"Not punish them?" Gus Riddle said. He shook his head like a mad bull. "Just let them walk away when they please?"

"No. Let them make up the time they lost here. Yes, maybe pay us a little interest on time," George said, smiling. "When somebody borrows in America isn't it customary to pay interest? Time is no different from money. It takes time to make money. Time is an important element to the pupil. It's his raw material. He is our raw material. So I'd like to let him pay a little interest."

"But he has to ride the buses," Gus said. "There's a conflict. If little Tom doesn't get home on time we'll be hearing from Poppy and Mommy. And, boy oh boy, the county super and his board members will hear about us."

"That will be wonderful," George said. "We want the parents to know most of the things they do."

"Any problems you don't want the parents to know about?" Marcella Waters asked.

"Yes, certainly there are."

Fred Laurie tapped his chair arm nervously and smiled at George.

"What are these problems?" Gus Riddle asked.

"We have student teachers with us," George said. "I wouldn't care to go into these just now. But there are problems parents don't need to know. We can solve them here. The policy of this school will be to help the pupil."

"Mr. Gallion, then I suppose you're against laying the wood to a few of these hoods," Charles Newton said.

Don Webber, who had been quiet throughout the meeting, burst into a roar of laughter.

"I'm not against that, Mr. Newton," George said. "I just don't tell that either. I might be calling on one of you men at any time to help me administer the board of education."

"I never used a board of education in my life," Gus Riddle said. "I'm against it."

"You've never been principal," George said. "What would you do? Kick them out?"

"Certainly I would."

"That's the difference in us," George told him. "I'm against kicking them out. I'd rather use the board if and when I have no other choice, and keep the pupil in school. That pupil needs the power of life we're going to generate in this school. Since I'm principal, we will follow my policy in this matter."

"Just don't call on me ever to help use the board of education," Gus told George. "I couldn't do it. I never whipped an animal in my life."

"I never have either," George said.

"Then why a human being?"

"The animal is guided almost wholly by instinct," George replied. "He can't reason very well. We are guided by reasoning over instinct. So why shouldn't a student who has been given a chance be corrected?"

"You have everything worked out, don't you, Mr. Gallion?" Gus said sarcastically.

"Not everything, but I try to stay a jump ahead of my pupils."

"Then the pupils who left school early today are to make up their time?" Elizabeth Haskins put in.

"Yes, I think that is the best thing to do with them."

"What about smoking?" Don Webber asked.

"Do you let your football players smoke?"

"No."

"Do you smoke on the schoolground in front of them?"

"Yes."

"Is that fair?"

"Well, I'm through high school and college and I should have that privilege."

"Before I comment on this I'd like to put that to a vote. I want the student teachers to vote on this too. How many of you agree that students should be allowed to smoke?"

"Well, I smoke," Shan Hannigan said, holding up his hand. "I'd say if they had someplace to hide out it would be all right."

"I agree to that," Don Webber said. "There are times I have to have a smoke."

"You'll never break that here, Mr. Gallion," Gus Riddle said. "I've been here too long. We have more vital problems."

"We have to meet every problem," George said. "We can't skip one. We either do or we don't. If we condone one problem, when we know it is wrong, we condone all, and, believe it or not, we'll have trouble with all the others. How many of you think we should not smoke?"

Some hands went up slowly among the teachers. The hands of the student teachers shot up instantly.

"Now let me ask you if you think it is fair for teachers to smoke and not allow the pupils."

Not a hand went up.

"Mr. Gallion, may I ask you if you smoke?" Elizabeth Haskins said.

"Yes, I smoke cigars when I get home. But you'll never see me smoke on a schoolground. I couldn't smoke on this ground unless I let everybody else smoke. At assembly in the morning I shall set down a few rules, and one is: *Smoking will not be permitted.*"

"It won't work, Mr. Gallion," Gus said, shaking his head.

"It will work," George said. "If you teachers work in unison to enforce this rule, we can make it ninety-five percent good."

"But there will be that five percent," Gus said.

"Yes. That's a problem. We have to take our problems as we come to them," George said. "We are faced with teacher and classroom shortages. We have hardly half enough space and half as many teachers as we should have! Maybe we should have a teachers' meeting in front of our student body sometime. Maybe it would be good for our pupils to know our problems. Maybe they'd go home and tell their parents what we are up against here."

"No, no, no, Mr. Gallion," Gus said loudly, shaking his head negatively. "That would only cause gossip. And we've got too many hoodlums who would try to create more problems. I'd be against that."

"I still believe our youth like a challenge," George said. "They would still have enough of their ancestors in them, men and women who challenged a continent, fought for it and conquered a wilderness."

"Nice words, patriotic and sweet," Gus came back at him, "but we now have another wilderness to conquer, Mr. Gallion. We have a wilderness of youth. If all of the teachers in here feel as I do they're plenty tired of trying to save some of the culled trees."

"Mr. Riddle, why are we here?" George asked, rising from his chair. He hit the table with his fist. "We can't give up! A youth should know where he is going while he is still young, so he can get a head start. If he doesn't know where he is going we should help him find his way. His mind should not be left a culled young tree in the wilderness, but he should be given some attention. As teachers it is our duty to help cultivate these half-choked and half-starved trees and give them a chance to grow."

The student teachers' eyes were fixed on George.

Gus Riddle shook his head.

"I've been waiting an hour for you," Grace said. She rose slowly from her chair in George's office. "You look tired, George."

"You don't look too rested yourself," George told her.

"Mr. Gallion, don't forget your basket," Sadie Markham said. "Nora typed the letters you dictated."

"Oh, yes," he said, smiling; "thank you."

The basket was on the floor by his desk. George didn't know how many letters the basket would hold, but it would hold fourteen dozen eggs. It was a willow basket with half-lids on hinges that fastened in the center near the handle and opened in opposite directions. When George picked the basket up from the floor he raised one of the lids and looked in. The basket was half full of letters.

"You must have answered mail all day," Grace said.

"No, Mrs. Gallion," Sadie said pleasantly. "He dictated letters all day on the run. Nora Wallings, our best pupil here in shorthand, has followed him around, taking dictation. Two of the office girls helped her type the letters."

"Stacks of letters, Grace," George said. "We owe bills. I'm putting off creditors."

"Mrs. Gallion, things are in a bad way here," Sadie said.

"I'll see you in the morning," George said, as he and Grace left the office. "Don't work too late."

They passed Herb Hampton, who was sweeping the corridor.

"Mr. Gallion, look at the missing tiles in the floor," he said. "Some of our students are going to get hurt if we don't repair this floor."

"When Mr. Caudill gets up here I'll show him the floor," George said. "The county board of education should do this. Look at the lockers, too!"

"Mr. Gallion, I know they look bad, but I haven't had time to scrub them yet," he said.

"What is that stain on the lockers?" George asked.

"Tobacco spittle. Mr. Gallion, have you ever raised up one of the chairs to see what is under it?"

"No, I haven't, Mr. Hampton. What is under them?"

"Just a minute and I'll show you if you've got time."

Grace walked slowly toward the corridor door.

The custodian stepped inside a classroom. He picked up the first chair he came to and carried it out and laid it upside down.

"They are all like that," he said. "The new and the old ones, in all of the rooms. The library tables are worse."

"Come here, Grace," George called. "I want you to see something you won't believe!"

"What in the world?" she exclaimed in disbelief . . . "How . . ."

"That's what I thought, too," Herb Hampton said. "I couldn't believe that much chewing gum could be stuck under a chair!"

"Wonder if it has ever been cleaned off since the chairs were put in here?" George said. "In places it's an inch deep. Solid chewing gum. How can we get that off?"

"Mr. Gallion, I just can't take that off all the furniture," Herb Hampton exclaimed. "The only way to get it off is to use screwdrivers and wood chisels. It's slow work, too."

"Maybe you'd better throw the chairs away," Grace said. "That one doesn't look too good."

George took his notebook from his pocket and made another note.

"People used to think I was a crank when I wouldn't allow pupils to chew gum in school. You know," he said, "I can't walk ten steps in this school without running into a fresh problem! Why is it I see so many problems? Why haven't others seen them?"

"Mr. Gallion, I hate to tell you this," Herb said. "But paper left in all the home rooms was just about ankle-deep."

"They won't go into their own homes and throw paper on the floor," George said. "They've got by with throwing it on the floor here. My pupils never did this. If one I used to have in this school were to walk in one of these rooms and find a piece of paper on the floor, he'd pick it up now!"

Grace laughed. "Are you sure of that? You said these pupils were the sons and daughters of the pupils you had."

"And that's right, but training has to be a continuous thing."

"And teaching is a continuous thing. Our day is getting too long, George; we'd better be on our way. Janet will be waiting for us.'

"I'll be working late tonight, Mr. Gallion," the custodian said as he picked up a chair.

"I'll get help to you as soon as I can," George told him. "Don't bother with the chewing gum. I'll take care of that. Have you got wood chisels, screwdrivers, and cold chisels here? If you don't have, order a dozen of each and charge them to the Greenwood County board of education. Get in an extra supply of soap and paint the same color that has been on these lockers, paint brushes, scrubbing brushes. Get some wax, too, to shine the chairs and tables."

"Who'll do all this work, Mr. Gallion?" he asked. "I can't do it all."

"You'll have help," George assured him. "We'll have crews working all the time. This place has to be cleaned from floors to ceilings. I'd be ashamed to have anybody visit this school. No wonder the pupils try to destroy it. They'll work better and be happier in a clean house."

George and Grace walked out to the car. Several cars were still parked in the schoolyard. Down on the athletic field Don Webber was coaching the first team, and Fred Laurie was coaching the second team. A small group of hot-rod messengers whose cars were parked on the schoolground were waiting for practice to be over so they could take the players home.

"We've had to change a lot of things around here today," George said. "We'll have to change a lot more. Then change what we have already changed. Then change them again. We'll have to change, change, change, until we get everything as near right as we can under the circumstances and handicaps under which we have to work. How did you get along today?"

"George, I've never seen anything like it," she said. "Believe me, we've had problems. I still wonder why we left a good home and a way of life and pleasant living to get into this."

She turned onto the highway. George rolled his window down and looked out at the quiet, breathless late afternoon sky.

"You didn't climb any steps today, did you?"

"No, I didn't, and I wondered what went on in the corridor above me. I haven't seen the library yet."

"Then you are following your doctor's orders?"

"Right."

"But suppose you overwork and you get sick again," she said. "Look what a schedule we have. When we get home there's Janet all alone in the house, and you have only Old Charlie to look after the farm and cattle. So the destiny of your school hangs on a slender thread, doesn't it?"

"Pick up that boy yonder, Grace," George said. "He's flagging us. Looks like one of our high school pupils."

Grace slowed and stopped.

"Going up the road?" George said. "Say, didn't I see you at school today?"

"Yes, sir, but I missed the bus," he said.

"What's the matter?" George asked him. "Didn't you get out of the building on time? Didn't the driver wait?"

"No, he didn't wait," he replied evasively.

At the top of Anderson Hill, three more youths stood by the highway flagging a ride.

"Pick them up, Grace," George told her.

They were reluctant to get in the car when they recognized George.

"I've seen you fellows before, haven't I? Weren't you at school today?"

"Yes, we were," one of the boys answered after he had glanced at the others.

"Bus leave you too?"

"Yes, it did," one said.

"Well, let's get acquainted," George said. "I'd like to have your names."

He put them down in his notebook.

"I'm going to get after that bus driver tomorrow," George said with a wink. "I don't want any pupils left on this highway. It's dangerous out here walking. You might get hit."

They picked up two more and George put their names down.

"We'll be running a school bus, too," Grace said, after the last one was dropped off at his house. "Poor boys! I feel sorry for them though. . . . You should bawl that bus driver out, George."

"You won't have to worry about using this car for a bus," George said. "They didn't know our car. They'll soon be finding out! We won't be picking up many who ran away from school."

"What?"

"I'm sure I'm right," he said with a smile. "When I get the absentee list in the morning, I'll check these names against that list. It's clicking, Grace!"

"I don't understand."

"This year they won't get away," George told her. "Solving the little problems stops the big ones. My policy is to get the problems before they get us."

It was eleven o'clock. George, in his pajamas, was working on the short speech he wanted to give in assembly the next morning when he heard someone pounding on the door. He switched off the radio, went to the door, and switched on the porch light. A man stood outside.

"Are you Mr. Gallion, of the Kensington High School?" he asked in halting English.

"Yes, I am," George said.

He took his wallet from his pocket and took a clipping from it. "I read you look for teachers. I am a teacher."

"Come in, come in," George shut the door behind them.

The man didn't come up to George's shoulder. He was dressed in a frayed brown suit, a soiled shirt, and a twisted, faded tie. His floppy black hat was several sizes too large. His shoes needed shining, but his face was clean and his short reddish mustache was trimmed neatly.

"I am Karl Hegioland," he said. "I am a minister and teacher."

"Have you a degree?" George asked him.

"Two of them," he replied. "I have degree from University in Denmark, and master's from University of Illinois."

"Where do you live now?"

"In Ohio, north of Dartmouth," he replied. "I married my wife in Ohio and I stay with her people."

"Ever teach school before?" George asked him.

"Yes, I have taught four years," he replied.

"In high school?"

"One year in elementary school and three years high school."

"What do you teach?"

"Spanish and history," he said.

"Where have you been preaching?"

"In Mexico. I have been holding revivals down there."

"How about your pay for preaching in Mexico?"

"Not so good," he said. "That's why I am here again. We, my wife, two daughters, and I, could not make enough to live. We did well to get back to Ohio."

"Did you try to get a post in Ohio?"

"Yes, but we got back too late," he explained. "All positions were filled."

"Can you speak Spanish?"

"*Sí, hablo español.*"

"I don't know what you are saying."

"Translated, Mr. Gallion, that is: 'Yes, I speak Spanish.' *Hablo español mejor que el inglés.* Translated, that means: 'I speak Spanish better than English.'"

"I'm short on history teachers," George said. "I'll want you to take junior history and two or three classes in Spanish."

"*Ha ud. enseñado español antés en su escuela?* Translated, that is: 'Have you taught Spanish in your school before?'"

"No, this will be the first year."

"*Me alegre que ud. vaya a enseñar español allí este año.*
Translated, Mr. Gallion, this is: 'I am happy you are going to
teach Spanish there this year.' "

"You report for work at eight o'clock in the morning at
Kensington High School," George told him.

"This soon, Mr. Gallion?"

"Yes. You are hired right now."

"Won't the school board have to pass on me?"

"We can do that later."

"This is the quickest I ever got a position in a school or a
church in my life."

"You are hired, Mr. Hegioland."

"*Vendré! Vendré!* I will be there! I will be there!"

"It's past my bedtime, Mr. Hegioland," George said. "I need
rest. And you will be needing yours too from now on. Goodnight."

"*Buenas noches, buenas noches,*" he said, opening the door.
"*Le veré a ud. mañana.* Translated, Mr. Gallion, I have said:
'Good night, good night, I will see you in the morning.' "

From his office window George looked out at the solid line of
buses and automobiles, almost bumper to bumper, moving
toward the Kensington High School building. As George
watched the long caravan of buses and automobiles loaded with
teachers and pupils rolling in, his mind flashed back to a time
from nineteen to twenty-three years ago. It was different then,
when only a few came in buses over the dusty roads. The
majority came on foot. He remembered the long lines of those
boys and girls, who came up the Hill, carrying books, holding
hands, laughing, talking, and having the time of their lives.
George remembered how he had walked a mile up the road
from Kensington with them and how the dust swirled up in the
dry autumn and late spring when a car passed them.

There were not many cars then. Only two teachers, the
coach and math teacher, rode to school. There was no one pupil

that he could remember who drove a car to school. The teachers didn't make good salaries. That was the time following the depression, and people didn't have jobs. There were ten teachers for every opening in Kensington High School. He remembered that he didn't own a car then, couldn't afford a car and couldn't drive one. But they had a telephone then. Some of his pupils then walked distances of fourteen miles to school. There were no roads and no buses for these but they came to school. Many of those living miles away never missed a day. They waded the deep snows, came through rains, sleet, and icy winds. They got there. Going to school was not a duty then, it was a privilege.

George followed the students and teachers to the gymnasium and walked onto the stage, where he thought his voice could best be heard. They didn't have a loudspeaker. They had had one, which a class in the school had purchased, but it had been destroyed. At the end of the platform, a podium had been placed for him to stand behind and a place where he could put his notes.

"Pupils and teachers of Kensington High School," he began in a deep full voice that carried out to the far corners of the gymnasium, "William Shakespeare, whom you English pupils will read in your junior year, made a great mistake when he characterized the schoolboy as a creature 'creeping like a snail, unwilling to school.' What he said then, about three hundred years ago, might have fitted schoolboys of his day in Elizabethan England, but it doesn't fit the schoolboy or schoolgirl of the public schools of America. I've been watching you ride in here, packed in buses and coming in cars, and a few of you walking.

"You are full of excitement and laughter," he said, as he looked out at the fresh young faces, "and you're bubbling over with enthusiasm. Maybe this will wear off in due time. Maybe this is the excitement of just getting together again in this beginning of a new school year. You come rolling in here in a hurry on big and little wheels. Those of you who walk come running, for I've watched you. And if even one of you has crept in here slow as a snail I haven't seen you. For you come with energy and you come with bounce."

Almost all the pupils were looking up at George, listening.

"Mr. Riddle, are you out there?" George said.

"Right here, Mr. Gallion," he replied.

"To my left on the second row of the bleachers are two boys who are busily engaged matching some object," George said. "Since they do not want to listen and are more interested in matching coins, will you please take these young fellows to my office. I will see them later.

"We are just having a little get-together here this morning, pupils and teachers. But I want to tell you a few things, ask you a few questions, and introduce you to your teachers."

Then George asked the teachers to stand as he read their names. Each name brought a round of applause, a few hisses, catcalls, and boos from different areas of the crowded student body.

"Now, the last one to be introduced is Mr. Riddle," George said, smiling. "Here he is standing before you, and you know him better than I do!"

Gus Riddle knew about everyone already. He had taught these pupils or had taught their brothers and sisters or visited their farms during the summer months.

"Hurrah for Old Gus," someone screamed. There was a roar of applause, whistles, screams, shouts, and shuffling of feet on the gym floor.

George held his hands up for their letting-off-steam to subside. "Since we do not have enough teachers, we have had to get help from you so we could open this school yesterday," George said. "So from among you we have selected a dozen student teachers, who will teach first- and second-year subjects. These are our unpaid teachers, who are going all out to help you, to help us, this school, county, state, and country. I want them to stand."

There was a moderate round of applause, and many students whispered to one another as the twelve arose.

"Now, while we are here together, I heard somebody a while

ago, when I introduced Mr. Riddle, scream, 'Old Gus.' That
was plain bad manners. You will not call any teacher by his
first name. You will address them as Mr. Riddle, Mrs. Waters,
Miss Wallingford, and as for your student teachers, you will
address them as Miss or Mister in the classroom as long as they
teach you! Now I want to say one thing more about the
teachers. And this is partly due to your conduct here last year.
We don't want to talk about that. But I'll assure you,"
George's voice rose with confidence, "this year will be different."

There was a buzzing of voices, then calm spread over the
student body. They looked up at him with questions written on
their faces.

"I wonder if there is anyone among you who can do work in
metals?" George asked. "If there is one or more among you
who can, and if you have a B average in school and two study
halls, will you come to my office? I want to assign the job of
fixing lockers which are in need of repair."

A tall boy stood up.

"I have a B average," he said. "But what have my grades
got to do with it? I know I can repair those lockers."

"I'm glad you brought that up," George told him. "Only
honor pupils will be permitted to work at the many assignments we have for you. You who have grades under B need
your time in the classrooms to pull your grades up. Now, our
custodian, Mr. Hampton, will need help on the inside and outside of the schoolhouse. For example, one of you young fellows
will have charge of this gym, to see that it is clean at all times.
Only A students will be permitted to work outside the schoolhouse, such as running the lawnmower and cutting the grass,
picking up papers and keeping this place clean. You know,
pupils, work is honorable. You will never be assigned any
laboring task as a punishment. Just as soon as we get going
here, I will want crews to scrub the lockers, scrub the walls
down, remove chewing gum from under the chairs and tables
and anywhere and everywhere it may be found. We are going

to have plenty to do. Probably twenty-five to fifty of you, if you can qualify, will be working your study periods on these assignments until we clean this house and this yard!"

The entire student body was giving George their undivided attention.

"You learn by doing just as you learn from books," George told them. "Books come first, for you are behind and you need mental training most of all."

"Now, something more," George added, "and listen carefully to this. I'm not going to write rules and tack them up on your bulletin boards. You are no longer little children out there. The majority of you are young men and women, and the rest of you will soon be. There will be no more chewing gum or smoking in this school. This applies to all pupils in this school. Teachers will not be permitted to smoke or to chew gum either.

"Something that will not be a written rule, but will soon be an understood one, is that gambling will not be permitted," George added. "Gambling is a rash that has broken out among you. Why? When you gamble you have something taken from you or you take something from somebody. Nothing is created. A person who does not create is as unsuccessful as a drone bee. So you can be the judge. I don't like don'ts. But I have four to mention to you. Don't steal. Don't gamble. Don't lie. Don't skip school. If you do one of these you'll run into trouble.

"Before we leave this assembly, I would like to ask you to hold up your hands out there if one or both of your parents have gone to school to me," George said.

About eighty percent of the pupils held up their hands.

"This goes to show that the pupils I used to teach here have not moved away," he said. "Little did I know when I taught youth here nineteen to twenty years ago, who looked very much like you . . . and I will tell you later after I see the way you act . . . if they acted like you . . ."

The audience laughed.

"Your parents got a very young high school principal," he said. "I was twenty-four when I came here and twenty-eight when I left on a scholarship for European study. Now, at forty-nine, I have been asked to return to help you. Like every person on this faculty, I am interested in you. I can't believe all the things I have heard about you and what has happened at this school. You know, I have heard it said you can't get something from nothing. Now you think this over and see if you don't believe it is true. But I do believe we can get something from something. Your parents were fine youth, as fine as I've seen in all of the states in this country and abroad. Then, why is it that you have had so much trouble here? Maybe I can explain that for you. Let us take one of these fertile river bottoms where the soil will produce one hundred bushels of corn to the acre. Let us plow that bottom in the spring, disk, and smooth with a cultivator, get it in the best preparation for planting. Then let us buy seed corn and plant. After this, let's not do any more to it. Let it grow up uncultivated with the weeds. Let springtime pass, summer come and go, and autumn come for harvest. Do you think we will have one hundred bushels of corn to the acre?

"In the meantime plant another bottom beside it, prepare it the same way, use the same seed corn, cultivate that piece of corn in the spring and early summer and spray the weeds and what will we have? We'll have those hundred bushels of corn to the acre, won't we? Has Kensington High School become the uncultivated bottom of corn? How these two fields can parallel your own lives! You are the good seed. Your homes, churches, and this school make up the surroundings wherein you take root and grow. We teachers are here to help cultivate you. The weeds that are trying to choke you are cheating, lying, gambling, stealing, skipping school, and too many more to mention. Now we are going to spray these obnoxious weeds that try to choke you and stunt your growth. We are here to do everything in our power to produce that hundred bushels of corn to the acre.

"Now, this is your springtime, your season to grow," George

said in a higher voice. "You have only one spring season wherein to grow. Now is the time to prepare yourselves. You have heard older people wish for a new springtime and say, 'Oh, if I knew then what I know now, my life would be different.' I never want one of you to have to say this. I want you to be prepared so you can amount to something in life. Amount to something in life," he repeated for emphasis, "for there is a place for each one of you. It is not always the A- and B-average pupils who amount to the most. If you work hard and just can't make those grades, but if you have another kind of grade that each of you can make, and that is an A grade in character, you will never be without work."

In a lower tone of voice he said, "You are living in a new world. That new world began shortly after World War II. It's not the world your parents, your teachers, and I knew. You know my age now. Well, I am not old. And I have seen every foot of hard road come to this county. I used to drive a horse and buggy to school. I have ridden horseback and muleback to school. I have walked five miles to and from school and some of your parents have walked fourteen miles to this school. Now you ride buses just about all the way. In a world in which I grew up, I remember the first car I ever saw. My sister and I ran over the hill, hid behind a bank and peeped up to watch it pass."

There was laughter.

"I wasn't born when the first automobile was made and the first plane was flown," he said. "But I have seen them come just as you have seen television come. I was a pupil in a one-room rural school when I saw the first plane go over. I remember what an old man said to me: 'Son, it won't be long until the world comes to an end. If God Almighty had intended for man to fly He would have given him a pair of wings as well as his pair of legs.'

"Planes of all kinds fill the air and the world hasn't come to an end," he told them. "Flying planes and dropping of bombs won't bring an end to this world. If you want to know, if the world ends I think I know what will cause its destruction. And that is ignorance.

"I have seen three wars, a depression, automobiles, planes, radio, television, and movies come in my day. Now if these things have come in your parents' and your teachers' time, what will come in your time? There will be wonders unheard of to come. Do you think it is proper that you should grow up like uncultivated corn or that you go to school and cultivate the talents you have? In your new world a high school education is a must. If you don't finish high school the big steel company over across the river won't employ you as a laborer to dig a ditch.

"In the world your teachers and parents grew up in, we didn't need the high school diploma and the college degree as you need them now. When I finished college there were not over ten people with college degrees in this county. Now you are sitting out there wondering what kind of a world that was. What did we see, read, hear! In my home we didn't take newspapers or magazines and we didn't have books. I read my first novel after I got to high school. About all the books we had to read were our textbooks. I walked over the hills, along the paths in all the seasons of the year and read the green hills, the brown autumn hills, and the winter's desolate land. I read the skies, watched signs for weather, since we didn't know about radios then; I hunted over the hills at night and listened to the wind in the trees and the sounds of water in the streams. The music I heard, except on special occasions, was nature's sounds. And, of course, I learned a lot.

"You are living in a new and different world. Isn't your world a smaller world? Shouldn't you be taught languages in this school and all other secondary schools . . . yes, even before you reach high school! Am I wrong in trying to get all the scientific subjects for you that I can when the world is going scientific, when one of our exploratory objectives is to put men on the moon, to reach the planets and see what is on them? Each pupil in this school should be so wide awake in your new exciting world that we should never have to punish one in this school. He should be so busy preparing himself when there are so many things out there in that future for him to do that he would be kept too busy to get into mischief. You should be working us more than we are already worked instead of our insisting that you work."

George halted to look at the small sea of faces looking up at him. There wasn't a sound from student or teacher.

"But here is one of the advantages we had in our world that you don't have. We had time to grow up. We had time to think. I had time to walk over the hills, listen to the winds, observe the seasons, learn the different species of trees, shrubs, and flowers that were native to my region; I had time to observe all wild life, animals, reptiles, and birds; time to learn how they had lived and reared their young and what kind of parents they were; how the gray lizards and the nonpoisonous snakes laid their eggs in the soft loam for the sun to hatch them, how the terrapins make nests in the sand and hide their eggs for the sun to incubate them. Who can tell me he doesn't need to go to school? There is a place waiting for each of you. Each of you must amount to something.

"Think about this too, that beyond your world today, this one that you know around your home, your school, and Kensington and Greenwood County . . . beyond your state and county, there are other countries and peoples. Remember, you will have to co-exist with other peoples of this world. And the place to start being tolerant is right here and now. You will have to start getting along with one another here. This is the place. This is the time."

It was late, well after five o'clock, when Grace and George Gallion got in the car.

"How did you get along?" he asked.

"I have thirty-two in my room," she said. "They're sweet children. But they are so serious. They don't know how to laugh. They've never even heard some of the little stories we used to have in the first grade. So I'm going back and reading and telling them stories. Soon they will be sharing their experiences, I hope."

Then Grace began to laugh.

"Why are *you* laughing? What's so funny?"

"I can't get them to laugh but they make me laugh. I'm thinking about what my little Jason said today."

"Who's little Jason?"

"Jason Boggs," she said. "He's a darling little boy."

"What did he say that was funny?"

"When all the class was busy he looked up at me so innocently with his big blue eyes and said, 'Mrs. Gallion, what makes little girls so nice?' "

"How did you answer that one?"

" 'Because they have nice mothers,' I told him. That pleased him; he loves his mother."

"What else happened over there?"

"A lot goes on over there," she said. "Sometime I want you to come over to see the kind of shoes two children in my room are wearing. Honestly, you won't believe it. Old canvas shoes pinned up at the heels with safety pins!"

"What?"

"It's the truth," she said. "A poor little boy and his sister, and I don't believe they get enough to eat. They keep saying to me, 'Mrs. Gallion, when do we get our dinner?' And I say to them, 'Not long, children.' They start asking at ten in the morning. They don't have any pennies to get candy, but Old Gordie gave me pennies for them today. He's such a kind old man."

"It's been a long time, Grace. How do you think you're going to get along?"

"You'd think I'm bragging if I told you, George," she sighed, shaking her graying curly hair. "Honestly, half the teachers are no better trained to teach children than I am. I guess the Kensington Elementary is an advancement over the one-room schools, but I must say," she sighed again as they sped up the broad highway, "I'm not out-of-date, George."

On their left were the vistas of the Ohio River flowing like the world of young humanity to some inevitable destiny to join other waters of the world. On their right were unsullied hill vistas where the leaves greenly streamed in the wind-mad places. This scenic quiet slowly removed them from their world of new-found problems.

They drove up the Valley now where their meadows were green leaves and early turning of leaves were miniature sails amid green-rustling clouds of leaves. In the distance they could see their silent house. Janet was sitting at the window, waiting. When she saw the car she came running across the porch and down the steps.

"Did you have a good day, Janet?" Grace asked her.

"No, Mama, I didn't," she said sulkily. "We have to leave so early in the morning and you don't get back until so late!"

"Janet, I'm sorry," Grace said softly. "I think a mother's place is at home with her children, too."

She held her daughter's hand as they went into the silent house.

"I remember how Daddy used to take me to school and come and get me," Janet said, smiling. "When Daddy was sick Uncle Whitie used to take me and come and get me. But it's so dull in the house now when no one's there."

"I've tried to be a good mother to you, Janet." Grace's voice faltered. "You're the only child we have. And I suppose I'm neglecting you."

"You're right this time, Grace," George admitted. He moved over closer to her. He put his arm around her shoulders. "Maybe I don't understand life and living, but I . . ."

"George, I hope you don't think I'm nagging because I watch over your health and Janet."

"I know, darling," he admitted in a soft voice, "if it hadn't been for you . . ." He didn't finish what he had started to say.

"Your editor has begged you to finish your book," she said. "There are articles you want to write. How long can you go on ignoring these things? Don't you know. . . ?"

"I know one thing," he interrupted her quickly. "I know I love you—no matter what you say. I can't help teaching, Grace. I love it—especially where I'm needed and wanted and there's a challenge!"

"Grace, what are you going to do with these jugs?"

George looked quizzically at Grace. He had never seen her as pretty as she was this morning. She had always dressed well and had kept her figure. Her pretty face had never looked better to him than when she came to the car this Monday morning carrying two glass gallon jugs.

"This morning I'm going to stop by the pond so you can fill these for me," she said, smiling. "My children will love what I'm planning for them."

"You look wonderful this morning."

"You sure do, Mama," Janet said.

"But why do you want that old brackish, smelly water from the pond?"

"Oh George, it's filled with frog eggs," she said. "We've got a glass aquarium to put it in and we'll keep the swamp water at room temperature so the frog eggs will hatch into little tadpoles. We'll watch them grow until they lose their tails and become little frogs. We're going to have fish and turtles and terrapins. You ought to see our room now, George! We've got the nicest room in the school and all my children work like beavers to help with it."

George put the jugs on the front seat between them. He was afraid to put them on the floor, lest they break as the car rolled over Washboard Valley Road. In Greenwood, Grace stopped to let Janet out at the high school. At the Greenwood post office they stopped again so that George could get his willow basket filled with mail for the school and for himself.

"More duns," he said, as he sifted through them, "duns, duns, duns!"

"Won't the county board of education pay for these bills?"

"No, the school made them last year."

"Why didn't they pay them?"

"Your guess is as good as mine."

"But why should you have to pay these?"

"The school is obligated and I'm principal of that school and therefore I'm obligated. Believe me, though, all the money will go through my hands this year."

Grace began to slow down as she pulled off the highway. The sun was a dingy half-lighted lantern globe up in the mists that sealed the broad valley from palisade to palisade.

"Oh, that pond," George said.

He got out with his jugs and crossed the highway, where the odor of stagnant water filled his nostrils. There was a green slime over its surface except where the waterlilies and swamp grass protruded above the brackish scum. There were little paths going down to the edge where the grass was worn into the dirt. In the first were the imprints of little bare feet. George chose a little path less steep than the others, and he started down. The force of his weight almost carried him into the water. He got one foot wet and his well-shined shoes were caked with swamp mud. He breathed as little as possible of the sour-scented air while he filled each jug. His shoes slick with mud, he struggled back up the little path and across the highway to the car.

"Here are the jugs, baby," he said. "I wouldn't be surprised if there aren't ten thousand frog eggs in these jugs."

"Your shoes, George," she said. "I'm sorry. There's Kleenex in the glove compartment."

He put the jugs on the floor and took the box of Kleenex from the glove compartment and went to work on his shoes. By the time she had reached Kensington High School he had used the entire box, and his shoes didn't look as good as the old pairs they had seen piled on the Greenwood dump.

Sadie Markham and Nora Wallings, her assistant, were already in the office when George arrived.

"Answer the duns, Nora," he said. "Tell them we'll pay as soon as we can. You know how to do these. I'll read your replies and sign them sometime today."

"I want to see the first-period absentee list," he told Sadie. "See that they are rounded up first thing. Any complaints from drivers of supply trucks?"

"No, Mr. Gallion, but there are complaints from some of the students. Somebody is stealing books."

"What? Any idea who?"

"No, but a lot of sophomores and juniors have been missing books."

At that moment George saw the signal lights flashing on the first bus turning from the highway into the Kensington lane. He walked out onto the schoolyard. He liked to watch the buses roll in like a convoy toward the schoolhouse. Here he stood, a small-town high school principal on a spot of sacred earth, amid the unsullied high hill and river vistas under an overcast sky where shafts of sunlight were splintering through. To him beams of sunlight were shafts of learning's light bursting through an overcast of darkness which was ignorance. He watched the convoy of buses, loaded until there wasn't standing room, with fresh young faces looking from the windows as they bounced dramatically over the pockmarked lane amid the blend of exhaust fumes and road dust.

He also watched one youth as he strutted toward the schoolhouse. He was coming along while pupils in the buses shouted and waved and called, "Wild Bill!" At the foot of the hill, Wild Bill departed from the convoy, took a short cut up toward the schoolhouse while the buses moved on around the loop. He walked rapidly up the steep short hill.

"Hiya, Mr. Gallion," said the tall freckled-faced youth. His reddish-brown hair was disheveled like a rag mop in the morning wind. His face was animated, like those of so many other happy young people who knew the world belonged to them. "You know me, don't you, Mr. Gallion?" George looked him over, wondering if he had ever seen him before.

"Well, I ought to know you," George said doubtfully.

"Maybe you don't know me because you haven't seen me for eight or nine years," he said. "The last time I saw you was at a football game. I was eight years old then."

George smiled at the eager youth as he looked him over. "I'm Bill Nottingham," the boy said. "Now do you remember me? Ah, shucks, Mr. Gallion, you used to teach with my mother, Alice Nottingham."

"Oh yes," George lied with happiness. "I remember you now. What are you doing now? How's school?"

"Well, I hate it there, so I came up here to see if you needed a good English teacher."

"Let me hear you say that again," George said, laying his hand on the boy's shoulder.

"I thought you might need a good English teacher and everybody says Mom is the best. Thought she might teach English for you and I could play football."

"Bill, listen to me," George said, slapping him on the shoulder. "If you'll bring your mother here to teach English, I'll guarantee you that you'll play football! I see Coach Webber up there at the corridor steps now."

George turned and yelled, "Coach Webber, got a minute?" He motioned to him with a sweep of his hand. "You know this boy?"

"Sure do," he said smiling. "Hello, Bill."

"How is it, Coach, that we don't have him on the football team here?" George asked with a sly wink. "He wants to bring his mother here to teach English for us if he can play football."

"I've always wanted you, Bill," Don Webber said gravely.

"And now we need your mother too. Boy, you'll make one of the best halfbacks on my squad. And I've got a two-hundred-pound line to open the holes for you."

"Gee, that's great," he said excitedly. "I told Mom I could make the team up here. I told her this morning I'd never go back to school if I couldn't come here. So I took off running. She was awfully upset."

"You'll make my team, Wild Bill," Coach Webber said. "I can tell by looking you over. You look like a man to me."

"I'm not chicken, I'll tell you," he said.

"Coach, now listen," George said. "Mum is the word on this deal."

"I'll get him a uniform right now," Coach Webber said. "He can come out for practice this afternoon."

"Wow!" Wild Bill shouted.

"Not now, Coach," George said. "We've got to work fast. I've got to get assurance from his mother that she will be here."

"Oh, Mr. Gallion, you don't have to worry," Wild Bill said with a broad grin. "She doesn't want me to quit school. She cried this morning when I told her I was coming back here. I told her I belonged up here. I know everybody here. Mr. Gallion, you heard 'em hollering at me from this bus, didn't you?"

"I sure did."

"Those voices made me feel good again," he said.

"All right, Coach, you have assured him he will play football."

"My word is my bond, Mr. Gallion," Coach Webber said in mock seriousness.

"Thank you, Coach," George said. "I'll take Bill with me to the office. I've got an idea. Can you get back into Northwest High School and deliver this note to your mother?"

"Sure can, Mr. Gallion; they have a principal over there and four assistants, but I'll get the note to her. I'll get past them all right."

"Don't let anyone see you give the note to your mother," George said. "I like to be as ethical as possible. But they took her, and I'm bringing her back if I can."

George took young Wild Bill Nottingham through the front door and into his office.

"Mrs. Markham, get me the fastest and safest hot-rod messenger up there on that list," George said. "Have him here and ready in three minutes!"

George hastily scrawled a note:

"Dear Alice: Your son has been here this morning. He wants to come back home. He's an upset boy and he needs you and he needs us. He wants you to come back too. And we want you and we need you. We have never wanted a teacher more than we want you. We will pay you all we can. If there is any way I can find to raise your salary I'll do it. But in this situation, more is at stake than your salary. Your only child is in open rebellion. We think we can help you save your son if you'll only come back and work for us and with him. Come today if you can. If not today, come tomorrow. By all means, come. Bill wants to play football. I've talked to Coach Webber and he has agreed to let him play, because we think this will give him an interest and hold him in school. Will you reply to this note and return it by him? Sincerely, George."

George put the note in an envelope and sealed it and scribbled her name on the envelope. Minutes later George saw a car with two eager young boys in it race from the Hill, followed by a cloud of dust

The morning passed. There was no word as yet from Bill. George was looking over absentee reports when Sadie Markham announced a visitor.

"Mr. Gallion, there's a man waiting to see you, Mr. Kale Manning—Ted Manning's father. Ted's a senior here this year. Mr. Manning seems to be very angry about something."

"Where is he?"

"Out there in the yard walking up and down in front of the schoolhouse."

"I know Kale," George said.

"Did Bill Nottingham find you?"

"No. Where is he? I've been waiting for him."

"He's hunting for you. He has a message for you."

"I'll find him."

"Mr. Manning has been in the office twice. He seems to get madder all the time."

"I must see Bill Nottingham first."

At the office door, George met the smiling tousled-headed youth. "I haven't read this, Mr. Gallion," he said. "It's sealed. Mom didn't tell me what she was going to do. But she doesn't want me to play football."

"Why?"

"Afraid I'd get hurt."

"What's happened to Alice?" he asked as he ripped the end off the envelope.

"You go into the office and ask for a registration card," George said after reading the note. "Mrs. Markham will help you with your schedule. Report for football this afternoon. Coach Webber will issue you your equipment."

"Oh, boy," he shouted, jumping up and down. "Oh, boy! That's great! Then Mom is coming. When?"

"Next Monday."

He ran from the office, waving his arms and shouting, "Oh, boy! Football!"—and collided with Kale Manning, almost knocking him down.

"What's the matter with that crazy boy?" he said. "Wild as a buck, and a teacher's son! Alice had better get a headlock on him. If she doesn't he's going to get the upper hand!"

"Kale, I feel the same way 'Wild Bill' Nottingham feels," George said. "I feel like jumping up and down too. I'm going to get another teacher. I'm going to get a great one."

"You'd better fire some you've got," he said. "You'd better get rid of that Coach Webber! That's the reason I'm up here."

"Have you got somebody to replace him?" George asked.

"No, I haven't, George," he shouted irritably. "But he's no good."

"How do you know?"

"I played football for Dartmouth High School back in the days when there wasn't a high school on this side of the river," he shouted, waving his arms up past the broad rim of his Texas-style hat. "I played back when they had teams."

"Now tell me what's wrong with Webber."

"Well, what I'm trying to tell you is that I know a little about football."

"Sure, you knew the old methods."

"Well, I've kept up with football, too, I'll have you know." His voice rose. "I know enough to know Don Webber's not any coach."

"Don't just tell me, Kale. Give me a reason."

"He's got Ted out there playing end and receiving passes when he ought to be a fullback and doing the passing," Kale shouted. "Take a look at the hands my boy's got on him. He can throw that ball!"

"I don't doubt your word, Kale, but I leave the coaching up to the coach."

"I've got a boy on this team," Kale said, waving his hands. "I'm a big taxpayer in this country. And of course I like to watch football practice. So the other evening I made suggestions to him and he ordered me off the field. Damned insulting like," he said, his face coloring. "That made my blood boil, George."

"Maybe you made his blood boil." George spoke softly. "I've known you a long time, Kale. You know you're good at making other people's blood boil."

"I'm right about my son, damn it," he shouted.

"Shhhhhhshh," George said. "Watch your language. School is going on here!"

"I don't care what's goin' on here," he shouted. "Enough is enough!"

"Coach Webber is head coach of the team," George said.

"What he says goes. If you go back and he tells you to get off the field, then you get!"

"You'd stand up for that whippersnapper?"

"He's the coach, Kale," George said. "That's all there is to it. Come to the game Friday week, played under the lights in Kensington. That game will be a test of his coaching. We're playing Rutland. We haven't beaten that team in twenty years."

"After the way he talked to me, I won't support his team," he said. "I won't pay a dollar to see a game."

"The place will be packed," George said. "Your son will be playing.'"

"You might lose that game," he said in a lower voice. "George, there's talk!"

"What kind of talk?"

"Don Webber is playing ineligible men," he replied. "You've got an ineligible ex-convict on that team!"

"And who is he?"

"Champ Burton! You've got everything in this school, George! I'm ashamed to tell people my son goes to Kensington High School. I hate to defile his character by having him associate with a teammate like Burton! Stop this smoking, gambling, carousing, stealing up here! Kick them out of this school! Clean this place up! What are we taxpayers paying you, this coach and teachers, for?" he asked as he pulled a large cigar from his pocket. He peeled the wrapper, lighted it in the corridor.

"You've said enough, Kale," George said. "You're nothing but a deflated bag of ill wind. You gamble yourself. Your wife has left you a few times. Now pinch that cigar. We don't allow smoking up here. Then get the hell out and off the Hill. I'm on Webber's side!"

"You mean you're running me off? I'm a taxpayer!"

"I don't care what you are," George said. "Get the hell out!"

"One thing more I've come up here to tell you," he said.

"Stop those kids from riding my fence down. I'll have them arrested!"

"Please do that," George said. "If you'll stop our runaways from crossing your field there won't be any leaks on this schoolground. I wish you would arrest a few of them!"

"If it will help you to have them arrested I won't, after the way you've talked to me," he shouted, waving his cigar. "I'm leaving, but you'll hear more about the investigation of your ineligibles. I'll guarantee you that much." He turned in the corridor, shaking his fist at George.

"And you're talking," George said. "You're stirring it up. Stir all you want to, but we'll be playing eligible men!"

"I want a decent school," Kale spoke defiantly. "They didn't have any ex-cons in my day."

"I've taught them, Kale," George spoke softly. "I've taught several youths just back from the reformatory. But that didn't give me or anyone the right to call them ex-cons. They were kids who had made mistakes. And I believe in giving them a second chance." Then George said in a low voice, "The third and fourth chance, if that will save them."

"I'm warning you, George," he said.

George was now alone where he could relax for a few minutes. He had had a busy day, one problem piling on top of another. In this small office which was the safest place in school, perhaps the only safe place, he looked around at the books, umbrellas, balls, gloves, and other items that pupils regarded as valuable possessions which they had fears of putting in lockers they couldn't lock. His office didn't look like a high school principal's office, but very much like a junkshop. His chair, which he seldom had time to sit in, was a creaky antique that might collapse with him any time.

The discipline desk, which had already been the scene of many a drama pupils would not forget, was a battered old thing that the principal of a modern school plant would phone a used-furniture dealer to come and get. There were few things in

Kensington High School for the pupils' or the teachers' comforts. But the thoughts, the dreams, the plans swarmed over and around him.

"A penny for your thoughts," Gus Riddle said.

"You'll have to give me that penny," George said. "You are to conduct a pleasant surprise. In just a minute pupils will be coming in here who have lost books. Now you're to conduct this surprise. A locker inspection!"

"Oh, no," he said. "This soon?"

"Just for sophomores and juniors," George explained. "Have sophomores and juniors lined up before the lockers. Don't let anyone open the lockers. Don't let anyone get into his unlocked locker. When they are lined up and you are ready, send me word. Some pupils have been missing books, and I'll bring them here. After it's over you can give me the penny. I need it."

The pupils who had missed books drifted into the office very quietly. There were twenty of them.

"Now each of you has reported one or more books missing," George said. "We think these books could have been misplaced. Maybe one of your classmates got your book by mistake."

Sighs went up in unison from the pupils. One said, "They don't get books here by mistake. Pupils wait until their classmates buy books, then they steal them. They spend the money their parents gave them for something else. It was that way last year, Mr. Gallion."

"Hold up your hands if you marked your books so you could identify them."

All hands went up.

"That's good," George told them. "You sophomores will line up and go among the sophomore lockers while Mrs. Markham takes the books out of the lockers for inspection. Books the sophomores are carrying will be inspected, too. You juniors will go along the junior lockers, where Mr. Riddle will help you. We want to do this in a hurry. Now check the books fast! Look for your identification marks."

"I found my history book," one of the group shouted. "Here it is! How did it get here?"

In ten minutes nineteen of the twenty missing books had been found, and the locker numbers where they had been were noted. The thieves would be easy to trace directly through the students who had, in many cases, bought the books innocently from the students who had stolen them.

George was tired. He sat on the edge of the large desk while the teachers came slowly in carrying briefcases, books, and armloads of papers.

Following Garrett Newall through the door was Charles Newton with chemistry and Latin books and a sheaf of papers. Don Webber was directly behind him. His pants and sweatshirt were dotted with blotches of clay. Just as soon as the teachers' meeting was over, he would be back on the athletic field.

Gus Riddle walked in looking at everybody at once. He was grinning and swinging a battered old briefcase. Pretty Mary Wallingford followed, stepping as lightly as a cat on dewy grass. Fred Laurie grinned as he walked up the aisle and took a back seat, holding a bulging briefcase on his knees. Fred Laurie was known to be a collector of old newspapers. He spoke to Mary Wallingford when Karl Hegioland, wearing a soiled shirt, and a disheveled tie which he had worn every day since his arrival, jumped into the room like a grasshopper. He needed a shave and his hairbrush mustache needed trimming. He said something in Spanish to which Charles Newton quickly replied. He was followed by dark-skinned, gentle Leonard Ossington, part-time bus driver, full-time teacher.

When Shan Hannigan came in carrying a horn almost his own size, there was a little trickle of laughter from everybody in the room but Gus Riddle. Gus' face colored and he pursed his lips.

Next to arrive were the student teachers. They came in quietly and sat together in the back of the room.

Gradually, the meeting assembled.

"Everybody's here," George said. "We don't have such a

small faculty after all. We have twenty-three teachers now, although twelve are just part-time. A most interesting faculty, too," he added with a smile. "The age difference between the youngest and the oldest is over a half century. I know all of you are tired," George continued. "This will be a short meeting. And there will not be a teachers' meeting tomorrow afternoon unless an emergency arises."

There was laughter, and light applause.

"We are in our second week," George said. "I want to compliment you. Under the circumstances, you have done a marvelous job! We're on the one-yard line. We have a first down and ninety-nine yards to go."

"Beginning Monday, Mrs. Alice Nottingham will be back with us."

There was a roar of applause.

"How on earth did you get her?" Gus Riddle asked.

"She's certainly taking a financial loss to come back here. I'm glad she's following her son. I'll admit she's just about the best I've seen in the classroom."

"Beginning next week, we're cutting out this noon hour," George continued. "We don't have the teacher personnel to police this schoolhouse and sixty acres of ground. We're teachers and not a police force. Do I hear any objections?"

"It's a radical change, Mr. Gallion," Leonard Ossington said. "I hear pupils on my bus talking 'strike' if their noon hour is taken from them."

"A strike of pupils would ruin us," Marcella Waters said. "We're making a good start here!"

"Why not an assembly meeting where you could explain this," Gus Riddle said. "I was against this at first, but after a few days out there on the grounds I'm willing to try something new. That's punishment out there!"

"I'd thought about an assembly program to explain this," George said. "But I've changed my mind for two reasons. Why should we let the pupils decide our policy? Someday they'll be initiating policies. They'll have their chance. So why shouldn't we have our chance? Then, too," he added slowly, "the more this thing is stirred up, the more our destructionist pupils will foment trouble among the good ones. I suggest we say nothing about it. That we make our plans and ease it into force. I think the pupils will like it."

"The smokers won't," Gus said.

"What about the gamblers?" Fred Laurie said. "I say let's not fool about it. Put it into force!"

"How many of you agree we try it?"

They all voted for the change.

"That was a clever way to find stolen books, Mr. Gallion," Charles Newton said. "We ought to have done something like that last year."

"I'm not through with that yet," George said. "I'll be calling eighteen pupils from your classes and study halls in the morning. I want to find out where and how they got those books."

"I'd like to know the ones who stole them," Gus said.

"But you won't know," George told him. "Not a person on this faculty will know."

"Why shouldn't we know?" Fred Laurie asked.

"Stealing is something that follows a youth all of his life," George explained. "A school is to help youth. I'm not making this public, not even to their parents. I'll find out who got the books. Many bought those books innocently. And you can announce in your home rooms there's liable to be a locker inspection at any time."

"Stealing was considered a sin when I used to come to school here," Fred Laurie said. "I could leave a pencil on my desk, go to my other classes, and go back at the end of the school day and find it on my desk, or in the lost-and-found box. What has happened here?"

"Mr. Laurie, when people in a community saw down telephone poles at night, when they cut telephone cables and destroy personal property, what can you expect?" Gus Riddle said. "The good people in Kensington, who are against this, are afraid to open their mouths. They are afraid of reprisals that might be taken! Look at the windshields of cars smashed here last year belonging to the people who lifted their voices against wrong!"

"I want all of you to speak out this year," George said. "Let's face the problems. Let's be frank and face any problem before us. We can win, and I'll tell you why. People know this little band of teachers stand between the public and disaster. We are all who can save this community. So take time in your classes and speak against evil. Our community cannot help this school. Kensington High School, as poor as it is, has to help this community. These people are like other people too. There's good stuff in them. The field lies fallow and uncultivated."

"You know, Mr. Gallion," Gus added, "if you want to see where crime is generated just drop down to the 'Corner' in Kensington. Go there at midnight and you will see. We don't have much trouble with the rural pupils. They're different."

"Why is Kensington so lawless?" George asked.

"There are five thousand in Kensington," Gus explained. "It's unincorporated. No marshal. No law. This place is wide open."

"Have any of you who live there ever thought of getting it incorporated?" George asked him. "This is the largest unincorporated town I know of in this state."

"It's been up two or three times to vote to incorporate it," Gus said. "But a few of the big taxpayers have enough power to defeat the measure."

"Have you ever led the fight, Mr. Riddle?"

"No, I've stayed out of it," he said. "I don't like messes."

"That's the trouble with us teachers. We're not aggressive enough. Incorporating Kensington and getting a marshal for day and one for night would work wonders for this school. That would be the spray to kill the weeds on the uncultivated field."

"It's an idea." Gus said.

"I have a big problem to bring up, Mr. Gallion," Mary Wallingford said. "This one is important because it deals directly with this school. We need a full-time librarian almost as much as we need police in Kensington. I can't leave my classes and go over there often enough. Pupils are destroying the magazines. They're cutting up books and tearing pages from them with knives. Yesterday one of the litter cans was filled with books. Pupils just can't handle this situation. We have teachers in the big library study halls only three periods out of six. We just don't have teachers to go around!"

George took his notebook from his pocket and scribbled "Library."

"How's the team coming along, Coach?"

"We invite one and all to be down at the Kensington Stadium Friday week to see what we've got this year." He spoke up quickly. "We'll be playing Rutland High School, a team we haven't beaten in twenty years! This will test our strength. You be there and judge for yourself."

"What about Latin, Mr. Newton?"

"I hope you visit my classes as soon as you can," he said. "I'd like to show you what we've accomplished in these few days under adverse circumstances. Most fortunately, we found a supply of old Latin books this school ordered and couldn't sell. We've put them to use and ordered more."

Gus Riddle looked around at the teachers, grinning and shaking his head.

"How are you getting along, Mr. Riddle?"

"I always get along," he replied positively. "I produce farmers. I produce men of character!"

"Better watch your bragging, Mr. Riddle," Shan Hannigan warned him in fun. "Someday when you are out, somebody might slip in there with a hatchet and work your paradise over!"

"That somebody might not be too far from me either," Riddle snapped. The color rose suddenly to his face like angry clouds before a storm. "I wouldn't be surprised if a hatchet isn't used on my desk," he continued as he pulled a ring of keys from his pocket. "I always use one of these on my door when I leave. When I have reasons to be suspicious I play the game safe. This year I have that reason, and I lock my door."

"What have you been doing, George? What kept you so long?"

"Teachers' meeting," he replied. He got in the car beside Grace. "We've had a longer meeting than we planned."

"You have long days over here, don't you?"

"But we won't have a teachers' meeting tomorrow evening."

"Why not?" she said. "You ought to make it one hundred percent."

"How many meetings have you had?"

"One, Monday afternoon."

They drove past the hot-rodders' cars parked waiting for the end of football practice.

"How are your pupils?"

"Wonderful."

"Are the frog eggs hatching?"

"Not yet."

"How's the turtle?"

"He's a naughty pupil and bears watching."

Now they reached the U.S. highway, which ran parallel to the Ohio River. Above the palisade ledges on their right, the late afternoon sky was unbelievably blue. The palisades were fissured endlessly toward the Ohio River. As the violet evening darkened, the landscape melted into luminous haze in the distance while on their left the waters of the Ohio glowed intense, electric blue-green. They moved silently up this road between the river and the palisades.

"I wish my problems were as simple as yours," George said, breaking the silence.

"But you asked for it, George."

"Admitted for the hundredth time," he said. "Sure I asked for it. Now they're destroying books. And I can't find a librarian."

"But George! I know where there's a librarian you can get. She's not a college graduate but she has had library science."

"Who in the world is she?"

"Your niece, Taddie Sue Gallion."

"Oh, why didn't I think of her? Three years in college, drove the county Bookmobile! And she's a pepperpod! Reckon I can work with her?"

"You know you can."

"That's a wonderful idea. I'll see John Bennington tomorrow about it. I'll try Taddie Sue. She's never worked in a high school with me before."

"Look what an assortment you are working with," she reminded him. "I've never seen a high school faculty like that one. You know she'll be better than your student teachers," Grace told him.

"You know she's explosive and she's my niece," he said.

"She's just the one you need in a library where they're destroying books," Grace told him. "Let her explode! She's the best for that position. You'll see. She has no equal!"

"I'm going to kiss you for this," he said. "That suggestion might solve another problem!"

The next afternoon there was a knock on the office door. When George opened the door there stood Herb Hampton with Volume 10 of the *Encyclopaedia Britannica* in his hand.

"I thought this book might be valuable," he said. "I just managed to keep it out of the furnace."

"It sure has value," George said. "Where did you get it?"

"Library trash basket," he said. "May've burned some smaller books, but this one was bigger and I caught it in time."

"Thank you very much, Mr. Hampton."

George took the book and went to the library. When he walked in carrying the book the noise simmered down.

"Pick up the paper around you," George said. "Pick up every little piece of torn paper. This place looks like a pigpen. You and you over there, come over here and take these two paper cans, and carry them around for them to put the paper in. I hope there aren't any library books in that paper," George added. "Now you boys may carry that down to the furnace room."

George stood there looking the students over until they were quiet.

"Now that you are through," he said, "I have something to say. I want to know who threw this valuable book into the wastepaper can!"

He held the book up so they could see it.

"We don't have many books in the library, not one-tenth enough for you, and yet somebody is trying to destroy what we have. Would the one who threw it in the can own up to it?"

The pupils gave one another furtive glances.

"Hold up your hands, those of you not guilty!"

All hands went up.

"Somebody is lying," George said. "There are girls and boys in this study hall who know I will find out who did this. It had to be done this period. I like a brave and honest youth who has the courage to tell me when he has done a wrong!"

Brave and *courage* were old-fashioned words in Kensington High School. George's use of these words provoked a snicker in his audience.

In these first days of the school year, George had learned that a pupil who squealed on another was "chicken." The language he knew in high school had changed. *Brave* and *courage* had changed to *squeal* and *chicken*.

"Will all of you write down the name of the person who threw the book in the can," George said. "I won't know who gives me the name. The guilty person will not know who reports. All of you belong to this school. You are an organization. It is not right for one individual to try to destroy this school. You must stop him."

George sifted through the papers hurriedly. Many of them were blanks. "I don't know," or "I wouldn't tell you if I knew," or "I won't squeal" were written on many. "None of your business" was written on one, "You go to hell" on another. Three could not be read in public.

"Well, no one knows," George said. "Somebody is lying. Thanks for all these nice scribbled notes."

When he said this he looked quickly to see whose smile was the broadest. Not one who had ever been in his office for disciplinary reasons was smiling.

"Yes, come right in, Mr. Gallion," John Bennington said. "A lot of things I want to talk to you about. But first I want to ask how you've been getting along."

"Monday we crossed the Rubicon," he replied. "This week we've made a beach-head for the invasion. Next week we'll start the big push; we'll be on the firing line."

The two men sat down at the table. They faced each other.

"What kind of reports have you been getting about me?" George asked.

"Well, to be frank with you," he said, looking at George with owlish eyes that revolved behind his thick-lensed glasses, "I've been getting varied reports. I've had a complaint from one of the parents. John Renfroe came to see me; he said you paddled his boy too high."

"Yes, his son Bascom told Miss Wallingford to kiss his rear," George explained. "I've never struck a pupil's tailbone yet with a paddle. I guess John Renfroe told you you'd lose his vote."

"You guessed it."

"If I were running a school board, I wouldn't want his vote."

"I need every vote I can get," he said. "From the reports I get, I don't believe Orman Caudill will be re-elected in that district. I'm sorry to tell you, Mr. Gallion, the way you've stirred up things, you won't be of any help."

"You mean I should soft-pedal the situation until after the election?"

"That might be better," he replied.

"I can't work that way," George said. "It's now or never down there. These first weeks are the toughest. Either the principal and his teachers are in command or the pupils will take over. We are in command. Shall we continue tightening our command or shall we turn it back to them?"

"Soften a little until after the election."

"I don't know what kind of reports you are getting," George said. "But where you lose a few votes in one place you'll be gaining in others. Food trucks are coming again. The drivers will report to you that they have been unmolested. Not a windshield has been smashed with a hammer this year. Without enough teachers, we are moving along."

"That's good news, Mr. Gallion, but can't you go easy until after the election? I am spending a great deal of my time on the road now, laying up fences, so I can get support."

"I'll do my best to cooperate with you," George said, "but I doubt that I can stand the situation that long."

"That will be fine, Mr. Gallion," he said. "We might be getting someplace now. Anything else you have in mind?"

"Yes I want my niece, Taddie Sue Gallion, for a librarian," he said.

"Why didn't I think of her!" he said excitedly. "That's a fine idea."

"My wife thought of her. Acute necessity compelled me to have to do something about the Kensington High School library. I need a full-time librarian down there. Had eight books burned this week!"

"What?" he said astonishedly.

"That's right," George said.

"Fortunately now," Bennington said, "we have the answer for the library. However, Charlie Aiken, principal of Taddie Sue's school, will hate to lose her. He says she's an excellent teacher and disciplinarian."

"Can I have her Monday?" George interrupted him.

"Yes, if she is willing to change," he replied.

"She'll go down there for me. She'll be interested in being a full-time librarian in a high school. Maybe we'll halt the destruction of books. Then, too, she'll command a study hall. I have teachers in only three of the library study halls. We don't have teachers to go around. Not one of our teachers has a rest period during the day. Each works the six hour periods, noon hour, evenings and mornings at home, and probably over the weekends!'

"And what about you, Mr. Gallion? Are you overdoing? I know there was some concern over your health."

"I've never thought of my health since the morning school began. I've not had time."

"I wish I could furnish you with more teachers, but you know the situation. But getting Taddie Sue Gallion will be a help. I'm just wondering how I will replace her."

"I've got seniors down there who could do it until a teacher is found," George said. "I don't believe there is another high school in the United States where more student help is used. They're doing everything down there from teaching classes, cutting grass, washing walls, cleaning chewing gum from the seats, repairing lockers, working in the cafeteria, and our hot-rod messengers are furnishing their cars and buying their own gas to deliver our telephone messages. You'd be surprised how fine they are and what a great job they're doing, Mr. Bennington!"

"They were a headache last year," he said. "Maybe the telephone strike has been a blessing in this respect."

"I can't agree with you on that, but we have found a way to deliver messages and get the sick to doctors."

"That school has been a thorn in my flesh," John Bennington sighed. "You know what I told you once. If the line isn't held there all my board members will be defeated."

"You are showing signs of weakness by not facing the situation, Mr. Bennington," George told him frankly. "You are my superior and I hate to tell you this. If I were not your friend I wouldn't tell you. You can't fool the students and you can't fool the people. They might criticize you when you are doing a job, but they'll respect you for doing it. Fear is the major weakness in our schools today," he said, and he rose from his chair. "Teachers are afraid because their principals are afraid and principals are afraid because their superintendents are afraid. Superintendents are afraid because the politically appointed state departments of education are afraid. A scared dog going round and round chasing his tail gets nowhere. It's the same with schools.

"I've made Gus Riddle dean of boys," he said. "Mrs. Nottingham's going to be dean of girls. But the big thing, Mr. Bennington, is that we'll do away with the noon hour, which will relieve us of such problems as gambling, smoking, no-goods slipping in on the grounds and mingling with our students."

"Are you sure that will work?" he asked. His enthusiasm was waning. "Watch for a strike down there! I had one once. It can be terrible!"

"We have to do it, Mr. Bennington," George said. "I don't have time to tell you and you don't have time to listen to the problems this will solve. Gus Riddle was afraid of this change, but after a week of school police he has come over to the idea. I don't think there will be a strike. You see, we can sell this idea to the students because it will shorten the school day by thirty minutes. If we can't sell this idea, we'll do away with the noon hour just the same."

"That's a radical change, Mr. Gallion," he reminded George. "Since that school was built twenty-five years ago they've always had a noon hour."

"Mr. Bennington, one time you didn't show signs of weakness," George reminded him. "We had one-room schools in this county for over a century. This year, for the first time, you are sending elementary pupils by bus to ten big consolidated schools. You have done what others failed to do, including myself, although I tried, but we didn't have roads for school buses then. You have made the most radical change of all, upsetting a tradition of a century. The progress of the county necessitated this change. This very change, despite the ulcers you get, is going to re-elect all three of your board members! So why would you be reluctant to accept changes I see are needed at Kensington High School?"

The school day had just begun when there was a flurry of hammer-loud knocks on the office door.

"Just a minute," George shouted. "Don't batter it in. We need it!"

"I'm Enic Zimmerman," spoke a loud gruff voice. "You sent for me. I'm here!"

"Oh, yes, Enic." George spoke happily. "I sure did send for you!"

Then George whispered to Sadie Markham, "Get Don Zimmerman's permanent record out for me."

George jumped up and went to the door. "Come in, Enic. Glad to see you! Thought that must be your old hard fists hitting the door. I remember how you used to use them in the ring."

"Not any more, though, George," he replied, grinning, showing broken and missing teeth. "Never in the ring any more, but I've had a few knock-down drag-out affairs with some pretty tough guys over at the Labor Hall."

"I have seen you in many fights," George said. "I can't remember you ever losing one."

"I'd have gone far if they hadn't found my weakness," he said. "I got too much pounding in the middle. I finally lost out, and—look where I am—not very high in the game, either," he said, grinning again, "but I've got ambition of climbing higher. It's rougher than the ring, George."

"Enic, did you go to Kensington High School?"

"Naw, I never went to high school a day in my life. That's the reason I'm so interested in my son. How's he getting along?"

"We'll discuss that in a few minutes."

"You see, I'm about your age, George," Enic said. "We didn't have a high school in this end of the county when I grew up. Only two high schools in this county, one up at Greenwood and one in the east end of the county at Roston. Too far away for a country boy on a farm with only dirt roads leading out, and they got impassable in winter. Now, look . . . this fine school where they are hauled in by bus over the hard roads. Things have changed, which is what I tell Don every day."

"Enic, let's go somewhere and talk," George said. "I want you to look around just a minute. Come with me."

The two walked out in the corridor. Enic was a square, stumpy, muscular man with a scarred face, a flat nose, and enormous hands. He had beady shoebutton-black eyes.

Enic followed George to the west corridor door, where they turned and walked back. At each classroom door, closed now while classes were in session, George asked Enic to take a quick peep and look at the crowded classrooms. They walked up toward the west corridor door, past a scrubbing crew cleaning lockers. "Enic, these are honor pupils," George said. "That's why they are allowed to work. No pay, no time-and-a-half for overtime and no double time on Sunday." George slapped Enic on the shoulder and laughed. Enic looked up at George and grinned faintly.

"Look in here," George said, opening the cafeteria door. "Class going on on one side, while they cook on the other. We have to double up here, Enic."

"Packed in here like sardines," Enic mumbled gruffly.

"I'm not through with you Enic, George said. "Come on down to the gym."

They went down the steps. "See, there's a class going on up there on the stage. There is one down on the gym floor. There's a class up in each bleacher," George continued, pointing toward a door in the rear of the gym. "There's a class up in that small projection room. Five classes down here. Spaced as far apart as we can get them!"

"Don't you use the gym for other things?"

"We sure do," George said. "We use it for assembly, games, classes, a place to eat. It's our all-purpose room. There was never a gym used for more things than this one or used as much. Our schedule has to go like clockwork. We move classes out while others come in carrying their trays. It's this way all day long. But I'm not through showing you. Let's go outside."

They walked out to the Ag building where Gus Riddle was teaching, then hurried on.

When Enic looked in at the first pre-fab, he shook his head. At the second pre-fab, he looked in and turned and sighed. Then at the third, where two teachers had two classes, he walked away.

"This is something," he mumbled hoarsely. "How can you do it?"

"We don't do it very well," George told him.

When the bell rang, they watched the line of pupils running to their next class at the main building, crossing the lines of pupils from the main building out to the Ag shop, band room, and pre-fabs.

"This school is getting too big for the space you have," he mumbled. "How many do you have?"

"Six hundred and twenty-five," George told him.

George and Enic walked on.

"Something else I want to show you," George said. A young boy came from the west corridor with a key in one hand and an envelope in the other. This youth came running toward the cars of all makes, descriptions, and kinds that were parked in the schoolyard.

"Where's he going?" Enic asked.

"To deliver a message," George said. "Pupils move out on the hour, sometimes as many as six in an hour, to deliver messages. They stand by to take those who are sick or get hurt to the doctor. They stand by at football practice. The students furnish their cars, buy the gas to help us. All drivers have their driver's licenses. We have forty-one hot-rod messengers."

"I'll be damned," he said laconically. "Put the hot-rodders to work! Making good use of the hoods, huh?"

"They're not hoods to us, Enic," George spoke quickly.

"They are lifesavers. They are helping the school. Not one week has gone yet and you'd be surprised how this is working out! But, Enic," George said, "how long will they be willing to help us? It's a new thing now to them. They'll soon grow tired of doing all of this for nothing. And this is where you come in."

"How do I come in?" Enic Zimmerman asked innocently. "How can I be of any help?"

"Look, Enic," he said, bringing Don Zimmerman's permanent record from his pocket. "We're busy up here on the Hill. You see what we have. But if you can help us we'll have more time to give your Don some special attention. He needs some, Enic! Look at this."

George gave Enic Don's card.

"We need a telephone line in here, Enic," George said. "We're not strikebreakers, but we need a telephone."

Enic didn't answer; he was too busy looking at his son's card.

"He's only got ten and a half credits," Enic said. "He needs sixteen to finish, don't he?"

"Right," George said.

"He can't make five and half credits in a year, can he?"

"I'm afraid he can't."

"Damn that boy to hell nohow," he said. "I didn't know that."

"Don't damn that boy for what he's done," George said. "Now is the time to give him a boost."

"But how can you do it?"

"Special work in the evenings, to get him over two English classes he has failed. He needs to pass English, Enic. Who knows but what Don might not be a fullback at Ohio State in the future? He can lug that ball, Enic!"

"Wouldn't it be great to have a son who would be fullback at Ohio State?" Enic said, beaming.

"It sure would. That would be as great for you as it would be great for us to have a telephone in here. But we'd be as proud of Don up here on the Hill as you'd be proud of him. A boy from this school!" He slapped Enic on the shoulder. "Yes, we'd be proud! *If* we had the telephone which would give students more time to stay here and study. This would give teachers more time, for they wouldn't have to write messages. We could give more individual attention to Don and some others who need it. Can you help us?"

Enic stood there looking thoughtfully at the parking area reserved for the hot-rodders.

"You're the only one who can help us, Enic," George flattered him. "Why do they want to cut the telephone cables, destroy telephone booths, cut lines, and saw poles off even with the ground, breaking wires and playing havoc in the night? You know Enic, that's not right!"

"Sometimes you have to get rough to get a fair shake," he mumbled, not looking up at George.

"But if one of our hot-rodder messengers wrecks while on duty for this school, kills himself or somebody, whose fault is it?" George asked. "People in Dartmouth have died because they couldn't call an ambulance in time. Couldn't get a doctor. They don't have a fleet of hot-rodders standing by like we have."

"You've got a good point," Enic admitted. "I've had the same thoughts about this you have. But I can't speak them out openly." He looked up at George quickly and then back at the hot-rods. "I certainly see your point. I see what you're up against here. You're on the spot and I'm on the spot. And Don is on the spot!"

He handed Don's permanent record back to George.

"But we can help each other," George said. "We can work together and work out these problems."

"You know schoolwork and I know labor. I've never heard of a schoolteacher getting his throat cut for doing his duty. Do you read the papers?"

"Sure do," George said.

"You remember reading about a guy that got his throat cut at the atomic plant?"

"Yes, I read that."

"The fellow lived but he ain't no good no more. Well, he was a little guy like me. He tried to be fair. It's gone too far to be fair. This telephone strike will last a long time, and the workers and company both will lose. Wait and see!"

"But can't you get phone lines restored to the schools, hospitals, and doctors' offices?"

"George, I'd like to work with you. You've got my son in this school. But I can't risk it."

"Enic, all I've asked is reasonable. This strike will finish this whole area."

"You can talk to me, George, but don't say it on the streets in Kensington and Dartmouth."

"Enic, I have to say it."

"I'd advise you not to do it. I know what I'm talking about."

"Well, Enic, I've got to get back to another problem," George said. "It's been fine to have you up here to talk to you."

"Sorry I can't help you, George."

"We'll still do as much for your son as we can."

"Yes . . . my son," he said. Tears welled up in his dark eyes. "I'd help if I could. But I'm afraid. You don't understand, George, but I'd be ruined. I don't want my car blown up or my throat cut."

"I don't either, Enic," George said. "Use your influence all you can to get us a line, to stop destruction of property and speak up unafraid against what you believe is wrong. We have to do it here or we wouldn't have a school. They were afraid to speak of it last year. And look what happened! The school went to pot. We're fighting back this year. Telephone line or no telephone line, we're going on. Surely we can't be held accountable for the youths who might die this year!"

"I can't do it, George." George held out his hand. Enic took it, then hurried out, and George watched him as he stood at the car door, wiping his face with a handkerchief.

George stripped to the waist and sat down. The leather chair felt cool to his naked back. Dr. Vinn pumped the bulb to inflate the cuff to cut off the pressure in his arm. Then, the white hand began jumping from number 300 back toward 20, on the face of the sphygmomanometer.

"How are you feeling, George?" Dr. Vinn asked him.

"Very fit, Doc," he replied quickly.

"Is that work pretty simple in Kensington High School?"

"Yes, sir, very simple. Lot of routine, like this checkup. Very similar."

"Not doing a lot of exertion, are you?" he said. "I mean physical exertion."

"Not an extraordinary amount," he replied. "Say, would it hurt me to give a spanking?"

"What, in high school?" Dr. Vinn said and laughed.

"I've got several who need the board of education, Doc!"

"Your systolic is 158," he said. "This is very good. Your diastolic is 88, and this is very good, too. Schoolteaching must agree with you."

"It does," George answered, pleased.

Dr. Vinn went over to his filing cabinet, where he turned to the record he kept on George.

"Six weeks ago it was perfectly normal," he said, "124 over 74. It's up a little."

George looked over at Grace, whose solemn face said to him, I told you.

"Maybe the excitement of the first few days," George said.

"Now if that's too much for you, my advice will be to resign," he told George. "I suggest you come back in five weeks for another checkup.

"Watch about climbing stairs, physical exertion of any kind," he warned George. "I had you in perfect shape. After you have a heart attack like that you're never the same. Take care of yourself and you can live a long, useful, and normal life."

George had heard this many times before. *Normal life for what?* went through his mind.

"That's what I've told him, Dr. Vinn," Grace interrupted. "You know George doesn't have to do this."

"Yes, I know, but he's been a busy man all his life," Dr. Vinn explained. "It's better for him if he can do something so he won't be thinking about his health."

"That's a sensible statement, Dr. Vinn," George said. "You're right about that. I've thought about my health so long I'd like to forget about it. I tell Grace that all the time."

Dr. Vinn looked serious. "But you want to live, too. Grace is right. You've got to the place where you can live comfortably and well. You have a wife and daughter, remember!"

Yes, and six hundred twenty-five others flashed through his mind as the nurse drew blood from his arm. I stand between them and disaster. The nurse pumped the bulb and inflated the cuff around George's arm again.

"See, I told you, Grace, work wouldn't hurt me," he said as he got into the car.

"Yes, but you mustn't undo what has been done," she said. "Dr. Vinn was right when he said you had reached the place where you could live comfortably. He was right, too, when he said you had a wife and daughter. Your first obligation is to us."

At five o'clock George got the final report that his cholesterol and blood clotting time were within normal limits.

Chapter Four

Third Defense and Lower Frame

Monday morning of the third week, when George and Grace left the Valley, Taddie Sue Gallion was riding beside her cousin Janet in the rear seat. She was twenty-three, a clever and pretty young woman of strong contradictory moods. Five feet eight inches tall, with large blue eyes, brown hair, and a tight little mouth, she didn't look as old as many of the students at Kensington High School. When Taddie Sue was six, her parents had separated, divorced, and both had re-married. Though she was constantly being moved about when she was a child, she had rated second in intelligence and achievement tests in her senior year in high school. When the Greenwood County library board sought a woman Bookmobile driver, who knew something about books and one who could drive the Bookmobile over rough terrain to one-room schools, Taddie Sue's qualifications were better than all others'. She could carry books, and she could change a wheel or fix a tire herself. Even if the engine went wrong, as it often did, she kept her tools handy and could repair it. Once when her brother, who drove a trailer truck, couldn't take his cargo from Columbus, Ohio, to Boston, Taddie Sue dressed in slacks, a leather cap which she wore at a rakish angle, took his place and drove the big trailer truck through the cities to its destiny.

On Saturday afternoon when George returned from his medical checkup, he went to see Taddie Sue. "I want you and I need you," he told her. "They are burning the library books in Kensington High School. Can you organize the library and stop the book-burning?"

"Uncle George, I'd be delighted."

"Taddie Sue, I can tell you you'll never teach in a more interesting school than Kensington High School. There are so many problems there."

"Must be," she said. "How many books have they burned?"

"I don't know," George told her. "One boy got by with destroying eight."

"What did you do with him? Expel him?"

"No, we didn't expel him. If I'd expel all the teachers want to expel, or those who want to be expelled, we'd cut our enrollment down to half."

In Kensington High School George had often heard the sympathetic remarks of teachers and pupils who made excuses for the bad behavior of many students from broken homes. The students themselves often used this as an excuse for their misconduct, and George felt he could use Taddie Sue to talk to them. Certainly she would be popular with these young people, since she was so near their age, and she would also be a most effective weapon against the assumption that pupils from broken homes were somehow not responsible for their behavior.

George knew, too, that if and when some one behaved badly to her, Taddie Sue would strike back faster than a copperhead. She could fold her little fists and use them like a man. She wasn't a hair-pulling woman but a fist-punching one. Yet she was the most feminine of women, despite her truck-driving talents.

"Uncle George, one thing bothers me," Taddie Sue said. "I don't know what to call you at school," Taddie Sue said.

"Call me Mr. Gallion," George told her. "Something I forgot to ask you," he added thoughtfully. "Do you smoke?"

"Not regularly," she told him. "I've smoked when I've driven a truck all night. Why do you ask?"

"I want you to be a model in front of our pupils," George told her. "You're young and you're my niece and you'll be watched carefully. Maybe you'll be imitated. So be against chewing gum and be against smoking. Our school, as you'll soon learn, is an emergency situation. I forbade teachers to smoke. No smoking in the ladies' lounge. Oh, I forgot, we're using that for a classroom. Teachers have to use the girls' rest room."

"I think I'm going to like this school," Taddie Sue said.

George and Taddie Sue turned from the main corridor toward his office. The glass in the front door was broken out. "That's funny," George said, pulling the key from his pocket to open his office door.

"You'd as well put the key back in your pocket," Taddie Sue said sharply. "Your door is unlocked. Looks like there's been a break-in."

"Don't touch anything," George said.

He took an envelope from his basket and scribbled a note.

"What are you doing?" Taddie Sue asked.

"Writing a message to send to Dartmouth to the police," he told her. "Just as soon as the first messenger arrives the message will be off in a hurry."

"Why not phone?"

"You don't read the papers?" he said. "We've had a strike here since early August. We don't have a phone."

"What?"

"That's right," he said. "Phone cables have been cut, telephone poles sawed off level with the ground, wires mangled and broken. This place is in a hell of a shape."

"Isn't it too much for you, Uncle George?—Mr. Gallion, I mean," she said.

"No, Taddie Sue, this is what I like. I like to see schools go forward, and that's the only way this one can go. This break-in is a matter of routine for us. We'll eventually get the offenders. But we'll need another lock on that door. If we can get the fingerprint men here first period we'll have a lock on this door and be back in business second period." Taddie Sue looked at her Uncle George, blinking her eyes and smiling.

"But why a lock on the door this morning?"

"We need that lock," he told her. "That's important. You'll learn later that we hold closed sessions behind a locked door. We don't want any intrusions when we have certain serious problems to settle."

They stood looking at the slivers of broken glass in the corridor.

In the office George found a crowbar lying on the floor, which had been used to pry open the filing cabinets. Records had been thrown in a heap on the floor. The door to the small press inside the office had also been pried open. Books that had just arrived late Friday had been tossed in a mixed heap on the floor.

Hunting for money, he thought. A school official is a fool ever to leave money in a schoolhouse. It happened here once when I was principal years ago, but it will never happen again while I am here.

When he walked out of the office he had to step around the fence Taddie Sue had erected with chairs.

"Much damage?" she asked.

"Very little," he replied. "I don't believe a thing was stolen. Certainly not a book. The thieves were hunting money. Our records are messed up, but they're intact."

George looked down the corridor, and to his delight he saw Alice Nottingham walking up the corridor. She was smiling as if she had had a very amusing trick played on her, one in which she had been quite pleasantly trapped.

George's stride lengthened as he approached her.

"Welcome home," he said. "I am happy to see you! You have never been as welcome any place in your life as you are now."

"I'd thought I'd better get here early," she said. "I wanted to go over my schedule with you."

"This is my niece, Miss Gallion, Mrs. Nottingham," George introduced them. "She's the new librarian. She begins work this morning, too. Our faculty is growing."

"You're getting things worked out around here, aren't you?"

"After a few weeks, I figure discipline will let up a bit."

"Say, what are the chairs doing up there?" she asked.

"Just a little break-in over the weekend," George replied casually. "You know these things happen in any school."

"Same old problems," she sighed. "Don't soft-pedal, George! I knew what I was returning to when I decided to come back."

"Well, we haven't any serious damage. Taddie Sue, you keep an eye on anyone crossing those chairs. I want to step outside and watch for messengers."

"Messengers? What messengers?"

"Hot-rodders," he replied. "They carry telephone messages. I've got two to send in a hurry. Come along with me, Mrs. Nottingham."

"George." She looked up into his face. "You haven't changed. But I have. I'm fifty, George. One of these days I'll be ready to retire. I'm not the teacher you've always thought I was. I am not a young pretty teacher . . . the popular kind. I'm the one they dread. I have standards, and they go with me. If they can they'll dodge my classes!"

"You've got them this time," George said. "They can't dodge you. You're to take all three classes of senior English and two in junior English." He talked fast.

There were a few seconds of silence. George went on. "I've got more work for you. Somebody has to coach a couple of plays. And I want you to be dean of girls."

"So you're organizing here, aren't you?" She spoke softly.

"We trapped the son and thereby got his mother," George said, his face beaming. "Gee, I'm happy you're here today. I'll begin this week with new courage. Girls' problems are tough ones for me. I'll want you to work that angle. You know the students and you know their parents. I have Gus Riddle for dean of boys, you know."

"Oh, good old Gus," she said, chuckling. "Good Old Poppie Gus!"

"Alice, I can speak confidentially with you," George said. "Tell me something. Gus Riddle is a man I can't figure out to save my life! I have never known a man whose dislikes and likes are so strong. I have never known a man of so many different moods! I can't figure him out. He got peeved at me from the very beginning over my giving the block building to Shan Hannigan, our new bandmaster here."

"So typical of good old Poppie Gus," she sighed. "I'm amazed you don't understand him."

"To tell you frankly, I thought he might have wanted the principalship of this school. He couldn't have handled it if he had been chosen. Not with his ideas of discipline. He would have had to change. Expulsion of pupils I have learned is not the answer! And my methods are insufferable to him."

"I know how he is," she said. "But I am sure he doesn't want to be principal here. He's a natural-born teacher and an adopted father to many of his boys."

"He's so quarrelsome at the teachers' meetings," George sighed. "Riddle is the right name for him."

"Don't be afraid of Poppie Gus," she said. "He expresses himself more here than he does down in Kensington. He's a very diplomatic person there. I heard someone say the other day Gus could carry a bucket of water on each shoulder and never spill a drop."

A car was turning off the highway into the lane.

"Here comes a messenger. Say, others will be coming, and I've left Taddie Sue in there and she won't know what to do. Will you go back and warn whoever's coming in to be careful what they touch. Set up a desk out in the hall where we can check excuses for pupils who have been absent. You handle this until I come. You know the way we used to do it."

She turned to go while the messenger skidded to a stop.

"You got a message, Mr. Gallion?"

"Yes, a very important one," he said. "One for Dartmouth. You know where the police department is?"

"No, sir, but I can find it," he said. "I don't have money for toll."

George fished into his pocket, pulled out his billfold, and gave the boy a dollar. "Turn left at the end of the bridge and go two blocks, then go one to your left. Tell them we have had a break-in and we want fingerprint men."

"All right, sir," he said, and was gone.

A teacher's desk had been borrowed for temporary duty and placed in the corridor under a clock. The clock was also a casualty of last year. The glass face had been broken and its two hands bent like fishhooks. It had never been repaired.

When George got up to the desk, Taddie Sue, Alice Nottingham, and Sadie Markham were in the corridor.

Gus Riddle came up the corridor, grinning pleasantly. "Ah, look who's back," he said. "Welcome home!"

"Yes, back again," Alice Nottingham said cheerfully.

"They've started on us," Gus said. He blinked as he looked at the chair-fence. "When I read in the paper last week about the robbery at South Dartmouth High School, I thought it would be our time next. Say, have you ever read of so many break-ins over in Dartmouth? They're not escaping either."

"Any ideas, Mr. Riddle?" George asked him.

"Oh, it's a gang," he replied. "Crowds that gather and stay up all Saturday and Sunday nights like they have down here in Kensington will do anything! No law! So why wouldn't they get into something? What are you going to do about this?"

"Fingerprint men will be here any time," George told him. "Do you think any of the students had anything to do with this?"

"Sure," he replied.

The police department of Dartmouth sent two men, who arrived just as the last bell rang.

"Anybody been in this office this morning?" one asked.

"Yes, I was in there," George said. "But I didn't touch a thing. My secretary went in to ring the bell."

"That's okay," said one, surveying the situation. "It's the same pattern as a lot of other break-ins we've had."

Both men were in uniform and carried kits of tools.

"I want to thank your chief for sending you over here," George said. "We don't have any fingerprint men very close on this side of the river."

"We're very close and your troubles are our troubles," one of the men said. "Maybe the same gang works both sides of the river."

"We've got more than one gang," said the other. "No one gang could do all this."

"What do you think accounts for this wave of break-ins?" George asked.

"This telephone strike is partly responsible," replied the first policeman. "Our police department can't even get word in time. We've had to add men to our force and add extra cruisers which we keep moving all night long. If we didn't we'd have to declare martial law in Dartmouth. We've even sent a business delegation to the governor, urging him to intervene and settle this phone strike. If you've read the paper, you know the result. He won't do anything but dodge issues because he's afraid of antagonizing labor. So we live in a state of perpetual fear. People are afraid to walk on the streets in Dartmouth at night. Have you read about all the purse-snatching?"

"Yes, when I have time to read the paper," George said.

"I was born in Dartmouth; I've lived there all my life. I've never seen a situation like we have now. Who would have thought telephone service could mean so much?"

"We have a plate-glass front in one of the stores smashed about every night," said the other. "We have a purse snatched or a man beaten and robbed. Everybody seems to be afraid. Every citizen ought to try being a policeman for about three days!"

"Or a schoolteacher," George interrupted. "Unfortunately,

we also have the telephone strike and no police force . . . not even a night watchman for the five thousand people in the Kensington area!"

"I don't see how you do it," said the first policeman, shaking his head.

"Do you suppose young high school boys have done this?" George asked.

"I don't know," said the short man. "But I doubt it. It looks to me like a professional job."

"We'll get a couple of fingerprints and see. I'll let you know when we're through so you can come back to your office."

"Sadie, round up these three boys," George said. "Send them to my office."

Toy Glover, Bertice Oliver, and Coy Hardin, all three honor pupils, were on the work details. Coy was on the chewing-gum-removal detail and was working in the gym. Toy Glover and Bertice Oliver were in the corridor scrubbing and polishing lockers. They had been caught stealing milk from the cafeteria while the cooks were busy preparing lunch. George shook his head sadly. Hard to believe, he thought.

When the boys came in, George asked Mrs. Markham to leave the office. Then he went over and snapped the new lock on his door.

"Fellows, I'm surprised," George said. "I never thought you would get into the milk in the cafeteria."

The color rose in Toy Glover's face. Tears welled up in Bertice Oliver's eyes. Coy Hardin's lips trembled. They were not well-dressed boys, but their clothes were neat and their hair was simply cut.

"Why would you do this?" George asked.

"I was hungry," Coy said, looking at the floor.

"Don't you eat any breakfast?"

"Yes, when we got something to eat," he said. "The three days I got milk, I hadn't had any breakfast."

"Coy, does your father work?"

"I don't have a father."

"Dead?"

"I don't know; I never knew him."

"Any brothers or sisters?"

"Yes sir, two sisters and a brother."

"Where are they?"

"Two sisters in this school."

"What are their names?"

"Clara Martin and Edith Tomlinson. I got a small brother, too young to go to school."

"What's his name?"

"Fred Reffitt."

"Are you giving me double names?"

"No, sir, real names," he replied.

"Your mother been married four times?"

"No, sir, never married," he said, scuffing the floor with his tattered shoes.

"I'm sorry I asked you those questions," George said. "Are you hungry now?"

"Yes, sir," he replied.

"You've been working and not had any breakfast?"

"Yes sir, not any breakfast or any lunch."

"Well, I'm glad to know your story. From now on you will have lunch."

"But I don't have the quarter to pay for it."

"Your work in this school will pay for it. You'll have milk, too."

He looked up at George.

"You'll have it if I have to pay for it," George smiled.

"Mr. Gallion, I didn't have any breakfast either," Toy Glover told him. "I've been reading where the Spartans were trained to steal when they were hungry. I've got so hungry I didn't think I could make it."

"Is your father living?"

"Yes, sir, but when the Sinton Shoe Factory closed in Dartmouth he lost his job," Toy said. "He's not been able to get work. Everywhere he goes they tell him he's too old."

"How old is your father?"

"He's forty-five."

"How many in your family?"

"Seven. I'm the oldest."

"Are you the only one in Kensington High School?"

"Yes, sir; Dad wanted me to quit school."

"What for?"

"Because he can't let me have a quarter to buy my lunch. Besides I have to borrow books."

"And you're an A pupil; you won't have to quit school. What about you, Bertice? Why did you slip into the cafeteria and get milk?"

"For the same reason," he said. "I was hungry. Sometimes I don't have breakfast, and I never have lunch. I don't have the quarter either."

"What does your dad do?"

"Works when he can find work," he replied. "He's forty-eight years old and there are eight of us. Six of us are in school."

"Are you hungry now?"

"Yes sir, but the carton of milk stopped the gnawing in my stomach some."

"Now, fellows, you'll never have to take any more milk," George told them.

"What are you going to do with us?" Bertice asked.

"Come with me," George said. "I'll show you."

He unlocked the door and the three boys followed him to the cafeteria.

"If you have the food ready, serve these boys right now," George told Edna Sexton. "From now on they will be put on the free lunch program. Not free to them—they work for their lunches. See they get plenty of milk."

"Why don't you come and eat with us, too?" Edna asked him.

"I'm too busy to eat," he said. "I'll be in later."

George looked at his watch. He crossed the corridor to the library study hall to see if Taddie Sue had the pupils under control. There wasn't a sound. This is becoming more like a school should be, he thought.

At the foot of the stairs he stopped at Mrs. Nottingham's English room. He eased the door open and motioned her out. She was teaching and he didn't like to disturb her. She came out, looking back at her pupils.

"They need something, Mr. Gallion," she whispered. "They need to snap out of a rut. They need a hard-rock foundation. They haven't had it."

"In other words, they need teaching."

"They certainly do," she said. "English, discipline, education, manners. They need ambition. They need inspirational teaching."

"Now you're talking," George said in a low tone. "You said what I knew you'd say. But I want to ask you a question. This is confidential. Do you know Coy Hardin?"

"Sure, I know him. Why?"

"Is it true that his mother has four children and has never been married?"

"That's right," she said. "How did you find that out?"

"We have to know about a pupil before we can work properly with him," George said. "Did you know Coy is an honor student?"

"No; you see, he's a sophomore and I left shortly after he entered as a freshman last year."

"Did you know he has two half-sisters here this year? Here are their names," he whispered, giving her a piece of paper. "I want you to check on these girls to see if they're eating properly."

"You know, Mr. Gallion, if Coy's mother handled her pension right, she could probably get along. I feel sorry for the children."

"Coy might make something of himself," he said softly. "The mother is compelled to keep her children in school and get aid, which also creates a school problem. Yet good pupils can come from the strangest places. Our Saviour was born in a manger. Abraham Lincoln was born in a one-room log cabin. I just wanted to ask you to look out for Coy's half-sisters."

"I'll do it," she said, returning to her room.

As George walked down the corridor he met Les Bowdin, who had proven himself to be an excellent student teacher.

"I've been trying to see you," he said. "It's about that break-in in your office. I can't prove it, but I think I know the man who did it."

"A student?" George asked him.

"No, sir, not a student," he said, giving George a piece of paper. The name Wes Herring was written on it. "He had help, but I don't know who they were. Two helpers."

"How did you find this out so soon?" George asked.

"I heard whispering at the locker, sir," he said. "They didn't know I was listening. They broke in early Sunday morning. This man was seen with two others."

"Thank you for this name," George said. "Are you guessing about this fellow?"

"No, sir," he said. "I'm not guessing, but I'm not exactly sure he's the right man."

"Where does he live?"

"Just up the road a piece from this school. You pass his house morning and afternoon on your way to and from school. He's been in the pen before, sir. He's already served a sentence for breaking and entering."

"Well, thank you for giving me the tip, anyway," George said.

In the office, George wrote a letter to the police department in Dartmouth, and sent it by a hot-rod messenger to the county sheriff.

The lunch period had come. Pupils had eaten hurriedly, though a few of them lingered on in the gym. Almost five hundred pupils and teachers gathered on the west schoolyard where they could look down on the practice field. Between the schoolyard and the field was a steep bank that slanted down to a road which wound around and up to the higher level, past the corridor door, then down the steep bank again. This loop was a perfect letter O, dry-earth-colored brown on this September day. Beyond the athletic field was the vast field of ripening buff-colored corn, which had been planted and cultivated by Gus Riddle and his ag students. Beyond the cornfield flowed the Tiber River in a graceful blue and silver hook, around the upland where the schoolhouse stood like an ancient castle. Beyond the Tiber River were the palisades where dwarfed trees clung tenaciously to rock crevices.

Behind the schoolhouse, where the formation was taking place, everyone could hear the occasional sound of an instrument. In a few minutes the school band began to play the *Washington Post March.* Dressed in her handsome regalia, a baton-twirling senior girl led the band. The baton went upward, twirling and spinning, pulling the bright sunlight from the air.

Behind her were a dozen majorettes, twirling smaller batons in unison, keeping time as they marched down the loop road toward the athletic field. And behind these came the band. Running alongside it, cupping his hand over his ear to catch some minor off-key instrument, was a shabby little man, his loose hair flying as if it were trying to leave his head. His blue coattail was riding behind him on the wind while he danced, jumped, leaped like a frog running from a snake. They marched down to the football field and followed the dim outline of the oval-shaped quarter-mile track around the field.

"Well, if we had that out here every day at noon we wouldn't have to police the yard, would we?" Fred Laurie said to George.

"Shan's worked day and night since he took over in August to do this," George said. "I say he'll have a winning band this year if he keeps that up!"

George looked to see where Gus Riddle was, then saw him walking slowly away from the crowd, toward his ag room. He unlocked the door and went in, shutting it behind him.

"We'll be proud of our school band Friday night," Don Webber said.

At the end of the number the band received great applause. Even those pupils who had taken off to the Tiber River bank jungle, perhaps to smoke, hurried back to join the crowd gathered in the schoolyard. A few cars pulled up from the highway onto the lane road to park and listen.

"Did you know the noon hour was over?" Gus asked George some minutes later.

"Yes, but the band concert isn't," George said. "You've missed something by not listening to what we have here. If we don't have much of a school we certainly have the beginnings of a great band."

The pupils fell in behind the band and followed them to the rear door of the gym. There were shouts and laughter as they followed Shan Hannigan like children following the Pied Piper.

"I'm certainly ready to get rid of the noon hour now," Gus Riddle told George later.

"If we don't get rid of it," George told him, "I'm going to suggest we have a band concert every noon hour."

George had watched the rise of Kensington High School through the years, from its inception on paper to its present state. Mrs. Nottingham's return and getting a librarian had helped put new spirit into his teachers. As they came in the office to sign for the day, each had a kind word and a smile. School had been open almost a month now. This was the day when the noon police force would be, they hoped, eliminated. The teachers had voted unanimously to abolish the noon hour.

Mrs. Nottingham had staggered time departures from the classroom to the cafeteria. Her English class was the first called. Immediately they were up and out of the classroom on their way to the cafeteria. The cafeteria personnel brought the food from the kitchen over to the tables. Everything else was done by the students themselves or by student help who were served free lunches for their labor.

With relief George watched the new program function. He knew they had the noon-hour problem solved. He had listened to pupils' whispers and murmurings when they passed him in the corridor, and had heard little dissension. In a matter of minutes, the students had been served and had returned to their rooms with loaded trays. The yard, the cornfields, the jungle were silent now.

Grace had just let Taddie Sue and George out of the car, when Gus Riddle, who had arrived earlier than usual, met them at the top of the steps.

"Did you see yesterday's *Dartmouth Times?*" he asked George.

"No, I haven't," George said. "Sometimes I get a paper and sometimes I don't."

He gave George the folded paper he was carrying. George unrolled it to look at the front page. "WES HERRING, EX-CONVICT, CONFESSES TO BREAKING AND ENTERING KENSINGTON HIGH SCHOOL." And, in smaller letters, "Charged with 12 Other Robberies. County Sheriff Acts on Anonymous Tip."

"That's something, isn't it?" Gus said when George returned his paper.

"It really is."

"That anonymous tip," Gus said smiling, "turned the trick."

"Do you have any idea who gave it?" George asked Gus.

"Some hoodlum who spends the night at the Kensington Corner, would be my guess. He probably got a small reward for doing it. With those fellows it's dog eat dog, you know."

"Yes, that's right, I suppose," George agreed. "Any method used to trap them is fair enough."

George sat down on the corner of his desk in the crowded little office. Outside the window beyond a flying bird, a cocoon in the spirea bush, and a rabbit on the grass, he saw the trees responsive only to the wind. Grass beneath these trees and over surrounding fields rippled in the wind. Legions of grass, like people, ran with the wind and not against it. When the fickle wind changed its course so did the legions of grass. They followed the senseless wind.

People are like grass, he thought, made of the same substance. Whenever and wherever grass and trees are not controlled there are jungles. *Character* was a key word. Whatever it took to put character and its associates, honesty, decency, and integrity, back would unlock the door to his problem here.

Outside he watched the rabbit hop cautiously over the grass. This rabbit's flesh-and-blood mechanism was more involved than the jets that thundered overhead and left their vaporous scribblings on the skies. The rabbit had been here longer than the jet, too. There was the tough interwoven fabric of a cocoon hanging to the bush by his office window. This cocoon now held a worm that would be transformed, if left alone, to a beautiful butterfly in the spring. A bird that passed his window was a learned thing. It knew the seasons. It knew when and where and how to build a nest and how to rear its young. Didn't people, the most intelligent of all flesh-and-blood creatures, have this much intelligence? Why didn't parents push their children from home and make them walk as birds pushed their young from nests and make them fly? Why not teach children to work as the parent birds taught their young to work? Could he and his little crew of underpaid teachers weather the storm, he wondered. So far they were making good progress, surrounded for the most part by a hostile world.

"Well, well," he said, opening the door and walking in. "I've finally made it."

"Glad to see you, Mr. Caudill. Funny thing: We listened to the news this morning and the weather report said something about rain."

"I listened to a later newscast," Caudill said. "But I didn't hear anything about rain."

"An immediate rain will defeat you in this forthcoming election," George sighed. "You know teenagers have a tendency to exaggerate anything that happens at school when they report it to their parents. If one umbrella has to go up in a pre-fab, by the time the news gets down to Kensington it will be ten umbrellas, and by the time the buses unload them along Shannon Creek, it will be a hundred umbrellas. Shannon Creek votes in your district, I believe."

"Quite right," he replied. "There's a lot of hostility built up out there against me, anyway. And one of my opponents is from Shannon Creek. Say, I'm sorry I didn't get here sooner," he added in a louder, more serious voice, "but it was the old ticker, you know. Fluttered like a young bird getting ready to fly from the nest."

"If anything comes up here, where will I find you?" Sadie asked.

"Out at the pre-fabs," George replied.

"Hear you're getting this school under control," Orman told George as they walked down the corridor. "Last year they even stopped the commodes so they could go home."

"You know, Mr. Caudill, since you couldn't get up here I got a plumber to fix the commodes. We had two out on each side. Students might have been working fast, but I was working faster. The sinks wouldn't work in the cafeteria but I got a septic tank cleaner and we cleaned the big septic tank."

"He didn't clean it in the daytime, did he?"

"Yes, he couldn't have found it at night."

"But it's against the state law, isn't it?"

"I wouldn't know. All I know is the cafeteria would have had to be closed the next day, as water was backing up in the drains. I might have broken a state law but I didn't break a health law.

"I thought of the pupils and I thought of the election," George said as they walked across a clean yard toward the pre-fabs. The cleaning crew worked on, never looking up at George and Orman. One was mowing, two were searching for scattered debris, and a fourth was pruning a shrub. "I knew if we had to send the buses away from here early it would hurt your chances. It would hurt me, too. You know I want to make good as a principal. I don't want to lose that reputation I left here eighteen years ago."

"I'm proud you're working for my re-election too."

"Yes, in a powerful indirect way," George said. "See, your two opponents have children up here in school."

"I know it," he said, shaking his head. "And they've said so many nasty things to my daughter about me."

"Well, here we are," George said. "You go in and I'll wait outside, for the rooms will be too crowded for two big men."

George waited while Orman went in the first pre-fab. Each pre-fab had once been a hastily constructed dwelling for an average family of four. It had had four rooms and a bath. Now forty to sixty pupils, depending on the size of different classes, occupied the flimsy structures.

"You're right," Caudill said as he slowly emerged. "Worse than I thought. That roof must've been busted to pieces in moving it over here from the A-plant."

"And of course no water, toilet facilities, no heat, no roof, no underpinnings," George said. "But fix the roof first. Then get stoves. Voters must know we're making a valiant effort."

"Mr. Gallion, are the others like this one?"

"I hope your seeing that won't have any ill effect on your health," George said. "We need you, Mr. Caudill. You're the only man on the Greenwood County board of education who can turn a wheel."

"Thank you for that compliment." His high-pitched voice shivered like broken window panes. "I'm puzzled," he added, "as to what to do. You know we need another pre-fab building. Two teachers in there, and I didn't ask the number of pupils. But they were just about on each others' laps. One sitting down in a chair and others sitting on the chair arm! I wonder if they can get enough air?"

"See, all the windows are up," Geroge said. "They're getting air, all right. Too much fresh air. They have to wear their coats."

"But what about winter?"

"Your guess is as good as mine," George replied. "We'll have the autumn rains first and then winter will be right on us. It's cold up on this hill."

"Is there any room, any place to take half the pupils from that pre-fab?"

"Not unless we put them on the roof," George replied. "We're using the women teachers' rest room for a classroom. We're using the gym, both bleachers—and the center floor for physical education. I'm willing to cooperate with you in any way I can before this election," George continued. "Maybe if you can get the roofs fixed, stoves in, and water and gas lines out there . . ."

"Tomorrow morning the roofers will be here," Caudill said.

On Friday Grace and George arrived early for the game between Rutland and Kensington. They took their places in the already crowded bleachers. On the opposite side of the field was an even larger crowd from Rutland. Rutland was an independent district, in one of the most industrialized areas of the state, and the fourth richest school district in the state. Rutland High was smaller than Kensington, with twice as much money to spend—for teachers, equipment, buildings.

The game was about to begin. The teams poured through the gates. Don Webber had put a team on the field as large as any small college team. George knew the players well—Ted Mannings, Les Bowdin, Don Weston—all of them. More than one of them had been disciplined in his office. One had stolen books.

In the backfield, George noticed Champ Burton and "Wild Bill" Nottingham. The fullback was Frank Fairman, his part-time student teacher. But while Kensington's starting lineup was big, Rutland's was bigger.

Shouts went up from each side of the field. The ball was teed up, the whistle sounded, the Kensington team moved forward, and the ball rose, end over end. A Rutland back pulled it from the air on his 7 and started upfield. The game was on.

Fourth down, with three to go, and a shout came through a megaphone from the Rutland side: "You play your teachers! Frank Fairman is ineligible!" The Kensington fans responded with shouts and boos.

This time Rutland started marching up the field on long sweeping end runs. They made one first down, a second, a third, a fourth, and a fifth, and the ball was resting on Kensington's 20-yard line. Coach Webber put in Don Zimmerman, a fullback. On the first play, he knifed through and threw Rutland's ball carrier for a five-yard loss.

"Watch a pass," someone shouted from the Kensington side. The Rutland quarterback dropped back and looked for his receiver. But Champ Burton leaped over men sprawled on the field. He was closing in on the quarterback, who couldn't get his pass away. He chased him back and nailed him back on the 35-yard line. The clock was running out; it was fourth down and twenty-five yards to go for a first down. Rutland was held on the 12-yard line, two yards short of a first down. The gun sounded ending the first quarter and Kensington took over on their own 12-yard line.

After the first play time was called for changes in the Kensington lineup. Champ Burton was pulled out of the game. George walked up behind the bench to hear what Coach Webber was saying.

"Coach, I've hit 'em hard," the Champ said.

Coach Webber said, "But you're not getting through there."

"Man, I'm hittin' 'em hard enough to knock 'em out. I'm softenin' 'em, Coach. Second half, they'll weaken."

"But now and not the second half is the time," Coach Webber shouted, biting his fingernails. His fingernails were blunt now, long since bitten into the quick. "When I put you back in there the second half, I'll see how soft you've got 'em!"

"You don't know what I'm doin', Coach," he said. "You don't know how hard I can hit a man. You might have to put me back before the second half."

Play was resumed.

"Let me back in, Coach," Burton begged. "If you don't, they'll score!"

"Shut up!" shouted Webber. "When I want you in, I'll put you there."

In the crowd George saw two state policemen and three of Greenwood County sheriff's deputies. He was glad they were here, because there could be trouble before this game ended. Four players had already been carried off the field on stretchers.

The first half ended, with neither team scoring.

The players limped from the field. The game had been vicious.

The fighting spirit surged high again in the third quarter. "Wild Bill" got the ball on the first bounce and started upfield. Champ Burton was on his feet running interference for Wild Bill. Two Rutland players were cutting across the field to meet them. Burton got the first one with a good block. The second man kept coming as Wild Bill reversed his field. While he swung around the Champ got to his feet and blocked the second. Wild Bill was over! The Kensington crowd went wild.

In this third quarter Kensington scored again. Burton crossed the 5, to the 15, 20, and up to the 25 before he went down. He got the ball again, went seventy-five yards, and scored.

In the fourth quarter fighting broke out between players all along the line. The referees ran in but couldn't stop it. People started to surge onto the field. The two state police and three sheriff's deputies rushed out and tried to wave the people back. The fighting stopped, and the game resumed. Rutland did not score. The day was Kensington's.

Monday morning opened a new era of good feeling in Kensington High School. There was a clipping from the *Dartmouth Times* sport page—KENSINGTON POWERHOUSE OVER- WHELMS STRONG RUTLAND—on every bulletin board.

Nothing could have lifted the spirit of Kensington High School students like winning their first football game with Rutland in twenty years. Defeat had hovered over Kensington High School for years. The Rutland game was a turning point.

George watched their faces and listened to their conver- sations. "Why haven't we beaten them before?" he heard one say. "We could have done it if we'd tried," another replied. They had won spirit, pride, and integrity enough to meet other challenges. They had sharpened the big ax to cut through harder wood.

"My students are watching a conservation film this period," Gus Riddle said. "Thought I'd come over and talk to you this morning about some things you ought to know."

"Have a seat, Mr. Riddle," George said. "Glad you've come over. Is this private?"

"Yes, I'd like it to be," he replied.

George asked Sadie to leave the office.

"I read Les Bowdin's article on the game in Saturday's *Times*," he began talking, "and you know, Mr. Gallion, that made me a little ashamed."

"Why?"

"Well, he's one of the players," Gus replied. "Then I came up here and there's a clipping on every bulletin board."

"Why shouldn't there be?"

"It looks bad for us," he said.

"It looks good to me," George interrupted. "How many foot- ball teams in this area will have two student teachers, probably a class valedictorian, and a school reporter on the first team! I just put my finger on the boy because we had no reporter and told him to write school news. Look at this! And he'll get paid for it. And what boy in this school needs the money more? I believe he's a lucky find," George added.

"Well, it just doesn't look right," he said. "It's like bragging."

"Did you see that game Friday night?"

"No, I didn't."

"Well, I was there," George said. "I watched every play. You'd know it's not half scandalous if you've seen Les Bowdin work at center. Yet he never mentioned what he did in the write-ups. Now our little achievements should be published. Believe me, when something goes wrong around here, if a pupil gets in jail or has a wreck or something, it will make the front pages. And, if you can find me a better reporter, one who can get material in four big papers, send that reporter to me. Les Bowdin is the best we have. And I'm holding on to him."

"All right, all right," he said. "Now, something else I want to mention here in private. I don't want you to tell I told you."

"Let's have it. I won't tell. I need to know what's going on."

"Well, I know you'll think I'm trying to take away Webber's glory but I'm not," he said. "And I feel that you think Webber is a wonderful coach and teacher. Well, there's a side to him you don't know."

"Spill it; I want to know his other side."

"He's the biggest spendthrift this school ever had," Gus said, his face getting red as a turkey's snout. "You think this school's indebtedness is approximately $5000. Wait until you know about the big athletic debt. Just add about $2000 more."

"What?" George asked. His face clouded with a frown. "Are you sure about this? Why haven't I heard about it?"

"Coach Webber won't let you get the bills," he replied. "I know this much; I get around. Now, if you think I'm wrong, wait until you're in Auckland and drop in at the Auckland Athletic Company and have our account checked with them. See for yourself. See if I've lied. You'll go up through the ceiling when you see that bill! You don't believe me, do you?"

"I've been round here a long time, you know," Gus continued. "Don't build your hopes up too high in your coach. There will come a day of reckoning. Mr. Gallion, there are a lot of rumors flying about Champ Burton and about school-teachers playing on the team. Something is bound to come of it."

In the afternoon, George visited Mrs. Nottingham's junior English class. Now that they were well into the academic year, he planned to talk to one of the classes each day.

"How many of you have time to study? How many of you have time to think? How many of you have a place to think? How many of you have time to be what you really are? Nettie Dillow, you held up your hand that you don't have time to study? Will you tell us why?"

"I live twenty miles from school," she replied. "I have to get up at four in the morning and help Mom get breakfast. Dad has to get off to work, because he drives to Dartmouth and works in the steel mills. Then, I have to help get five more up and get their breakfasts and see they get ready for their bus to Morningside Elementary. I leave at seven in the morning, and I don't get here until eight-thirty. You want me to continue, Mr. Gallion? I guess what I have to say will sound silly."

"Continue, Miss Dillow," he said. "We want your story. You have a problem that's similar to scores of others here."

"Well, after I get here I go to study hall, which has a student teacher in charge. Since we are his classmates we don't make it hard on him. But he can't help us with our lessons. So we have to figure things out for ourselves. When school's over, I go back in a crowded bus. When I get home at five, I'm worn out. I take my books with me and study all the time I can, but I get home in time to help Mom with supper, and there's not much time left."

"You should have some time to study after supper," said Claris Walker.

"How can I study then?" she asked, turning to Claris. "Dad

can't read. He turns the TV up so high we can hear the news in every room in the house. After the news he turns from one program to another until he goes to bed. None of us can study at home. Where can we go?"

"Learn from TV," Don Zimmerman snickered.

She shrugged her shoulders. "Learn what? Bang! Bang! Bang! I'm so tired of that stuff I want to run and scream every time it's turned on!"

"Well, I'm not a good student, Mr. Gallion," said Coy Hardin. "I try to be. I study all the time I can and I'm just average. I'm not an athlete either. So I can't be of much help in a new world!"

"You can do as much as the next one," George said. "You can put in more time with books. You can learn a trade. You can be a farmer. The country is filled with things to do. If one of your classmates invents a machine, somebody has to operate it. There's a place on the team for all of you."

"But, Mr. Gallion, about our having time to study," another student began, "do you have any ideas to help us? What Nettie Dillow told you is the same problem I have. Where can we find a quiet place?"

"Now, don't laugh when I tell you," Nora Wallings said timidly. "Our TV is blasting away and Dad and Mom watch programs until they fall asleep. Well, my brother John, who's a sophomore here, wired a henhouse we don't use any more. He learned how to wire a building over there in Mr. Ossington's shop class. He bought a little electric stove at a used shop in Dartmouth. So he and I study in the old henhouse. That's the only place we have."

"Nora, you and your brother John are going to amount to something," George said. "Two young people who find a way and who are that eager will do something. What do you say, Mrs. Nottingham?"

"I agree with you," she replied. "Nora is in the upper five percent of this class."

"What you've said brings up a point," George Gallion said

animatedly. "The eager pupil will find a way under adverse circumstances. If a pupil knows what he wants, has average ability, and is ambitious, he will reach his objective. You asked me how to help you find a place where you can study. If you have so many distractions that you can't study, look around your homes like John and Nora Wallings have and see if you can't find a cellar, a garage, an attic, smokehouse, a corncrib, or even build yourselves a little house outside. My brother and I built ourselves one in the backyard because our father compelled everyone to be in bed at a certain time. We wanted to study, read books, and be ourselves. Now some of you are fortunate enough, though, to have parents who furnish you nice quiet rooms so you can study. You are fortunate enough to have parents who request you to study. But look at the number of you who aren't that fortunate.

"But too many of you expect to be entertained all your lives," George continued. "You expect to be entertained by your teachers in the classroom. You are entertained by watching games, movies, TV, listening to the radio, reading papers, magazines, and books. When and how are you ever going to think for yourselves? You will *have* to think for yourselves someday. When you're alone with your own thoughts, you might even learn something new about yourselves!"

"But what can we do, Mr. Gallion?" Mary Rose asked.

"You have to be better prepared to meet this new world you are in than we had to be to meet the problems of the world we entered," George replied. "Your new world is so far advanced over our old one. You have more opportunities than we had. You will be going places and seeing things in your world we never dreamed about. This high school is only one step. You should learn to study and to think here. There is so much ahead for you. You will have to know how to think. I believe that being alone with your thoughts for one hour each day will help you toward your goals in your new world. Since we cannot afford these places at public expense when we need teachers, new buildings, library books, and other equipment so badly, I hope each of you can find your quiet place to be alone for an hour by yourself so you can think; I hope you get acquainted with yourselves. I hope you *know thyself, control thyself, improve thyself, be thyself, and amount to something.*"

"You're going to the game tonight, aren't you?" Coach Webber asked.

"Can't make it, Coach," George replied. "I'm sorry."

"Why can't you come?"

"Look here," George said, taking a letter from his pocket. "Read this."

"Congratulations," he said. "Say, this is something! You're getting the Golden Apple!"

The meeting of the East State Teachers' Association began this evening in Auckland, and George had been chosen to receive "the Apple," an annual award for the teacher who had performed service to education. The award was a block of lucite with a golden apple in its center with words engraved on the apple: TEACHER FOR LOYAL SERVICE TO EDUCATION.

"You know there's a lot of lawlessness over in South Dartmouth," Don Webber said. "This telephone strike, railroad strike, steel strike, and everybody just roaming the streets without anything to do! Have you been reading the *Dartmouth Times* about the fights and robberies over there? My problem is going into that area where there is such lawlessness," Coach Webber said. "I dread going. We've always had good relations in the past, but I'm afraid it will be different this year."

"Sorry I can't go with you," George said. "Don't start anything. Caution your players about rough stuff. Don't permit it."

"It won't be our team. I've cautioned them. We're going over there to play ball. And we're going to win that game! It's going to be tough and rough. You've seen the powerhouse we have. East Dartmouth has one, too, and when they meet head on, sparks will fly. Something tells me this game will be rough. Not even a phone to call the police if we should have a riot."

"But you're not expecting that."

"No, I'm not anticipating a riot, but anything can happen when two teams like we have clash. See, they hate to lose to a team from over here. And we hate to lose to a team over there. You know, Mr. Gallion, the Ohio River flows between two worlds."

"But it shouldn't separate a country into two worlds," George said. "They don't have telephone service and we don't have it. Their men are out of work because of strikes and our men are out of work because of strikes. Ever stop to think, state lines don't mean anything any more. They're just about all rubbed out!"

"Not in athletic competition when teams get fired up."

"Straight as the crow flies, their school is not over two miles away," George said. "If it weren't for a few houses we could see their school. They can see us perched up here on the Hill. They're our good neighbors. What's a river between us? Now don't back down, Coach! Go on and play that game and stop worrying."

"I can't help being superstitious," he said. "Somehow I feel things. I get a hunch when to throw a pass and we win. But all my signals point to disaster this evening."

Saturday morning, George and Grace were eating breakfast when they heard on the radio about a riot at the close of the hotly contested grid game between Kensington and East Dartmouth high schools. The game had apparently ended in a free-for-all between the teams and the fans. The fracas had gotten out of police control, and in the fierce fighting that had taken place many boys had been badly injured. The Kensington fans who had followed their team across the river had to be escorted across the bridge by the police to insure their safety.

George switched the radio off. "Don Webber had the right hunch about that game. I should have been there."

"What could you have done in the face of a riot?" Grace asked.

"I don't know," he said thoughtfully. "That's bad publicity. We try to build the school up and then what we build up is torn down again. This sort of thing will bring repercussions against both schools. Regardless of how the trouble started, we'll get the blame!"

"I wish you'd never taken that school," Grace said. "If you can't even take the time out to go receive an honor . . ."

"Oh, to hell with the honor."

"I'd be ashamed to talk like that."

"I should have been down there with the coach and the team," he said. "Coach Webber had a feeling he'd have trouble. I let him and the team down. I let the school down. A personal honor isn't worth it!"

George took the little block of lucite from the table and looked through its transparency at the golden apple. "What's a thing like this," he said, laying it on the table and looking across at Grace, "compared to broken bones and all the ill will that we'll have between our schools? Years ago we had wonderful relations with the school. What in the world has happened to people?"

"Don't let it worry you too much, George," she said.

"I've got to go down there right now. I have to get at the bottom of this trouble."

"You need to take Saturday off. You can't teach seven days a week."

"Running a school requires more than seven days a week," he said, getting up from the table. "I'm going to Kensington to see Coach Webber."

The Webbers' house was a modest neat white cottage in a run-down neighborhood near the railroad tracks.

When George knocked on the door, Webber's pretty, blonde, blue-eyed wife, Teenie, opened the door. "Oh, you've heard," she said. "Honest, it was awful the way we were treated!"

"Come in, Mr. Gallion, and have coffee with us." Coach Webber rose from the table where he was having breakfast. "I couldn't go to sleep until about three this morning," he said. "This coffee hasn't wakened me yet. Sit down and have breakfast with us."

"How did you hear so soon about this?"

"It was on the radio this morning."

"Doggone it, it'll be in all the papers and over all the radio and TV stations," Webber said. "I hated to have it happen. But we couldn't help it. You know I was uneasy yesterday when I talked to you."

"Yes, I know; I shouldn't have gone to Auckland last night."

"But I can't blame you for going," he said. "Honors don't come very often to teachers. But I had a feeling we needed you with us last night. Yet nobody could have stopped what happened. So please don't feel badly about it."

"Tell me what happened."

"The riot started toward the end of the game."

"Tell me what took place from the beginning to the end. How many people were there last night?"

"About two thousand."

"How many from this side of the river?"

"About seven hundred."

"How many in the free-for-all?"

"Everybody was in it, either fighting or trying to separate those who were were fighting. Yesterday we got permission from Orman Caudill to bring four school buses loaded with our Kensington students until there wasn't standing room. Then parents came bringing Kensington students. And every hot-rod car that comes to the Hill came loaded with students. If we hadn't had about seven hundred I don't know what might have happened to us.

"I'll tell you what happened and you be the judge," he continued. "In the first half of the game neither team scored. It was played on even terms by evenly matched teams. Neither side threatened the other. Actually, the first half was played within each other's thirty-yard line."

Teenie filled George's and Don's cups with coffee.

"Late in the third quarter East Dartmouth scored on a sustained drive. They passed for the extra point but the pass was incomplete. The score was 6 to o in favor of East Dartmouth. Then Ted Manning took the kick-off on our 10 and went to the 30. On the third down, with seventeen yards to go, the Champ got loose and went all the way. Then the Champ ran the extra point. The third quarter ended with the score 7–6, our favor.

"The fourth quarter was a seesaw affair until the last two minutes of the game. East Dartmouth had the ball at midfield. Here we held them to the third down and seven yards to go. They gambled with a pass on the fourth down and pass interference was called on us on our 25-yard line.

"When East Dartmouth came out of the huddle we shifted to pass defense. Their quarterback dropped back, threw a wobbly pass which was caught out of bounds. One of our men had hit the referee and knocked him down. A partisan fan of East Dartmouth ran in and threw up his hands signaling a touchdown. When the referee got to his feet and saw the civilian waving a touchdown he threw up his hands, too. Then all hell broke loose.

"Our fans booed and protested," he continued. "Fighting started first on the sidelines near where the fellow caught the out-of-bounds pass. Our players who had seen the ball caught out of bounds stood stunned. They couldn't believe a civilian could come onto the field and make a decision. I looked up and saw East Dartmouth fans storming down from the bleachers. Our side was silent for a few seconds and then they started leaving our bleachers and going to meet them. Laurie and I ran to the players, where both teams were now swinging with fists and headgear."

"Where were the police?"

"We had only two there, and one of these, I learned later, had gone for help. By the time we got on the field Don Weston and John Salyers were standing with their backs to each other and were using their fists. Players were piled up around them like they were trying to recover a fumble. Champ Burton was upending fans and players until somebody addled him with a helmet. Mothers of the football players were screaming and swinging with their pocketbooks and umbrellas. One policeman couldn't do anything with that howling, screaming, hair-pulling, fist-cuffing mob. He ordered the lights out to stop the fight. But in the darkness on that field they still fought. East Dartmouth and Kensington fans floored each other—they couldn't see whom they were fighting! I'll never forget that fight until the day I die.

"That isn't all," Webber went on. "We got our players to the dressing room and East Dartmouth got theirs to their dressing room. And our fans went through the darkness, screaming and hollering and fighting all the way to the buses and their cars. They got in them as fast as they could. The first ones to their cars switched on lights so others could see. Women from both sides of the river knocked each other down. When the fans got away, about three hundred rowdies gathered around our dressing room. We didn't have any police protection but that one policeman. He drove our school bus up to within about thirty feet of our locker room and opened the emergency door in the rear for us. He said we should wait until police reinforcements came, but we were too scared to wait. Then I said, 'We're going to try to make the bus. Everyone of you players hold on to the chin guard of your headgear and use it if attacked.' Then we walked out in front of our team and told them to back off. These hoods called us every kind of a sonofabitch. We made the bus, though, and what a battered and bloody lot we were. Rocks were thrown at the bus, and three windows were smashed. Before we got to Dartmouth four police cruisers met us and escorted us to the bridge. I didn't even know how the game came out until this morning. I heard over the radio that they gave them the disputed t.d. on the grounds that we removed our team from the field one minute and forty-five seconds before the game officially ended."

"What else could you do?" George asked.

"Some of them would've been killed if we'd left them. Now what would you have advised if you had been there?"

"Exactly what you did."

"But the athletic rules of both states are strongly against this," he said. "We had the game won if that fan had stayed out and let the referees make the decision.

"I'll never take another team there," Webber sighed. "That used to be a good school, but the police and school officials can't control the lawlessness."

"Let's think this over until Monday and then decide what to do."

"It's not a conference game, and it was played in another state."

"Do you have another game scheduled over there?"

"No, but we play Dartmouth Northwest over here next Friday evening—that is, if our team is able."

"I'll guarantee them they'll get protection on our side of the river," George said. "We'll have the county sheriff, his deputies, and the state police down here. Then I'm going to talk to all of our students before that game."

"It will be another hard-fought game," Coach Webber said. "And after our experience last night, we can't use enough precaution!"

"In all my teaching I've never had a thing happen like this," George sighed, getting up from the table. "But I guess there has to be a first time for everything."

Monday morning was different at Kensington High School. There were more swollen cheeks, split lips, blacked eyes, and bandaged hands among the boys than he had ever seen in one of his schools. Several of the girls had scratches on their faces and broken nails. And for the first time that season no athletic clippings from the papers were posted on the bulletin boards.

When Alice Nottingham arrived for the day, she went directly to George's office, "I must say I've been upset all weekend about that free-for-all at East Dartmouth. Bill got a terrible beating," she said. "He was so sore Saturday morning he could hardly get out of the bed. And all that awful front-page newspaper publicity. It was all over the radio and TV."

Everyone was discussing the game. Students showed each other their bruises, while the teachers speculated about the ill effects this would have after the good relations these neighboring schools had enjoyed over the years. Many blamed the situation on the strikes which had followed in the wake of the telephone strike in Dartmouth and which had spread to its cosmopolitan areas. With the strikes men were idled, many of whom were young, and they roamed the streets without anything to do. In addition to the strikes, many large industries in the area were closing down or were moving away, and this contributed to the general tension. The Sinton Shoe Company, which had provided thousands of workers with jobs for many years, had been sold by the management to a company which in turn was breaking it up into parts and selling each for a huge profit. Almost three thousand people were out of work as a result. Among these, many were from the Kensington area. George came into daily contact with the hungry, the under-nourished, and the underfed. He observed pupils who had only one change of clothing, pupils who couldn't buy books, paper, or pencils.

This once calm and settled area was rapidly falling apart. Both labor and management seemed to be out of control. The only bright light George could see was the young with whom he could work, to help them perhaps make their world a better one.

"If you didn't throw it, who did? Every time you come to my class the throwing starts! "I'll take you to the office. You can tell Mr. Gallion what you did."

"I didn't throw nothing," the boy sassed. "I ain't never throwed nothing in your class."

"And you never brought a book, either," he shouted.

They knew in the office who the boy and the teacher were before they came into the office. Charles Newton, who was often referred to as "Sir Isaac" by the pupils when he wasn't around, came in with big Lefty Goldiron walking a step ahead.

"Mr. Gallion, he is yours to keep," Charles Newton said. "He's no good in my class. He won't bring a book, as I've told you before. He won't do anything but cause trouble. My class is better off without him."

"He don't like me, Mr. Gallion," Lefty said. "He's never liked me."

"Does anybody like you, Lefty?" his principal asked him.

"I don't reckon they do," Lefty answered, looking sullenly at the floor.

"Do you like anybody?" his prinsipal asked.

He didn't answer.

"I don't want him back in my class," Charles Newton said, getting his breath more easily. "I have too many students to have to spend all my time on this one. He hurts my class. As I've said before at the teachers' meetings, we need to weed out a good ten percent."

"Which ten percent?" the principal asked.

"I could give a list from my classes," he replied quickly.

"I don't want it now," George said. "If I got a list from all the teachers how many would we have left?"

George didn't want to argue with Charles Newton now. He was afraid of losing this excellent teacher. George had dreams of expanding his science department, making it the best of any high school in the whole surrounding area, maybe the best in the state, by putting this brilliant young man at the head of it. He wanted to hold him on his faculty and promote him, delegate more authority to him, as long as he was principal of the high school; yet their ideas clashed painfully on methods of discipline.

"Lefty, I've got to make a trip down in Kensington," George said. "You want to go with me? While I go on this errand we can talk."

"Yeah, I don't care."

"Well, let's go," George said. "Sadie, if anything comes up you can't handle, call Mr. Riddle."

"All right, Mr. Gallion."

Pupil and principal walked out of the office and down the corridor.

"Man, we know this little old truck," Lefty said. For the first time his sullen face showed animation. "We know its make and color!"

"What if I have it repainted?" George Gallion asked.

"That wouldn't do no good," Lefty said, grinning faintly. "We know the sound of the motor."

They got into the pick-up and he drove over the Hill very slowly, with Lefty resting his big arm where he had rolled down the window glass.

"Lefty, I used to teach your mother." George Gallion began talking slowly. "Daisy Watson was a good student. We never had any trouble with her. Then I taught your stepfather. Well, they went to school here at the same time. He was a very nice fellow."

"Don't mention that sonofabitch to me," Lefty snarled. "I hate his guts. If he ever comes back here and fools with me I'll open his belly with a knife and see what he's got on the inside. I hope he's better on the inside than he is on the outside!"

"Well, let's talk about your mother then," George said. "You don't seem to care too much for your stepfather."

"What about my mother?" Lefty said.

"She finished Kensington High School and made very good grades," George told him.

"But I don't want to go to school," Lefty said. "Why'n't you kick me out? Go ahead. I'd rather you did. You know, I'll think more of you. Who cares if you knew my mother; that don't mean nothing to me. All I want to do is quit. So why don't you leave me alone?"

George Gallion pulled the truck over to the side of the road. "What will you do if you quit? You know you have to stay in school. So let's do a little talking."

"What for?" Lefty asked.

"I want to talk to you before it's too late," George told him. "If you don't want to talk, I'll talk and you can listen. First: You are an important person growing up here. I've heard about the reputation you have of starting fights down at the drive-in theater. I've heard about your whipping everybody you've fought. I need you to do some fighting at Kensington High School. The coach needs you! How much do you weigh?"

"Hundred ninety-six."

"Got me beat by one pound," George Gallion told him. "And you can run a hundred yards in ten seconds, I've been told."

"Yeah." His voice was icy. "But I don't want to play football and I don't want to do any running either."

"You'd make an All-State Fullback before you're a senior," George told him. "I expect to start a track team like we used to have up on the Hill. I'd like to have you for the dashes, low hurdles, discus, and shotput. I'll make a one-man track team out of you!"

"Oh no you won't," he said. "That's too much like work!"

"Well, just what do you expect to do when you grow up?"

"Nothing."

They sat in silence, there was little left to say.

"Are you going to expel me?" he asked George Gallion. "Grandma and Grandpa just keep talking school to me."

"I'm on my way to your grandparents now. I want to talk to them about you."

"No need to go today. They ain't there."

"But we'll drive past the house anyway in a few minutes."

"You don't believe me, do you?"

"Why yes, I believe you. You've never lied to me."

"Why are you wasting your time with me when you got six hundred up there on the Hill, Old Man?"

"Don't you call me Old Man," George Gallion said. "Never let me hear you call me that again. I'm Mr. Gallion to you. If your mother and your stepfather were to see me now, they wouldn't call me George or Old Man. They'd call me Mr. Gallion. That's what I am to every pupil upon the Hill and to every teacher."

They sat in silence a minute. George Gallion looked at his wrist watch, a bright round yellow-gold case set against the dark background of his hairy wrist.

"We'd better be moving," he said, turning the key and pushing the starter.

He pulled onto the road again, and they went down the highway and crossed the railroad tracks.

"Your grandparents live in the same place?"

"Yes, Mr. Gallion," he said sarcastically."

George Gallion drove over to Front Street and stopped in front of a small weatherbeaten house that looked as if it were about to fall down. He got out of the truck, walked slowly up the steps, and knocked on the door. No one answered. He knocked again and again. No one came.

"I told you they were gone," Lefty said.

He came back down the steps and got into the truck. Lefty glared at him with icy blue eyes that were narrowed down to tiny slits.

"You know this town, don't you?"

"Yes, I used to know it," he said. "I used to walk all over this town. I knew everybody here then. I used to take walks at night; right up there is an old graveyard."

"You know about the graveyard?"

"Yes, why?"

"It's not all there now."

"What happened to it?"

"I dug part of it up." He said this with pride.

"You did! Why?"

"Oh, just hunting for something."

"That's hard to believe. Find anything?"

"Yes. Bones. No money, no old guns!"

"You know that's dangerous business?"

"I'm not afraid," he said. "I'm not afraid of anything or anybody. Now you don't believe I dug into the grave up there, do you? You think I'm lying. You think I'm afraid."

"Yes. I believe you," he said. "But we'll drive up there. I want to see the place again."

"If you can believe the dates on the tombstones them old bones have been in the ground over a hundred years. That's something, ain't it?"

"Yes, that's a long time."

George Gallion drove up to the end of the street which trailed off into a narrow dusty road over an Ohio River bottom now abandoned to dead weeds and sawbriars. He continued driving over the little ridges where there had been rows of corn until he reached the old pioneer cemetery. He stopped and got out.

"You ain't very strong since you had that heart attack, are you?"

"Neither am I very weak," George replied. "Why?"

"I just wanted to know," he said. "I was just thinking you couldn't dig down there on a moonlight night until you reached them old bones, could you?"

"I know *I* wouldn't; these are graves of pioneers that settled this land. I wouldn't disturb their sleep. They deserve their rest. Look at that stone. One is a Revolutionary soldier."

"So what? What do I care?"

"You'd better care," George said. "If anybody reports you, you're a goner."

"You're tryin' to scare me like Grandpa and Grandma do."

"I'm not trying to scare you."

"I ain't afraid of iron bars either," he snarled. "I been behind them before." His small blue eyes narrowed, fastened on George Gallion. He sized George up like a fighting rooster maneuvering for advantage.

"You don't believe me, do you?" Lefty said. "You don't believe I been in jail. You don't believe I dug them graves. Go in there and look and see. That grave over on the back side is one . . . I ain't filled it up yet. When I didn't find nothing I filled the others up."

Lefty walked across the small cemetery. George followed. Lefty was right. There was an exposed human skeleton down in the deep hole.

"When are you going to fill up that grave?"

"Thought I'd do it tonight when the moon is up."

"I think you're going to do it now," George Gallion said. "Go to your house and get a shovel."

Lefty stood looking obstinately at his principal.

"Go on, I said. Go in a hurry. Double-time."

Lefty Goldiron walked off slowly at first. Then he increased his speed to a slow trot until finally he was running toward his home at the edge of the weed field.

Old bones . . . George's thoughts tumbled over and over in his mind as he looked down into the grave. Disturbing the bones of the pioneers! George wasn't sure whether Lefty would return. He decided to wait. When these bones were put here this was a cornfield. People lived from the land then. They loved the land, because it fed and clothed them. Now there was not a tree here. A yellow, fallow field that would hardly grow weeds! We have been the despoilers of our own earth. Have we taken from our youth, putting nothing back, until they won't produce? Old bones. Dry bones. Bleak bones. Pioneer bones. Old bones uncovered by a youth in my school! Old bones exposed to the air and sun in this unfruitful land . . .

Once in this area there were four villages, each rivaling the other, but in the last two decades, when it became industrialized, lines between the villages had been erased and all the villages had grown into one. Level areas where there was mechanized farming had quadrupled production, which meant hillside farmers could no longer compete. They were forced to leave the land and move where there were industries. The breadwinner of a family could work by day at industry and buy more good food than he could grow. There were fewer

farmers each year. Small farms were eliminated in the competitive farm markets. Yet farm production rose higher and
higher. Despite the strikes, Kensington was one place where
the mountaineers came and brought large families. Others
came to Kensington from other parts of America, and here
they mixed with the descendants of these who had pioneered
this area.

He looked at his watch again. Time was passing. Here he
was with one boy when he needed to be with six hundred
twenty-four pupils upon the Hill. One youth. Was he worth
saving? He was a part of a young human jungle. He knew he
couldn't give him up, no matter if Charles Newton did disagree
with him. He looked down the road again. He saw Lefty coming with a shovel over his shoulder. He was trotting up the
road, too.

This has never happened before, he thought. Never among
the thousands I've taught. Shoveling in a graveyard, digging
up old bones. The thought horrified him.

"Shovel them under, Lefty," he said. "Shovel them under. I
can't stand to see them any longer."

"Sorry, Mr. Gallion, that it hurts you," he panted. "Guess
it's about to turn your stummick! This don't bother my
stummick. It takes more'n this. Guts of cats and dogs strung
along the highway bother me more than these bones."

Then he began shoveling the dirt over the bones.

"I didn't know it was against the law to do this," he panted
as he shoveled.

"It certainly is," George said. He looked at his watch
again.

"I know it ain't right, but I wondered what was here, so I
went down in the ground to find out." He shoveled faster. "I've
always thought there's a lot of things hidden in the ground. So,
I been trying to find them."

"You're right," his principal agreed. "But not in cemeteries.
Gold, silver, iron, coal, and plenty of metals."

He pushed the high-piled dirt down into the hole. He could do it faster this way than by shoveling it. He was so powerful he bent his long shovel handle until George Gallion thought it was going to break. After he had pushed the pile of dirt into the grave, he pushed his shovel down with his foot and lifted full shovels of dirt and threw them into the hole.

"You're good with that shovel," George Gallion said. "Maybe, one of these days, I might recommend you to a company who needs a good man with a shovel."

Lefty grinned and wiped sweat from his face with his shirtsleeve. Then he went back to work. "I don't think I'd want to do that," he said.

The bones will be hidden, George Gallion thought. When spring comes again and the grass grows it will hide the scar. Bury the old bones and what they stood for long ago. We need to chart new paths. We need to know where we are going, and why and how.

"Well, I've got it, Mr. Gallion. Okay?"

"Yes, Lefty," he said. "Get in and let's get back up the Hill."

They got in the truck and Lefty stuck the long-handled shovel out the window so he could hold it. George Gallion gunned the truck off to a fast start. He stopped in front of Lefty's grandparents' and waited until Lefty put the shovel in the toolshed. Then Lefty returned and got in the truck and they were off to Kensington High School.

"We've been gone nearly an hour," George Gallion said.

"I've filled up that grave, Mr. Gallion," he said. "Now kick me out."

"You're just joking, Lefty. You really don't want to be expelled."

"That's what *you* think. I don't want to go to school. I don't want to do anything."

"I want you to get your textbooks and start work," George told him. "I want you to dig into books instead of graves. I want you to be prepared for the future. I want you to know what you want and then go after it. I want you to amount to something in life."

As George drove across the railroad tracks, they bounced up from the springy seat, bumping their heads on the top of the cab.

"Yes, amount to something," he continued. "I want you to read a book."

Lefty was sullen again. "I hate books.".

"I'll find you one you'll like," he said. "I want you to read it and tell me what you found in the book. You didn't find anything in the old graves but bones. I know you'll get more than old bones out of the book I'll bring you."

"Why won't you kick me out?"

"I'm not going to kick you out," George Gallion said firmly. "I don't want to hear that again."

They had now reached the top of the Hill and George parked near the schoolhouse door. Lefty got out very slowly. He looked icily at his principal again when they went inside the building.

"Come with me to the cafeteria," George invited him. "Lunchtime is over and we're late. We'll get some food."

George bought Lefty's lunch for him and left him in the cafeteria eating while he took a sandwich and went into the office. There was a long list of things for him to do that Sadie Markham had written out and left on his desk. He ate while he read the list. He was trying to figure a way to meet each task when Lefty walked in.

"Old Man," he snarled with clenched fists, "you can't buy me with a little cafeteria grub! You couldn't buy me with a big steak, let alone this rotten high school stuff. I won't be bought! I've asked you a dozen times to throw me out. I talked to your face like a man. I'm not asking you another time."

"What are you saying," George asked, rising quickly. "What are you saying to me?"

Lefty's face was as red as paint. His cold blue eyes seemed

to have shrunk until they were no larger than little peas. He was standing squared off and slouched as if he were in the ring.

"I said you couldn't buy me with a rotten meal from this dump," he said. "Are you deaf? Didn't you hear me the first time? I've asked you like a man to expel me. You keep putting me off. Since school started I've looked at you so many times. I've looked at your face and chin. What a target you'd made for a knockout! The only thing that's held me back is that you wear glasses."

George jerked his glasses off and pitched them on a stack of papers piled up in the corner.

"If that's what you've been waiting for . . ."

Lefty's right went back like a well-oiled piston. His fist shot out like a frog's tongue after a fly. George dodged as the fist whistled past his cheek. Lefty put everything behind that blow, and it pulled him off balance. He couldn't follow with a blow from his left. His right missed the target and struck the plastered wall. George drew his fist and struck with everything he had. Lefty's unguarded jaw got a direct hit. The weight of George's shoulders, which were as broad as Lefty's, was behind the short quick punch. This lick jarred George all the way back to his shoulder. The pain ran up his arm like electricity running through wires. Lefty went sprawling over on his desk. His arm went limp. Blood was oozing from the broken skin on his right fist.

"I won't expel you either," George said, though Lefty could not hear. "You wanted to hit me. You've had your chance. You had the first lick. Now!"

Coach Webber, who was walking down the corridor, looked through the open office door. He saw Lefty sprawled across the desk, and George standing over him with his fists still clenched.

"What's the matter?" he shouted, running into the office. "What happened?"

"Lefty has wanted me to expel him," George said. "I wouldn't do it. He then came in and demanded that I expel him. He said he had wanted to hit me since school started but I wore glasses, so I threw them over there on that paper. He struck and missed. I struck and connected."

"He's out now," Don Webber said. "I've tried to get him to play football. That boy could do everything but won't do anything. And you, Mr. Gallion, shouldn't be fighting."

"What else could I do?" he asked. "I've had him out riding around this morning and talking to him. I've done everything I know to do. Yet he attacked me."

"You'd better let him go," Don said.

"I won't let him go either," George said. "I still think he's got good stuff in him. He's like a dull ax. I'm going to work with him until he's sharp enough to cut through hard wood. I had to give him what he needed."

"When you need any fighting, call on me," Don offered. "I told you once if you were a principal in hell I'd want to follow you there and work for you."

He looked at George and grinned. "You know I've done a lot of boxing too," Don Webber added. "You knocked out a good man here. I'm surprised he didn't get you."

"A lucky lick," George said. "Strange—when you have to do something and know you're right you're usually lucky."

"I'll stay a minute if you don't mind," Don Webber spoke softly. "He's waking up."

Lefty groaned and shook his head like an addled rooster.

The two men watched the big youth rise slowly to his feet. His blue eyes looked sleepy behind their pea-shell slits. His heavy shock of hair lay disheveled over his head like clusters of dark-brown ragweed.

His broad shoulders shook. His whole body trembled. Tears tumbled down each cheek.

"I can't believe that, Lefty," his principal said. "I can believe almost anything else about you, even that you threw that eraser some time ago in Mr. Newton's class, but I can't believe that you are a crybaby! I've always thought you were a man, not a baby. Did you throw that eraser?

"Lefty, stop that crying," George said. "I'm not going to

send you to the study hall like that. You are too much of a man to go in there before the other fellows bawling like a little calf just weaned from its mother. Dry your eyes and straighten up your face. Go wash it in cold water. Then comb your hair!"

Lefty took off running from the office, his shoulders still heaving.

"First time I ever saw him cry," Coach Webber said. "Maybe it's good you're not sending him to the study hall. He's bullied many of the boys I have in there. If they see him crying just once they'll know he's not invincible. He's knocked a lot of them out. They're good to him because they are afraid of him. Now if some of the follows could see him . . ."

"I don't want them to see him now," George Gallion said. "What happened to him in here was a shock. I think he'll be all right from now on. He'll never ask me to expel him again!"

Outside the office window Coach Webber and George watched Lefty Goldiron pace up and down in front of the schoolhouse, under the windows where the pupils inside couldn't see him. He was still crying.

"Just as soon as the shock wears off he'll be all right," George said. "Are you going upstairs now?"

"No, but I can go," he said.

"Tell Miss Gallion when Lefty comes in to the library study hall to put him up front where no one can see his face."

"A lot of time to give just one student," Coach Webber said.

"But he's worth a lot of time," George said. "Tell Miss Gallion to give him a book. See that he has one that is easy to read, one with a lot of interesting pictures. Books are new to Lefty, and we have to go easy with him at first."

Monday morning there were newspaper clippings from the three tri-state papers thumbtacked on all the bulletin boards—except in Gus Riddle's ag rooms. KENSINGTON SURPRISES DARTMOUTH NORTHWEST. Les Bowdin had tacked his columns on all the bulletin boards.

Prearrangements had been made to have the police at the

games, and this had prevented a recurrence of any trouble.

It was apparent to everyone how highly charged was the atmosphere. From a chaotic collection of youth, Kensington was becoming a school. The spirit of youth was taking hold of the teachers, too, for they were far more relaxed with the students than they ever had been.

Among the swarm of faces this Monday morning, George saw two strange men trying to push their way through the crowds of students up the crowded corridor. George waited. Why didn't they wait for the bell, when the corridor would be cleared and the classrooms would be packed instead of the corridors? One of the men George recognized. It was Jock Sutherland, who had once been basketball coach of Auckland High School, and who was now selling textbooks for a publisher.

"Good morning, Jock." George welcomed him with a warm handshake as if they had always been close friends. "You're seeing us at our most hectic time."

"I'll say we are," the stranger put in. "I've been in a lot of schools, but I've never seen or heard anything like this. Sounds like a football school!"

The stranger looked up at the clippings of victory on the bulletin board. "See where you've just taken another one," he said. "Nice write-ups up there."

"Yes, they should be, I suppose," George said. "Our center is our reporter."

"Mr. Gallion, I want you to meet Marvin Dinwiddie, assistant director of the state's Athletic Control Board," he said.

George instinctively disliked the man. Now he could understand why he had called this a "football" school.

"Let's go into my office," George invited them.

"Yes, let's get out of this crowded mass," Marvin Dinwiddie said. "You can get trampled on in this corridor."

Inside the crowded office George offered Marvin and Jock chairs. Just then Coach Webber came in.

"Good morning, Jock," he greeted an ex-coach and friend.

"Don, I want you to meet Marvin Dinwiddie," Jock said. "He's assistant director of the state Athletic Control Board."

Don Webber's face colored and he broke out in a sweat. "I've heard of you, Mr. Dinwiddie," he said, shaking his hand. "I'm glad to meet you."

"You might not be glad you've met me by the time this is over," he told Webber. "My duties are never pleasant, but they must be performed."

"Yes, I understand that," Coach Webber said.

Miss Markham pushed the bell. School had officially begun. The students hurried to their home rooms, and soon the building was silent. "We push a button and that makes a little difference," George said to Marvin. "It's best for them to let their steam off early in the morning."

"I'm ready to let some steam off here too when you're ready," he said to George.

"What are the charges you've brought against us?" George asked.

"Same old question and same old story," he replied. "You have been playing ineligible men."

"We have not," George said emphatically. "We want your proof."

"I have it," he replied.

He spread out on George's cluttered desk the football eligibility lists for players for the past three seasons. Coach Webber and George looked at the lists.

"Are there inconsistencies in these?" George asked.

"No, but in recruiting," he said.

George and Webber stood silently and stiffly at the table, like two mummies.

"You know it's recruiting," Marvin Dinwiddie said. "Look where your players were born."

George and Don looked at each other and smiled.

"Sure, most of our players were born in Dartmouth," Coach Webber said. "We don't have a hospital on this side of the Ohio River and our women go to one of the Dartmouth, Ohio, hospitals to have their babies. So our football players were born in Dartmouth, Ohio, and we have to record this on our eligibility lists."

"Mrs. Markham, get the permanent records of every football player," George said.

"But I've done this before," she said.

"Well, do it again," George told her. "We want to show our records to Mr. Dinwiddle."

"I particularly want to see the record of the boy you call the Champ," he said. "And what about this boy you call Wild Bill? Quite a football player, isn't he?"

"When you came into this office you intimated that our school was guilty of playing ineligible men, didn't you?" George asked Marvin Dinwiddie.

"I intimated no such thing," he replied. "I say you are guilty."

"When an individual is on trial in our courts a man is not guilty until he is proven guilty," George said. "Why is the method of procedure used by the state Athletic Control Board so different?"

"We have received what we think are authentic reports," he said.

"May I see those reports?" George asked.

"I'd like to see them too," Coach Webber said.

"These are confidential," he said.

"But they have no right to be kept confidential in a trial," George said. "We are on trial. We want to know who has indicted us."

"Not just one person but several," he replied.

"As long as we didn't win a game, we could have got by playing ineligible men," Coach Webber interrupted, "but we didn't play them then and we don't play them now."

"No, I have made it a point to check each man in this office," George said.

"You have not explained about the Champ," Marvin Dinwiddie said. "Now did he come to school here last year?"

"No, he didn't," Coach Webber said.

"Did he play football last year?"

"Yes, he did," Webber replied.

"Where did he come from?"

"The principal will explain this," Coach Webber said.

"Where did he come from, Gallion?"

George didn't answer.

"Where did he come from, Gallion?" he asked loudly.

"Address me correctly," George told him. "I'm not Gallion to you. I'm Mr. Gallion. You should have manners, Mr. Dinwiddie. Very few pupils in this crowded noisy school would be as unmannerly as you are!"

"I've seen nothing fancy in your mob out there," he sneered. "I've seen better-looking pupils in other schools!"

When Marvin Dinwiddie and George looked savagely at each other, Jock Sutherland shook his head and winked at Coach Webber.

"Mr. Gallion," he said with sarcasm, "if you can't tell me where the Champ went to school last year, I'd like to see the boy myself. He will tell me."

"Mr. Gallion, he's absent today," Sadie said.

"He would be," Marvin Dinwiddie said. "Where does he live?"

"I'll answer it this way," George said. "He's eligible."

"Where is the transcript of his grades for last year?"

"Locked up, in a file," George said.

"Unlock the file," he demanded.

George shook his head negatively. "I won't do it," he said. "I don't like your attitude."

"A lot of mystery surrounds this football player. Where does this boy live?"

"Where does the Champ live?" George asked Coach Webber. "Where can Mr. Dinwiddie find him?"

"He doesn't have any certain home," Coach Webber replied.

"Did you know, Coach, he has to live in this school district?" Marvin Dinwiddie asked. "Just one ineligible player on your team and I will have to suspend Kensington High School for one year from the state Athletic Association and forfeit your string of victories."

"There's no string of victories yet," Coach Webber replied. "We've won two and had one stolen. If we have to forfeit those we've won, it will kill the spirit of my team. My players may just as well turn in their uniforms."

"If we have a man ineligible we'll have to do this anyway," George said. "But I say we don't have an ineligible man on the team."

"I say you had better forget the rest of your schedule!" Marvin Dinwiddie said. "I'm sure you won't be playing any more games."

"We're not putting the schedule away yet. We'll fight this thing to a finish."

"How will you fight the state Athletic Association?"

"We'll take your charges against us to the county, state, and Federal courts," George said. "We don't like to be guilty until proven innocent."

"There is no record of our problems going into the regular courts," Marvin Dinwiddie said. "We have our own athletic laws and our own directors to decide."

"I went through this once before, as you know and have reminded me. I know what it means to be suspended. I'll never go through it again. It kills the spirit of the school. This is a crippled school trying to rise. Why do you think most of us are teaching here?"

"I really don't know."

"Mr. Gallion has a very serious heart condition and was given orders not to climb the stairs when he came here," Coach Webber said. "I can cross the river for $1500 more salary, coach one sport, and have a lighter teaching schedule. We're what Mr. Gallion calls do-gooders, Mr. Dinwiddie. Why should I, as a coach, want to play ineligible men?"

"To win," he retorted. "That's why all coaches play ineligible men. I have your record, Mr. Webber. You are out to win!"

"You are exactly right, but not out to win with ineligible players."

"And you back him up," Marvin Dinwiddie said to George.

"All right, you prove it," George said. "You prove one man ineligible, and I'll resign as principal of Kensington High School."

"I'll go with you," Don Webber said.

"You wouldn't do that," Dinwiddie said. "I've heard that before, too. You wouldn't leave your jobs."

"If I allow Coach Webber to play ineligible men and he plays them to win over eligible players, we do not deserve to be here. I want a decision by trial and jury for this school."

"I've never run into anything like this."

"We've never had an accuser like you, either," George said. "You've been fed horrible lies from some source which you won't reveal. And you expect me to turn over a transcript which I have kept locked in a file for a purpose."

"I'll find out about Burton," Dinwiddie said. "I'll find out where he lives. I want to see what kind of people he's from, anyway."

"They're good people," Don Webber said. "He's from a broken home. There are five children in the family. One or two of the four children are college graduates. One of these is a teacher. All but the Champ have finished high school. Unfortunately for him, his parents separated and his mother, who is remarried, lives in Ohio, while his father, who has remarried too, lives here. He tries to stay a little with both of them because he loves them. He sometimes stays with an uncle and sometimes with his grandfather, who lives in this county. You'll get the information you're after, but I'm not giving it to you. We're trying to play down the youth's mistakes and give him a chance in life."

"That's very noble talk," he said. "Very kind of you, but I want the facts. Everybody knows he's a good football player.

People are wondering how you got this boy. Maybe, Coach Webber, you can answer that. You know it's against the state rules to recruit players."

"I know the state rules well enough to quote them to you," Coach Webber told him.

"To know them and to abide by them are different."

"Here are the permanent records of all the players, Mr. Gallion," Sadie said. "And here are the grades turned in by each teacher for each week of this year."

"That information is for Mr. Dinwiddie," George said. "I check it all before each game. Judging from the facts I have, an ineligible man never plays on a team where I am principal, and never will."

Sadie looked at her watch, then she pushed the bell for the first period to end. Marvin Dinwiddie gathered the stack of cards and other information and started to put it in his brief-case.

"Don't take those cards," George said. "They don't leave this office. You can have all the other information to take with you. You ought to know a set of permanent records cards never leave the principal's office."

"Won't you trust them with me so I can look this over at the hotel this evening?"

"I will not," George said.

"You're a most uncooperative man."

"I don't like to be accused. I don't like your attitude. You have no diplomacy or manners. You're the rudest man that's ever been in my office."

Marvin Dinwiddie stiffened and his face flushed. For a moment George thought he was going to strike him. Slowly he laid all the material back on the desk. Sadie rang the bell and the corridor grew quiet again.

He then laid on George's desk a letter from the Ohio Athletic Association. Coach Webber picked up the letter and began to read it with him. "You see, I know what I am doing," Marvin Dinwiddie said as they read.

The principal of East Dartmouth High School had reported Coach Webber for taking a team off the field one minute and forty-five seconds before the game ended. He had also accused the seven hundred Kensington fans of starting a riot with fourteen hundred East Dartmouth fans.

"He doesn't mention our team had to be escorted from East Dartmouth with police protection," Coach Webber said. "We had to take the team off the field or have them hurt."

"But you did take the team off the field, didn't you?"

"Yes; we had no other choice."

"Now, quote the rule."

"You quote it."

"You know the penalty, don't you?"

"'Yes."

"That's my last exhibit and my clincher," he said. "I knew I had you when I came this morning."

"You want us, don't you, Mr. Dinwiddie?" George said.

"I didn't say I 'wanted' you," he said. "I said you were guilty of rule infractions enough to be suspended and your game forfeited. See, when you boasted," he added reflectively, "about taking this to the courts, I knew that was so much hot air."

"That's where you're wrong," George said. "It will still go to the courts. Yours is an athletic law, made by a few. There should be a provision in the law that when a team is in danger said team might be allowed to leave the football field or basketball court. That would be better than getting a boy killed or maimed for life. I don't believe any court will condemn us for taking the team from the field in East Dartmouth."

"I'd do the same thing over," Coach Webber added.

"You forgot to report the incident to us, Mr. Gallion," he said. "Wouldn't this forgetting of yours be an indication of your guilt?"

"No, I didn't forget. I met with the coaches and we decided what to do. We were ashamed of what happened. The game wasn't a conference game, and since it was played in another state we thought the best thing to do was to forget it. We planned to have them come here next year and show them real sportsmanship."

"Did you write the East Dartmouth principal?"

"Yes, I did. I asked him to forget the incident and to come and play us next year, and there would be no trouble. Now he's suggesting to you he was canceling the game with us."

"Still, you should have reported this to us," he said. "It looks like you had something to hide. That's the way we interpreted this nasty situation."

"You want to believe them instead of us," George said. "Isn't that it?"

"We'll discuss this later," he said. "I have some checking to do. I'll be back to show you my findings and ask you a few questions."

When he picked up his briefcase and walked out, Coach Webber went with him. George sat down at his desk and Jock Sutherland stayed behind.

"I think you talked a little rough to Marv," he said.

"According to Marvin Dinwiddie we were guilty the minute he walked in this corridor," George said. "The fact is, we aren't guilty."

"The fact is, according to the state Athletic Association's laws he has you for taking a team from the field," Jock Sutherland said. "You know I have had several years of experience in this state."

"Mr. Sutherland, you're different from that fellow," George said. "Had you been in his place we might have worked everything out satisfactorily."

"See, I know him and I'm a friend of his," Jock Sutherland explained. "When he contacted me in Auckland I figured I'd better come along. Don Webber is a good friend of mine and he's a fine coach. I hate to see him in trouble. I've really come to help you and Webber all I can."

"Not the Coach and me," George said. "You'll be saving this school if you can get that fellow away from here, or else we'll have to go to local courts to get justice!"

"You don't really expect to take this to court, do you?"

"I certainly do. I'm not bluffing."

"Taking this to our regular courts would cause a lot of bad newspaper publicity."

"That's what we need to air this situation to the public," George told him. "Maybe we can get new athletic rules. This will cause more publicity than he expects, and you'd better tip him off. The state department of education will have to find a new principal and new coaches and a new faculty if we are suspended."

George and Webber stood at the window in silence and watched the car leave.

"We were reported by someone up the river," George said. "He's going back for more information."

"He won't find the Champ, no matter where he goes," Coach Webber said. "The Champ has left school."

"What?"

"When I went to my class this morning I saw him in the corridor. He asked me who was in the office and I told him Marvin Dinwiddie had come to investigate him and other ballplayers, and he didn't take time to get his books," Coach Webber explained. "He took off running and I couldn't stop him. I ran to the end of the corridor and he was out in the yard going over the Hill, across the loop, down through the cornfield. He swam the river and I saw him climbing up the other bank in his wet clothes."

"Why would he do that," George asked. "He didn't have to run."

"Don't you get the connection?"

"What connection?"

"His hearing the name Dinwiddie again. After all, he was in the Dinwiddie Reformatory. He must have thought they'd come to take him back there again."

"Could be," George sighed. "He told me he'd slash his wrists before he'd go back there again."

"They'll never find him," Coach Webber said. "He won't stop running. We've lost him."

"Poor boy. He'll have a rough time. We might have done something for him here. He liked me and I liked him. I don't believe he would have ever broken faith with us. Now he'll get in trouble again. And whose fault will it be? Where will he go? What home will he have?"

"And now what will *we* do?" Coach Webber asked.

"Fight to a finish."

"How? This is going to ruin me. I can see it headlined in the *Dartmouth Times:* KENSINGTON KICKED OUT OF THE STATE ATHLETIC ASSOCIATION. My name will make the front page this time!"

"I don't think we'll make the front page."

"But I did take the team off the field," he said. "I ordered them to the dressing room. It's against the rules and I knew it, but I was afraid."

"You did the right thing. Don't worry when you do right."

"If I had a losing team, I could play ineligible men and get by," Don said.

"If you didn't want to be a winner I wouldn't want you for a coach," George said. "If you tried hard and failed I wouldn't hold your losing against you. You'd still be my coach. Now you're giving up. But this is the time to fight!"

"How?"

"Like your team fought against Rutland."

"That game will be forfeited."

"Will you work with me?"

"Tell me what to do!"

"Get word to all your boys and tell them what has happened. Tell them to keep cool. Tell them to come to school tomorrow wearing their best suits. Tell each one to wear a white shirt and tie."

"What's that got to do with it?"

"Plenty. I'll send a special message to all the classes requesting pupils not to drop a piece of paper on the floor for three

days. I'll ask Mrs. Nottingham to tell the girls to look their
best. In the next two days, while Marvin Dinwiddie is here investigating us, I want to see if this entire school can rise to an
occasion the way I'd like to see them rise for the entire year."

"Why not have a teachers' meeting?"

"No. Not for this. It's better to pass the word."

Coach Webber stared at George.

"I've got a tip, Coach," George said. "I got a tip, when I
heard Marvin Dinwiddie talking about the way the pupils were
dressed, about the paper on the floor and the general appear-
ance of the school. Let's make his coming do us some good."

"I'll get word to the boys," he said. "But will they understand how this can help us?"

"Can you keep a secret?"

"Sure can."

"I know he can't make the final decision," George said. "He
has to take his findings back to the state office. Otis Sandburn
is still Marvin Dinwiddie's superior, and Sandburn, who is a
very decent man, will have much to do with the final decision.
Otis is a friend of mine. I'll write him just as soon as I'm
through talking to you, and I'll tell him the truth, all of it."
George added, 'I'll tell him you knew it was wrong and you
broke state athletic rules to save our men. Let's try it this way.
If it works, we won't have to go to court."

Early the next morning, when George heard the car pull up
at the corridor door, he left the office and went out to meet
them.

"Well, I see you're back," George said. "Let's go in the
office."

"Yes, the bad penny has turned up," Marvin Dinwiddle said
as they went into the office. He pulled a pack of cigarettes from
his pockets.

"Sorry, Mr. Dinwiddie," George cautioned him. "No one
smokes here: teachers, students, coaches, cafeteria workers, or
janitor. Not even our guests."

"No lounge room for teachers?"

"Yes, but it has been taken for classrooms."

"We've been to see the Champ's father," Marvin Dinwiddie said. "He says he has custody of his son all right. He told us his son didn't get along with his mother's new husband. Said he didn't like his stepfather."

"Did you see the Champ?"

"No, but I think he's hiding out," Marvin Dinwiddie sighed with a shrug of his shoulder. "I made inquiries in Kensington and talked with people who had seen him get on the school bus this morning. You know, this situation looks rather suspicious."

"What else did you learn?"

"His father said he and the boy's mother were still married then and living together in Ohio when the Champ got on a cop's motorcycle and rode off. He told me his son was caught and they gave him two years. And that's what his jail record amounts to. Is that right?"

"Yes, that's right. I have the transcript of his schoolwork there," George said. "He was here this morning, but when he heard there was a man named Dinwiddie here he took off running and we don't have a man in this school who could have caught him."

"But I have no connection with that reformatory."

"Yes, but your name's the same," George said. "That's the only reason we can think of to explain his behavior."

"I didn't know he had this kind of background," Marvin Dinwiddie said. "He's not the most desirable type to have in school."

"I wouldn't say that if I were you," George said. "How many boys have stolen something who never got a reformatory rap? Look at men in high places today who got into trouble in their youth! I was determined to keep his name clear of the charge and give him a second chance."

"Have you ever taught boys before who had been to the reformatory?"

"Several of them."

"How have they turned out?"

"With the exception of two, they're fine citizens today. Young people have to find themselves and make adjustments. They have to belong, and feel not merely wanted but needed. Then give them responsibility. We had trouble with the Champ early this year, but not now. He knew he was needed to carry the ball for this school. He carried it, too."

"Now, I want copies of your eligibility lists for the past two years."

"We have a game here Friday evening. Shall I go ahead and let them play this game?"

"Certainly," he said. 'Continue your schedule."

"Mr. Dinwiddie, you said yesterday you'd like to look this school over," George said. "Would you like to look around this morning? I'll be glad to take you and Mr. Sutherland around."

"Yes, I think the setup of a school has some bearing on an investigation," he said—"although I have recorded my first impression to turn over to the committee."

"Regardless of what you have recorded, I'd like to take you around," George invited him. "Of course we put more emphasis on the student body than we do the physical properties around here. We think we have a fine family."

"That's not what I've heard," Marvin Dinwiddie said. "But I would like to take a little time and look around. Wouldn't you, Jock?"

"I certainly would," Jock Sutherland said.

They went out into the corridor and stopped at a classroom door.

"Les Bowdin, center of our football team and school reporter, is teaching this class," George whispered. "Since we have several places to go, and since your time is limited, we won't stay long, but you can see the type of student we have and what goes on in a student-teacher classroom."

When George opened the door and they went in, the rows of seats were in order. There wasn't a piece of paper on the floor. Boys were dressed in white shirts and ties and looked well-scrubbed. The girls, too, looked fresh and neat. Les Bowdin was standing up behind the desk, lecturing. He was wearing what was obviously his best suit. It was slightly short in the sleeves.

"Would you like to say something, Mr. Gallion?" Les asked him.

"No, we don't have time," George said. "We're just visiting a few rooms this morning."

After they went back into the corridor, Jock Sutherland commented, "That's amazing."

"Say, you've got a fine-looking group of young people in there," Marvin Dinwiddie commented. "I must have missed my judgment yesterday morning."

"Sometimes we do that," George said casually. "We can't be accurate all the time. I've visited towns in the rain and thought they were terrible. When I returned later in the sunlight, they were altogether different."

They passed the chewing-gum crew removing gum and polishing old chairs.

"They're honor students," George said. "Only honor students are permitted this honor."

"What?" Marvin Dinwiddie exclaimed. "Looks like you'd have trouble getting students to do that kind of dirty work."

"But we have only one janitor for this big building," George said. "We have student crews organized and working all over this building and out over the schoolgrounds. You'll see them."

"Here in this room is teaching at its best," George bragged. "Mrs. Nottingham is dean of girls and she teaches five classes. She's a veteran teacher. Her English students who make at least C average here don't fail English in college."

They followed George into the classroom.

"Will you football players rise and let a couple of former coaches see you," George said.

Seven husky seniors rose and stood stiffly. On their way out the men eyed a large bust of Shakespeare that was standing on a table near the door.

"A fine-looking class," Marvin Dinwiddie said. "Those high school senior girls are downright pretty. Nicely dressed, too."

"Don ought to have a good team here," Jock Sutherland said. "He's got college material."

"Yes, we've had poor teams around here long enough. It won't hurt us to have one good season. We've never been football champions of this district."

On the upper corridor they hastily visited Mary Wallingford's typing classes, where pupils were so busy they never looked up from their typing, and just across the corridor they looked into a science laboratory room where Charles Newton was teaching Latin. Everywhere it was the same. Teachers were busy, pupils were well-dressed and serious, and the rooms were neat.

"I'll have to change my report on this school," Marvin Dinwiddie said. "I'll admit I didn't use the best judgment when I came in here yesterday. I never saw a better dressed, more handsome lot of boys and girls than I have seen here. I don't see how I overlooked them yesterday."

They passed the outside cleaning crew picking up paper in the yard. "Now these boys you've just passed here are straight A students," George said. "Only the very best students are permitted to work out here. This is the highest job our student labor can attain."

"We're running late," Dinwiddie said. "We might not be back this afternoon. We're on our way to Ohio to investigate."

"We'll look for you anyway," George said. "We want to know what you find."

The day passed and the two men didn't return.

On Wednesday Marvin Dinwiddie and Jock Sutherland returned during the second period, while Don Webber was in the office talking to George.

"Good morning," Marvin Dinwiddie said and smiled. "We won't be here more than an hour. My work is done and I want to give you a report of my findings."

He took a sheaf of papers from his briefcase and laid them on the desk. He and Jock Sutherland carried their chairs over to the desk and sat down.

"All right," Marvin began; "the eligibility lists. I have not found a single inconsistency in these. Since only a river divides Kensington and Dartmouth and since the hospitals are over there, I know why the athletes were born in Ohio. Kensington is really a suburb of Dartmouth because the state line is erased. Of course," he added, with a glance at Don Webber, "not being familiar with this area, and seeing one of these eligibility lists, one might surmise you had recruited players from over there. Bill Nottingham is very eligible."

"If he's not eligible we don't have an eligible player on the team," George sighed.

"Now," he said wearily, "and this is your tough one, Coach. One of the Ten Commandments is: Thou shalt not lie. Our code of rules says a coach cannot take a football team from the field. You admitted doing this, and therefore what shall I say? Shall I lie?"

"No, you shouldn't," George spoke up. "But that's one rule that should be modified. When players' lives are in danger, no rule will ever bind me to keep a team on the field!"

"This is a fact that I am afraid will cause you to be suspended from the state Athletic Association, thus forfeiting the two games you've won."

"But that's not fair," Don protested.

"We don't like to resort to other means to prove our innocence," George said.

"Then I take it for granted you weren't bluffing when you said you'd take it to the courts?" he said to George.

"You're right," George said. "Then if the court decides in the state's favor I'm ready to resign."

"I will report this is the finest-looking high school group I've ever seen," he said. "The house is crowded but it's kept clean, and your schoolgrounds are the prettiest and cleanest I've seen anywhere. I'm amazed how much responsibility of running the school is placed on your students."

"We have no one else to do it," George said. "We had to do this, or not open the school this year."

"I blame myself for the way I acted when I came in here Monday," he said apologetically.

"Just forget that," George told him. "We all make mistakes."

"But you see, actually," he said, "by all the rules you're still guilty by the book. What am I going to tell the Athletic Board when it meets this evening and I lay this information before them?"

"Please explain what I was up against," Don Webber said. "I've been on the battlefield using a flame-thrower and I never saw a situation more dangerous than over there. Strikes, robberies, and no form of communications except from police cruisers, and they're limited for an area of that size and on the move all night long. Don't blame the police. God help them in their responsibilities over there! Their responsibilities over there correspond to the teachers' responsibilities in this school. Explain this to the state Athletic Board."

"Yes, do," George said. "If you decide against us, even if we don't resign in a body, this school is ruined. It can't stand this calamity. Athletics help us. Winning two football games has lifted our spirit here. I believe, Mr. Dinwiddie, you have it in your power to make recommendations. And I hope you will recommend that this school be spared this calamity and more problems."

"Marv, isn't there some compromise?" Jock Sutherland asked.

"I was just coming to that, Jock," he said. "I was thinking maybe we could make Champ Burton a borderline case, since he lives at four different places. He has four parents and he lives at four places and in two states. He is doubtful, isn't he? Then, too, there is his unfavorable background and he's a poor student."

"I'm not sacrificing that boy," George said firmly. "These pupils are my children and he is my son, too, even if he has been wayward."

"But this would be a most effective compromise," Marvin Dinwiddie said. "I've got to show some reasons why I had to come here to investigate."

"I can't see this reasoning," George said, sitting down again. "Although we are not guilty, we have to show some guilt because we have been reported and you were sent to investigate us. A man is indicted. His accusers appear in court against him. Our accusers do not. We are tried and have to defend ourselves, not knowing or seeing those who have accused us. The man who is indicted and faces his accusers in court has a right to a jury, to hear his pleas of innocence and the charges of his accusers. In our cause it is not this way! And yet, what I do here helps decide the destinies of six hundred twenty-five young people. I can't sacrifice one of our sons or daughters! I can't do it!"

Coach Webber broke the silence. "The Champ will never be in this schoolhouse again. He's gone for good."

"What are you talking about?" George said.

"He's said he's quit school and won't be back!"

"Where is he now?"

"Gone to Ohio. He left yesterday."

"Well, then, there isn't any problem," Marvin Dinwiddie said.

"Except for Champ," George snapped. "Poor boy. He was happy here. The pupils liked him, and he liked them. They cheered him when he carried the ball for this school, and he loved that. He didn't have to be told he belonged to us. He knew he belonged. This school was his anchor in a world he didn't make and didn't quite understand. He'll come back sometime," George sighed. "Maybe not now, but later, but I have a feeling he might get into more trouble."

"But he won't be back this football season, will he, Coach?" Marvin asked Don.

"No, I'm certain of this."

"Are you certain you won't be playing him any more this season?"

"Yes, very certain. He's gone," Coach Webber replied.

"All right, I can work it like this," Marvin Dinwiddie said. "I'll recommend that this school not be suspended but, since there is some controversy over Burton's residence, that he not play any more football this season for Kensington High School. I recommend this to counteract your breaking one of our strictest rules of taking a team from the field and to counteract your own mistake, Mr. Gallion, of not reporting the incident the following day,"

Jock Sutherland gave George a knowing wink, but George did not respond. He was thinking about young Burton's future.

The absentee problem at Kensington was still acute. As the fall months went by, it was becoming increasingly clear to George that absenteeism was not unrelated to organized pinball machine gambling. It was early in November when George and six youths had gone into Greenwood. The boys had been discovered gambling in Kensington on pinball machines. George appeared with these boys before Cotton Dysard, the Greenwood County Attorney, to indict the operators of the machines. Gambling was spreading throughout the school. George was convinced that if the doors didn't close on gambling, the doors of Kensington High School might have to close. The operators were successfully indicted for using pinball machines for gambling purposes.

The story broke in the newspapers, and it included several statements George had given to the press.

"George, after all these statements of yours on pinball machines won't you be afraid to go back to Kensington High School?" Grace asked him. "This is dangerous!"

"Sheriff Lonnie Biggers got the credit, and I'm glad he did," George said. "I'm glad he's willing to accept this as an honor. He must be going to run for another political office. Over a hundred boys have been staying out of school, Grace, doing without lunch money to play these machines! That's been at the heart of our absentee problem all along. And some of them were the boys I'd put on the free lunch program."

"The meeting will come to order," Alice Nottingham said, and smiled. "I seem to be conducting this meeting today, and I understand your time will come next. Each regular teacher will have to conduct a teachers' meeting this year. Now I shall come to the point immediately," she said. "Mr. Gallion wants to up our scholastic standing equivalent to what he believes the athletic teams and the band will be."

Les Bowdin held up his hand. "I've just read in a book where people used to pay just to hear the writers of the Concord Group talk to each other in general conversation," he said. "I think Concord reached a high civilization, one like I'd like to see us have in Kensington."

"What book did you find that in, Les?" Marcella Waters asked.

"I don't know, because the backs and the title pages are gone," he replied. "It's one of the old books Miss Gallion gave me when she discarded it from the library. But I feel if they could do that in Concord a century ago, we can do it now."

"I agree with you, Les," Alice Nottingham said. "And the purpose of this meeting may help us along that way. We want to enter pupils in the Greenwood County Scholastic Contest. I understand Mr. Riddle was the only teacher here last year to enter anyone."

"Now, we don't have a float for School Day at the County Fair. We have only tomorrow to build a float and we can't spare a teacher to supervise it."

"Let the seniors try to do it themselves, Mrs. Nottingham," Les Bowdin suggested.

"What do you teachers think of letting them try?" Mrs. Nottingham asked.

"Why not?" Fred Laurie said.

"There can't be a teacher to supervise you." Mrs. Nottingham spoke directly to the student teachers. "You'll have to originate your own ideas and carry your plans through yourselves. All the other schools have their floats ready."

Mrs. Nottingham counted the teachers' hands for votes. "Well, we seem to be all for you."

"Now for the scholastic contests," she said. "That's another matter."

"I doubt we can get one first place," Charles Newton said.

"Then let's get second place," Fred Laurie said. "If we can't get a second, then let's get a third."

"Remember, these contests are held tomorrow," Mrs. Nottingham said. "We don't have a teacher to spare to send to Greenwood with our pupils. We'll have to send seniors with the underclassmen."

"Who'll we send with the seniors?" Gus Riddle said.

There was laughter.

"No one," Les Bowdin said. "I'll go with a group and help them. I want to put my rock collection on display."

"But the pupils won't know until morning they're going," Fred Laurie said.

"So much the better," Mrs. Nottingham said. "They won't have time to fret about it."

"We'll have some tough competition in the freshman class scholastic contest," George said. "You teachers select our very best to enter that one."

"Why competition in that one?" Mrs. Nottingham asked.

"My daughter Janet is in it," George replied. "She's entered this contest four years, taking two firsts and two seconds for Greenwood."

"But you'll want to see your daughter win," someone said.

"My daughter has already had honors," George replied. "I want to see somebody in Kensington High School win. We need a scholastic win badly here, the same as we needed the football victories over Rutland and East Dartmouth."

Mrs. Nottingham tapped the desk again. "Each of you must recommend certain pupils for certain tests tomorrow. You have just tonight to do it. Have the names by morning, and we'll send those named to Greenwood High School, where the tests will begin at nine o'clock. We don't have any time to lose."

Sadie Markham hurriedly compiled a list of the pupils, and a list of the seniors selected to go to the fairgrounds to make the float.

The next day passed slowly. Late that afternoon, when one of the buses that had been sent to the fair came around the loop, George rushed out to meet it.

"Mr. Gallion, we made it all right," Les Bowdin said, grinning. "We didn't have a bit of trouble!"

"That's fine, Les," George complimented him. "I was sure you could get them there and back."

"Where's the other bus, Les?" George asked.

"Oh, I forgot to tell you," Les said. "He's coming behind me. He ought to be here now. The seniors didn't get the float finished and some of them are staying. You ought to see that float, Mr. Gallion! It's a beauty! You know we got some help on it?"

"No; who helped you, Les?"

"Mrs. Timmons, who teaches at Greenwood High," he said. "You know, she's a wonderful lady. And I think she was disappointed because her own school hadn't chosen her to help them with the float, so she saw us there alone without a teacher. We told her why we didn't have one and then she said, 'I'll help you if you want me.' She even found some throwaway stuff to give us."

"How do you think you came out in the tests?" George asked the other students. "Do you think we'll get one first place?"

"I don't know, Mr. Gallion," Nora Wallings volunteered. "That essay was awfully difficult to do."

"How many did we have in it?" George asked.

"There were forty-three in this contest, and nineteen were from our school."

"Well, we ought to place," George said.

"We'll know tomorrow how we came out," George said. "Papers will be graded today. Tomorrow the winners will be announced at Greenwood County School Day."

On the morning of the Fair, when Grace, Janet, and George left the Valley, white clouds were stacked like fluffy feather-beds on the western rim of the hills.

"Daddy, you certainly tried to beat me yesterday," Janet said irritably.

"I certainly did," he replied. "We're trying to beat everybody."

"Nearly half of the pupils taking the ninth-grade scholastic contest were from your school," she said. "Everybody was talking about the number you sent."

"Don't know my pupils well enough down there yet," he replied. "So we didn't know who to send. We sent everybody we thought might have a chance."

"Sent them without a teacher, too," she said.

"We couldn't spare a teacher. How did they act?"

"They acted all right," she replied. "They really acted better than many who came with teachers. Of course I want to win," Janet sighed, "but I hope one of your pupils does!"

"It's nice of you, Janet, to have such an unselfish attitude," her mother said.

"Kensington hasn't won anything scholastically in so long that if we can only get one first place we'll be happy," George sighed. "We'll have a special assembly and honor the winner."

"Oh, Daddy," Janet laughed. "It's not that important."

"It will be with us," he told her. "We need to emphasize the scholastic achievements more in our school than in any school along this river. And," he added reflectively, "our entering that contest was an all-pupil affair. They've had to do everything for themselves. Could you send your pupils out without teachers?"

"I don't believe we could, Daddy," Janet replied. "What if I beat all your pupils, Daddy?" she said, smiling.

"Then you will just beat us," he said. "If you get first in the big contest, maybe we can get second."

"Contests are not that important in Greenwood," she said.

"They should be that important," George said. "Our whole school gathered around our buses and cheered our pupils before they left as if they were a team going to play a game to decide a championship. And scholastics should be the number one game we play!"

"Oh, Daddy, I never heard of anything like that," she said. "Honest, I dread winning something in my school. Everybody gets jealous. It's not popular in Greenwood High School to be a 'brain' and make good grades. If you are, you're very unpopular."

"Something is wrong in your school," George said. "When I went to Greenwood it wasn't that way."

"Well, it's that way now," Janet said. "If I win this scholastic contest many of my classmates will quit speaking to me," she sighed. "Many of them won't speak to me anyway."

"You ought to have gone to Kensington High School with me," George told her.

"No, she shouldn't," Grace said. "Not with student teachers teaching."

They had now arrived at the courthouse square in Greenwood.

"We're early," George said. "My school hasn't arrived yet."

"I see a few of my teachers and some of my friends over there," Janet said. "I'll go over and join them."

By nine o'clock an armada of loaded school buses had already delivered almost 6000 pupils from all over the county.

There was always an atmosphere of gaiety at this School Day at the Fair, a day which all the pupils in the county looked forward to almost as much as Christmas. There were a merry-go-round, a ferris wheel, a merry-mixup for them to ride. Confetti, tinsel, balloons, and colored streamers brightened the warm autumn air, and the fairgrounds were filled with the sounds of laughter and shouts.

The first of the Kensington High School buses moved up Main Street carrying the school band. The musicians poured out of the bus and began to play.

"Got some awfully young teachers," a man said.

"George Gallion out there marching," someone said. "That won't do him any good."

"I thought he was nearly dead," said another in a low tone.

"He's teaching school again, nearly dead or not," came from another.

Now the students roamed around the displays in the large fairgrounds building—displays of farm products, quilts, canned goods, farm products, from tobacco to turnips, livestock, poultry, hogs, sheep—just about everything and anything people produced on their farms throughout the county.

All of these displays had been judged by a team from State University and a blue ribbon for first place, a red for second, and a white for third were now pinned to their displays. George watched Les Bowdin as he made straight for the fairgrounds building and came running out again. "My rock display got a blue ribbon," he shouted. "What about that? Don't you think that's great, Mr. Gallion?"

When George entered the building, he was surprised to see a Kensington High School booth that the seniors had arranged yesterday while they were making the float. The booth had a red ribbon for second place, in a field of six. But the big event came when the floats were displayed on the fairgrounds. George heard screams and shouts of familiar voices outside. He walked out of the building in time to see Kensington High School awarded the first place for their float.

Gus Riddle's FFA youth made almost a clean sweep of the first-place trophies. "I told you what we'd do," Gus said to Coach Webber. "I'm glad you and Hannigan heard that announcement. There's something besides a band and athletic teams in Kensington High School!"

Where George and Don Webber stood outside the broad

entrance door to the fair building they could see the Kensington High School pupils mingling among others, going around the circuit inside, checking blue, red, and white ribbons. The winners of the scholastic awards were about to be announced.

A voice from the loudspeaker called, "Attention please for the announcements of the scholastic winners." The crowd was silent.

"The high school freshmen winner for this year. The highest score a pupil could make was 165 points. I'll read the winners by points."

Only the music coming from the merry-go-round on the far side of the fairground broke the silence while everybody waited for the winners.

"Janet Gallion of Greenwood, 159 points," she read. A trickle of applause went up from a few Greenwood pupils.

"Bill Wills, 142 points! Bill Wills is from Kensington High School." There was deafening applause from Kensington students.

"Sadie Sheets, 132 points," she said. She had to stop again for the third round of applause. When it subsided she said, "I guess you know where she's from by this applause! Kensington High School!"

"As you know, we don't have scholastic tests for the tenth, eleventh, and twelfth high school students," Mrs. McNair explained. "but we have two important essay contests given each year in which only high school students compete. The Soil Conservation Essay, and the Good Citizenship Essay sponsored by the Greenwood Junior Chamber of Commerce."

Now the music of the merry-go-round had stopped and there was silence among the crowd.

"Adrian Tennett, Greenwood High School, first in the Soil Conservation Essay." There was a light patter of applause. "David Nicholls," and a roar of enthusiastic applause went up again.

"I don't know him but he must be from our school," George said.

"He is," Don Webber said. "I know him. He's one of Mr. Riddle's ag boys."

"It's a great day for Gus," George said.

"Now for the Good Citizenship Essay," she said. "Hold your breath."

"Nora Wallings," Mrs. McNair announced. The applause was overwhelming. Kensington had come through.

"We've got to thank Mrs. Nottingham for that," George shouted to Don Webber. "She's a teacher! She directed our pupils in this contest."

"Now a bit of explaining," Mrs. McNair continued. "Miss Wallings is a senior. The second-place winner is a freshman. Here is a note from one of the judges saying it was a hard decision to make when only three one-hundredths of one point separated the two essays. I don't know how they could judge that closely. Janet Gallion of Greenwood High School is second!"

There wasn't any applause that went up for Janet. George looked over where a few girls, dressed in white and green sweaters, were standing around one whose head was bent and who held a handkerchief to her eyes. George saw Grace standing there. He knew the weeping girl was Janet, who was a fierce competitor and a hard loser.

"Three-hundredths of one point is going to make a change in our school," George said. "With that first-place win, we can change the entire attitude of our student body. This is the beginning of a new day for us!"

"Third place goes to Naomi Bradley, Kensington," she said.

Kensington had made almost a clean sweep of an important contest.

Chapter Five

The Educational Firing Line

"Fellow teachers, I have never been upset in my twenty years of teaching as I have been this year," Gus Riddle began. "We go right out of one problem into another. We get to the place I think we are going to coast along smoothly and then another problem arises to upset us. I have never done as much work in my life in as short a time."

Shan Hannigan sighed and moved uncomfortably in his chair.

"You ought to try a full teaching schedule and in addition coach three major sports," Coach Webber mumbled disgustedly in an undertone.

"Now, you might wonder why I have requested this special meeting," he continued. "As a teacher here, my turn to conduct a teachers' meeting would come around shortly, so I'm choosing my time now. I want to save this school. I want to lay down a few disciplinary rules which I think should be enforced here. Kensington High School isn't a reformatory. This idea 'save the student' applies only to a few and neglects the many. I'm not for it. And I shall come to this later."

His face was very red. Beads of perspiration popped out over his face. He gave George an uncomfortable look, then looked up toward the ceiling.

"I am in complete disagreement with the principal in his ideas of running a high school," he said. "I've signed when I had time, and just initialed when I didn't have time, over a hundred faked excuses where boys claimed they had been ill or faked other excuses. Has one of these boys been suspended for lying? No, they're still coming to school now. Sure they are. It's a pleasure to have less than the normal number of absentees for a school this size. But did this great change come through the head of our high school? No."

Teachers began to shift nervously in their chairs. George sat silently and listened to this fine classroom teacher who so violently disagreed with his philosophy of teaching.

"Where would we be right now if it hadn't been for Sheriff Lonnie Biggers?" he asked. "Now, when the county sheriff has to clean up a school problem it is a reflection on our school. And I have some things I must say to get them out of my system. As you know, I am for law and order. Right now, in the face of criticism, I am working to get Kensington incorporated. It's the largest unincorporated village in the eastern part of this state. Five thousand people in Kensington and it's called a village. It is without law and order. I solicit all your help to aid in the incorporation of this village. Look at the headlines in the papers about our students! It's bad publicity: we need good publicity. What do you think. Mr. Hub-of-the-Wheel?" he asked in a sarcastic tone, turning to George. "You got anything to say for yourself? Will you state to us teachers your reasons for not punishing the pupils who stayed out of school and gambled? What about the boys you were giving free meals, who gave you a sob story you believed about why they gambled away the money their poor hard-working parents had given them to buy lunches, books, and school supplies?"

"Yes, I can defend my policies," George said, rising and standing by his chair. "I agree with everything you said about getting Kensington incorporated. I give you my support. I'll help in any way I can. If Kensington were incorporated and had a day policeman and a night policeman, then much of our trouble would end. We have not had sufficient law to protect Kensington where parents of pupils of this school have become law violators. There are people who will make a dollar any way they can. I think perhaps, Mr. Riddle, you should talk to these parents the way you're talking to us."

"But you're dodging the issue I have brought up," he reiterated. "You have not punished any of these pupils."

"I think they have received sufficient punishment," George said.

"Punished," he repeated. "When? How?"

"By their parents," George replied. "Many have received unnecessary beatings by angry parents, and, Mr. Riddle, I'm telling you the weapon of suspension you constantly bring up will not work. They've already missed a lot of school. They need to be in school. I don't want to turn them loose in Kensington and the rural communities over the western half of this county. They're better off here."

"You'll defend a student in spite of everything," he chided George.

"Maybe I'm sentimental," George said. "Sure, I defend them; I can't do anything else when I think about what might have happened to me if it hadn't been for my teachers. I had a good home and good parents. Yet the teenage years are tender and crucial ones. Now is the time to save them. This year a pupil will be an obnoxious weed, while next year you won't know him. He'll blossom like a flower. So I like to hold on to each pupil and hope for the best."

"Yes, and some of them will always be obnoxious weeds, and if they are allowed to remain they'll make obnoxious weeds of the flowers. You know the old story about a rotten apple in a barrel of good ones. The whole barrel may soon be rotten."

"Not if the teachers don't go to sleep," George said.

"Mr. Gallion, you mean well," he said, shaking his head sadly. "We have what you call a flexible program in this school, but you don't have a flexible mind. You are rooted like a tree in your thinking. Your policies of discipline are tree-rooted on top of the ground. The trees will soon all topple over."

"No, most of them bend downward, take roots, and grow in earth," George replied.

"You're talking to a man who has spent his life in agriculture," Gus replied admonishingly. "I'd rather set young trees in the ground. We just can't see eye to eye, Mr. Gallion."

"Maybe we'll come closer before the school year ends."

"Yes, if the school continues through all these upheavals. I've never seen anything like what has happened here. I've never heard tell of such problems as we have encountered this year!"

"If you are through with me I'll sit down," George said.

"I'm through," he said in a tone of dismissal.

Charles Newton interrupted from the back corner of the room. "Some progress has been made here. We have made good arrangement by reclassifying the good and poor students."

"But it is discipline I am speaking of," Gus said. "Mr. Gallion doesn't inflict the proper punishment. It's time we removed the chaff from the wheat."

Fred Laurie, who had until now agreed with George, spoke up, "I sanction every word Mr. Riddle has said."

"What's so wrong with his discipline, Fred?" Alice Nottingham snapped, turning around in her chair to face Fred Laurie. "I remember when you were a student here, Fred. You were an outlaw then. He handled you, didn't he? Where would you have been if it hadn't been for him?"

"I've said many times Mr. Gallion used to be as rough as a crosscut saw," Fred Laurie added. "But I believe he is slipping in discipline."

"No, I've just lived longer, had more experience, since then," he told Fred Laurie. "I still like a working noise in school. We must have discipline, but much of this we can get by giving our pupils enough work and inspiring them to do the work and to amount to something in life."

The teachers, who had been listening quietly until now, began talking to one another. Gus Riddle pounded on the desk for order but the buzz of their voices continued.

"Mr. Riddle, I would like to ask something if you don't

mind," George said, rising again. "I would like to have you put this to a vote of confidence just to see how many of you believe I am wrong in discipline. I'll leave the room when you vote."

"That request is fair enough," Gus said agreeably.

George left the room.

When he returned some minutes later, Alice Nottingham was standing. "I have the pleasure of announcing this to you because I wanted to make this announcement myself," she said. "Mr. Gallion, there were only three votes cast against you. And I want to add that I've never seen anything so silly as giving you a vote of confidence." She sat down quickly. When she looked at Gus Riddle her lips were trembling. "Silliest thing I ever heard of, but maybe some of you will get something off your chests," she snapped. "Did you give your principal a vote of confidence last year? What kind of discipline did you have last year? Did they play the pinball machines last year? I'll bet they did. And none of you ever found it out. I'll find out for my own satisfaction by going over the old absentee lists. Where were you last year, Mr. Riddle, when this school fell apart? It hasn't fallen apart this year, has it?" she continued heatedly. "And I say it won't fall apart. Shame on you, Fred Laurie," she said, turning around and looking at his flushed face.

"All right, thank you," George said. "We'll continue from here on the educational firing line tomorrow. You are dismissed."

"Mr. Gallion. I'd like to speak to you," Don Webber said.

"Let's go inside the gym," George said.

Don Webber followed George upon the stage behind the heavy curtains, one of the few private places left in the crowded schoolhouse. "I want to talk to you about this school election," he said. "Has anybody approached you?"

"No. What do you mean?" George asked.

"Have they asked you to contribute?"

"No, but I got a letter from Superintendent Bennington," George said. "He asked me to stop at the office this afternoon after school. He didn't say why he wanted to see me. Has anybody approached you?"

"I'll say somebody approached me last night," he said. "Ephraim Potters, who is on the county payroll repairing school buildings, drove down to see me. You see, he's one of John Bennington's men and he lives in this district and is strong for Orman Caudill. I was preparing my class assignments when he knocked on the door. He told Teenie he wanted to see me outside. Of course we know Eiph real well. So I stepped out in the yard and he asked me if I'd take a drive with him. He said he had some things to talk over with me. Well, I got in the car and we drove up the road to Greenwood and back. He told me he heard I was out of line with the administration. Then he said everybody who was working in the system was invited to give a voluntary contribution."

"How much?" George asked.

"Well, from the way I got it he's supposed to tithe," Webber said. "You know Mr. Bennington has made a big change in the county system, don't you?"

"No, I'd better not hear anything about it," George said.

"I'd better tell you this, because it leads up to my problem," he said. "Wendall Phelps is no longer principal of Winston Elementary!"

"What?" George said. "He was one of the better principals in this county. I used to teach him. What happened?"

"He wouldn't cooperate," Coach Webber said. "Since he has a lot of relatives in this county, which is a lot of votes, they didn't fire him at the office but shifted him to Clifton Elementary. Mr. Bennington sent Parker Dunnaway from his office over to Winston and brought Delbert Ludlow to his office to replace him. Delbert Ludlow is a politician in your party."

"That's correct," George said. "I know him very well. I used to teach him, too. What's Del Ludlow doing in John Bennington's office?"

"Mr. Gallion, don't be naïve," he said. "You know what he's reported to be. He's the check-off man. Since his former assistant superintendent, Dunnaway, wouldn't or couldn't do this very well, he moved him out and Ludlow in as assistant superintendent. Ludlow may not be much of a principal, but brother, they tell me he's a good politician and money collector!"

"He's a good politician," George admitted. "But I don't know about what kind of a collector he is."

"He must be good or John Bennington wouldn't have him. I was just as good as told last night if I didn't cooperate I wouldn't be coach next year. See, it doesn't matter what you do and how well you do it here, it's who you're for or against that counts. Mr. Gallion, I love teaching and coaching but I'm disgusted. Say I'm for Mr. Bennington, say that I tithe and I drive a car for him on election day. If he wins, then I win. But say that he loses. I lose, too. It's just too complicated. And what's it got to do with teaching? What's happening to our profession?"

"A lot of wrongs," George replied quickly. "But we can't give up. The profession must right itself and go on. The wheels still spin. Not every place is like here."

"But who'd ever believe this county would get this way? When somebody starts putting the pressure on me something in me boils. It boiled over last night. I told Eiph plenty. So, if John Bennington's board members win, I'll be away from here next year."

"I'll have something to say about that," George said. "I'll be principal here. The Greenwood County board of education can't hire anybody I won't recommend. And I'll recommend you. Now take it easy. Vote the way you please."

"I'll bet he's calling you to the office to ask for a contribution," Coach Webber said. "I'll bet they're going to put the pressure on you."

"No, he won't," George said. "He knows me too well. Del Ludlow might be the check-off boy, but he won't approach me either. I'll see them this afternoon."

When George walked up on the porch of the old office, he didn't have to open the door. It was opened for him by Del Ludlow.

"Hello, Mr. Gallion." He greeted George with a big smile, grabbed his hand, and pumped it three times. "How are you?"

The big smile remained fixed on his face. Though four years younger than George, he looked much older. He had known victory and defeat in many a county political tussle. He knew the people of Greenwood County better than he had ever known the contents of a textbook, for he had studied them more than any book.

"Mr. Gallion, you look well," he said. "I know you must be feeling well."

"Yes, very well."

"Schoolwork must be agreeing with you. Go right in, Mr. Gallion. Mr. Bennington has been wanting to see you."

"Where is he?" George asked.

"Back in his private cubbyhole, Mr. Gallion," he replied.

George found his way back along the long corridor to the little windowless room where John Bennington held court. John Bennington was sitting behind his desk like an ancient Egyptian king on his throne.

"Glad to see you, Mr. Gallion," he said when George entered. "I've been waiting for you." He rose from his chair and the two men shook hands.

"Have a seat, Mr. Gallion. Much has happened since I have seen you last," he said. "Many of the ups and downs you've had I thought would cost us votes. Such as, for instance, you've used the 'board of education' on the boys pretty often and you had that athletic investigation down there. Then, of course, that gambling situation had me worried, but it has turned in our favor. And, as I have explained to some who came here asking me to fire you, Sheriff Lonnie Biggers, not you, did the investigating and cleaned up that situation. Of course, Mr. Riddle's trying to incorporate Kensington might make a few enemies. I wish he'd wait until after the election to do this."

"That deal is already ten years late. I've encouraged Mr. Riddle to carry through. He has my backing."

"You've kept that high school going, Mr. Gallion, in the face of defeat. I think what you have done down there will save Orman Caudill. We have a chance of getting him re-elected. He's a fine board member. I don't believe I could get along without him. Now, one of the reasons I have asked you to stop in is to tell you I have another teacher for you."

"That's great. Who is he, and how did you get him?"

"He is Ralph Sizemore, and he went to Menton State College with my son Delbert, but unlike my son, he didn't stop to sell insurance," he said. "He will get his degree at the end of this quarter. He's a young man and his major is math and biology. He's never had teaching experience before, but he's a dedicated man."

"We'll give him plenty of math and biology," George said. "Just don't let anybody else grab him."

"Right now, Mr. Gallion, what concerns me most is the election next week. Now, I want to say you have done your part in your improvement of the school. I want to tell you so you can tell your teachers at a meeting: there will be no school on election day."

"But what about our records? The state is very particular."

"We'll have to make that day up somehow. I want all schools dismissed, since several of the schoolhouses will be used as voting precincts."

"Can't you find other places for this?"

"I'm afraid not. This is going to be the biggest election we ever had in this county. It's a presidential election, state election, as well as the school-board races. I'm going to give that crowd opposing me something to think about. I've had to grant some concessions to the opposite party, but watch me slice into the vote there. You see, I have a lot of relatives on that side. My blood kin will never turn me down. Blood is thicker than politics in these parts. I plan for my board members, in three of the five precincts of this county, to win."

"What about your financial kitty?"

"It's getting sounder and sounder," John Bennington replied, and smiled. "People want this program to go on. Voluntary contributions, you know. And," he whispered, "one textbook company that we patronize hasn't forgotten us."

"Oh, John, no wonder," George said. "Those terrible books they've loaded on us! I suppose that's a way to sell them. But I'm so glad to have a new teacher."

"I'm so grateful Kensington High School hasn't fallen apart this year," he said as George rose to go, "That is why I believe Orman Caudill will be re-elected. Still, he'll have a fight. I wish you could encourage the teachers to do what they can on election day."

"That was a quick meeting," Grace said, when George got back to the car. "I expected you'd be gone for hours."

"We transacted all of our business in a hurry," George said. "Everyone in that office, superintendent included, should be forced to sit in one one of our teachers' meetings. The difference between the two places is that one is politics and the other is education."

Grace started the car.

"Do you know we have to close school on election day?"

"Yes, I've already heard that," Grace said. "Mr. Withrow told us he wasn't going to close Kensington Elementary."

"Yes, he will too," George said. "The die has been cast. We're really in for an election this year. Preparation for this election and vote-getting began the day the schools opened last September. Even before."

George worked in the office checking absentee lists, to keep track of the youths who had been gambling on the pinball machines. They were coming to school now, and most of them were improving their poor grades. The boys who had stolen books and sold them hadn't missed a day of school, and were now making far better grades. Slowly all of them were getting a feeling of belonging to the school—and, George hoped, a sense of right and wrong.

The pupils in Kensington High School were getting to know George better now, and they were beginning to trust him. Many of these pupils had never known the love of a parent. Even his spankings were becoming popular events, and pupils were actually beginning to do things just to be paddled so they could say they had had "The Gift of Gallion." George never wanted his pupils to fear him, and they didn't. Instead, his pupils were perhaps getting too close to him, were becoming too dependent on him. Most of their questions were ones their parents should have answered.

Pupils would ask him the most unusual things at the most unusual times.

"Mr. Gallion, do you believe there is a God?" a young girl asked him one day when she met him in the corridor. He didn't know her name. "My father says there is no God, but Mother says there is. This troubles me. If I don't have a God, I see no use of living."

"Then believe your mother and go on living," George told her.

A junior came to the office one day and asked to speak to George privately.

"Mr. Gallion, if some no-good boy should blackguard your sister, what would you do?"

"One did that once to my sister and I beat the hell out of him," George replied.

"That's all I wanted to know," the boy said.

The following day George noticed another junior with a pair of black eyes.

Pupils asked George if they should marry while they were young and in love, and, being against extremely young marriages, George advised them to wait awhile just to be sure. Often he asked them to wait six months or a year, assuming that the romance would probably not withstand the pressures of time. George knew that young people were searching and trying to find a way. They were, many of them, ambitious and prideful, and they wanted to do something that made them shine before their classmates, teachers, parents, and neighbors. He did his best to help them find that one little thing that could often change their whole lives.

The 1960 presidential election was mentioned less often by the voters in three districts of Greenwood County than that between "Little John," also known as "Our John," or "Honest John" Bennington, and Mrs. Irene Carpenter, a teacher and a high school classmate of George and Grace Gallion's. John Bennington had once been a member of her faculty in Kensington High School. There was much enmity between the two when he was a teacher and she was principal. And now fierce charges and countercharges were made in this last week before the election.

While the air was charged with this electric atmosphere. George thought this was a time to speak to the pupils. During all the spare time he had before election, he went from room to room, where he sat informally on the teacher's desk and talked.

"How many of you students believe it is right to sell a vote?" he asked them.

"I think, Mr. Gallion, anyone who would sell his vote ought to be disenfranchised!" Don Weston said.

"Don, you've got good moral values, honesty, and integrity," George said; "I agree with your answer."

"Mr. Gallion, what about the man who buys the vote?" Frank Fairman asked.

"One of you answer his question," George said to the class.

"He is just as guilty as the one who sells," Nora Wallings replied.

"Why?" George asked.

"Plain ignorant," Nora Wallings said.

"Why are they ignorant?" George asked.

"Lack of education," Bert Wilson said.

"Yes, education is needed," George said. "We talk about other ignorant areas of the world. Believe me, we've got some to wipe out at home. I've traveled in countries where youth are much better educated than our own. But there's something just as valuable as being educated that you have failed to mention. There are men and women who know right from wrong who cannot read or write. They won't sell their votes and they won't buy votes either."

Nora Wallings said, "That's moral training and character, I guess."

"How do we get that?"

"Some people seem to be endowed with it," she replied. "Then of course in our homes, our schools, churches, and our associates."

"Yes, so much character is acquired," George said. "So much of everybody else you contact, whether good or evil, rubs off on you. You either have to put up a defense against it or accept it. Often the weak will accept and the strong will rebel and sometimes conquer those who are trying to conquer them. We are always tempted to take the path of least resistance. Do not ask me why, unless it is a weakness in all of us. What would happen if we didn't have the honest, the strong, and the courageous? If we didn't have parents, teachers, friends, churches, homes, and schools?"

"We'd be barbarians," Don Zimmerman said. "We'd work on each other, too."

"We certainly would," George said. "What you are now has taken you thousands of years to come by, and you ought to profit from this. And what makes the difference between uncivilized and civilized people is education."

"Will there ever come a time when we don't buy and sell votes in elections, Mr. Gallion?" Don Weston said.

"When all people reach the stage you have reached in this one class," he replied. "There's not a pupil in this class who would buy or sell a vote. Can we get everybody to become like you are here? If we can, we'll have honest elections. Remember, each of you in here is something special for the future. You have gone to school and you can read and write and think for yourselves, so you're going to be leaders in this new area."

"They buy men's votes with whiskey, too, Mr. Gallion," Don Zimmerman said.

"Such people don't care for their country, who runs it, or what happens to it, do they?" George asked. Then he added, "You in this class are as free to ask me a question as you would feel free to ask your parents. I'll give you an honest answer if I can. I would give you the same answer as I would give my own daughter, for I want you to grow up and be real men and women in this world. You are needed now as never before at any time in the history of this country. It's up to you to save us. When you are old enough to vote, don't vote as a group. Think and even pray before you vote to cast your vote for the better candidate, whose interest isn't selfish but is for the welfare of our people, for honesty in public affairs and in our government. Vote for a man with vision and courage, if you can find one. Use your heads. Don't vote as Pa, Ma, Brother John, Sister Sue, your church, or your boss, or your labor union directs you, but use that head and brain and conscience that is directed by your own heart. If any one of you ever sell your vote for money, a job, or a bottle of whiskey, never tell anyone you once came to school to me."

"Oh, what a relief to have a day like this at home," Grace said. Hand in hand, she and George walked beside the Valley stream. George carried the picnic basket filled with sandwiches and Grace carried a thermos of hot tea. Janet ran after Birchfield, their cocker, who poked his nose in holes where he thought there might be a chipmunk, a lizard, or a mouse. The bright November winds sang up the Valley, over the little green meadows. These winds carried multicolored leaves like flocks of southbound birds. "To have Saturday and Sunday free," Grace spoke softly, her face lit up with joy. "This is like it used to be, George, before your illness. And it could be this way again!"

"Look, Grace," George said "There goes a squirrel! Birchfield is after the squirrel. And Janet is after Birchfield."

"Stop it, Birch! Stop it, Birchfield!" she shouted. "Leave the squirrel alone! You're a naughty boy!"

"Don't worry about the squirrel, Janet," George said. "Birchfield can't catch it. It's going home."

The squirrel ran up the side of a giant beech, one that stood in a grove where Byrnes Hollow joined the Valley. George and Grace stood laughing while Birchfield, a very disappointed cocker, stood with his forepaws on the tree, watching the squirrel disappear into a hole.

"Look at that lizard lying over there sunning on that log," George remarked. "Not many more days of sun for him. He'll soon have to hibernate."

"And there goes a butterfly!" Janet exclaimed. She took off after it with Birchfield at her heels. George walked down the creek bank first, then he turned to Grace.

"Here's a narrow place where we can leap the stream together," he told her. "One for the money, two for the show, three to make ready, and four to go!" Then they leaped over the stream together hand in hand. On the rocky bluff above where the stream flowed at the foot of the hill, they stopped below a patch of purple and white farewell-to-summers.

"These never bloom until frost," George remarked. "And they last until snow falls."

"How pretty," Grace sighed. "I want a bouquet of these."

"No, no," George teased. "If I gather these for you I won't get to hold your hand. You'll have both hands full."

They laughed.

"Mama, you and Daddy act like some of the kids in Greenwood Elementary," Janet said in her most grown-up voice. "You're schoolteachers, but you act like children."

"We're not teachers today," Grace told her.

"I can't be selfish with you today, Grace," George said. "I'll gather you a mixed bouquet of farewell-to-summers."

He put his basket down and climbed clumsily up the bank like a big groundhog. He plucked a small bouquet of white and purple farewell-to-summers. He scooted back down the steep bank to Grace and gave her the flowers.

Now they walked under the giant beeches where squirrels denned in the hollow tops. Here the thin, dull-silver and light-brown beech leaves slithered down from the iron tracery of branches, like slow drops of leaf-rain, to the ground. Bright November sunlight filtered through the holes amid the interwoven branches and remaining leaves and made pencil-sized lines, dots, and splashes of shifting light on multicolored carpeted ground.

"No worries, no problems today," Grace said happily. "We're free as the wind and the flying leaves!"

They walked alongside the smaller Byrnes Hollow stream, which was humming a monotonous lullaby, mocked by the autumn winds overhead among the leaves of the interlocking branches.

"Listen to this, won't you?" Grace sighed. "Those are not problem sounds. You need to hear these sounds more often, George!"

"Maybe," he said, smiling. "Maybe both of us do. Maybe we need to hear them together."

"Here's a good place," Grace said. They had come to an ancient log where a tree in the folds of forgotten time had fallen across this narrow valley. It was covered with a carpet of moss. She sat down on the log and George dropped down beside her. Janet sat at their feet. Grace put the stems of her flowers in a knothole on the log, which served as a vase. The moss covering the top of the log, green as paint, was a bright tablecloth. Grace poured tea in the cups while Birchfield stood before them looking up. Here they ate their sandwiches and fed Birchfield, who was always hungry.

"Oh," Grace said pointing. "There's a little holly tree. I want to dig it up and take it to the house and set it in the yard! I have a place for it."

"We'll do that," George told her.

"Mama, look above it," Janet exclaimed happily. "There's another holly bush."

"Then we'll take two home with us and set them in the yard," George said.

The autumn winds were blowing up and down the hollow, coaxing frost-ripened leaves from the beeches, oaks, and poplars—filling the air with multicolored swirling leaves. George sat close to Grace on the log and held her hand.

"Every day we have free, let's have a picnic," Grace said, her face beaming. "I'm so happy out here!"

"Thanksgiving will soon be here," George said. "And we have to have turkey. But this log, darling, won't be table enough for our turkey and everything else!"

"Oh, George," she laughed, "we'll have the turkey at home! There will be turkey too for the picnic basket."

Birchfield had stuffed himself on sandwiches. Grace put the cups back in the empty thermos bottle and George picked up the empty basket and got her bouquet from the hole in the log. They walked slowly up the slope to the two small holly bushes. George picked up a stick which he used as a tool to dig in the soft, rotted leaf-loam, and dug up the two young holly bushes with great care. Grace put them carefully inside the picnic basket. The free day with autumn splendor was coming to an end. The western wall of the Valley was obscuring the sun; tree shadows, in grotesque ghostly forms, were beginning to lengthen. Slowly George, Grace, and Janet walked back hand in hand while Birchfield ran ahead as if he might be trying to protect them from the harmless lizard, chipmunk, and mouse.

On Monday after school. the day before the elections, Ackwell Kent, George's brother-in-law, drove up, parked, got out of his car, and came up the walk.

"How does it look?" he asked, frightened.

"How does what look?" George asked. He had come out to take a few sticks of wood to lay a fire.

"The election for Honest John Bennington," he said.

"Oh, I couldn't tell you about that," George said without too much concern.

"Ain't you interested in your job?" he asked George.

"Sure, I'm interested in my work," George told him. "I'm more interested in my school than I am who's going to be the next Greenwood County School Superintendent. Who's going to be elected President?"

"I don't know about that race," he said. "I'm innerested in this school race. See, Honest John's wife is my first cousin, and boy, blood is thicker than water any old time. Thicker than politics, too. All I have to do to get my two daughters and my wife a school, any school, is go ask Honest John Bennington! George, I'm goin' to be in that Beechwood precinct before daylight in the morning. I'm goin' to dynamite the place, an' I got the tools to do it with! See here," he said, taking out a billfold too stiff to bend with five-dollar bills. "Votes will be higher than a cat's back tomorrow. I hear they're going thirty dollars now on the absentee votes, but we're going higher. We got the money and we got the half-pints."

"To use in a school election?"

"You guessed it."

"Where did you get all the money?" George asked.

"Our Honest John's got friends, buddy," he replied with confidence. "All us fellows had to do was contact. The family was only too glad to shell out the lettuce. Now don't pretend you don't know about this when you're a member of the family with one of the biggest jobs in the county system."

"I don't know about the money," George said. "No. No one has ever asked me to contribute."

"What?"

"No, no one has ever asked me," George repeated.

"Then it might be your hide next year."

"Let it be my hide. I'm not paying for my job. I don't believe in that."

"Quit feedin' me that malarky, George," Ackwell Kent said. "The good things in life ain't free. I wouldn't have all these hundreds if a lot of people didn't think the same way. I know the people around here. Got plenty to pay them for their time off from their farms and all. They'll make more outa voting than by selling corn at eighty-six cents a bushel, you can bet that. Well, I got to be goin'," he said, turning back down the walk. "Tomorrow is the day for all who cannot help pull the plow to hold onto the handles and help guide it through the rooty ground, like the man said."

George drove his truck over earth frozen harder than a man's fist. A white thin blanket of frost covered the colors and scars on the corrugated surface. Bodies of trees stood stiffly white like statues of imaginary ghosts. Three branches were white outstretched arms with their tip branches frozen like thin fingers spread stiffly apart but ready to bend to clutch their imaginary prey. What a beautiful, silent world, with birds and crows slicing the clean ice-cool atmosphere beneath the blue canopy of sky!

George drove up the Valley farm road, up the winding staple-curved road, until he reached Laurel Ridge. The rising sun was as large and round as a wagon wheel.

Maybe Grace was right, he thought as he watched white clouds ascending as the warmth of the sun melted the frost. Here was his own world, where he could forget the never-ending pressures of his school. George looked out over the gigantic folds of eternal hills that would outlast all living creatures.

Up here on Laurel Ridge where he'd not been since Kensington High School began, high-wind coolness flowed like water.

Colors had gone from most of the trees except where leaves still clung to the branches of the oaks; these the sun had soon dried, and they rustled mournfully in the rising morning winds. Colors had crept downward toward the valleys. The sumac, first to color, and the dogwood, not far behind, were barren here, but down under on the steep slopes they were holding on to some of their leaves. The ash below was yellow and blue and the elms were touched with rusty-russet leaves. Maples on the slopes were still ablaze with every shade of red and yellow. The leaves with their season's work almost accomplished hadn't given up their brief season's span in their last fling of glory. Their once green lush of spring and summer growth had become the lavish gold and potent wine of maturity achieved. Wasn't this the same true parallel of man's existence? Could the leaf in its maturity and last fling of glory give more to beautify the earth than man could do to keep it from falling apart? He could see each leaf left on the boughs doing its part in this whole beautiful spectacle, clinging tenaciously to give, in its last brief fling of existence, despite winds and storms, before it dropped onto earth to become a part of the whole again.

When he went back to the truck it was midday. The hard-fisted frozen earth had thawed to sloppiness. He headed down the muddy road. The trouble with people was, they were getting too far removed from the land of which even their very bodies were made. He was often struck by the fact that his rural pupils had stronger bodies, less confusion in their minds, and, for the most part, more ambition than those from the town. He stopped the truck and made a note. Since there were many vacant lots in Kensington, once the town was incorporated, couldn't the town buy these lots and make parks throughout the city, so the young in the city could still be close to nature?

Tuesday afternoon, just before the polls closed, Grace and George left their house to vote. When they reached Greenwood there wasn't parking space for all the cars. The courthouse yard was filled with people who were looking up expectantly at the loudspeaker system waiting for the announcement of votes from each precinct. The streets were lined with people and cars.

The square remained crowded all day and night, and even the morning after the election, when Grace, Taddie Sue, and George reached Greenwood there were still crowds on Main Street. Election was in doubt. School-bus drivers, elementary school custodians and their relatives, repairmen—everyone who had some job with the Greenwood County schools was there.

Honest John was a hero to many people. And he enjoyed it.

Grace had to drive with great care, for several of the people were tipsy this early in the morning, and staggered across the street heedless of the traffic. They were all on their way to the courthouse to get news on the loudspeaker, and they would be there, day after day, hour after hour, until the Greenwood County vote was counted—usually four days behind the rest of the country. They had always done this, even when tobacco was in case in their barns and it was time to prepare it for market or when corn stood ungathered in the fields. They let their farm work go, and if they had industrial jobs, they let that go, too, until the vote was in. Many were armed should trouble arise over the legality of a vote.

This was a way of life that only the younger generation could change. This was a county and a state where a dollar of state or county money seemed to have twice the value of the dollar earned from farms or industry. This was a state and a county where it was an honor for one to hold a state or county job, do as little work as possible, and get as much salary as possible. The salary one got was a measure of his height in society and his popularity.

George was handed his mail through the window. He stuffed it into his egg basket. When he turned to leave the post office he met Willie-Slim Arvin, who faced him with his broad smile and an outstretched hand. Little Willie-Slim stirred early in these busy vote-counting days.

Willie-Slim Arvin was the dogcatcher. He got only one hundred dollars a month and he was a respected man. He maintained a modest enough apartment in Greenwood, but he and his wife were close to the county and state political bigwigs. Willie-Slim's father was a small-time politician. His son had hardly enough education to write his name, and since he couldn't qualify for any kind of work except hard labor—which he refused to do—his father had got him the position of dogcatcher. Though the state had passed a law that dogs should be tagged, hundreds of unlicensed dogs lived in the streets. The aged hunting dogs that had outlived their usefulness, the unwanted canine females, the puppies no one wanted —many of them from other towns—were turned loose in Greenwood to find homes or go wild, sleep in the cliffs, run in packs, and attack cattle and sheep.

Willie-Slim was on his way to something higher. He was elegantly dressed, had a good grip of the hand, a ready smile, and a nice set of white teeth. He also knew the "right people."

"When I get to be governor, I'll do something for you," he would confide to the voters. The governorship was not out of his reach, either, and the people knew this. Why couldn't Willie-Slim Arvin be elected governor when qualified men, well-known educators with doctors' degrees, had been defeated for State Superintendent of Public Instruction by political hacks who could hardly read and write? One could rise in this state from dogcatcher to a position of great power. And people in Greenwood County knew that someday they might live to see Willie-Slim Arvin in the governor's mansion, and it behooved them now to treat him with deference.

"Morning, George," Willie-Slim said, pumping George's hand seven or eight times. "How's our Little Honest John coming along?" Willie-Slim belonged to a different party from John Bennington and George. He understood at once that the superintendent was getting his extra help "by tapping the other party" for votes. With the help of little Willie-Slim and a powerful faction of his party, Honest John would be elected.

"Well, it looks like he's going to be elected," George said.

"I'm for that man," he said; "he's come a long way. Man, I've walked these streets for him."

Willie-Slim's wife taught in the county system, but this wasn't all the sap that had been squeezed from the educational turnip. He knew his ex-classmate, Irene, who wasn't a glad handshaker, and who had the unfortunate political stripe against her of being a woman in this man's political county, had lost the election.

"You know, Uncle George." Taddie Sue said as Grace sped down the highway, "I'll never work in another election. I can't get over what happened yesterday."

"What happened?" George asked. He dropped an opened letter back into his basket.

"Plenty happened," she said. "Back in the Beechwood precinct where Uncle Ack worked, he bought votes like you'd buy cattle. I didn't know people were so helpless, so poor, and so ignorant. I didn't know there was a place in America like Beechwood. Talk about sending money to the underdeveloped parts of the world! Some of these high officials who advocate changing the world with American dollars had better visit Beechwood first. I've always thought you talked fancy and highfalutin to the students in Kensington about the old world falling apart and how they were entering a new world—until yesterday. Now I'm beginning to believe what you have been saying. If the world has more undeveloped and ignorant areas than where I worked yesterday, all I have to say is, God pity the world."

"No, you're wrong, Taddie Sue," George said. "Why should God pity the world? Why should God pity his children who live in corruption, become a part of it, and accept it? If God were among us He couldn't be elected to a political office in this county, and I doubt that He could beat our Little Honest John for Greenwood County School Superintendent. Not if the Greenwood County dogcatcher was against Him. And the mighty American dollar isn't the answer either."

"American dollars did it yesterday," she said. "Uncle Ack paid as high as sixty dollars for a vote!"

"That much?" George said. "What did they pay on the other side?"

"Uncle George, that's what makes it so sad," she sighed. "They went higher than Uncle Ack. But you know what a horse trader Uncle Ack is. Besides, he knows Beechwood better than anybody. So he said 'Go on and take the seventy-five dollars they offer you. They've got the money to throw at the birds. But remember, Minnie or Tom,' and he'd call the voter by his name—he knew all of them—'after you take his money, go inside that secret poll and vote the way you please. But please vote for your own Honest John Bennington. He's one of us. He comes from right over yonder hill. And when you come out of the polls come around and see me. Because I've got sixty dollars more here for you. It's better than raising corn and tobacco on these poor old hillsides. We don't want that cranky woman in there; besides, she holds her head high with pride except when it's raining.' Then, somebody asked why she didn't hold her head up when it was raining and Uncle Ack would say, 'Her nostrils catch rain and tickle her.' Then they'd all laugh and the voters would do just as Uncle Ack told them to. And then they'd go off and collect their sixty dollars. Uncle Ack had some money left after the election that he's going to turn back to the teachers and bus drivers and janitors who he thought contributed too much. You see, Uncle Ack underbid the other side and got their votes anyway. You wait and see who wins. Naturally, Mr. Bennington's board member—and I don't even know who he is—will win!"

"We're rotting at the core. We'll fall apart if the young people we're teaching now and those to come don't save us," George said. "No one had better ever tell me again how rotten the young generation is or use the word 'delinquent' again!"

"George. George," Grace said. "Your blood pressure!"

"No wonder I have high blood pressure," he shouted. "I love my country. I hate to see it go to hell. Why do you think I'm back teaching school? It's our only way out. I'd like to teach in some other part of the world, to see if it is as corrupt as it is here."

"You have to be practical, George," Grace said. "You have to wait for things to right themselves. It takes time. You can't change the world overnight. You can't even change this county!"

"I can change this county," he said. "Not one of those people selling their votes ever went to school to me. I'll tell you that. If I'd taught all the people in this county it would be different, and don't you tell me I'm egotistical, either. The young people we have now should be taught. And it's not old-fashioned to tell them to be honest, to live right and amount to something. I'm disgusted with some of the teachers we have too. Don't tell me a principal or a teacher can't change things. I know we can. We can clean this damned mess up and we ought to jail some of the corrupt parents. Their children would be better off without them!"

"Taddie Sue, why did you ever bring it up?" Grace said.

"Aunt Grace, he's right," she said. "I came home and couldn't sleep. I honestly cried. I can't get over it. What he's saying is the truth. You don't know our problems on the Hill. Honest, you don't, Aunt Grace. They'd got to the point where they even accepted stealing. It was the smart thing to do, if they could get away with it. Uncle George is changing that attitude by degrees. The Hill is changing. I pray Uncle George's health will hold up even for a year. Aunt Grace, he's fearless! He's teaching me to be too. Teachers have ideas and they're allowed to express them and no one is afraid—even to criticize Uncle George. Isn't that right, Uncle George?"

"Don't let's talk about what's been done. Let's talk about what there is to do. How much money, Taddie Sue, do you think was used in this school election?"

"I can't estimate it," she said. "If they spent in all three districts as they spent in the Beechwood District, there'd be thousands and thousands. How much do you think, Uncle George?"

"At least $30,000," he replied. "That would be $10,000 in each district. But there might have been $30,000 spent in the Kensington District alone. It's twice as large as the others, and people are plenty hard up, what with all the strikes and unemployment. It might even be as much as $100,000, and yet," he sighed, "we can find this much money to spend in an election but we teach over six hundred boys and girls in a building not safe for more than three hundred, our pupils have to eat in classrooms with trays on their laps. We got a $300 appropriation for the band, one of the best in the county, but none for books. We're beggars and we're hypocrites, because we have to be! What if the people who sent us books knew how money was spent on the election?

"We have the philosophers of sweet education advocating education for 'the few bright ones.' Heaven forbid," he was almost shouting. "What will become of a handful of these Sons of Light when the Sons of Darkness are left ignorant? Educate all or we perish."

"You can't change this county, this state, this country all by yourself," Grace said quietly.

"The hell I can't," he shouted angrily at Grace. "I've heard that too many times! If I could only speak to all the people, if they would listen . . . if I could be man enough for just one hour to face every man who walks, breathes, eats, and sleeps with his eyes open and just shake the hot water out of him once until he wakes up, you'd see!"

"You'll kill yourself trying to do the impossible," Grace said sadly.

"Mr. Gallion, there are two things you had in mind and forgot to do," Mrs. Markham said. "Do you remember what you said about money earned by classes and school organizations having to go into a central fund?"

"Yes, I remember."

"I thought maybe, since Mr. Riddle was dean of boys and took such an active hand in this school's management and since his viewpoints and yours so often clashed, you were not going to challenge him on his keeping a separate fund."

"Whether I want to challenge him or not, I'll have to. Why should he be exempted?"

"Not that I am telling you what to do, Mr. Gallion," she said, "but if Mr. Riddle's separate fund is to be put into the central fund it is time this was done. I've made out two monthly financial statements and will soon be ready to make out the third month's report on the central fund, but Mr. Riddle still keeps his money in his own fund."

Kensington High School's central fund included money from athletic games, cafeteria money, money from the freshmen, sophomore, junior, and senior classes, the various clubs of the school. Within this central fund, each organization's money was kept as a separate unit, money which could be spent only by that organization. But there was a large separate fund, of money earned on the Kensington High School's farm, which was kept by Gus Riddle. Heretofore, rumors had flown like sparks from heated steel over the community, of how money was being squandered in Kensington High School. A few of the teachers and the coaches were even accused of misappropriating funds.

Each check that went through the office had to be okayed by George Gallion. Mrs. Markham, who took pride in never making a mistake, watched over the school funds like an English pointer watching a quail.

"Of course, Mr. Gallion, I am not sure you want to go through with the second thing you wanted me to remind you about—to replace the worn-out tile on the main corridor?"

"I tried to get a promise about this before the election but couldn't get it. That's the time to get promises, and now the election is over and we won't get it done unless we pay for it ourselves."

"If you don't mind my advising you, Mr. Gallion, I'd say try to get them to do it. The five hundred dollars it would cost would mean so much to us right now to pay off our old debts. We're really getting the old debts paid, Mr. Gallion."

"But look at that corridor out there. And look at the floor! It's a disgrace and it's dangerous. The loose tiles lie like loose stones, and one of these days a happy, skipping girl is going to get her toe caught under a tile and get a spill and be maimed for life. Out of the million and a half budget they won't allow us five hundred dollars to repair the corridor, so we'll have to do it ourselves. And we'll do it, if I have to pay for it myself."

"What you have to say to me must be very important," Gus Riddle grumbled. They walked upon the stage together, where George switched on the light. "You know I have good boys in my classes, but still I hate to put a student in charge. You yourself have said a good teacher never leaves his post."

"It's important what I have to say, Mr. Riddle," George said. "It is most important, and I don't want anybody to hear us."

Beyond the heavy curtain that divided the stage from the gym, a teacher was conducting a class in each of the bleachers. A physical education class was in session in the gym itself.

"This place is not too private here," Gus fretted. "Listen out there!"

"But it's the most private place we have left. Suggest another place."

"All right, spit it out," he bellowed. "If you've got something to say to me, then say it!"

"Before I start you feel as if you're being accused of something drastic," George said.

"It is, or you wouldn't have asked me to come here."

"Mr. Riddle, you believe in cooperation, don't you?"

"Yes; what has this got to do with it?"

"If you were principal you'd ask for it, wouldn't you?"

"Yes, but tell me what you're driving at. I'm a grownup and

a teacher. You don't have to talk to me as if I were a student."

"I have to build up my case with you," George said. "You are an important man in this school. I like you personally, and this school needs you. You're one I've had to lean on heavily. You're the one who finds my mistakes. But in one thing you haven't cooperated. When I mentioned this to you before, you lost your temper."

"Oh, oh, I think I know," he said, his face turning color. "If that's what I'm here for I can tell you now: no soap."

"What do you mean: 'no soap'?"

"You want me to put my fund in the general fund."

"That's exactly right," George spoke positively. "Every organization has cooperated but you."

"Do you mean to intimate that I am dishonest?"

"Not at all."

"I've got the best-kept financial books in this school," he said. "They're better kept than Sadie Markham's. And I don't mind anybody in this school's seeing them."

"All you have said might be true," George said. "I'm not disputing your word. But why shouldn't you, dean of boys, who expect cooperation from others, be willing to cooperate? Somebody might think you're hiding something. Talk can get out in the community, you know."

"Why, what have you heard?"

"I've heard plenty, but I don't believe anything I've heard."

"You'd better check the athletic fund," he said. "You'd better check the old debts the coaches have made here."

"I know about the athletic debts that were made before I came here. The statement of what we owe comes into the office too often. We're using all the money we get from games to pay them off. I don't have to, Mr. Riddle, but I'll show you what we're doing."

"But, I don't owe anything. Everything I buy is paid for with cash."

"And you have a good backlog of $2,900, too, haven't you,

while other organizations are poor as blacksnakes resurrected
in the spring."

"Do you mean to intimate that I have to share with these
pauper organizations?"

"You don't understand the setup. When your money is put in
the central fund, it is still your money. That money cannot be
spent for anything, cannot be loaned to another organization,
without the approval of the organization that has made it."

"Yes, you know it will soon be time for us to sell our corn,"
he said. "You know more money will be added. Other organizations need money, and I have it. So they're after mine."

"That's not true, but I want to know what you have and
what you spend it for. I'm principal, and that's my duty."

"You listen to me, George Gallion," he snarled, leaning over
and facing George and pointing a trembling finger in his face.
"That building I teach in out there—funds we made here built
that. We bought everything in it. That shop Mr. Ossington
uses—we built it. He didn't do it. And it burns me up to feel
I'm not welcomed in that shop. We bought our tractor, our
truck, our farming tools. Now, what do you have to say to
that?"

"Very good, very good," George said. "But I didn't know
this until you told me. What could I tell some parent out in the
county who asked me what you did with all the money you
made from the Kensington High School farm? I have no
record. I don't know."

"You can tell him to go straight to hell as far as I'm concerned."

"But he has a right to know. Everything here should be in a
central fund, and we should keep the books open for any person
interested to have a look for himself."

"Well, I'm not going to do that. I never have, and I'm not
going to start now."

"Now is the time you're going to begin, Mr. Riddle," George
raised his voice. 'You don't own that land you're farming. You
get student help free. And you get the highest salary of any

teacher in this school. You build buildings, buy tractors, trucks, farm equipment. You're in a better position to make money with less expense than anybody else in this school. Why in the hell should you be treated as a special case? I want your financial books."

"I've never seen anyone like you!"

"I won't say that about you," George told him. "I'll say you're a good man—one of the best. One I'd hate to do without, but one I will do without if you don't cooperate with me. If you refuse, you and I will sit together and give this story to the *Dartmouth Times*. What will people think? Will they think I'm asking something unfair of you, when every organization in this school but yours cooperates? To be frank with you, Mr. Riddle, I've let time pass thinking you'd change your mind, but now there is so much talk I am forced to have a showdown. You, not I, will be the loser. Hand over your books in my office tomorrow."

George started toward the steps. Gus Riddle stood there with his arms folded, gazing into space.

"Sometimes I can respect you," he said thoughtfully. "Other times I can't."

"You can respect me when things go your way," George said. "When they don't go your way, you have doubts about me. Think this over, sleep on it tonight, be honest with yourself and see if I am wrong."

That afternoon, Gus Riddle took his agricultural class and went to the field to husk corn. The corn was husked by hand. Gus Riddle was a frugal man, too. A corn picker was expensive, and anyway, he believed, as he often told his pupils, there was no substitute for work, and the human hand was the greatest machine ever created.

George stood at the west corridor door and counted Gus Riddle and nineteen student farmers walking across the lane-loop, the athletic field, and into the forty-acre field of dry buff-colored stalks that were left out so the ears would dry. The group was soon hidden in the tall stalks, and George followed them. He had not had time before to see what these FFA youths and their teacher had grown on these fertile acres. After the morning conflict with Gus Riddle, he thought he might compliment him on his work and salve the ill feeling Gus obviously felt.

Once within the cornfield, George walked slowly to listen to the warm November winds sing lonesome songs among the dry fodder blades and tall stalks, bending with one, two, and sometimes three ears of corn. Young eager voices were audible above the music of the wind. He could hear the tearing husks, the snapping of the ears from the stalks, and the thuds of the husked ears hitting the ground. He could see cornstalks shaking below where the bottom slanted gently toward the Tiber River. In one place he thought first he was watching wind-blown furze over the field, but the grayish-white thinned above the buff-colored corn on the shimmering haze. There was only one row shaking in this area, and George thought one of the boys had left the others for the privilege of smoking. One puff after another was rising up now as George walked in this direction where one of the youths had strayed off to himself. Where was Gus Riddle that he wasn't watching this? George thought, as he came closer to the unsuspecting husker.

When George crossed another row of corn and looked up the balk between two rows he couldn't believe that the lone corn husker was Gus Riddle with a cigarette in his mouth. Would he walk up after what had taken place between them over the funds? Why not? If he were a student he would walk up. The rule applied to both student and teacher. George walked slowly toward Gus Riddle.

"Oh," Gus said, jumping back as if George were a poisonous snake he had almost stepped on. His mouth was open but the cigarette stuck to his lower lip. "Snooping, huh, and you've caught me." His voice trembled. He pulled the cigarette from his wind-dried lips, threw it on the ground, and stepped on it.

"No. I'm not snooping," George said. "I just came down

here to look at the corn. You've really got some fine corn. Much better than any I've seen."

"You came to see who was smoking."

"And I found you. None of your boys is smoking."

"How do you know they aren't?"

"The smoke rises up," George said. "I didn't see you, but I saw your smoke. I thought you might be one of the boys and so I came over this way."

"Looks like I've had a bad day," he said.

"Yes, you once told me I'd have enough to do to get Shan Hannigan for smoking," George reminded him. "I never dreamed of ever catching you."

"Well, you have; what's the verdict?"

"If I were to tell anyone that I caught you smoking in the cornfield, Gus, you, Gus Riddle, dean of boys in Kensington High School, do you think anyone would believe me? They'd think I had seen a mirage."

"So what?"

"Moral issues are involved," George said. "We can't be hypocrites and set up a rule for the pupils and let the teachers break the rules. If we let you smoke we're going to let everybody smoke."

"But I was down here by myself."

"That's no excuse."

"I didn't pay any attention to what I was doing," he said. "It's a force of habit."

"You were conscious enough to isolate yourself from your students. You didn't forget either."

"I've thought over what we talked about a while ago." He quickly changed the subject. "In fact, that was what I was thinking about when I automatically put that cigarette to my lips. I'll send my books over to the office in the morning."

"Mr. Riddle, let's consider all incidents closed," George said. "I'm willing to overlook what has happened here, but never let me catch you again."

Gus grinned and looked up at the shimmering, haze and extended his hand. George shook it. The two men smiled conspiratorially.

Gus Riddle brought his financial books in the next morning and gave them to Mrs. Markham. "Check these thoroughly," he said, grinning good-naturedly. "See how much money we've confiscated."

"What's come over Mr. Riddle?" Sadie Markham asked. I've never seen him so cooperative."

"He is wonderful at heart," George told her. "Make no mistake about that. He likes to argue and pretend once in a while."

"Just to get attention," she said.

"Yes, perhaps," George sighed. "I couldn't do without him. He tells me my faults and I have them. Every school in this county needs a man like him. He's everything but a 'yes man'; I really depend on him when the chips are down."

Now often on the short days in December when Grace, Taddie Sue, and George drove to Kensington High School they could see the first peep of the weak red ball of sun rise up over the white valley like a bloodshot eye, and the blue river, where lay the gentle murmur of silence. Now the undulating brown of the earth was gone and when the snows melted there was the dark disconsolate earth where sleeping, naked trees on the cliffs and the palisades were silhouetted against the lilac blue. When they returned from Kensington in the afterglow of an early winter sunset, they watched the violet evenings deepen into darkness before they reached home.

On the morning of the last day of school before the Christmas holidays, the road had been cleared by snowplows. When Grace drove down the slushy-frozen dark ribbon of highway, the morning sun winked gold and red in the morning sky. The stiff winter winds blew in from the valley and slapped at the frosted white car. Grace was the first to drive over the lane road except for Herb Hampton, who arrived at 4 A.M. to fire the one furnace which was providing heat for the entire school. The other furnace was out and beyond repair.

It was on one of these bleak December mornings when Gus Riddle reported a new incident of stealing.

"Something has happened to mar our holidays; I never heard of anything like it."

'What now?" George asked.

"A boy in this school broke into the jar where I kept the donations for the Korean Orphans," he said. "This is the worst place for stealing I've ever seen. And besides," he sighed, "it's bad when a boy who has plenty steals."

"When did it happen, and who did it?"

"Yesterday, but I didn't know about it until just before we went home," he said. "I know it was Sid Blake."

"Have you got proof?"

"One against one," he said. "But I'd take Minnie Purcell's word over his any time. You know her, I think. She is the daughter of Reverend Charles Purcell and one of the finest girls in this school. You know I've warned you about Sid Blake before. He's a hoodlum, Mr. Gallion. He hasn't any business in this school. Just think how many of the students in this school dropped pennies into that jar!"

Gus Riddle was always working for some cause. He had collected funds, groceries, and clothes, and had personally driven a truckload of these supplies 150 miles to a flooded area in the heart of Appalachia in the eastern part of the state.

"Did you know how much money was in the jar?" George asked him.

"I counted that money every day," he said. "Yesterday morning we had $27.43."

"How is it that you didn't know about it until school had turned out yesterday?" George asked. "Why didn't you tell me then?"

"I had the jar in my ag room," he said. "I had to rush over here to the main building just as my last class ended. I have

Minnie Purcell's brother Fred in that class, and she ran out there to see him about something and Sid Blake was in there stuffing the money out of the jar into his pocket. Sid grabbed Minnie by the hand, bent her arm back and said, 'If you tell this on me I'll break your damned neck.' When she got loose from him, she came running to the main building. By this time Sid had gone around the back of the building to the bus. He was already gone when I got out there. Minnie Purcell missed her bus. She was crying and in a terrible state of mind when I took her home."

"Yes, quite a mess," George said. "I'm surprised at Sid Blake."

"Why are you surprised?" Gus asked. "Haven't I warned you about him? He's of low character. He shouldn't be permitted to associate with decent youth."

"His mother, Ethel Carrington, was a classmate of mine," George said. "There was never a finer girl in this county."

"Come to think about it, he had a brother and two sisters who graduated from this school who were fine, respectable students," Gus admitted. "But this is not the point! It's not what they are but what he is. Anybody who would steal charity money should be out of this school."

"I'm glad to have the information," George said. "I'll go to work on this just as soon as the pupils get here. Don't publicize this any more than you can help, Mr. Riddle."

"I won't for one reason only," he said. "The boy has an artificial eye, and, you know how it is around here. We have a lot of boys in this school who might take it upon themselves to do something about this. They might try to work Sid over."

"You don't think Sid could be reformed?"

"Oh, Mr. Gallion, don't start that again," he sighed. "We've had enough of that 'saving the youth' stuff. As I've said so many times to you, this is a high school and not a reformatory!"

"But you believe in 'saving the war orphans of Korea,' "

George reminded him. "Just what is the difference between saving children over there and here? Anyway, I promise you to get to the bottom of this in a hurry."

"Sid, you know what you're in here for, don't you?"

"No, I don't," he said.

"Come on now, don't tell me that. Truth will make this easier for you."

"I don't know what you're talking about."

"Mrs. Markham, go to the door and tell Minnie Purcell to come in."

Sid Blake was a 190-pound, six-foot, seventeen-year-old sophomore. He was an awkward youth and had lower than average grades.

"Have you ever thought about playing football, Sid?" George asked him.

"Sure have, but Mom and Dad won't let me," he replied quickly. "I wanted to play baseball too, because it's my favorite game, but they won't let me do that either."

Minnie Purcell walked into the room.

"Minnie, did you see Sid take the Korean War Orphans' Fund from the jar?"

"Yes, sir, I did," she whispered.

"It's a lie," Sid shouted. "You didn't see me either."

"But I did, Mr. Gallion," she said. "He bent back my arm until it hurt and told me if I told on him he'd break my neck."

"What a lie!" Sid said.

"Sid, what were you doing out in the ag room?" George asked. "You don't take any courses out there."

"I went out there to see a guy."

"Who was the guy?"

"Bert Phillips."

"What for?"

"He owed me money."

"Did you get it?"

"No; he'd already gone to the bus."

"Why, didn't you have any money?"

"No, sir, not a cent in my pockets."

"You mean you went from the time you left school yesterday until now without any money in your pocket?"

"Yes sir."

"Then what were you doing at Sey Madden's place last night setting up soft drinks and sandwiches for your friends?" George asked him. "Where did you get the money you were spending there?"

Sid flushed.

"How do you know I was at Sey Madden's place?" he asked.

"I know what goes on there," George said. "Where did you get that money you were spending? I don't like a liar, and you are one! And you've been a thief. You know you aren't telling me the truth. You want this to go to court? This offense is a grave one. I could abandon school punishment and turn you over to the law! Minnie, you are excused to go back to your class."

"Yes, I took the money, Mr. Gallion." There was no remorse in his voice.

"Did you know if this gets out among the students some of them might get sore and take it on themselves to punish you?"

"Yes, but you know I got a glass eye, don't you?"

"That's no excuse for your stealing," George said. "That's not something for you to hide behind. Your having a physical handicap is all the more reason you should come to school, become a man of character. That glass eye won't keep you out of prison. And if you keep on stealing that's where you'll be. I don't think we can save you, no matter how hard we try. Now, you live up by the Tinton Post Office, don't you?"

"Yes, sir, but you're not going to tell Mom, are you?"

'Yes, I've made up my mind to try to save you from going behind the bars," George said.

"Spank me for it," he said.

"Spanking you for something like this would be too mild," George said. "You don't realize what you've done. You've stolen the bread right out of the mouths of children whose parents were killed in the Korean War—a country 22,000 American soldiers laid down their lives to defend. Sid, you are in a serious predicament. Those older professional bums you bought the drinks and sandwiches for last night don't think anything of you! Why do you run with such hoodlums? Not one of them is your age. Not one of them goes to high school. Do you want to be noticed by that kind of man? Just why did you do it?"

"I don't know."

"I'll find out."

"Go to all this trouble over me when you've got hundreds of good ones here?" he said. "I'm no good, I guess," he sobbed.

"Hundreds of others don't need me right now, but you do," George said. "And you can be of some good if you quit hiding behind that physical handicap."

"You're not going to spank me?"

'No, I'm not. But we do have to start working on your case. I do have to ask that you do something for me. First, I want you to go to the ag room and call Mr. Riddle outside and apologize to him. We know how much money you got, but you tell him the amount. Then I want you to apologize to Minnie Purcell. I'll be checking on you, Sid. I'm not too busy to go into the details of your problem. Then you must go to the library and see Miss Taddie Sue Gallion. Tell her you want a history of South Korea. You read of the struggle that country has had for its independence. I want you to copy that in longhand for me. You're excused now to return to your classes."

In the sixth period the whole school crowded into the gymnasium for a Christmas party. There was a huge tree which reached from the gym floor to the iron beams across the top of the gym, which had been decorated by the senior girls. Under the tree presents were piled—each of the students had drawn by lot the name of another student to whom he was to give a present. In this way, all the students received gifts. The teachers got presents, too. George received a dozen inexpensive presents—a pair of socks, a bag of candy, a pencil that had cost a nickel, handkerchiefs. Many of these were from students he had disciplined in his office. One was a little paddle which he held up before the audience. There was a roar of laughter.

"My little Henry said to me, 'This present I'm giving you is not an old handkerchief, Mrs. Gallion. It's something nicer than that,' " Grace said. "Bless that little boy's heart. It wasn't a handkerchief, either. He got me a little fruit plaque, made of plaster of paris. It must have cost a dollar! He didn't have that kind of money to spend on me. He's from such a poor family!"

As Grace chattered, George saw Sid Blake getting off the school bus ahead of them.

"Grace, I want you to pull off the road up here at the Tinton post office," George said. "Keep the motor going and keep the car warm. I might be gone a few minutes."

"But this is Christmas," Grace said. "Forget your school problems now."

"I can't; this is a new problem and I've got to work on it right now."

Grace parked in front of the little post office and George got out.

"George Gallion," Ethel said, getting up from her sewing machine. "Fancy you here!" She shook his hand warmly. "I've been wondering when you were going to stop and say hello to one of your old classmates."

"Ethel, I've a big family down there and it takes all the time I have, and more."

"I've heard the school is changing. I know something had to be done. I told Bill you would be able to handle the school last August when we heard you were taking over. How's Sid getting along?"

"That's why I've stopped, Ethel."

"Don't tell me he's into something again." Her smile faded. "I've prayed he'd get along all right this year. What has he done now?"

"He took the Korean War Orphans' Fund our school had collected to send to Korea."

She turned pale and George thought she was going to faint. She dropped her work-worn hands on her lap. Life had dealt harsh blows to this once beautiful young woman.

"Oh my, what is the answer, George? Can you tell me? What's happened to this generation?"

"The parents have had too much money for themselves and for their children," George said. "They go around mooning, 'We don't want our children to work like we have.' Have you ever said that?"

"Yes, I have," she admitted.

"Would Sid walk five miles to high school through all kinds of weather?"

"No, he'd never get there. He hasn't any ambition. My other three did fairly well, but not one of them made near the grades I made in school. I took harder courses than they did, walked ten miles a day, and had chores to do at the farm too. But tell me, how serious is this?"

"It's stealing, Ethel," George said. "You know what stealing is here."

"To think that I have a son who would steal."

"Tell me, Ethel, why is he this way?" George asked. "Your son is a product of two good families. There are teachers, doctors, ministers, and nurses among Sid's people on both sides. I don't know of any who have ever been in court. Never knew of one on either side for three generations. Your son Sid is intelligent enough, if he would only apply himself."

"I don't know what's wrong."

"Why does he run with these older hoodlums?"

"George, how well do you know my husband, Bill?"

"Not very well," George said. "I know all of his people better than I know him."

"He used to be a fine man," she said. "But something

happened to him. He got to drinking. He went from bad to worse, and those men you call hoodlums are worse than that. They're the bums who used to take Bill's money when he was helplessly drunk. Sid met up with them through his father. He won't associate with boys his own age. These men have ruined my son!"

"What about Bill?" George asked. "Has he reformed?"

"Yes, by the help of God and Alcoholics Anonymous," she replied. "But now his hands are crippled with arthritis. If Sid wanted to, he could push Bill all over the place. Sid knows he can, too."

"But he wouldn't do that, would he, Ethel?"

"Yes, we think he would. We never punished him like we did the other children, since he's the youngest and you know he's got only one eye."

"Yes, I know he has an artificial eye," George said. "He hides behind it. You know, Ethel, I've a physical handicap, too, but no one should ever hide behind one. I told Sid that since he has a physical handicap he should be more ambitious than ever to prepare himself so he can make a living in the future. And, Ethel, the majority of our pupils who have enough heart in them to give a few pennies to those unfortunate children overseas might forget Sid has an artificial eye, if they find out what he has done."

"Oh, George, it's the sins of the fathers." Tears welled up in her eyes. "This is what it all goes back to, and now Bill can't handle Sid. What can I do? Are you going to expel him?"

"If I should expel your son from school he'd be very happy," George said. "That's what he wants. What would he do if I'd expel him?"

"I know he wouldn't stay home."

"Of course he wouldn't. He'd spend his days and nights in Kensington loafing with his crowd."

She wiped her eyes with her handkerchief. "If he doesn't change I don't know what will happen. Can't you help me, George?" she pleaded. "You are a classmate and a friend."

"His associates in Kensington High School could lift him

up. But the point raised here is how many of the youth in our school will your son corrupt? The fact is, I don't think many, since he doesn't associate with boys his own age. He likes older people. There's no point in expelling him. We do use the board in Kensington High School, but not on a problem that goes as deep as this one."

"I keep this post office, which brings me a small salary, but I have to stay in the building, so I'm not home enough, I suppose."

"How much spending money do you give him a week?"

"Most of the time ten dollars a week, and never under five dollars."

"Why don't you let him work for his money?" George said. "You have to work for it, don't you?"

"Yes, but he's our youngest and has had this handicap since he was six years old, so I have to help him more than the others," she said.

"Parents make a mistake trying to buy their children, Ethel," George told her. "You can't buy them with money. The good ones are those who work for their money. I'd say a hundred students in Kensington High School do odd jobs and make their own money; not one of these is ever up for stealing. They just don't do it. They have learned the best way to get money is to work for it. And they know the value of money and don't spend it foolishly. You're giving your money to the hoodlums in Kensington. Let them work for their money instead of taking it from your son. After he took the money from the jar, he set them up at Sey Madden's last evening."

"How much money did he get, George?"

"There was $27.43 in the jar the day before he took the money."

"I want to replace that money," she said. "And I'd like to make a contribution to the fund."

"That is a nice gesture, Ethel," George said. "Your contribution to the fund will please Mr. Riddle very much. I suggest that when you offer to replace his money you have Sid along with you and that you do it when no students are around. They might not respect the handicap he's hiding behind. A few others are handicapped down there, but they don't hide behind it. There's a girl who had polio who climbs the steps on crutches. She plans to go to college. She's much worse off than your son and she has only a mother, because her father is dead. While you're down there I'd like to take you around and let you visit the classes—and something else, Ethel. Sid knew I was going to stop to see you so he got off the bus down the road and started walking up. He won't get here as long as he sees our car parked out front. I also suggest that you visit Reverend Charles Purcell and take Sid with you. His daughter Minnie was the one who caught Sid in the act of taking the money. He twisted her arm and told her he would break her neck if she told on him. I think you should go with him there and see that he apologizes to Minnie Purcell."

"Won't you keep him in school, George, and give him another chance?"

"Yes, I promise you that. This visit with you has given me more understanding."

"Do you think this will solve the problem?" she asked. Her tired blue eyes were dry now, but ringed with wrinkles. "Do you think Sid will behave?"

"I don't know," George said. "I'm not sure. He's done several minor things before. But this is the most serious. When a seventeen-year-old robs a poorbox . . . Well, you know, Ethel . . . say, for instance, one of us in our class had done this in Greenwood High School!"

"Oh, George," she sighed, looking down at the bits of cloth and pieces of thread that littered the floor beneath her sewing machine. "I know, I know. And thank you, George."

"It's up again," Dr. Vinn said. "Let me see the other arm."
"I've told you, George," Grace said. "I've warned you."
Then there was silence, for George didn't answer Grace.
"It's the same in this arm," he said; "200 over 100. It's too

high, George! Remember, George, you've got a crippled heart!"

"But a most valiant heart," George said, smiling. "I can still trust it to carry me through. I talk to it and pet it."

Dr. Vinn stood back and looked at George. "If I didn't know you as well as I do, I'd say maybe you need a psychiatrist."

"I think he does," Grace said.

"Are you still taking those little white pills I gave you?"

"Not recently," George replied. "It slowed me down until I couldn't think."

"Now when you go back home take one morning and night for a couple of days. I think they will put you back to normal. You won't be teaching now for a couple of weeks. You'll have a good rest. Fool around on your farm. Visit your cattle barn. Throw hay down to the cattle. Forget teaching. Get a change in your work. You'll have fewer problems with cattle than you have with the young. I've been reading the papers when I have time," he sighed, lifting his hand high and gesturing, "and I've never seen so much stealing and trouble as they are having around here. Where has the honor of our people gone? Down the drain? Who's to blame for all this?"

"Dr. Vinn, if I tell you our parents, our churches, corruption in our law and too much money are to blame, would you believe me?" George asked him while he put his shirt and tie on. "Maybe the whole world is corrupt, but these youth you mention are all we have to save us if some of us will only save them. And, so help me, save them from their parents!"

"You might have something."

"Come on, George; others are waiting to come in," Grace said.

"She teaches the little and the innocent, Dr. Vinn," George said. "Their little innocent world is most refreshing because it's not contaminated. I know youth, and I know it's our old world that's contaminating them. They're entering their own new world and they have to be prepared!"

"Now, you see about George's blood pressure, don't you?" Grace said.

"I know, but I'll work carefully with him," Dr. Vinn said. "I'm on his side, Grace," he sighed, lifting his big surgeon's hands. "I save their bodies and we need men to save their minds. He's right, Grace."

"Sure, I'm right," George said. "I know I'm right or I wouldn't be doing what I'm doing."

"Dr. Vinn," the nurse interrupted, "the waiting room is full."

The snow came down Sunday mornng like white grains of sawdust. By afternoon there were sixteen inches of snow, the greatest fall in years, covering the scars of the drab world. If only something like this could hide the scars in the minds and hearts of youth, George thought. If only the old world we parents could give them could be this clean, so they could get a fresh start! He waded through snow to the tractor shed, where he put a blade on the tractor and began to open the road to the cattle barn.

He didn't need the white pills now when he was doing this peaceful work which soothed his nerves. The snow still came down thick and fast and he had to use his tractor light to go through the storm. He broke a path to the cattle barn. Then he cut a swath to Old Charlie's cabin where the woodsmoke curled up from his stove to integrate and disappear in the fluffy flakes falling from dark skies that rubbed the upheaved belly of the earth.

Old Charlie, who took care of the farm, came out onto the porch.

George asked him, "How about feed? We got plenty?"

"Shore have."

"What about the cattle?"

"Brought 'em down from the hills and put 'em in the barn. Brought the horses too and put 'em in the old barn."

"Have you got plenty of wood to last you through this spell?" George asked him.

"Sure have," he replied. "Got wood and groceries. I'm lucky."

Then George turned his tractor and, following the way he had come, he broadened the road through the snow. He drove back past his home, opening the lane road down to the Valley Road. Then he opened two miles of the Valley Road over to the highway. He fastened a towline to a small truck and pulled it up the bank. On his way back home, he broadened the road with another furrow from the tractor blade. When he got home the storm had subsided and there were a few dim stars and a large moon in a sky that was as satiny and velvety blue as hollyhocks' petals in spring.

George, Grace, and Janet had a white Christmas. Before the blazing firelight, Grace sat at the organ, and George and Janet sang Christmas carols. The Christmas spirit in the Gallion home rose almost as high as the school spirit was rising in Kensington High School. The storm winds, the high snows could not crash their citadel in the Valley, a place of warmth and love where they could be together after the trials of the day.

The storms that had blown up in Kensington High School had less chance now of crashing the walls of the school than they had in September. Unlike George's own home and the homes of many of his pupils, there were homes in the Kensington area where youth escaped the storm crashes in high school during the day only to face them in their own homes when they returned from school. Unfortunately for them, Kensington High School, not up to the teaching and disciplinary level of many schools, was still the only home many of the pupils had. And these students who had begun to love the warmth and friendliness of this school would fight along with their teachers against anything that threatened it.

On Saturday before New Year's, George went back to Dr. Vinn for a checkup. His blood pressure was the same as it had been when he was a young man, and his prothrombin and cholesterol were normal too.

The pupils' attitude after the holidays pleased George. The whole atmosphere was electric with friendliness. Gus Riddle wore his biggest smile of the school year. Alice Nottingham's home room filled up with eager pupils long before the first bell rang. Pupils from the algebra classes followed Ralph Sizemore, the new teacher, as if he were their coach.

Sid Blake passed along in the current of Kensington youth that swirled between the clean corridor walls. Sid's face was as white as dough and he looked like a walking mannikin in long white, tight-fitting beltless jeans that hung low over his swivel hips. He turned his head to keep from looking at George. Les Bowdin passed with books under one arm and a handful of rocks.

"Mr. Gallion, I've found some new species," he said, opening his hand to show George. "Had a wonderful holiday. Hope you did." George went into his office.

Mrs. Blake was waiting for him there.

"How about our walking around and looking the school over?" George suggested. "As we walk we can talk."

As soon as they were out in the corridor, George asked, "Have you seen Mr. Riddle yet?"

"Yes, and honest, George," she said, "he was as nice as could be. I returned the thirty dollars and then I gave him a five-dollar donation for the cause. I thought he was going to hug me he was so pleased. Friday night after you visited me, I took Sid straight to the Purcells. We had a couple of hours' visit with those fine people, and when we left we were friends."

"Getting together can iron out problems," George said. "Ethel, I think if this had been done ages ago there wouldn't have been the disrespect for human life, wars, the mass murder of peoples in this world. Wouldn't it be hard to take a life of someone you'd sat down with at a table?"

"I can't imagine anything more horrible," she replied. "But why bring that up?"

"We bring this sort of thing into our teaching here," he said. "Ninety percent of the pupils you see here will travel in other parts of the world. The young today will be world citizens as well as Americans. They'd better get some understanding here before they get out into a new world, a world you and I could never even dream of."

Ethel Blake went with George out past the Ag building toward the pre-fabs.

"I'm so pleased this is working so well," she said thoughtfully.

"Yes, I hated to see you have to replace that money," George said. "I know how you came by it."

"I don't mind how hard I had to work for the money if it will help my son."

"I'm afraid this is not the answer, though, Ethel," George explained. They had stopped in front of the first pre-fab. "Your son has to change from within, and the minor little punishment I prescribed, well, that's not the answer. Sid should have to work with his own hands and pay that money back, Ethel. Why shouldn't he? He's big and strong. Earning money will teach him something of its value."

"But, George, what if something should happen to his other eye?"

"He'll come nearer to losing his other eye out loafing than he will by working." George snapped. "You hide your son behind a physical handicap. One of the best men we ever had on Greenwood High School football team was Frank Shelton, who had one eye out and was nearsighted in the other. Played four years of football. Now he's a minister. Not only your husband, but you are a lot to blame for your son's troubles, Ethel. Give your son some responsibility. Nothing wrong with him that can't be corrected if you'll cooperate."

They went through the pre-fabs where George introduced Sid Blake's mother. Many of the pupils who disliked Sid stared in disbelief at the sweet-faced, dignified Ethel Blake.

"This is a large school and I don't envy you your job," she said. "You've certainly helped me."

"No, not you, Ethel, and I'm afraid we haven't helped your son in the right way. We've just saved him for the time being. Let him earn his own money and you stop hiding him behind his handicap. Let him go out for baseball this spring. He wants to be a catcher. A mask will protect his eye. Let him go out for football, too."

"Oh, no, George, I disagree with you."

"Well, he's your son; I'm just giving you some free advice."

"George, thank you again," she said. "I'll think about all this. I know you're busy now, and I must be going."

When Ethel Blake got in her old car and drove over the Hill George walked slowly to his office. He thought of the striking contrast between the two boys, Sid Blake and Les Bowdin. Les Bowdin was perhaps the most enterprising and mature boy in the school. George had met Les' father once, a short, stocky, tobacco-chewing farmer who had driven to the school in a truck that would hardly hold together. "I can't help my boy Les much as I'd like," he told George. "You know it's hard for me to do without him when he's in school. Les is a good farmhand. See, the old lady and me, we've got ten others besides Les and we just can't make that thirty-three-acre hill farm go. We can't make a thousand a year to save our lives. So, like I tole the old lady, our young-uns would have to do a lot of scratchin' on their own."

When Les Bowdin plowed his father's hilly acres, he used to stop to pick up stones. He found a geology book in the school library and he learned to identify them. He started a collection. He won prizes for his collection, and had lectured to the Greenwood Woman's Club on his hobby. When he went to work in the fields in summer, he carried a football which he would snap back to his brother. He wanted to be center on the football team, and though he wasn't a natural athlete, he made the football team. He had volunteered to be a student teacher to sharpen his own knowledge by reviewing what he'd been taught, and he added new knowledge of teaching experience.

English composition was his weakest subject, but when George selected him to be sports editor and publicist for the school, he had improved his writing by the practice, and he was paid, too. Despite all his outside work, he stood first in a class of eighty-five pupils. Ethel Carrington had been like Les Bowdin when she went to school, too. By mental and physical inheritance, Sid Blake should have been like Les Bowdin! Yet poor but wise parents made the difference. Les had to assume responsibility at an early age. Les Bowdin was like a hungry chicken who scratched for food for himself, while Sid had grown fat by sitting on the nest while his mother did the scratching for him.

More snow fell and the thermometer dropped to two degrees above. All the following week, buses were late. The inclement weather was at its worst, stark and forbidding. George, Grace, and Taddie Sue left home when the stars were still shining, and when they got home the stars were out again. The little pond where George had stopped so often to fill Grace's jug with scummy water had frozen over, and the ice was scarred by the many skates that rang in the winter moonlight.

After the home basketball games were played in the Kensington gymnasium, a hi-fi was moved in, and the teen-agers played records. George had suggested they hold these dances. He and Grace attended often and danced the slow ones. Even Mrs. Nottingham came often with her husband.

There were a few of the teachers who were against dancing. Karl Hegioland, who had never attended one of the hops, said to George one day, "I am surprised you permit dancing, Mr. Gallion. I think dancing is the work of the Devil, and will send our young people to hell and damnation."

"I don't think so," George told him. "I think poor teaching and wearing dirty clothes and never taking a bath will come nearer to sending a man to hell than anything I know."

It was on a Monday morning after one of these dances that George found Orman Caudill waiting for him, pacing the floor with his hands behind his back.

"Good morning, Mr. Caudill," George said. "You act like a worried man. Remember, worry isn't good for the old ticker."

"Yes, I know," he muttered. "I know. It's something I hate to bring up, but it was brought up in my church in a sermon Sunday morning."

"I know what it is," George said. "Sit down and take it easy. Let's do some talking."

Orman dropped his two hundred twenty-five pounds onto a very weak chair which cracked ominously under his weight.

"You've done a great job here, and perhaps you saved my skin in the board members' race," he began, "and . . ."

"No, I didn't save your skin in the board members' race," George said. "I might have helped you by working to make this a respectable school again, but money saved you in this last board race. Go ahead, I just wanted to correct you on this point."

"Well, you've paid bills here this school owed from last year. And you've just about policed the streets in Kensington looking for absentee pupils who lose us money when they don't attend! But this is something that's a mark against the school. It's these dances after the games."

Sadie Markham stopped in her tracks and looked puzzled. Then she began to smile.

"Mr. Caudill, what have you got against dancing?"

"This bodily contact among young people leads to something else," he replied. "It is of a sinful nature."

"I've danced all my life, Mr. Caudill," George replied. "As sinful as I am, I'm principal of Kensington High School and when I was superintendent of the Greenwood County schools I was always tipped off where there was going to be a barn dance, and believe me, I was there if possible, and I rode horseback in those days. The Devil hasn't got me yet."

"When cold Death holds you with his clammy fingers don't

be too sure," he said. "You've not passed through the Gate yet."

"I've been awfully close," George said. "And I have no fears."

"I certainly would if I had dancing in my feet," he said. "I will not let my daughter stay after a game and attend one of these hops. I'm thinking in my mind whether I should let her attend any more games."

"We don't have a hop after every game. We'd lose too much sleep. But that's the only reason we don't. See, Mr. Caudill, we believe a teacher or the principal hasn't any right to do anything in this schoolhouse that he won't let his pupils do. We eat the same food, and we don't smoke because the students aren't allowed to. Quite a number of teachers dance here, and we dance with the students. They're well supervised. They dance so fast there's little bodily contact, anyway. Why don't you come to a hop and bring the other board members, the superintendent, and even your minister. See what's going on here."

"Not me. I wouldn't be caught in this house when dancing is going on here. I tell you it's evil and will send our children to hell as sure as I'm in this office!"

"I'm not going to argue with you."

"No need to argue," he interrupted. "I've been requested to come up here and tell you to put a stop to this dancing."

"By the authority of the Greenwood County board of education?" George asked. "Have they taken any action?"

"No, they haven't, but Mr. Mannigan, our board member in the East County District, has put a stop to the dancing at East County High School. This is the only county school where dancing is carried on!"

"We're going to dance until Greenwood County board of education takes action," George said. "I want to be at the board meeting too when this is brought up."

"Can you give one reason why you let these students dance?" He looked at George coldly. "Just tell me one reason!"

"When I was here before we did all our physical education by folk dances," George said. "We had the gym filled with more people than ever came to a basketball game. If we had a gym large enough now, I would do the same thing, but our gym isn't half large enough, and besides, we have to use it for classrooms, cafeteria, assembly hall, and just about everything else. You should get us a gym instead of trying to stop us from dancing."

"I agree we need a gym," Sadie Markham interrupted.

"You stay out of this, young lady," Mr. Caudill said. "I'm talking to the principal now."

"But she's a taxpayer and has a voice," George said. "She has the right to speak."

"Maybe I spoke too hastily. I'm sorry. But this dancing has me worried. People are coming and putting the pressure on me to do something about this."

"Any of those people vote for you?" George asked.

"Yes, they're my constituents. I have to listen."

"Now a lot of those people took money for voting for you," George said. "All of us here on the Hill think about the most sinful thing a person can do is sell his vote. Not dancing but vote-selling is a mortal sin to us. So, I guess it all boils down to a definition of what sin is."

"I see I can't talk to you," Orman said irritably. He got up from his chair with his overcoat still on and his black umbrella hat in his hand. "I'll just put this before the board of education. I'll let them decide. But don't say I haven't warned you!"

"But don't go now," George said, standing up beside him. "There are some things I want to say to you. I hate to tell you, but I'm going to. You say your daughter doesn't dance. I know she does dance."

"Why? Where did she dance?" he asked. "How do you know? Where did you see her?"

"She's one of the best rock-and-rollers I've seen on the floor," George said. "Unfortunately, you won't let her come here where our hops are supervised by teachers. You asked me where I saw her and how. My wife and I were driving down State 1 one night and stopped for a sandwich and a cup of coffee at Bellman's Drive Inn. That's about thirty miles from here. And who did we see doing rock and roll to jukebox music? A group of my students who were not allowed to attend the hops here, and your daughter was among them. I suppose there were twenty students from this school there."

"I can't believe it," he said sadly.

"I believe it because I saw her," George said.

"Then she learned to dance here," he said.

"We don't dance here during school hours," George said. "She doesn't come to our hops. How could she learn here?"

"She got the idea here," he said.

"No girl could have learned to dance as expertly as your daughter in the short time we've had hops here. We began them last autumn after the football games. And you didn't say anything then, and I know why. You needed me then. The election was coming up. Mr. Caudill, you still need me. And I advise you to let your daughter attend one of our hops, since she's hiding out in unsupervised places. You don't know youth of today and your definition of sin isn't correct, and when you and I pass through the Gate, as we surely will soon—you've had three heart attacks and I've had four—I'll look you up in your reserved segregated plot of eternity! I'll come to you on dancing feet. Do you suppose I'll get in?"

"I don't like your humor," he said. "You haven't said anything about these pupils who won't salute the flag!"

"I don't worry about their not saluting the flag as much as I worry about your segregated righteous group! When those who come to this school won't salute the flag, I know after they get through the courses of American history under Coach Webber, they won't hesitate to salute the flag. They'll live and learn. And I don't say anything to those who don't believe in blood transfusions. When they get through taking health courses and biology courses in this school they'll believe in blood transfusions. Education is the only answer to these things."

"As a parting thought, I just wonder what will come out of this school," Orman said. He put his big hat on.

"Plenty will come out of here. Young people are beginning their preparations for a new world."

"The old world still suits me."

"You're satisfied with what is," George told him. "Your world has crumbled into dust but you don't know it."

The two walked to the door. "I can't get over my daughter," Orman sighed, puzzled. "That troubles me."

"Don't let it trouble you," George said. "Dancing is not sinful, and your daughter is a good student and a lovely girl. But don't drive her away. Let her dance before you."

"Youth of today!" he sighed.

"*They* don't puzzle me. Too many of their parents puzzle me. If we teachers can save them now from the corrupt world they have inherited from parents who don't know right from wrong, our youth will be all right. I have faith in them."

"Mr. Gallion, will you stop talking long enough for me to tell you something now?" Orman Caudill said, holding the front door partly open. "I hadn't planned to tell you this. You came to us a popular man. Everybody was for you when you came here in September. Now you're not a popular man. You know a lot of people down in Kensington are calling you a Hitler and calling some of the teachers little storm troopers."

"If we had come here and had just accepted things as they were heading—and that is straight for hell—then I suppose we'd have been called nothing at all."

Orman Caudill slowly pulled the door wider so he could get his thick body through.

"Maybe you'll think about this after I am gone," he said. "There are rumors in Kensington that your house will be burned, and everything in it."

George was dumbfounded.

"I didn't think you'd believe me, but it's true."

"Well, some of them do hate me, don't they?"

"Yes, they do. A lot of us are losing respect for you and your dancing teachers."

"Yes, even you," George told him. "The same people who would burn my house when I try to help their children don't believe it is wrong to buy and sell votes or to permit people to run gambling dens before their children. Even those same parents can't turn their children against their teachers and me."

"Since you're in such deep water already with other problems, I might not report this dancing until some later date."

"I have no intentions of resigning, Mr. Caudill. You're chairman of the Greenwood County board of education. You can tell the board members and the superintendent that I am staying."

"Charlie, I'll want you to feed the cattle early and work close to my house until we get in from school," George said. "First I want you to cut the wood and cord it near the toolshed."

"But you got more wood cut than you'll burn."

"Yes, but cut this wood and stack it. Then I'll want you to cut the worthless bushes on the hill above the house with a hoe so we can set twelve thousand young pine seedlings there."

"But I've already cut the field off back of the Gap for that," he said. "Are you going to get more trees?"

"No, it's too late to order more."

"I don't get it. It's too late to begin this now."

"Not too late. Now, I want you to feed very early and be down home at about the time we leave. I'll want you to be there when we get home, too."

"Why are you changing plans?"

"Charlie, can you keep a secret?"

"You know I can, George. What is it?"

"People are threatening to burn my house."

"Who in the world would want to do that?"

"I don't know why or who they are, Charlie. I want you to work around here where you can watch the house. When anybody drives up or walks up here and stops, you quit work and go see what he wants."

"I expect I'd better bring my shotgun!"

"No, you won't need the gun. You just be alert and watch."

"I sure will," he said.

"Treat people right, for most of the people who come here when we're gone will be our friends."

"I will, George," he promised. "But if anybody looks or acts funny I'll keep my eyes on him like a sparrowhawk keeps his eyes on a bird."

"All right, you start in the morning. Cut the wood first."

"You'll hear me chopping in the morning when you leave. Listen for my ax."

When Grace, Taddie Sue, and George left the house, George heard Old Charlie's ax up at the woodshed.

"Why are you having that wood cut up there?" Grace asked. "We've got more wood now than we'll get to burn in the fireplace."

"I'm having him work close to the house."

"Why are you doing that? Is something wrong?"

"Yes, I've heard rumors somebody in Kensington is going to burn our house."

"What?" She brought the car to a stop. "You mean that?"

"I think it's only a rumor but I'm not taking any chances," George said. "Drive on. I shouldn't have told you."

"Yes, you should have," she said. She started the car again. "I knew no good could come out of your taking that school. I've said it all the time."

"No good for us but a lot of good for them," George said.

"Uncle George, I think it's one of those wild rumors they start down there," Taddie Sue said. "More rumors can start there than any place I've been."

"When I hear a rumor I don't like to take a chance. When I

hear a rumor on a student I trace it down to see if there's any truth to it. I can't track this one down but I do have an idea where and how it started."

"Somebody must be awfully mad at us, George."

"Yes, somebody is. You ruin a big pinball machine racket and the owner is liable to get mad and brag about what he's going to do."

"We've worked for our home and built it with our own hands, George," Grace said. "Being do-gooders is not worth the price we're paying. Look at the trouble we've had."

"You don't have to worry," he said softly. "Old Charlie will be around!"

"What if somebody shoots somebody?"

"Old Charlie doesn't even have his gun. I told him to leave it at home."

"I've never lived in as much excitement and trouble in my life," Grace said. "This is one year I'll never forget."

"You wouldn't want to be one of our walking dead, would you?" George asked her. "How can people live just for full bellies, and soft beds? How can they?"

"All right, George, I'll say no more. No more arguments about the fate of the country this morning. I know how you feel. You know how I feel, too!"

"The purpose of this meeting will be finance," George said. "We're not through paying off old debts, and I want your ideas on how to make some money."

"I know one thing," Gus Riddle interrupted. "I will not stand for money to be taken from the ag fund to pay on old bills we didn't make. Why are school people so irresponsible with money?"

"It's because we've all got so much, Mr. Riddle," Shan Hannigan teased.

"This is no joking matter, Mr. Hannigan," Gus said irritably, shaking his head like a white leaf still hanging in the winter wind. Gus looked disgustedly up at the ceiling. "Teachers ought to be made responsible for the money they spend. This athletic situation needs looking into before it's too late."

"Mr. Riddle, we'll take care of that," Coach Webber said heatedly. "We're paying on bills now I didn't make. We're having a good year. People are coming out because we have good teams."

"Now, let's not have any arguments," Garrett Newall said. "Arguments won't get us anywhere. We owe money. Our problem is, as Mr. Gallion has just stated, how to make money to pay these bills."

"What became of that $8000 this school had in its school fund year before last?" Gus asked.

"That's no concern now," George said. "It was spent last year. Yet this school was plunged into an indebtedness of over $5000 which the Greenwood County board of education refuses to pay."

"They should pay it," Elizabeth Haskins said.

"What? Pay last year's debt for student pictures taken by two different photographers, pay for books never used, pay for flowers sent to the deceased in the community, pay things of no use which Tom, Dick, and Harry could order at will?" George said. "This is one time I agree with the Greenwood County board of education."

"What about putting the tiles on the corridor floor?" Fred Laurie asked. "Do you think the school should pay for repairs,"

"No, I don't," George said.

"We'll have to repair that furnace that's down," Marcella Waters said.

"No, we're going to manage with one," George said. "With body heat from pupils, plus what's generated from one furnace, we can manage. Besides, the pupils do better work in a cool house."

A few teachers shrugged their shoulders.

"I believe pupils do better work in a cold building," Delbert Bennington said. "Our little pre-fabs are easy to overheat. I've noticed overheating produces irritability among the pupils."

"The money we have to make doesn't go for heating," George said. "It will go to pay these old bills which we didn't make. Do you have any ideas on how to make this money?"

"Couldn't we solicit funds from the merchants in Kensington?" Ralph Sizemore asked. "I'd think they wouldn't want the school to owe bills! And what about the Parent-Teachers Associations?"

Gus Riddle sighed disgustedly and said pointedly to Ralph Sizemore, "You don't know, Mr. Sizemore, how merchants in every little town where there is a high school are hounded by solicitors and beggars. We don't want to turn our pupils into beggars. I wouldn't have any part of your idea. If I were principal I'd put my foot down on that suggestion!"

"I agree with Mr. Riddle," Garrett Newall said. "That's not the way to make money. I'm against handouts and begging! The townspeople aren't responsible for the school's financial mistakes. I think it best not to let them know how much the school owes."

"I disagree on their not knowing how much we owe, Mr. Newall," George said. "I think they should know and we should keep open books, which we do now, so any citizen can see our debits and credits."

"Now, Mr. Riddle, you could pay off a lot of our debt with that fat fund you have," Shan Hannigan prodded Gus again.

"When I buy a horn for your band you'll know it," Gus snapped. "I've got use for the money in my fund. Who buys the tractors, trucks, plows, machinery, and supplies for the shop? Who buys the seed and fertilizers? The horn-tooters don't do it. We are solvent, and we expect to remain that way. I'm the teacher here who has built the building where I teach and the shop where Mr. Ossington works, but even he doesn't appreciate it."

Leonard Ossington made no comment.

"Mr. Gallion, I thought I'd let everybody talk a little, then I'd come up with an idea," Gus Riddle said. "I've just been sitting here listening to the silly nonsense of those who would enjoy spending my fund. And since you've been nice enough to protect me, I'll tell you how to make some money. Not many here know I'm of Scottish descent, born of uneducated parents who had to scratch to make a living from the barren, rugged hills of Darter County. Well, all six of us have college degrees and three of my brothers are high school principals. Yes, I learned to scratch on the barren hills like a hungry chicken in the spring. I can tell you how to make money, and how to save it."

"Well, fine; tell us how," George said.

"Now, listen carefully. Since we have a flexible schedule, one which we can work in a matter of minutes, don't let a howl go up when I tell you. I suggest we order movies approved by and for schools. A film will cost from fifteen dollars to thirty dollars. We can advertise the film in advance on the bulletin board."

"But what about . . . " Charles Newton interrupted.

"Now you just wait a minute until I'm through, Mr. Newton. We cannot show any film over ninety minutes long. Here is the reason why. You see, I have figured this out long in advance, because I knew this kind of a teachers' meeting had to come. We operate here with six one-hour periods per day. Take fifteen minutes from each period and that gives you forty-five minutes, the state's requirement for the time of each class. This would give you ninety minutes' time for showing the longest film. Many of the films are only one hour. By selecting these, only ten minutes would have to be taken from each period."

"But, Mr. Riddle—" Fred Laurie began.

"Wait until I'm finished before you say anything," Gus shouted. "Your manners are atrocious! I know I'm rude, but I can be ruder. Now, what you started to say was that one of these would be shown in the afternoon or at a certain class period and the students would lose too much time away from class."

"What I started to say awhile ago," Charles Newton said.

"That was my question too," Fred Laurie added.

"Let me explain to you fellows," Gus continued. "Have a film each week and rotate to cover the six periods. By doing this we won't hurt any class too much. And, by the way, get scientific, historical, and other films with a love story maybe— one the pupils will like—but one that is analogous to some subject we teach. I'll just about guarantee you we'll fill the gym. We'll have 600 pupils to watch the film. This would be about one hundred dollars profit!"

"But coming from the poor student," Marcella Waters said.

"Most of the money we owe was spent for them," Gus Riddle said. "Be a little more practical, Mrs. Waters! Don't they see TV at home and movies in Kensington? Don't they spend money to see movies? Why not spend it here? And," he added, "you'd better have plenty of change when you sell tickets at both doors to the gym, because you'll never see as many tens and twenty-dollar bills in your life. You might even have a fifty- or a hundred-dollar bill sprung on you. One of my boys pulled a joke on me the other day by giving me a hundred-dollar bill which I first mistook for a ten. He asked me to change it. When I couldn't I never heard such laughing. Fellow teachers, I say this will work. We can wipe out all indebtedness by the end of the year."

"Thank you, Mr. Riddle, for a practical solution," George said. "How many of you are for it?"

"I don't like the idea of movies in school," Charles Newton said.

"I don't either," Garrett Newall said. "But since we have a problem where we have to meet just and honest debts made by this school, we have to pay. I'm all for it."

"I prefer we create our own entertainment from our own student talent," George said. "I don't like the idea of movies in a school either, but I like good movies. I'd like to put Mr. Riddle's idea to a vote. Hands up, those who are for it."

Gus Riddle beamed with pleasure when every teacher's hand and the principal's hand went up.

"Mr. Riddle, you've found the idea," George said. "I'm going to make a suggestion we let Mr. Riddle and Mrs. Nottingham select these films."

When George went to his office Gus Riddle followed him.

"Have you got something up your sleeve?" George asked him.

"A little tip I don't want anybody to hear," he replied. "I'm glad you put me on the committee to select the films. You remember that song, the best things in life are free? I've had some of the finest films sent to me to show my ag classes, and they don't cost a penny. My students have to watch them—they're a part of our classroom work. So when a good one comes along, I'll slip it over here and we'll charge to see it."

"I'm not so sure about that," George said.

"I'm positive about it," Gus told him with a wink. "Some of the films are on soil conservation. Some are on planting trees, beautifying homes . . . all of them are good films. If you show one free, you wouldn't get fifty pupils out to see it."

"What would you charge for films like these?" George asked.

"I've debated that in my mind," he replied. "Advertise it as something special, add probably a nickel, a dime, or even a quarter to the fee we'll charge for others and we can pack 'em in!"

"No wonder you have money in your fund," George said.

"Do you approve? We'll pay those bills and educate them at the same time!"

"But those films are supposed to be free."

"Yes, to my classes only. And because they're free they don't appreciate them. The whole school should see them, Mr. Gallion, and the only way to get pupils to see them is to charge a fee. You know most of the pupils have money to waste. So let them waste it on something good."

"We have about sixty pupils on free lunch. They can't pay to see these extra-special good films or the others."

"Any of them pinball gamblers?"

"I don't think so."

"You know what you got into before," he warned George. "You've got a good heart, but I think it's too soft at times. You want these debts paid, and we can pay them. Just Alice and I will know the secret of the special films."

"I'm thinking of the pupils who can't pay," George said. "I hate to keep them in a study hall! They'll want to see the movies and can't."

"But you'll have several who can pay who will want to study."

"That's right too. But what about those who want to see them, and can't afford to? I'd like to let them in free, but that wouldn't be fair to those who pay."

"All right, since you're so self-conscious on these matters, what about giving them I.O.U.s?" Gus suggested. "Let their I.O.U.s accumulate until they have a very good stack. Then let them do something, some little errand around this school, to pay off the I.O.U.s."

"Say, that's not a bad idea. Although," George added, "student labor has been free."

"I'll tell you we"ll issue I.O.U.s to them and work it out later. They'll feel better thinking they have to pay. They don't want to accept charity when they're young."

"I agree with that. We'll try your experiment."

Gus' plan went quickly into effect. He and Alice Nottingham selected a film and sent away for it.

"If we use one a week, we have to start now," Gus said. "Twenty-five hundred dollars is not easy to make. That's more money than some of the teachers make."

"All right, Mr. Riddle, we'll set up the showing for ninety minutes," George said. "We'll take the last part of the fifth and all of the sixth period tomorrow. You get your publicity on the bulletin boards."

"Ah, my friends, it'll be sensational."

A week after Gus' plan was proposed, Gus Riddle sat at one gym door and Alice Nottingham at the other. The film had cost twenty dollars, plus approximately four dollars for posting.

The box-office receipts would have been the envy of any small-town theater operator in the whole area—one hundred thirty-one dollars.

Now that the school was getting out of debt, it was also pushing up by inches, feet, and yards, from its tentative beginning in September to a virile, confident, husky secondary school by the first of the year. Inexperienced and unqualified high school teachers and student teachers, led and encouraged by a few veterans, were learning to teach by teaching. They were becoming more confident of themselves now.

Mrs. Nottingham and Garrett Newall had given the student body in the fall state-wide intelligence and achievement tests, and when these were compared with the state average, Kensington High School was three points lower. Each teacher was eager to pull upward to reach the state level when another achievement test would be given at the end of the year. But how could they raise the scholastic level of the school, when there weren't nearly enough teachers?

George was thinking about this one day early in February when Sadie Markham tiptoed up to his desk.

"Mr. Gallion, I've been looking for you all over," she said. "There's young man in the office to see you."

"He's a salesman, isn't he?" George said. "I don't want to see him unless he's selling teachers."

"I don't think he's a salesman," she said.

"Then send him to me."

She went back to the office and George walked up the corridor to meet the stranger. He was over six feet tall, with clear blue eyes and a firm mouth. He looked like a very young and inexperienced insurance salesman.

"My name is Otto Schubert," he said.

"What do you sell?" George asked him.

"Oh, not anything, sir," he replied. "I've come to see if you need a substitute teacher. I'm a graduate of Ohio State University and I have four majors. I also have my master's degree."

George laid his hand on the young man's shoulder. He

looked him in the eye. "Young man, do you believe in prayer?" George asked him.

"Well, I should, sir. I'm the son of a Lutheran minister."

"Mr. Schubert, will you be interested in teaching next year?" George asked.

"No, sir, I plan to return for more graduate work in philosophy this autumn. This summer I'll travel in Europe."

"How old are you?"

"Twenty-three, sir," he replied. "If you do not need me this morning I can give you my street address and all the references you want. If something comes up and you need a substitute you can let me know. I'd hate to be idle from now until the end of the school year."

"What about the Ohio schools?" George asked him. "Have you tried to find substitute teaching in them?"

"I thought I'd be more needed on this side of the river," he said.

"We don't need your phone number and address," George said. "We can't phone from here. There's the bell. You start work now."

"Mr. Gallion, I'm not prepared."

"That won't matter much right now," George told him. "In five minutes you'll be a regular teacher on this faculty."

"You know, I believe God sent me what I was praying for," George said. "I prayed for one more teacher to take over American history to free me from classroom work. I've scraped the bottom of the barrel to find student teachers to man the classes. You take over some of the American history classes."

"Then I came at the right time?"

"You certainly did. I can be free to go from room to room to help the student teachers. Mr. Schubert, you're going to fit into our flexible schedule. Come on, let's go," George said. "I'll introduce you to the first class. Then, from now on you'll introduce yourself. I can't be with you. I'll be going from room to room to visit the student teachers. Some of the staff is out with flu, and I almost thought I'd have to send the students home for the day. Tell me why you came here this morning," George asked, as they walked down the corridor toward Mrs. Nottingham's room.

"Something told me to come over here today," he told George. "The idea just came to me, so I changed clothes, got in the car, and came over from Dartmouth."

Chapter Six

The Second Defense
and the Middle Frame

It was a cloudless bright spring morning, and school had just begun when Shan Hannigan rushed into the office.

"We had a robbery last night in the block building," he said. "Somebody broke a window pane, unlocked the window, and went through. Unlocked the door from the inside! They broke the lock on my army footlocker I keep out there. Somebody took thirty-five dollars from that footlocker. Of all places for them to find money!"

"Do you have any idea who?" George asked him.

"No more than you had about this office," he said. "How many break-ins have you had here?"

"Too many to count," George said. "And the robbers didn't leave a clue. Say, what about your band members? Do you have one you think would have seen you put money in that locker?"

"Only one boy," he replied. "He's on free meals here and honest, he couldn't do anything like that."

"I want his name," George said.

"Tom West," he said.

"I agree with you about him," George said. "I can't believe he'd do that. But where money is concerned you can never tell. I've been fooled many times."

An hour after Shan Hannigan's report, Harvey Withrow, principal of Kensington Elementary, who rarely visited the neighboring school, came in.

"We're ruined," he shouted. "We've been robbed!"

"Over there?" George sighed. "We've had a robbery here, too. Thirty-five dollars of band money was stolen last night."

"I wish we had just lost thirty-five dollars," he said. "There was about fourteen hundred dollars in our safe. Some of it was your money."

"Eleven hundred dollars of that money was ours, Mr. Withrow," Sadie Markham said.

"Our movie money, athletic money, and cafeteria money," George said.

"Mr. Gallion, what do you suggest we do?" Harry Withrow asked. "Most of our money was from the cafeteria. You see, the government has part ownership in this."

"I suggest we clean house," George said. "The time is right. We want Lonnie Biggers, the state patrol, and the FBI. Not for your robbery, but the two might be connected. We should get the FBI because it's government money that's been stolen."

"Nothing has been touched at my school," Harry Withrow said. "The vault is in the section of the building that leads to my office. After taking a look at how they got in—they knocked the blocks out with a sledgehammer and went in from the top—well, such destruction of a new vault! I didn't touch it. I locked the door so no one could get in or touch it."

"Sadie, go get me a messenger."

He quickly dictated notes to Sheriff Biggers, to Pat Brannigan of the FBI, whose headquarters was in Auckland. "We need your help this time. This is your affair as well as ours."

Although Greenwood was twenty miles away, Sheriff Lonnie Biggers arrived forty minutes after the note was sent, and shortly after his arrival, Pat Brannigan came in with Joe O'Brien. Both were from the FBI.

The four men pulled up chairs in the center of George's little office and faced one another.

"Now with robbery in the band room and the elementary school on the same night," Joe O'Brien said, closing his eyes,

"I think this has been an inside job. I'd like to check a record of who was absent from this school yesterday and today."

The men drew their chairs closer and looked over the lists.

"I detect one incongruity here," Pat Brannigan said. "Not a boy absent yesterday is absent today."

George was relieved to find that Tom West's name was not on either list. Yesterday's list had seventeen absentees and on today's list there were eighteen, of whom ten were girls.

"Are these lists high or low?" Pat Brannigan asked.

"Very low," George said. "We have now approximately 630 pupils enrolled here. Our enrollment hasn't fallen this year. There has been a slight increase."

"All right, Mr. Gallion, maybe you can tell me something about each boy," Joe said. "Here's Don Zimmerman. Has he ever been involved in stealing?"

"Not to my knowledge," George said. "I wouldn't consider him a prospect."

"What about Delmar Blanton?" he asked.

"Definitely no," George replied. "I know his parents. They're deeply religious people. He's from a very good home. And he's seldom absent from school. Check his record, Mrs. Markham."

"What about Mark Woods?"

"He's a little freshman who lives ten miles up the Tiber," George said. "He wouldn't have the power to lift a sledge-hammer."

"Yes, but don't forget a little man might have gone down into the vault." Pat said. "You'll be surprised at what people will do, people you would never believe."

"I still say Mark Woods is out."

"Jason Perkins?" Joe asked.

"Freshman, with the mumps," George said.

"Mr. Gallion, Delmar Benton only missed one day last semester," Mrs. Markham said. "This is his first absence this semester."

"A commendable record," Joe replied. "He's not a likely

prospect. We have five of the ten. Now what about 'G.B.' Bear?"

"Not likely," George said. "He runs with some ruffians but has never been involved."

"I'll put a check mark here," Joe said.

There was a knock on the door.

Mrs. Markham unlocked the door and looked through the crack. "Mr. VanHoose, state patrol."

"Got your message, sheriff," he said. "Relayed from your office. Sorry I'm late."

"You know all these men, Mr. VanHoose?" George said.

"Sure do."

He got the last chair and pulled it up in the circle.

"Glad you're here, Van," Pat Brannigan said. "Think we're going to need you in a few minutes. We're going to do some rounding up."

"All right. Bud Peters?" Joe said. "What about him?"

"Senior from a good family," George said. "I used to teach his mother. Know both families. Never heard of one from either family ever being arrested and of being in court."

"Ralph Corrigon?" he asked. "He's the last boy. Maybe we'd better check some of the girls. Not many prospects here."

"But one could have done the job," Pat Brannigan interrupted.

"About Ralph Corrigon," Sheriff Biggers said; "he has a little record of seven minor offenses against him which his parents have made good."

"Ralph Corrigon has been very nice in school," George explained. "He is very mannerly among his teachers. But I've heard he's a Jekyll and Hyde."

"Maybe he was Mr. Hyde last night," Pat Brannigan said, smiling. "We'll soon find out about him anyway . . . now, what do you suggest, Joe?"

"I suggest we check each home and see why they're not in school," Joe said. "Van, you and Sheriff Biggers know this area better than we do. What do you say we divide and each take two homes? Do this as fast as we can and then report back here."

Before noon the four men were back in the office with their reports.

"You're right, Mr. Gallion, about Mark Woods and Jason Perkins," Pat said. "One is recovering from mumps and the other is home sick in bed."

"I visited the Benton and Zimmerman homes and their mothers told me both boys started to school this morning," Joe O'Brien said. "Looks suspicious to me."

"Well, I got bawled out when I went to the Corrigon home," Sheriff Biggers said. "Mrs. Corrigon really went after me. I went down to the plant to see Dan Corrigon and he didn't make any sense at all. I don't know whether he was there and went to school this morning or not."

"Grandma Bear said G.B. went to school as usual this morning," VanHoose reported. "And Mary Peters said she sent Bud to school. Do you suppose they're all together, playing hooky?"

"Something in the wind, fellows," Joe O'Brien said. "I can smell it." Then he added. "I'm sure that by tonight we'll have our men. Say, could you tell me where Ralph Corrigon hangs out? Where does he loaf when he has money?"

"I can't answer that correctly," George said; "but I imagine in men's clothing stores. He's crazy about clothes."

"What's your idea for this afternoon?" Sheriff Biggers asked Joe.

"Visit some clothing stores in Dartmouth," he replied. "We'd better get going."

"Give me a report as soon as you can," George said. "I'll be here waiting until I hear from you."

George escorted the men to the front door and watched them get into their cars. He walked back to his office with his head bowed. Could these be the ones? Could they have done this?

Coach Webber came into the office. His face was serious.

"I'm worried, Mr. Gallion," he said. "I'm just plain worried."

George gave Coach Webber the absentee list.

"Zimmerman, Benton, G.B., and Peters started to school this morning but didn't arrive."

"What about Ralph Corrigon?" he asked. "You know whether he started or not?"

"His parents wouldn't cooperate with Biggers when he checked the home and plant," George told him. "We don't know whether he started out to school or not. Coach, you got any ideas where these boys would be hanging out?"

"Yes, I think so."

"If you found Ralph Corrigon could you bring him in?"

"You bet I could!"

"All right, I'm sending you," George said. "Get in your car and see if you can locate him. I'll send Nada Fairman to take over your classes."

"All right; I'll see what I can do."

At the end of the fourth period Don Zimmerman, Delmar Benton, G.B., and Bud Peters came walking into the office.

"Have you seen Mr. Webber?" George asked them.

"No, was Coach hunting for us?" Delmar asked innocently.

"Sure, I sent him to find you. Where have you fellows been?"

"Down in Kensington," Don Zimmerman said.

"Did you start to school this morning, Don?"

"Yes sir, but I stopped in Kensington."

"Did you start to school this morning, Delmar?"

"Yes sir, but I didn't feel very good and I went down to Big River and watched the boats. I played hooky, I guess," he smiled sheepishly.

"And you, Bud?"

"I started to school but I got with Delmar," he stammered. "So I took the day off."

"What about you, G.B.?"

"I've been loafing with Don," he said.

"Did you know there was a big robbery of the Kensington Elementary School last night? Did you know the band room was robbed?"

"Heard about the robbery just a little while ago when Delmar and I got back from the river," Bud said. "We heard it down in Kensington."

"Did you know State Patrolman VanHoose, Sheriff Lonnie Biggers, not to mention the FBI, are hunting for you four right now?"

"No," Bud said. He flushed. "No, I didn't know that."

"You fellows get chairs and sit down in this office. I don't want one of you to leave."

"The FBI!" Don said breathlessly.

"I sent for them. Government money was stolen. This time we're going to find out who got that money. Have any of you seen Ralph Corrigon?"

All four denied that they'd seen him.

"Did you see him last night, Don?"

"Yes, I saw him down in Kensington."

"Anybody with him?"

"No, he was alone, walking down the street."

"Why are we being questioned, Mr. Gallion?" Delmar asked.

"Because you were absent from school today," George replied. "Now if you fellows were in any way implicated in either of these robberies I want you to come clean and tell the truth. If you don't we'll find out anyway, and the situation will be worse for you."

"I don't like to be accused," Bud Peters said.

"I don't either," Delmar said.

"I'm not accusing you," George said firmly. "I'm just warning you if you are implicated in any way come clean right now."

"My old man is going to be awful mad about this," Don Zimmerman said.

At that moment the door opened and Sheriff Biggers came in holding Champ Burton by the arm.

"Howdy, Mr. Gallion," he said, extending his hand. "I'm glad to see you. The sheriff picked me up down in Kensington and said I was a suspect in a robbery."

Sheriff Biggers stared icily at the Champ.

"Mr. Gallion, honest, I don't know where I was last night," he told George. "I was so drunk I don't remember."

"Shut up, you," Sheriff Biggers scolded him. "We'll find out where you were."

"Mr. Gallion, if it hadn't been for that man putting me out of this school," the Champ said with an infectious grin, "I would have played football, basketball, and baseball and I would have won the Golden Gloves. Gee, this was a great place and I liked you."

"Champ, when did you start drinking?" George asked him.

"Mostly since I left here; I'd drink a beer sometimes . . . but after I left here I'd go on binges, see? . . . And yesterday when I got to Kensington I reckon I drunk a whole case of beer. I don't remember nothin'."

"Nice to come back here and tell your teacher all that stuff," Sheriff Biggers said. "A young man like you . . . you ought to be ashamed."

"Let him talk, Sheriff," George said. "I want to know about him."

"I guess I've plumb gone to the dogs, Mr. Gallion," the Champ said. "But I'll say one thing. You were my friend. I just never could do anything I didn't think you would want me to do . . ."

"Maybe you're drinking now," Sheriff Biggers questioned him.

"No, he's not drinking either," George said. "I was good to the Champ and I did my best to keep him in school."

"But I'll never be in school no more," he said. "Nobody will have me. I'll remember the good old days I had here! You remember that old Kensington-Rutland football game last fall, don't you, Mr. Gallion?"

"I sure do, Champ," George said.

"I think of it all the time," he said. "That one was just rough enough to suit me."

"Sheriff, you stay in here a few minutes," George said. "I have something to do and I'll be back in a minute. Sheriff, you know these boys, don't you?"

"Yes, I know who they are," he replied. "Who rounded them up?"

"They just came in," George said, pulling out a drawer of the filing cabinet.

"You fellows know anything about the robbery?" he asked them.

Each one denied he knew anything. George found the card he was looking for. He put it in his pocket and closed the drawer.

"Nobody seems to know about the robbery," the Champ said.

"Shut up, I told you," Sheriff Lonnie Biggers said. "When I want you to bark I'll pull on your chain. You'll have your chance to talk after a while."

George went out of the office and asked for a sheet of paper and an envelope. He scribbled a note, enclosed, and sealed it. "Deliver this to the student to whom it is addressed," he told Myrtle Spence. "He is in Room 222. Thank you."

George went down through the boys' rest room, opened the door with a master key, and waited in the room adjacent to the furnace room. In a few minutes he heard steps in the rest room. He heard the door open, for there was an eerie stillness here. He heard the door shut gently and light footsteps on the stone steps.

"Tell me, did you see the Champ and Ralph Corrigon together last night?"

"Yes."

"Where?"

"I watched them leave Kensington and go up the road," he whispered.

"Where did you last see them?"

"Between the Tiber Bridge and Kensington Elementary."

"What time?"

"About nine o'clock. The Champ was staggering. I thought maybe Ralph was taking him home."

"What were you doing in Kensington?"

"I had to go see Uncle Ben for Dad," he replied. "He lives in one of the houses in that row above Tiber Bridge."

"Did you suspect anything?"

"No sir. But I have more to tell you sometime. Not now!"

"Lucky for us," George said. "You might have something. Thanks. Go back right now. Lock the door when you go back."

George went around through the furnace room and up the chute. Then he walked around and through the west corridor door and back to the office. He put the youth's card back in the file.

"Champ, were you with Ralph Corrigon last night?" George asked him.

"Mr. Gallion, I just don't remember rightly," he said. "I was so drunk I don't know where I was."

"Shut up about being drunk," Lonnie Biggers scolded him. "That's all I've heard out of you. Maybe somebody hit you with a sour apple."

"No, Sheriff, I had a case of beer in me."

"Let him talk, Sheriff," George said. "Maybe he was drunk. What I want to know is where the Champ was when he sobered up and woke up."

"Now, Mr. Gallion, I'd rather not tell you that," he replied.

"Yes, now where were you?" Sheriff Biggers asked. "That's a good question."

Just then the office door opened and Don Webber came in.

"I couldn't find Ralph," he said. "But look who's here! Where did you fellows come from?"

"The sheriff picked me up as a suspect," the Champ said.

"Shut up, I told you," Sheriff Biggers said. "Wait until you're asked."

"I played football for Coach Webber," the Champ said. "He was good to me. He was a nice guy to us players."

"We had some great games, didn't we Champ?"

"I'll say we did, Coach."

"These other fellows just walked in here about an hour ago after you left, Coach," George said. "Did you see anybody who had seen Ralph?"

"Step out here a minute, Mr. Gallion," Don Webber said. "I'd like to speak to you privately."

George followed Don Webber out and down the corridor.

"Any trace?"

"Yes, clerks in two stores said they waited on a young man buying sport shirts and shoes," he said. "It looks bad, Mr. Gallion. But I couldn't find him."

"There's a saying that the FBI gets their man," George said.

"I think they're back now. They have Ralph."

Ralph Corrigon got out of the car with two boxes of clothes.

"I told you I spent my own money," Ralph was saying as they came up the steps.

VanHoose followed them into the schoolhouse.

"They're trying to accuse me of robbing Kensington Elementary last night, Coach," he said. "I went to Dartmouth and spent my own money and got me some clothes and shoes."

"The other four are in the office," George said.

"Is Sheriff Biggers in the office with the suspect he nabbed?" Pat Brannigan asked.

"Yes, they're in the office too," George said.

They took Ralph Corrigon to the office and Don Webber turned and walked slowly back to his classroom. George locked the door.

The questioning began. Each of the four boys denied being with Ralph Corrigon the night before, though Don Zimmerman admitted that he had seen him walking down the street alone.

"I went down to Grandpa's Place to get me a soda pop and some ice cream," Ralph said. "Then I went home. And this morning I took my own money and went to get me some clothes."

"Were you with Champ Burton last night?" Lonnie Biggers asked.

"What? I never saw the man," he said.

"If I saw him I don't remember it," Champ Burton said.

"Don't play possum on us, Champ," VanHoose said.

"I ain't playin' possum, Van," he said. "I just don't remember."

"Didn't any of you see these two men together?" Pat Brannigan asked.

They shook their heads.

"My ma can tell you where I got the money to buy my clothes," Ralph said.

"I was over there and your mother wouldn't tell me anything," Sheriff Biggers snarled. "She talked to me worse than I'd scold a dog."

"Aw, Ma don't like for the law to come snoopin' around all the time," he said. "Why am I always accused of something? I mind my own business, don't I? Ask the teachers in this school about me. Ask them if I go around here a big shot a-raisin' hell all the time. Check my record. Go ask Coach Webber about me!"

"I know more about you, Corrigon, than you think I know," Sheriff Biggers said. "I know enough to know you're not telling all you know."

"You're a smooth talker, Corrigon," Pat Brannigan said, smiling. "Come on and tell us what you know."

"I told you I didn't know anything," he said.

"Ralph, do you have any idea who broke into the band room?" George asked him.

"No, Mr. Gallion, I don't."

"Have you any idea who has been breaking into this school-house hunting for money?"

"No sir. I don't."

"Ralph, you say you didn't see Champ last night?"

"No sir, I didn't."

"What time did you leave Kensington for home?"

"About nine or nine-thirty," he replied.

George motioned for Joe O'Brien to go outside with him.

"I have definite proof that Ralph Corrigon and the Champ went up the road together at about nine last night," George whispered. "I doubt those other boys are connected with these two."

"Can you furnish us a witness?"

"No, but I have good information."

"If you have this, we can break the robbery wide open," he said. "We'll take them to jail this afternoon."

"Don't take Zimmerman, Benton, Peters, and G.B.," George said. "I'm going to suspend them for playing hooky." George looked at his watch. "It's time for the last bell. Let's go back in the office, and wait until everybody clears out of the building."

George pushed the button. There was a crescendo of voices and a scurrying of feet down the corridor. There was the slam of locker doors and in a few minutes the noise gradually subsided to the occasional rhythm of a teacher's footsteps down the corridor.

"All right, Zimmerman, Peters, Benton, and G.B.," George said. "Get your belongings, books, and everything and go home. When you think you might want to return, bring your parents. That's the only way you can be reinstated."

The four got up silently from their chairs and walked out.

"All right, Corrigon and Burton, you can go with us," Joe O'Brien said.

"Where to?" Ralph asked.

"Greenwood County Jail," he said.

"You can't take me," Ralph said. "I haven't done anything."

Champ Burton was silent.

Next morning when George parked his truck in front of the Greenwood County Courthouse, Sheriff Lonnie Biggers was coming down the steps.

"Well, Mr. Gallion, Van and I have the unhappy task of picking up the other four boys this morning. Corrigon became a gentleman in jail and confessed he was the leader in both robberies. He said Zimmerman helped him take the money from the band room and Burton helped him rob the vault in Kensington Elementary."

"How are the other three involved?"

"By accepting stolen money," he replied. "Van and I are making the arrests this morning while Pat and Joe take Ralph Corrigon back to a dump outside Dartmouth where he buried the rest of the money."

George was barely listening. He gazed vacantly into space. "You were right about Burton's being drunk. He was so drunk during the robbery he didn't remember it," the sheriff went on. "Corrigon was too big to go from the top down into the vault after they knocked the blocks out with a sledgehammer, so he put Burton down that hole. How he ever got down there without being fastened is beyond me. Corrigon said Burton didn't want to go but he told him if he didn't he'd kill him. Strange about that Corrigon; he's a wild man at night and a gentleman during the day."

"How did you find all this out?" George finally asked.

"We separated the boys and told each of them what the other had said. You know the old trick. How did you know they had been seen together walking up the road at nine o'clock night before last?"

"I can't tell you that," George said. "If I did somebody could be hurt."

"That's the straw that broke the case wide open," Sheriff Biggers said. "Each made a confession. If you want to read something that will make the hair stand up on your head, read Ralph Corrigon's confessions. They fill pages. Our troubles and your troubles in Kensington and the western part of the county are going to end for some time. Your school won't be broken into any more for a while. We've got the right one this time. He's the ringleader."

"I'd like to see the boys. Where are they?"

"Behind bars! Right where they ought to be," Sheriff Biggers said, and he got in his car.

In the county attorney's office George read Ralph Corrigon's confession. He had never read anything like it. Ralph Corrigon was an almost classic case of a split personality. He hadn't spared any details in his confession. He described how Don Zimmerman had taken twenty dollars his father gave him to buy a class ring and how he had gambled it away on pinball and was afraid to tell his father. His cousin, Delmore Corrigon, had seen Shan Hannigan, the band master, put money in the bottom of the army locker, so Ralph had told Don about this easy way to get the money back. Then, after they had opened the door to the block building Don was frightened and wanted to back out, but he threatened Don that he would break his neck if he tried to back out. All of the other boys knew the money had been stolen, so he had parceled out six dollars to Delmar Benton, three dollars to Bear, and two dollars to Peters in bribes so they would keep quiet. He had paid Champ only twenty dollars for going down through the top of the vault because Champ spent his money unwisely for beer and not on "worthy" things like good clothes.

George went down to the jail where he was allowed to go in and talk to Ralph and the Champ.

"I'm sorry sir, I did it," Ralph confessed in his schoolboy role. "I worry more about the baseball team than anything. I hate to do Coach Webber this way. He's been so nice I hate to let him down! You've been nice to me too, Mr. Gallion; I hate to let you down, but I just couldn't help it. When night comes I dream of money in this place and that place and how easy it is to get . . . and how I need things. You know, nice things like sport shirts, nice pants, pretty socks, and neckties! The old devil gets hold of me or something.

"No, Mr. Gallion, when I went after money I destroyed as

little as I possibly could. I broke the smallest window pane I could so it would be easier to put back. And I never stole a book or paper or put chewing gum under a seat, either. I just wanted money. I never tore up your office, did I?"

"Not too much," George said.

"Mr. Gallion, that Ralph Corrigon is the biggest hog over green folding money I have ever seen in all my life," the Champ confessed. "I had to take my twenty dollars in nickels, dimes and quarters," Champ Burton grunted disgustedly. He sat on the side of his bunk with his feet hanging over.

"I was sober when we divided the money. See, you asked me where I sobered up but I couldn't lie to you. You been too nice to me. Honest, I don't remember doin' the job. Will they send me to jail? Can't you help me, Mr. Gallion?" he pleaded.

"In this case the government is involved," George said. "Part of the money you stole is government money. No, I can't help you! It's now up to the courts, I'm afraid."

"That's what I told Champ," Ralph said. "We're guilty, and we're not babies. We'll take our medicine."

"What about Don Zimmerman?" George said.

"I got him into this, Mr. Gallion," Ralph admitted. "He didn't want to go through with it after we started, but I made him. Poor old Don's not a bad fellow, he just can't get his guts up when night comes on."

When George Gallion left the jail he was deeply depressed. If something isn't done for Ralph Corrigon, he'll be in and out of prison all his life. He's a sick boy. Champ just doesn't have quite enough upstairs. He's a follower. How he followed me like a pet dog in school begging to get his D— raised to a D+! How I liked that boy! How I fought for him. . . . Maybe, yes, maybe if we had kept him in school we could have made a fair citizen of him.

That afternoon George drove his truck home. When he arrived in his own world, where there were still telephones, he phoned Circuit Judge Harrell and asked him if he could drop in that evening.

When George knocked on the door, the tall, cold-faced,

balding Judge Harrell opened the door. "Come in, George," he said, forcing a smile. "Have a chair."

He closed the door. "Pull those front shades," George said.

"Why pull the blinds?"

"I don't want anybody to see me here," George said.

The judge gave George a puzzled look. "Since you're my guest I'll try to make you comfortable." He pulled the shades.

"You've no doubt read the papers about the trouble we're having in Kensington High School," George said.

"Yes, it's in the headlines," he said. "Very unfortunate. Your own pupils have given your school unfair publicity. But you've had good publicity which I've read from time to time. That's the way of life . . . mixing the bitter with the sweet."

"I want to tell you a bit about the boys who are involved," George said. "I wonder if you know any of them?"

"Their names are familiar to me," he replied. "I know some of their grandparents and their fathers and mothers, but not the boys. I have heard about Ralph Corrigon and Champ Burton. I think Burton has been involved before, hasn't he? And isn't it true there has been considerable cover-up for Corrigon?"

"I didn't come to discuss these two," George said.

"Well, I'm telling you it won't do any good," he said. "They'll stand trial. They're in jail and without bond, aren't they?"

"So far," George said.

"I don't think they are through questioning those boys yet," he said.

"I've come to speak on behalf of Don Zimmerman, Delmar Benton, Bud Peters, and G.B. Bear," George said.

"Didn't that Zimmerman boy break into a building and steal? Seems like I read that."

"Yes, he did," George replied. "And just because his father is a rough-and-tumble labor leader, a lot of people hate him. I'm afraid for this boy!"

"He'll get a fair trial, George."

"Yes, but what if you do the sentencing?" George said.

"Now, you go ahead with the discussion," he said. "I do not care to discuss this with you. You do the talking. I'll listen."

"Judge, Don Zimmerman is not a criminal," George began to explain. "This is his first offense. I know he is not a thief. This is his first time in trouble. His grades are not so good but he stands tenth out of a class of eighty-five in achievement tests."

"Would you like to have a son like this boy?"

"Judge, I would like to have Don for a son."

A faint smile played over Judge Timothy Harrell's cold chalk-white face.

"Regarding Bud Peters, Delmar Benton, and G.B. Bear, I hope you admonish them only. Everybody has paid the money back but Dan Corrigon. The Champ's mother has paid back all he got. Enic Zimmerman was the first to come and pay the money his son and Ralph Corrigon stole from the band room. Sure as I'm sitting here, not one of these boys except maybe Ralph Corrigon and Champ Burton will ever get into something like this again."

"Go on," the judge said, looking coldly at George.

"You're a judge and I'm a schoolteacher. I've worked with youth since I was seventeen years old. I think I know them fairly well. I don't think they should be tried as criminals. They're teenage boys."

"Halt there," he said. "What about all this juvenile delinquency? I can't pick up a paper that isn't full of it!"

"Have you ever considered the ratio of youthful stealing as compared to the older people?" George asked him. "And why are pinball machines allowed to operate in this county where gambling isn't legalized? Who puts these devices before our youth? Their elders. And why hasn't this been cleaned up? Why should a teacher have to battle this?"

"Don't blame me," he said. "I'm not the sheriff or the state patrol. Ask them why it hasn't been cleaned up."

"Judge, the trouble with adults is they don't give youth credit for being great imitators. When you were a teenager, didn't you select somebody you wanted to be like when you grew up?"

"Yes, I did. Old Judge Rennigan, in fact."

"Youth are smarter than you think," George said. "Our youth of today are the smartest generation this country has ever had."

"I don't believe that,"

"I know it's true. I've seen them come and go. Youth will reason that if their elders can gamble and steal and get by with it, they can too."

"What you say doesn't make sense," the judge said.

"It does make sense." George's voice rose. "There are no more thieves now among the young in proportion to their number than there were when you were a boy."

"I don't believe that either," Judge Harrell retorted. "The papers are filled with thievery and delinquency reports."

"When you were a lawyer in this town, I have heard you sit at the counter in the Liston Drugstore and entertain your listeners with stories of slipping off from Greenwood High School. None of that was in the papers. Today that would be in the papers and you'd be branded as a juvenile deliquent. Many of the students in your youth would have been called delinquents today. As rough as my school has been, I don't have as many now."

Judge Timothy Harrell rose a flush spreading over his cheeks.

"You know what I'm going to do with your youth if I can," he said.

"No, I don't," George said rising.

"I'm going to send them to the pen," he said. "I'm tired of this stealing and juvenile delinquency."

"You know what I'm going to do, Judge, if I can?"

"No."

"You're coming up for re-election soon and I'm going to fight you to the last ditch."

"Now you just go ahead," the judge said blandly. "You're welcome to beat me if you can. I'm not afraid of you."

"I may not be able to turn the tide, but my conscience will rest easier with a lost vote against you than with a winning vote for you."

"Goodnight, George."

Bud Peters, Delmar Benton, G.B. Bear, and their parents, Superintendent John Bennington, and George appeared before Judge Harrell. The three boys didn't have to stand trial, but they and their parents were admonished sternly. Don Zimmerman, however, had to stand trial with Champ Burton and Ralph Corrigon. Ralph Corrigon and Champ Burton were released on bond, but George would not permit Ralph Corrigon to return to school or practice baseball with his teammates. Once when Coach Webber let him referee a game between the sandlot nine and the second team, George ordered Don to remove him. Nor could he permit Champ Burton to return even for a visit. George did allow Don Zimmerman to return to school until the trial was over, but he was severely criticized and even threatened for this.

There was no question about Ralph Corrigon and Champ Burton now. They pleaded guilty before Judge Timothy Harrell, and to George's sorrow Ralph Corrigon was given a four-year sentence in the state penitentiary. Champ Burton was given two. Don Zimmerman was given one year, but Judge Harrell commuted his sentence. After he was placed under a parole officer, George permitted Don to re-enter competitive sports, for he was sure that Don regretted his act. Enic Zimmerman was deeply grateful, and was now zealous to help the school.

On the Saturday morning following the trial, George went to Dr. Vinn's office for a checkup. His blood pressure had reached an all-time and alarming high. Dr. Vinn warned him that if he wanted to remain to finish the year he would have to slow his pace.

As the school year advanced, the seniors began to plan for their futures. Many pupils didn't have enough money to go to college, and of these many had excellent character but inferior grades, and colleges wouldn't give them scholarships. George tried to get them student aid and small scholarships and wrote many letters in their behalf. Even superior students had difficulty getting scholarship aid. John Salyers, the 228-pound fullback, who could run a hundred yards in 10.2 seconds but stood at the bottom of his class, was offered a $7600 four-year scholarship at a university outside the state, while Les Bowdin, who stood at the top of his class, was offered only a $300 scholarship from a small though highly reputable Methodist college outside the state. This contrast was indicative of the way the winds were blowing in higher education.

"All right, everybody around here is winning prizes," Shan Hannigan said one day to George and Gus Riddle. "Now is our time to try."

"What do you think you'll do, Mr. Hannigan?" Gus asked him.

"I'm not sure what we'll do," he said. "But one thing is certain, we're going to try."

On this Friday at noon in the middle of April, two school buses were parked and waiting at the west corridor door. Shan Hannigan was to drive one of the buses and Fred Laurie was to drive the other. George had dismissed the entire school to come out to cheer the Kensington High School band on to its competitive contest with bands from all the high schools in the eastern part of the state.

"Aren't you going out to lead the band to the buses?" Gus asked.

"Mr. Riddle, I don't have to do that," Hannigan replied. "If I am not with that band it can give a performance on the athletic field, or it can give a concert. I have trained leaders who can lead the band when I'm not there. Isn't that right, Mr. Gallion?"

"Correct," George said.

At that instant the band began to play over at the band building. They had assembled there, dressed in their freshly cleaned but worn uniforms, playing on old discarded instruments Shan Hannigan had bought secondhand and repaired.

"Wonder what Shan Hannigan and his band will do at Menton State College in this band contest?" George said quietly.

"Not much of anything," Gus replied. "He's overrated. He's never been in any competition. Wait and see what I'm telling you. I didn't miss on Ralph Corrigon, did I?"

"But there'll come a time when you will miss," George said.

"I can't warm up to that fellow," Gus sighed, looking up at the April sun. "I don't see how you can overrate him."

Sunday morning when George drove over the highway to get the newspaper, he stood by the paper box and scanned the headlines. Thumbing through the paper before he drove back home to give it a more thorough reading, he came onto a news item that caught his attention: KENSINGTON HIGH SCHOOL COPS REGIONAL HONORS.

As he read this story of his band's first achievement, he was deeply stirred. Playing on inferior instruments and wearing old uniforms had not dampened the spirit of these determined youth and their leader. They were from a region that could spend thousands of dollars for an election yet had to beg library books from all over the nation. Still, the sons and daughters of these people had music in their lips and fingers, in their hearts and minds. All they needed was a teacher and a leader to organize and teach them.

This was not the only honor that came to the school. Again the school took the statewide scholastic test, and this time

Kensington High School, which had placed three percent below state average, had risen to a point above the state level.

Kensington High School's finances were in a less desperate situation, too. The last old debt had been paid off. In addition to this, there were a new tile floor and countless new window panes.

Otto Schubert's arrival at Kensington High School had helped to change the atmosphere of the school. He introduced games in his physical education classes that Kensington High School students and teachers had never seen before. His physical education classes became model competitive games. Students who were not in his classes and couldn't get in them liked to sit in the bleachers and watch him conduct a class. Pupils who had never played or become a part in a group before played in his class, and he opened up a whole new world to those students. Often he took his physical education class on a hike, and required them to take notebooks and to draw pictures of spring flowers and leaves, and to be able to identify them. Students who were fortunate enough to take one of these hikes never stopped talking afterward about what they had passed over every day and yet had not seen.

Otto Schubert coached plays, and there were so many students who wanted a part that he was forced to turn many of them away. American history came alive in his classes. He was young and eager and full of the will to help others. George saw in this young man a great teacher for the future.

"Mr. Schubert, we're going to miss you next year," George said. "This summer you will be in Europe. Next year you will be studying philosophy. I wish there was some way of keeping you here as a teacher."

"Thank you; I like to work with you," he said. "We see things much the same way."

"We see things as nearly the same as any teacher I have worked with in my life. You wouldn't change your mind and stay with us next year?"

"Well, I hadn't thought about this," he said. "I am already making my plans for next year. What do you have in mind for me to do?"

"What is it you can't do?" George asked him. "I've used you in just about every teaching field and had you in almost every situation. If I don't find that extra teaching for you above your six full periods, you go out and find it yourself. You're what I call a teacher. You give yourself. And you care."

"Mr. Gallion, when I look on the great potential in these young people, I'm up in the clouds. When I see what little chance some of them have in Appalachia, and how hard they try to overcome it, I can't help being moved."

"You don't have to tell me this," George said. "I can see it myself."

Schubert changed the subject. "I have something to ask you if it isn't too personal."

"All right, go ahead," George said.

"I've heard you have informers in Kensington High School," Schubert said. "I'm told you know everything that goes on in this school."

"Well, I don't have a spy system," George said. "And I don't know everything that goes on. I get most of the information myself. But I have received some information from another source. Is there anything wrong with that?"

"I hear talk you don't hear."

"Yes, I'm sure of that," George said. "You hear plenty of favorable and unfavorable talk about me. You'll hear most of the unfavorable in Kensington."

"That's right, sir."

"If they were selling drinks to students, I'd know it," George said. "If students are gambling on pinball machines, I'll know this, too."

George was curious why Otto Schubert had brought this subject up. George wasn't aware that even a teacher knew or had even suspected his having a secret source of information. But Otto Schubert was extremely popular with the students and was closer to them than any teacher in Kensington High School.

"I don't want to administer this school through fear, Mr. Schubert," George added. "I want to administer it through firm respect and love. Mrs. Markham, will you send student teachers to take Mr. Schubert's first- and second-period classes? We have to go on an errand together this morning. Can we go in your car, Mr. Schubert?"

"Drive down to Kensington," George directed him, "then turn left on the Tiber Road.

"There isn't a house on either side of the highway that hasn't furnished a pupil I haven't taught," George told him. "And when you teach pupils, you get problems. There's not a street here where I haven't picked up a truant youth and taken him back to school."

"Not this year?"

"Yes, this year. This applies to all of Kensington."

"But why do you have to do it?"

"I have to do it when the attendance officer doesn't," George told him. "If a school doesn't have problems, it isn't a normal school."

They were on the Tiber Road now.

"Move along a little faster," George told him. "We have fourteen miles to go."

"Sir, what's this all about?" Schubert asked.

"It's something I've never told a teacher," George explained. "I've never even told my wife. Since you're an understanding man I can tell you."

As they drove up the Tiber Road, George pointed out the homes where his pupils lived.

"How do you know so much about this country and these people?" he asked George. "Do you know all your pupils?"

"I can call each by name," George said. "The better you know your pupils and their parents, the better teacher you are.

That's why you ought to be a principal someday. You like people. You go out and meet them. You stay around this country as long as I have and you'll know as many people as I do."

When they reached the foot of the Prater Hill, George directed Otto to turn left over a sandy, narrow-lane road and drive about a mile.

"Say, where are we going?" Otto asked. "I didn't know we got students this far away."

"Tom Langley comes twenty-four miles," George said. "He walks eight miles to the school bus and rides in sixteen miles. He's a good student. He's going to Benton College next year. He's an alternate on the list for West Point, too."

They came to a tiny two-room shack under some ancient trees. Here the lane road ended.

"What now?" Otto Schubert said. "I can't go any farther."

"See that little shack?" George said.

"But who on earth would live there?"

"Four youths we have in Kensington High School."

"Who are they?"

"Alexanders. Do you know Bruce, Bob, Bert, and Ben Alexander?"

"I know Ben and Bert. I have them in class."

"They live here."

"It's hard to believe four boys at Kensington came from this shack."

"It's harder to believe they live alone and come to Kensington High School, isn't it?"

"You mean they have no parents?"

"No, they live alone. Both parents are dead."

"How on earth do they live?"

"See this land around here? They farm it. See the cattle down there? They belong to these boys."

"Mr. Gallion, they're the neatest dressed and cleanest boys in Kensington High School."

"They wash their clothes and iron their own shirts," George said. "They sew buttons on their clothes. They plan and cook their own meals, wash the dishes, clean the house, feed cattle, hogs, chickens, and milk their cows. They buy their groceries, pay their taxes. Each one has his work laid out for him as soon as he gets out of bed. As soon as they get off the bus and walk up this road, their work begins."

"This is amazing."

"They're very clannish and hold together," George said. "Two of them played on the football team last autumn. If one brother got slugged the other brother would see that the fellow who slugged him got slugged himself. But that isn't why I brought you here. These boys love Kensington High School. Kensington High School means more to them than anybody we have there, except perhaps Les Bowdin. Kensington High School is both father and mother to the Alexander brothers. They'll fight and slug for the school. They're as determined as I am to see the doors of Kensington High School remain open."

"Those Americans who ate roasted potatoes at Valley Forge and nearly froze to death haven't anything on these boys," Schubert said.

"When somebody plans to deal Kensington High School a damaging blow, I hear about it," George said. "Let that person or persons be citizens or students. And I'm always there to meet the challenge with Bruce Alexander on my side. He's always with me. He's the oldest. He's my source of information, but he doesn't bother about petty things. Not a teacher but you in Kensington High School knows this. I expect you to keep this confidential."

"Well, Mr. Gallion, you have ways of getting things done, don't you?" Schubert said.

He turned his car and they were on their way back to Kensington High School.

"Yes, I suppose you're right," George said. "I have to. There are the Bowdins, Langleys, Alexanders, and Wallings.

and six hundred other potentials up there on the Hill. And help arrived every time to save that school when our backs were to the wall. And you know I'll never get over the day you came to this school. I was in despair about getting another teacher. And now, we'll go to the close of the year and the doors will not have been closed. I like to believe God sent you to us."

Otto Schubert looked seriously at George.

"Would you consider changing your plans next year if I can persuade our county school superintendent and county school board to make you my assistant?"

"You've asked me so suddenly and unexpectedly," he said. "Give me time to think this over. You see, this would mean a big change in my life. It would mean I'd be going into school-work instead of religious work."

"You can do either brilliantly, I'm sure," George said. "But there is so much to be done in our schools and a teacher like you is so greatly needed. Maybe when I ease out you can take over. Of course, you'll have to take on additional administrative work to qualify to be a principal."

"Yes, I understand that," he said. "I'd like to work a year with you before I'd take over a school."

"Think it over," George said. "I'll see what I can do. If you can be made by assistant next year I want you."

"Thank you, sir, and I'll give this serious thought. I'll let you know Monday."

Saturday morning George got up feeling sleepy. His feet were very cold, too. Grace took him to Greenwood where Dr. Connaught took his blood pressure.

"It's way down," he said. "No wonder you feel drowsy and your feet are cold. Your pressure is 96/62. Wait. I'll take it again to be sure."

He took his blood pressure again. "That is correct," he sighed. "I suggest that you get a checkup from Dr. Vinn this morning."

"Well, that's something," George said. "I've never had low blood pressure in my life. It's always been the other way around. I don't understand it."

"I'm not a heart specialist," Dr. Connaught said. "I think you should go to your own doctor and have him check you."

"What do you suppose has caused his blood pressure to drop, Dr. Connaught?" Grace asked.

"Oh, maybe he's tired, not getting enough rest," he said. "Maybe worry, tension, diet . . . I just don't know."

"We don't have an appointment," Grace said. "But I think we'll just go on anyway. Maybe Dr. Vinn can take him."

Before they got to Rosten, ten miles up the highway, George had really come alive. He felt a warm glow come over his face and his feet were no longer cold. In fact, they were so warm they felt as if they were burning. When they crossed the bridge over to Toniron, Ohio, and drove across the city to Dr. Vinn's office, he saw George at once.

"Dr. Connaught told me over the phone your blood pressure was low," he said. "Let me see what it is now."

He put the cuff around George's arm and inflated it to cut the pressure off his arm. Then he watched the white hand of the machine jumping from number 300 down toward 20.

"Are you sure your pressure was down to 96/62?" he said, shaking his head in disbelief. "If that was correct, it has risen to 201/120 in the last fifteen or twenty minutes! Something has gone haywire!"

Then he took the pressure again in the same arm, and it was the same. He took the pressure in the other arm, and the diastolic was three points lower.

"Doesn't look too good, George," he said. "What on earth have you been doing? That little school hasn't done this to you, has it?"

"I don't think so," George said.

"He's had a big job this year, Dr. Vinn," Grace said. "He's

had a lot of work and worry and he won't take it easy. He's in a place where he can't."

"He'd better take it easy," Dr. Vinn said seriously. "If he doesn't he'll be the best teacher in the graveyard. I told him when he went down to that school last September not to climb the stairs."

"But Dr. Vinn, you don't know the situation," George said. "I had to climb the stairs."

"He's even paddled the students, Dr. Vinn," Grace told him.

"Shame on you," Dr. Vinn said. "Students don't need paddling. Send them home when they don't behave."

"Dr. Vinn, you know medicine, and I know a little about school-teaching," George said. "You can't send them home. The power is in the schoolroom, and not in the freedom outside on the streets."

"Dr. Vinn," Grace said—and there were tears in her eyes— "I want George to live. But if he keeps on he won't make it."

"All right," he said. "We'll run a few more tests now. I'll give you a report at about six this afternoon. I'll call you. Now, George, I am going to be frank with you when I give you a final report on these tests," Dr. Vinn said. George was sitting on the side of the couch near the electrocardiograph, putting on his socks and shoes. "If I see this schoolwork is too much for you, I'm going to be frank with you."

George dressed and he and Grace left the office. They drove home and George spent most of the day lying down. Just before six the phone rang. George answered.

"George, your prothrombin is eighty-five percent of normal, and this is too high," he said. "It should be seventy-five percent of normal. Your cholesterol is 297, and you know that is too high. I have found something in your E.K.G. that I have not seen before. You are overworking, George. Your heart shows too much strain. Go back on that little white tablet I gave you to lower your blood pressure."

"What about school, Dr. Vinn?" George asked.

"Since you have only a few weeks, you can do it if you really take it easy," Dr. Vinn said.

"What about taking next year?"

"I recommend that you don't take it," Dr. Vinn said. "It's too much for you, George. You're getting too much strain on the heart from some source. You might not think so, but you are overworking."

"Then you recommend that I don't take Kensington High School next year?"

"That's what I've told you, George," he said. "I mean this."

"Then away go my plans," George said.

"Better let your plans go than to lose your life," Dr. Vinn said.

"I'm not so sure about that, Dr. Vinn," George said. "What's life worth if we can't do something that's worth doing."

"George, you are paying me to tell you this," Dr. Vinn said. "I know what can happen to you. All I can do is tell you. You have to have a physical each year before you can teach, don't you?"

"Yes, we have to pass a physical," George admitted.

"You can't pass your physical this time, George."

George hung up the phone.

"That's really a blow, Grace," he said. "That's cold water thrown in my face. What will happen to Kensington High School?"

"That school will go on without you, George."

"I know it will, Grace," he replied in disgust. "But how will it go on? I've got plans for every teacher I have. I've got plans for expanding science, adding more courses, and raising the number of units to graduate. We've got dreams to expand in Kensington High School."

Chapter Seven

Over the Hill Is Out

George Gallion wrote his resignation, to become effective at the closing of the school year.

"I want you to stop at the superintendent's office," he told Grace. "I'm handing in my resignation."

"All right, I'll stop," Grace said softly. She glanced quickly at George then faced the highway again. "George, I know you want to continue, but this is better."

George did not reply.

He found John Bennington in the back room.

"How are your ulcers?" George asked.

"I'm off my diet now, thanks," he said. "They've cleared up since I've been able to dodge a lot of petty problems. How is your health?"

"Here it is," George said, laying the single sheet of folded paper on the desk.

"What's this?" John Bennington asked. He unfolded the letter and read it. Then he looked up at George in disbelief. "You mean this?"

"Yes, this is it."

"But you don't say why."

"I can't pass a physical for next year," George said. "I'm permitted to finish the term if I'm careful."

"Is your condition that grave?"

"Dr. Vinn thinks so," he said. "Everything has gone haywire, but I know I'm going to live. I just feel that I am. I'm positive I have more years yet to live and work."

"You've done a fine job, Mr. Gallion," he said. "This is a terrible blow to me. I'm very sorry you are leaving. You must have done a great job. I've heard over half of the senior class is going to college."

"Just half of the senior class going to college isn't anything to brag about," George said.

"It's better than last year, when three went to college and two of them came home," he said. "I don't pick up a paper now that somebody from down there hasn't won something!"

"We've got some bad publicity, too," George said.

"Mr. Gallion, do you suppose we could get you an emergency health certificate? Sometimes we do get emergency certificates for our teachers. And next year you just be there. Don't do a thing. Just sit there in your office or in the corridor. Just see that school goes on."

"No, you don't run a school sitting in your office," George said. "I couldn't work under those conditions."

"Will you recommend somebody to take your place?"

"Let me think this over, and maybe I can recommend you one of my former students," George said. "You know this came as a blow to me, too. I'd like to have another year at Kensington High School to lift the program a notch."

George turned to go. "Then this is it," John Bennington said, gripping George's hand. "Thank you, thank you. You know I'd give you my position here if you want it." The remark surprised George, considering how hard the superintendent had fought to hold the office.

"No, not me," George said. "Here I'd be too far removed from the firing line. I want to be right in the thick of the biggest drive forward. I can't help loving that kind of teaching . . . right where the going is toughest and every inch, foot, or yard of drive forward counts!"

"No defeats, huh?"

"Setbacks, but no defeat," George said. "Consolidate the lines after one big drive and then move forward again! Teaching is the greatest life in the world. It's the light against the darkness, and if we try hard enough we can spread light over the world. And now that you've heard my little sermon I must be going."

"Ooooh," Sadie Markham groaned.

"What's wrong, Mrs. Markham?" George asked. "Are you ill?"

She was pacing the floor and wringing her hands.

"I've made a big mistake," she wailed.

"What kind of a mistake?" George asked.

"A big one. My first big mistake in figures!"

"What is it? Be specific. I want to know."

"The seniors are overdrawn," she said. "Each senior will owe this school $8.52."

"Everybody is entitled to one big mistake," George said gently. "I thought you were having an attack of appendicitis!"

"I would rather have had that than to have this happen to me."

"This isn't a matter of life or death," George said.

"They won't want to pay," she said.

"Why won't they want to pay an honest debt? I didn't want us to graduate any senior from this school who wants to skip an honest debt. He won't graduate either, if he doesn't pay. I have to sign the diplomas before they're valid.

"Mrs. Markham, will you check your figures again," George said. "Maybe you were right the first time."

"That's just what I *have* done," she said. "And I've found a mistake."

"Why don't you check again? Take your figures off to some quiet place where you won't be disturbed. Go to the kitchen," George said. "It's empty. Go in there and lock the door behind you."

Sadie Markham took her financial ledger and several loose papers filled with figures and went into the cafeteria kitchen, where she locked herself in. When she returned an hour later, the answer was written all over her round face. Sadie Markham, bursting into tears, had made her first mistake of the year.

The senior class was on a trip to Washington. When they returned, Mrs. Markham took her ledger and went to them in their home rooms to explain the shortage in their funds. Before she could finish pandemonium broke loose. Tempers flared, and there were catcalls and boos. Mrs. Markham returned to the office.

"Mr. Gallion, you're going to have to go up there," she said. "The seniors are acting up something awful. They're about to riot! Mr. Gallion, I've never been so humiliated in my life," Sadie Markham said. "To hear them talk, you'd think I stole the money."

"Mary, you go up there and tell Miss Wallingford to announce that the senior class will meet in the west bleachers of the gym immediately after their last bell," George said, and then he turned to Sadie.

"You will be heard," George said. "We'll go to the gym and they'll listen to you explain this shortage."

The senior class pushed their way among other students in the corridor, and went grumbling toward the gym. They looked as if they were ready to revolt.

George hastily summoned the senior teachers to the meeting.

"This is really something," one of the seniors said. "We take a trip, pay for it, and come back to find out what's happened to our money!"

"Yeah, what's happened to it?" came a shout from high up among the bleachers.

"All right, will you all come to attention?" George said sternly. "We'll explain to you about the money. You wouldn't give Mrs. Markham a chance to explain this morning. I suggest you stop acting like children and be grown-ups! After all, you're seniors and you want to graduate, don't you?"

There was silence while Mrs. Markham read her report on the finances of the senior class. When she had finished George asked her to go back to the office. "If we need you again, we'll call you."

"Mr. Gallion, I'd like to know what's gone on with our money," Frank Fairman said.

"You've spent your money," George told him. "In fact, you have spent more than you had. So what does anyone do when he overspends? Does he say he is not going to pay it back? If he has this kind of an attitude, do you think he is honest? If he is dishonest, do you think he should graduate from high school?"

"We already got our credits," Randy Miller, one of the seniors, said.

"No, you haven't, Randy," Mrs. Nottingham said. "All of you are in the senior class Tuesday and Wednesday until noon. No, you haven't got your credits yet. Many of you are close to the margin of not being able to make your standing."

"Now if you think I'm going to sign a diploma for anyone who owes this school $8.52, you're mistaken," George said. "You can't graduate until I sign your diplomas. If you owe this school any money we don't have to send a transcript of your credits out of here until your debt is paid. I am disappointed that you would refuse to pay a bill. If one of you whom I've recommended to college objects to this, I'll rescind my recommendation. Mr. Riddle, you know the seniors, perhaps better than any of us. I'd like you to say something."

"Yes, I know all of you," he said. He eyed them from the bottom to the top of the bleachers like chickens roosting in rows on the branches of a barren tree. "And you know that I know you very, very well! When you came here as little ninth-graders you didn't act like you are acting now. If I were principal of this school I'd send the last one of you home! Your attitude makes me ashamed of you! What do you mean by saying you don't owe the school? And what do you mean by saying you won't pay a bill you owe? Is that the training we have given you in this school?"

A number of hands went up.

"Don't be so rude," he shouted. "You wait until I'm through. I'll give you a question-and-answer period. I have a few questions to ask you. Did you know you are acting worse than little children crying for candy! I would be ashamed to have people know you have acted like this.

"I know what it is to pay off old debts in this school. Do you want the school to pay off a bill for you? Do you want to burden this school with one of your old debts? Anybody who leaves an old debt for a school from one year to the next is dishonest. I don't care if he is a principal, coach, teacher, or student. A student who would leave a bill for the school to pay for him should not be permitted to graduate. I think there is a school law and a state law regarding this. I shall look it up. Lots of things I don't go along with teachers and the principal on in this school, but let me tell you one thing, when it comes to honesty, I go all the way and maybe farther. I wouldn't graduate any one of you who fails to pay that $8.52."

More hands went up.

"Just a minute, please!" he said angrily. "Will you wait until I am through? Don't be thinking about what you are going to say, but listen to what I am saying. Right over there across that river are schools in Ohio that will not send out a transcript of one's credits or even graduate one until he pays for a library book he has lost. You young people have had the wrong attitude for so long that you've begun to accept it as being the right way of life. There are very few up there among you about whom I cannot go back into my mind and review some little shady incident in which you've been involved over the past four years. I know some little things Mr. Gallion and the new teachers here don't know. I am the only veteran teacher in this school. They come and go, but I remain. So I know you as no other teacher here, and I'm telling you to pay that debt and be glad to pay it and keep your mouths shut. Now, one more thing. Objecting to an honest debt is no different from stealing. And, this one year, stealing has been smashed in this school. Where are some of the thieves now?

Think, you people! Think twice, think three times! When you do some thinking you'll keep your mouths shut. Now, if you've got anything to say to me, say it!"

"We'd just like to know what happened to our money," Ethel Bush said.

"Didn't Mrs. Markham read the financial statement to you a few minutes ago?"

"Yes, but I didn't understand that."

"You're a senior and up for graduation this week," he said. "Why couldn't you understand it? Maybe Mr. Gallion is right in raising the standards in this school to a C average. Come to think of it, that's pitifully low. Now, if you want a financial statement, that can be mimeographed and each of you can have a copy. But it would be Greek to you. Mrs. Markham doesn't have time to go through each detail with each of you. She, like the rest of us, is a very busy person. And look at the time we are losing with you. Anything more you want to ask before I go back to class?"

No one stirred.

"Now, this final word before you go to your classes," George said. "You have not graduated here yet and you won't get your diplomas signed as long as you owe this school. This year we have had to pay over $5600 in old debts. I know what Mr. Riddle is talking about when he spoke of former teachers, coaches, principals, and students leaving debts for others to pay. This school will not leave any debts for others to pay. You certainly wouldn't think of doing a thing like that.

"I'll tell you seniors what I'll do," George added. "If one of you in here can't possibly pay your debt I'll pay it for you. You can pay me later when you get the money. I say we pay our bills. Let's be honest.

"I'm not asking who will and who won't," George added as eighty-five seniors gazed down from the bleachers at him with incredulous eyes. "I won't graduate one of you from this school who doesn't. This is in my hands, too. So this will be up to you to decide. If you want to throw away four years' work over

$8.52, which you can earn yourselves, borrow, or get from your parents, the responsibility is all yours."

When he was finished, George sat down exhausted.

On Tuesday morning classes were over and final examinations had begun for the entire school. Crews of seniors were getting ready for commencement exercises. Chairs had been borrowed from two local funeral parlors, and the gym was decorated so that it looked like a grand ballroom in a large hotel. The iron railings at the foot of the bleachers were interwoven with multicolored streamers and decorated with flowers.

Before the afternoon was over, Mrs. Markham sent a brief memo that George had prepared to all the teachers. It read: "Withhold all senior grades from report cards and permanent records until you are authorized by me to record them."

When all the preparations were complete, George and Grace drove home to the Valley, and George lay down on the sofa to rest. He had this evening and two more days to go and the year would be over. His health was a far greater problem now than any of his school problems had been. He knew the best thing to do with any of them, teachers and students, Janet and Grace, was to tell them he felt fine. He wanted them to think he was as strong as a bull. If the students at the beginning of the school year had taken him to be weak, they might have been as tough as a pack of wolves ready to move in for the kill on a weakened animal.

After supper, while Janet and Grace dressed, George went to a dresser drawer where he kept a number of hoods, one of which was his own university's colors that he planned to wear with his cap and gown on the platform this evening. There were five other hoods from other colleges, and he folded them neatly into his attache case.

Grace drove speedily back to Kensington High School. At this early hour people were already arriving; in the halls, seniors were hurrying in their caps and gowns.

Down in the combined kitchen-classroom-cafeteria, the

teachers walked in slowly, like seasoned veterans of a hard-fought campaign. They were smiling and talking about their summer plans. George laid his attache case and box on a table.

"Mr. Gallion, one of the students wants to see you out there in the corridor." Alice Nottingham said. It was Bruce Alexander. He dropped a piece of paper in George's hand and went on his way in silence. George unfolded the paper and read the unsigned printed note:

"Watch tonight when you start signing the diplomas in your office. There are threats against you. Parents are saying their sons and daughters don't have to pay Kensington High School $8.52 because the school took the money and if you don't sign the diplomas, you won't get out of the office alive. Be careful."
George pocketed the note and went to the cafeteria.

"Mr. Hannigan, you look good in that cap and gown," George said. "All you need is a little decoration. I have a hood for you to wear this evening."

"It might get in the way of my directing."

"No, it won't; you deserve this little decoration while you direct one of the state's three best bands."

George put around his neck a hood from the University of Texas, which hung low down his back. The bandmaster grinned broadly.

"Mrs. Waters, here's one for you," George said. "This is a West Virginia color."

"Here, Taddie Sue, is a color from your old school and mine, in Tennessee," George said. "Wear this."

"Thank you," she said, smiling. "But I don't have a degree."

"That doesn't matter; wear it tonight. We're going to have the nicest-looking faculty out there that ever sat on that platform. You deserve to wear this for one night."

"All right, Miss Rockwell, here's an Ohio color for you," George said. "This is the last one I have. And three of you don't have hoods."

"I have an extra one here, Mr. Gallion," Alice Nottingham said. "Here," she said. "Somebody can use mine."

"I'll take it," said Elizabeth Haskins quickly. "Thank you, Mrs. Nottingham."

"Everybody has hoods but Mrs. Barton," Marcella Waters said.

"Well, I know where there is a white scarf," Mrs. Nottingham said. "They'll never know the difference out there."

"Get it," George said. "She can't go on the stage with us without being decorated, too."

Alice Nottingham went over to a small valise and pulled out a white scarf. She pinned the ends together and placed it over Mrs. Barton's head.

"That's as decorative as any," she said, chuckling. "Besides, the pins won't show down your back."

"Just a minute until I get the speaker and the minister," George said. "Then we'll march in."

George went to his office, where John Creston and the Reverend Daniel Fox were waiting. John Creston, a handsome, six-foot man in his late thirties, was a well-known newspaperman in the state. Daniel Fox was a graduate of Kensington High School when George Gallion was first principal there years ago.

"Before we go in," George said turning to his faculty, "I want to invite you men into my office after the commencement program is over. I'd like to have two or three of you stronger ones. I might need you."

The teachers laughed at what they thought was a joke. The procession marched in and took their seats on the platform. The exercises began. Through the broad open doors out beyond the rear of the gym, George could see the sea of faces under the light out there and back against the darkness of night. And now, after everything was in readiness, the band stopped playing. There was silence. The seniors marched in.

Gus Riddle stepped up to the podium.

"It is a pleasure to introduce to you the valedictorian of this class of eighty-five seniors," he said. "Les Bowdin is one of eleven children. His parents have worked hard and earned little on their small hillside farm. Les Bowdin hasn't had the opportunities many other young people have enjoyed, but this had never daunted his spirit. How he has found time to do what he has done this year is his own well-guarded secret. Les Bowdin is one of the most versatile, determined young men in this school or any high school, and he gives great promise of doing something worthwhile in life."

George Gallion looked at his watch to see if the program was moving according to schedule. He then stepped up to the podium to introduce John Creston. Creston's talk paralleled what George had told the students in Kensington High School in his lectures from room to room, and it was well received.

The seniors then came forward to receive their diplomas. The graduation exercises were over, and the whole program had gone without incident so far. But a vast crowd was surging from the gym through the door into the corridor and on toward the principal's office.

George and Mrs. Nottingham hurried to the office. Mrs. Nottingham was to check off the names of the seniors with George before he signed the diplomas. With them went Grace, Janet, Otto Schubert, and Don Webber. When they arrived, the office was packed like a can of sardines. Many of the people gathered in this office George had never seen before.

The first name called was Don Weston.

"Sign his diploma," Mrs. Nottingham said.

"Don Zimmerman, sign."

"I'm glad to sign this for you, Don."

"Frank Fairman, sign."

"Nada Fairman, sign."

"Nora Wallings, sign."

"Les Bowdin, sign."

"Bill Newberg, sign."

"Kate Whittinghill, don't sign."

"Why not sign my daughter's diploma?" shouted a man

standing near George. While George was still on the platform he had seen this man pushing his way through the crowd toward his office.

"She owes this school $8.52. When she pays that her diploma will be signed."

"She passed her work, didn't she?"

"Yes, and I've got her scholarship at Menton State College so she can be a teacher someday."

"What did you do with that money? Did you pocket it?"

"Do you mean to imply that I took this money?" George asked, his voice trembling.

"Who did, if you didn't?"

"Yeah, who did take that money?" several more of the men shouted.

"I'm Dan Whittinghill; I'm Kate's father. And I know enough, because I went to Greenwood and consulted an attorney today. I know you can't steal money like this and get away with it."

George got up from his chair where he was signing diplomas. He started toward the man. "Here, easy," Mrs. Nottingham said, pulling at his coat.

"Stay where you are, Mr. Gallion," Don Webber shouted. He stood with his fists drawn. His lips trembled and his brown eyes flashed with anger. "You don't have to fight. I've got a good fist here for somebody! Mr. Whittinghill, don't you move a step toward that desk!"

"Come on out, George," Grace's voice trembled. "Don't stay here. Come on! Come on!"

Janet ran from the office crying. John Creston had heard the commotion in the office and, being a newspaperman, he squeezed through the door where the free-for-all was about to take place.

"I'm not a slugger and I don't believe in fighting," Otto Schubert said, "but I am a good boxer. And don't one of you hoodlums move toward that desk! I'm warning you!"

He took his coat off, threw it toward a window, and rolled up his sleeves.

Alice Nottingham quietly picked up a baseball bat that was leaning against the wall, and laid it on the desk beside her.

"When the first dishonest parent moves toward me I'll brain him," she said calmly. Her brown eyes were moving cautiously behind her glasses. "You're not bluffing anybody."

"George, come back tomorrow and sign these diplomas," Grace said.

"That would be better, Mr. Gallion," Mrs. Nottingham said.

A group of rugged-looking parents muttered and cursed at George.

Where are the rest of my teachers? George thought. United we could stand here, but divided we might fall. This hour is crucial.

George picked up his fountain pen and put it in his coat pocket.

"All right, seniors, you'll be back tomorrow, and I'll sign your diplomas if you have all your debts cleared with the school," he said. "If you haven't, don't ask me to sign your diplomas."

"We'll see our lawyer tomorrow," Dan Whittinghill shouted. "Besides, I am not sure you're going to leave this office."

"No, by God," said a bearded man. "You won't get out until we say so."

"Are you sure of that?" Don Webber asked. "I'll say he does leave the office or somebody will get hurt."

"One of you start something and you won't have a hair left in your head," Taddie Sue Gallion shouted.

"Come on, George," Grace said.

"Come on, Daddy," Janet screamed outside the door.

George pulled on his coat. "All right, move out," he said. "This is my office. I can clear it any time I like. Get out! Clear out!"

They moved slowly through the door and into the corridor. Mrs. Nottingham was still gripping her baseball bat.

"As long as I live, I'll never forget you four teachers," George said. "Thank you. You don't give up when the going is the toughest. You stand up and are counted."

Outside the door John Creston was waiting.

"Trouble, huh?" he said. "What's this all about?"

"John, it's a long story," George said. "I can't give it to you tonight."

"Maybe you'd better get out of here."

"John, will you do me a favor? Don't mention this in your paper. Please. We've had enough of this sort of thing here."

"It would be a wonderful story," he said. "But —well—all right. I won't use the story."

"Come out at the front door, Mr. Gallion," Don Webber said. "They're down at the west door waiting. All of you come down this way. You got those diplomas, Mrs. Nottingham?"

"Sure have," she said. "And my baseball bat, and I'm holding on to both."

"Stop sobbing, Janet," George said. "Keep quiet so they won't hear you."

"Daddy, I never want to come here to school," Janet said as they went out the front door. "It's worse than Greenwood High."

"Honey, you have to fight for things in life," George whispered. "I told you you might change your mind even about Greenwood when you get older. You've underrated this school. It's a good school—now."

"Give me that baseball bat, Mrs. Nottingham," Coach Webber whispered. She handed it to him as they went down the front steps. Don Webber and Otto Schubert led them around the rear side of the building to where their cars were parked behind the house. Grace started the motor at once. When they passed the west corridor door they saw a large group of men assembled there waiting.

"Give 'em a honk," George said.

"I'll give them nothing of the sort," Grace said. "What kind of people do you have here, anyway? I wonder what your blood pressure is now."

"If you honk at them they might follow us," Taddie Sue said.

"I pity them if they come tomorrow," George said. "I'll have plenty of help. Ninety percent of the boys in Kensington High are on my side. They'll chase them from the Hill like dogs after a fox."

"They're going to force you to sign those diplomas," Taddie Sue sighed.

"Maybe it would be better to sign them, George," Grace said.

"What are you saying? I'd see their parents in hell before I'd sign those diplomas until their children's debts are paid!"

Taddie Sue was belligerent. "None of us were good enough for the students we taught. Honest, they're so superior to our generation. Uncle George, I didn't believe you at first, but I believe you now. Our faults in this country are not with the young, but with the grownups."

"I've told a lot of people where the fault lies but they won't believe me," George said. "All this publicity about the teen-agers is just to protect their own shortcomings. The school has a long way to go yet."

The next morning George and Taddie Sue were back at Kensington High School before the others arrived. They were surprised to see a sheepishly grinning Sadie Markham.

"Oh, Mr. Gallion, I've got the grandest news for you," she said. "The seniors don't owe that money. I was right in the first place. I haven't made a mistake except that I made a mistake by thinking I had made one."

Taddie Sue stood there with her mouth open and her eyes wide. George was speechless.

"See, look here, when I rechecked a half dozen times I forgot to carry this number," she chattered on. "See here, that little figure caused all that trouble."

"It almost got me killed last night," George said. He had now regained his composure. "I wish you could have found out sooner."

"I wasn't here last night and didn't hear about what happened," she said. "I stayed home and combed these figures. What happened last night?"

"Wait until Mrs. Nottingham comes with her valise of diplomas," he said. "She'll tell you. We've got a lot of money that will have to be refunded to the seniors. I'm afraid you'll have to go before the senior class and explain all this."

All the seniors were assembled in the library.

"What now?" Bill Newberg sighed. "Do we owe more?"

"I am embarrassed," Sadie Markham announced. "I offer you my apologies first. I made a mistake trying to find a mistake and I was right in the first place. You don't owe anything."

An outburst of laughter and hand-clapping went up that was almost deafening. "What about the perfect Sadie Markham!" and "Fire your secretary!" came from the group.

"Just a minute," George raised his voice. "You be quiet for once, and listen. This is the best news I've had for some time. Now, you who have paid $8.52 will get your money refunded today. Mrs. Markham won't be fired. In fact, I'm recommending her for a raise in salary. I have never worked with a more competent secretary. In a way I'm glad she made that mistake. One thing about it, it tested your honesty and your parents' honesty. We've not always had a good time, but one thing sure we've had is an exciting time together, so all of you who have sixteen units credit bring your diplomas to me in the office and I shall sign them for you. You will be graduates of Kensington High School then."

By noon the seniors' diplomas had been signed. They cleaned their lockers, gathered their books and belongings, and went to their special buses to take them home. Many of them had tears in their eyes, and a few of them wept.

George was the only one left. He looked up at the sky where lazy white clouds drifted under the canopy of endless blue.

Then he looked again at the pre-fabs and the jungle on the Tiber River bank. Old memories were renewed while he took his last look at familiar scenes. The pre-fabs, Ag building, shop, and block buildings are lovely things, he thought.

He got into his truck. Before he released his emergency brake, he took a look at the main building. What is more lonesome than an empty schoolhouse? he thought. He switched on the key and the engine sputtered. He was on his way.

When he got home, George lay down to rest.

"Are you feeling all right, George?" Grace asked him.

"Never felt better," he replied. "I'm just resting for the big evening we have ahead of us. You be ready. We are going to have a great time. It will bring back memories."

"I'll be ready," she said. "By the way, did you ever recommend your successor to Mr. Bennington?"

"Yes, darling," he said. "I have three recommendations. I want Kensington High School to move as we have it moving. I love that school. Many years of the good years of my life have been given to it."

Tears welled up in Grace's eyes.

"May I ask whom you recommended?"

"Yes. Otto Schubert."

"But can he qualify, George? Has he had enough experience?"

"He qualifies with me, all right," George told her. "But I'm afraid he doesn't qualify with our state rules and regulations. He's brilliant and young. And one of his great assets is that he believes every youth is worth something and no talent should be lost. He works for young humanity. I've never had a better teacher. His moral integrity cannot be questioned. If he were to head schools all over America, we'd have a new country in one generation. But, darling," George sighed, lying on the divan looking up at Grace, "he won't get it. He hasn't had enough teaching experience to qualify to be a principal."

"What about Don Webber? Grace asked. "I know how well you like him."

"He doesn't qualify, either," George said. "He doesn't have

his master's degree. And, besides, Grace, I want him to remain as coach and teacher. But you guessed it. I have him down as second choice anyway. He doesn't have a chance. He wouldn't have a chance if he was qualified. You see, he never got out and worked in the school board election last autumn when the pressure was put on him. As for the third choice—and he'll probably get it—I recommended Banks Broadhurst. He's hard to get along with, but he will keep discipline and, I believe, improve the curriculum. And, darling, I've recommended all my teachers, for they've experienced problems this year they've never found in educational textbooks. They've learned to teach by teaching."

The students decided to have the graduation party on the *River Queen,* one of the last paddlewheel excursion boats left on the Ohio River. It was anchored by a clean shoal of river bank.

When Grace and George drove up to the pier they sat for a few seconds watching the twinkling lights and listening to the laughter floating on the soft night air. George was wearing a new dark blue suit with a white carnation in his coat. He looked approvingly at Grace. She was wearing a floating white chiffon dress and on the shoulder was pinned a corsage of violets. The sound of the boat's mournful whistle brought back exciting memories to many in the now-gathering crowds of parents and children. George and Grace watched a procession of young people pass by under the dry electric lights and the full moon above. River insects and the songs of whippoorwills mocked the talk and laughter of the gathering crowd. Kensington High School boys in evening clothes and white shirts were as handsomely dressed as any high school boys anywhere. Who had taught them?

"I thought you told me your young men in Kensington High School were sloppily dressed," Grace whispered. "I've never seen nicer-looking and better-dressed young men. Are these the same young fellows I used to see in the lower corridor?"

"Sure they are," George replied, pleased. "We haven't taught them how to wear clothes, but we have put something in their heads—and not only books. We've told them they could do anything. That's paying off tonight. I'm proud of them. Aren't they a handsome lot?"

"Look how well the girls are dressed," George went on. "They've come a long way! Some of those girls hoe corn on the hillsides during the summer."

"I don't believe it," Grace said softly.

"They do," George said. "Subrina Tolliver, who just passed by, hoes corn and feeds the cane mill to make sorghum molasses and helps to hand tobacco in the barn. Twenty-one percent of these girls do farm work! They milk cows, feed hogs, mules, horses, and cattle."

They sat watching in silence.

"Isn't this something? Brings back the old days, doesn't it?" George said, squeezing his wife's hand gently.

Every few minutes long mournful whistles came from the boat. A steady stream of couples were walking up the gang-plank to the deck of the boat.

"They don't know you won't be back with them next year, do they?"

"No, Grace, and don't tell anyone, not yet. I don't want anyone to know just yet I won't be back."

George and Grace followed the last couple now hurrying down the trail to get on the boat.

The Ohio River was at this point a half mile from shore to shore. The waters were placid except for little ripples, and the broad river looked like a silver ribbon on the moonlit night in May. Grace and George strolled along the lower deck. On the upper deck there was music and dancing.

"Let's be a part tonight," George said. "Come on, Grace."

They walked up the steps to the dancing. She came into his arms and he held her close. They were cheek to cheek. They danced slowly among the crowds of young couples. They passed the lights and the shore at Kensington, as the boat glided up the river. Night birds flew over the boat screaming their wild notes of exultation at being alive in another spring. Grace and George danced on with the students on the deck until the lights from Greenwood loomed in the distance.

"George, do you remember other springs when we went on river-boat excursions?" Grace asked.

"I sure do, darling."

A large group of students gathered around Grace and George. Boys who had seen George all day came up and shook hands as if he were an old friend whom they hadn't seen in a long time. George told them how he and Grace had danced on excursion boats on the Ohio River years ago when excursion boats were plentiful and they were students together in Greenwood City High School.

"Grace, many of the boys who gathered around me are ones you thought would go through life hating me," George whispered. "Almost every boy in that group I've had in the office at least once. I've gotten some of them scholarships and work and they're going to college. One is going to West Point."

"George, you can't mean you've spanked those big boys?"

"I certainly have; I had to. These are young men I battled with over who would control the school, they or the teachers! And they're going to college, too. Now, weren't they worth saving?"

"Who would ever know or even think they'd been problems?" she said. "It's hard to believe now!"

"Well, you are seeing the finished products. Before the boys were hewn and polished, a lot of chips were hidden in the dust."

"George, you're really one of them; I can see that now. And I'm sorry your health won't permit you to go back next year."

"Sure, I'm one of them," he said. "They know I'm one of them and they love and trust me for being one of them. They know I'm fair and honest with them. They know a teacher can't get by, doing something they are not permitted to do.

Remember, darling," he whispered, patting her shoulder, "kids are smart. They're smarter than we grownups, for they have more time to think. We too often make the mistake of underrating their intelligence. On this *River Queen* dancing tonight are young men and women who are going to amount to something in the world. And had they been let grow up like corn planted in fertile earth but never cultivated, they would have been outlaws instead."

There was a waltz now, and George and Grace glided over the dance floor in this atmosphere of youth and springtime. At last the *River Queen* swept downstream to its mooring by the shoal, under a trail of light. The music stopped. George had spent his last hour with his students.

"Slow, Grace; let me look again," George said. Grace slowed the car as they drove over the Tiber River bridge. "Kensington High School looks like a citadel up there on the Hill."

The moon was low on the dark green clouds of western hills. There was darkness on the flat bottoms in the Ohio River Valley. The school was silhouetted against a backdrop of white clouds in an eerie light, not of day or night.

"That's the citadel all right, Grace," he said. "One where products are shaped to change the world. You have just seen them, Grace. There it is, in a world of darkness, bathed in light."

About Jesse Stuart

Jesse Stuart is recognized as one of the most important voices of America. Poet, short-story writer, and novelist, he has written over twenty books, all of which have immortalized his native Kentucky hill country. Besides being one of the best-known and best-loved regional writers, he has taught and lectured extensively. His most recent book, *My Land Has a Voice*, the eighth volume of his collected pieces, was published by McGraw-Hill in 1966.